Willing Love

by

Mary Jean Adams

Willing Love

Cover Art by *Debbie Taylor*

The Wild Rose Press, Inc.
PO Box 708
Adams Basin, NY 14410-0708
Visit us at www.thewildrosepress.com

Publishing History
First American Rose Edition, 2015
Print ISBN 978-1-62830-790-0
Digital ISBN 978-1-62830-791-7

Published in the United States of America

"So how do you propose to catch a husband? I believe it would appear rather unseemly if you attempted to run one down." He gave her another head to toe inspection. "Besides, you don't appear to have the bulk to wrestle one to the ground."

"Money, Mr. Evan."

"Money?" Evan's blood ran cold, but he tried to make light of her words. "I'll admit, I am new to Rhode Island, but I am not aware of a market where young ladies can buy a husband."

"Aren't you?" She turned and started walking back down the hill. "Money has purchased more than one husband for unmarriageable ladies throughout the years."

"Unmarriageable? Are you speaking of yourself?"

Prudence shrugged. "Perhaps that is a bit strong, but I must be realistic."

"What about love?" Evan walked faster to catch up with her. "Your grandmother found it. Your mother found it. Why can't you?"

"Love?" She said the word as though it tasted sour. "Mr. Evan, I suspect you've made a wager or two in your life. Am I right?"

"On many things."

"Reality dictates that I face the fact that my chances of marrying for love were never that great to begin with. What odds would you lay on my chances of a man falling in love with me, or me with him for that matter, within the next three months?"

"I admit those are not odds I'd take, but then neither would I bet against it."

"Why not?"

"Because I prefer a sure thing, Miss Ashcroft."

Dedication

To my sisters, Cynthia and Lauralee.
There's a little bit of both of you in here.
Love you tons!

Chapter One

Newport, Rhode Island
April 1764

The British Crown, in an attempt to pay for mounting debts incurred in the defense of the American Colonies during the lengthy French and Indian War, barred her colonies from trading with other countries. The Americans, angered by increasingly burdensome oversight as well as taxes levied against them by a parliament in which they had no representation, turned rebellion into a profitable enterprise. Despite the best efforts of the king's representatives to collect duties and control imports, merchants up and down the coast managed to elude them. Perhaps, the most notorious of these colonies was Rhode Island where the seeds of the coming revolution were already being sown.

"But, Prudence, you have to marry eventually."

Prudence Ashcroft sat on the edge of the bed and stared at the soft hand her grandmother laid on her forearm. Through a vision distorted by unshed tears, she could see her grandmother's skin had grown even paler and more translucent in the past week.

Blinking away her distress, she raised her face to the old woman's faded hazel gaze.

"But, Grandma Rachel, I don't understand how you

could say such a thing. You ran Ashcroft for years by yourself."

Guilt nagged at Prudence. She shouldn't be arguing with her grandmother. Not at a time like this. She still held out hope, against the express recommendation of Doctor Willis, that her grandmother would make another full recovery.

Rachel Ashcroft just needed rest. Just rest. Nothing more.

A seed of doubt insisted on taking root. Her grandmother hadn't brought up the subject of marriage again simply to make idle conversation. They had argued about it before—many times. Talk of marriage had become as common as toast at breakfast. And like toast, it tasted bland on the tongue and was easily disregarded for more substantial fare.

But not this time. This time, there was a note of urgency in her grandmother's voice despite her weakening condition.

The shadows in Rachel Ashcroft's makeshift bedroom grew long, emphasizing the hollows in her cheeks and the purple stains under her eyes. Prudence longed to throw open the velvet curtains, oppressive in their opulence, and let in the fading light. She couldn't, however, as even the soft orange glow of the sun dipping below the distant hills would hurt her grandmother's eyes.

She left the curtains as they were, their fashionably long length piling against the golden carpet in crimson pools.

"I had your grandfather for twenty years after your great grandfather died." Rachel Ashcroft's voice shook, and her eyes grew distant as though she spoke of a world long past.

Prudence gave the older woman's hand a slight squeeze, bringing her back to the present.

"I was ten years older than you are now when my father died, so I already had a great deal more experience than you. Then I had your grandfather to help me do the kinds of things that I couldn't manage by myself."

Prudence gave a tremulous laugh. Rachel Ashcroft was the strongest woman she had ever known. Even now, lying back against her satin pillow, her grandmother's white hair fanned about her head like unspun cotton, Prudence could easily call to mind her once strong, clear voice and intense, hazel eyes. No one, not local merchant, not servant, not even the royal governor, could stand against Rachel Ashcroft when she had her mind made up. Prudence had grown up seeing one after another crumble before the matriarch of the Ashcroft empire.

The idea there was anything her grandmother couldn't have done on her own was absurd.

"You laugh, sweetheart, but I was young once, too." Rachel gave her granddaughter's hand a squeeze that wouldn't have killed a fly. "I had my share of challenges when it came to dealing with customs officials. Annoying little toads." A flash of the old spark lit Rachel's face for a moment, then faded into a soft smile. "Your grandfather had a way of negotiating that I just couldn't match."

Prudence laughed again, this time with real humor. From the stories she had been told, her grandfather's method of negotiating had been to dunk the customs officials in the sea if they didn't agree to look the other way.

"He also had a head for numbers that helped tremendously," her grandmother added.

Prudence ran the pad of her thumb against a delicate blue vein in the back of her grandmother's hand.

"But I have a head for numbers as well. Long ago, you told me that I got that from him."

Prudence cringed. Hers had been the voice of a little girl asking for approval. Not that of a young woman, ready to take sole responsibility for the family empire, an empire that employed half the county, perhaps even half the colony of Rhode Island in one fashion or another.

"So you do." Her grandmother patted Prudence's hand as though she were seven again. "But the ability to add a column of numbers or calculate cargo duties is not quite the same as negotiating with a suspicious customs official. You've only been out of school for a few months now. It takes years to develop the kind of wisdom you'll need to run Ashcroft by yourself." Her voice dipped low. "Hopefully, you'll never have to."

It had actually been closer to four years since Prudence finished her formal education. Most of her male classmates had continued their studies at schools like Harvard or Yale, venerable institutions of higher learning that were closed to members of her sex.

Her grandmother had insisted she continue her education and arranged for her to stay on in Boston at the home of the Reverend and Mrs. Sorenson, where she had access to the finest tutors her grandmother's money could buy and of whom the Sorensons approved.

Unfortunately, Mrs. Sorenson's idea of proper studies for young ladies had been in the languages and literature. Only very begrudgingly and at Rachel Ashcroft's insistence had she allowed a tutor of mathematics in her home. And a real world education was out of the question. Mrs. Sorenson had swooned and cried for her smelling salts the one time Prudence suggested she be allowed to go down to the wharf to talk to the merchants. The good Reverend had helped his wife to her bedroom where she stayed sequestered for three full days until Prudence gave her word she would never suggest such an immoral thing again.

Prudence's sigh expressed her inner feelings about all the innate injustices of a woman living in a man's world.

What she would have given for just five minutes with John Hancock. Although older than her by almost ten years, he too was in the position of having to take over the family import business with the failing health of his uncle Thomas. The difference was that while well-meaning adults had cloistered her away from the business world, Hancock had been primed to become the patriarch of his family's empire since the age of eight.

Determined not to feel sorry for herself, Prudence tried a different tack with her grandmother. "I have Richard. He has five years on me, and he will advise me."

Grandma Rachel trusted Richard so thoroughly that she had allowed him to manage the day-to-day business at Ashcroft for the past two years. Rachel Ashcroft only became involved when there was a particularly important decision to be made.

It was her grandmother's turn to laugh now. "Never forget, Richard may be your friend, but he will soon be your employee, sweetheart." When Prudence opened her mouth to protest, her grandmother quickly continued. "He'd never presume to tell you what to do. Even when you were children, he followed you around like a puppy. If you climbed a cliff, he was there waiting for you at the bottom, wringing his hands until you were on firmer ground. If you decided to swim in a pond, he would shiver on shore, holding your petticoats until you decided you'd had enough. When you rode Bolt for the first time, I found him praying in the barn for your safety. Did I ever tell you that?"

Prudence chuckled. Her grandmother hadn't told her that story, but she could easily believe it. Richard Bainbridge was so cautious as a child that she had taken great delight in finding ways to make him nervous. Luckily, as a young man, he had outgrown his timidity, or perhaps she had outgrown her delight in teasing him. She valued his friendship above all else.

"Richard works for you, now," her grandmother said with a certainty born of considerable thought, "and although he may advise you, he'd never be an equal partner in your relationship."

"So you want me to find a man who will tell me what to do?" Prudence could feel her frustration rising along with her voice. "One that will presume our family business is his, and I am some subordinate he can order around? Why on earth did you even bother to send me away to school if I am to spend the rest of my life doing my husband's bidding?"

The soft squeak of hinges interrupted her grandmother's response. Prudence turned to see Dr.

Willis's shiny pate and rosy cheeks peering through the opening.

"Is everything all right in here, Miss Ashcroft?"

"Of course, Doctor," Prudence said, in control of her tone once more.

"Very well." The doctor puckered his plump lips. "But you shouldn't stay much longer. Your grandmother is tired this afternoon, and she needs her rest."

Rest? You are the one who told me she would never recover no matter how much rest she had. Just this morning you said it wouldn't be long now. What if these are the last moments I have with my grandmother?

Those thoughts remained unspoken. Instead she said in a slow, measured tone that belied the anxiety tearing at her insides. "Yes, you're right, Doctor."

The doctor shuffled backward through the door, seemingly intent on shutting it behind him but leaving it ajar at the last moment.

"Prudence, I am not asking you to marry someone who is your superior," her grandmother said, drawing her attention away from Dr. Willis's obvious attempt to keep an eye on his patient. Her grandmother must have noted it too because she spoke now in hushed tones that had nothing to do with her illness. "Frankly, honey, I am not certain you could find anyone like that."

Prudence smiled at her grandmother's attempt to humor her. Grandma Rachel must have been born a diplomat.

"I want you to find someone who will be your partner in the business. But more than that, I want you to find someone who is a companion, someone with whom you can spend the rest of your life." Now it was her grandmother's turn to blink back tears. When she spoke again, her voice trembled. "I don't want you to have to suffer the same fate. It is no fun to grow old alone."

"Miss Prudence?" Doctor Willis said from the doorway.

"Yes, yes, I am coming." Prudence stood and smoothed her skirts. She leaned over and laid a kiss on her grandmother's silky cheek. "I will see you tomorrow."

She gave her grandmother a smile meant to reassure the old woman, but Rachel Ashcroft had already closed her eyes.

We will talk about this again, Grandmother.

****

"I do not need a husband." Prudence muttered and lifted her skirts to pick her way across the soggy grass.

She could not, would not, turn the Ashcroft family business over to a husband—even if she could find one she could trust, even if she could find one willing to marry her. There was too much at stake, too many lives depended on it. Ashcroft was her responsibility, and she would see it cared for.

Keeping her eyes on her footing, she paid scant attention to her direction, but as usual, her feet found their own way to the stables. Since she was a child, her search for solace always ended on the back of a horse.

A pregnant mare raised her head and nickered at Prudence's approach.

Prudence paused at Mazy's soft greeting, then made her way over to the fence.

"I do not need a husband to help me run Ashcroft." Prudence ran a hand down the horse's neck and came away with a palm full of winter coat.

The horse blinked caramel-colored eyes.

In her final weeks of pregnancy, Mazy was one of the few horses at the Ashcroft stables that was not a brood mare. However, her gentle nature had such a calming effect on the more excitable thoroughbreds that Rachel Ashcroft treated her as one of her prize possessions.

Prudence patted Mazy's mottled coat.

She didn't want to be calmed by Mazy's gentle nature. Not today. Today, anger bubbled within her, and she wanted to strike back at the world. A world that wouldn't allow her the time nor the opportunity to prepare for the responsibilities that would soon be hers.

She needed Bolt.

Prudence swept her gaze over the rolling, pastoral hills. She felt a tug at her heart as surely as if they had called her name. Racing across those pastures on Bolt's back, the sea breeze combing its fingers through her hair... It was the only time she truly felt free of the restraints her position and her gender placed on her.

Prudence gave Mazy's silky mane one last stroke as if to apologize to the little mare, then turned toward the stables. It was late, and the afternoon sun had already turned the dried grass in the meadows surrounding Ashcroft lands to gold. If she hurried, she could take Bolt out for a gallop across the meadow and be back in time for supper.

Prudence stepped through the open stable doors, then glanced around, looking for the stable master. Robert, her grandmother's previous groom, had left Ashcroft not a month before to move closer to his wife's family in Boston. Had her grandmother even found the time to hire a new man before she fell ill?

"Hello!" Prudence called out, standing on tiptoe to peer over the slatted sides of the nearest stall.

"Hello."

Prudence pirouetted at the sound of a deep voice. A tall man with a blue and white checkered horse blanket draped over one arm and a shedding blade in the other hand regarded her with cool gray eyes. He wore a plain woolen riding jacket and breeches, not the close-fitting uniform of the Ashcroft stable hands, but his boots and the back of his breeches were caked with mud as though he had spent the day working in the stables.

Was he one of the locals who boarded their horses at Ashcroft? Prudence mentally ran down the list of boarders in her grandmother's ledger. There had been no new names that she could remember.

She was also certain she had never seen this man before. Sizing him up, she ran her gaze from the top of his wavy brown hair over his broad shoulders, across his trim waist, down his muscled thighs, to the tips of his riding boots.

No, she would definitely have remembered seeing him before.

He must, therefore, be the new stable master. Prudence opened her mouth to return his greeting, expecting him to be just as eager to meet the woman who would someday be his employer. When he brushed past her without a second look, she clamped her mouth shut as though her jaw were hinged on a spring.

She pushed her irritation aside. Perhaps he didn't realize who she was. After all, she had yet to introduce herself.

But then, what other woman would be wandering

around, unaccompanied by servant or chaperone, in her grandmother's stables in late afternoon? Certainly not one of the housemaids and not another boarder.

So this was to be the first test of her authority? Prudence straightened her shoulders, determined to demonstrate the same steel spine that ran through all Ashcroft women. She assumed she had one. She was an Ashcroft. At least in name.

"You there," Prudence said in short, clipped tones, "saddle up my horse."

Had that been too harsh? She had meant to sound confident, not rude. Despite her irritation, she pasted a facsimile of her grandmother's benevolent smile on her lips.

The man turned, a slow graceful movement, as though he were moving through water while those around him had to be content with mere air.

"Pardon me?" His dark eyes seemed to see her for the first time.

Her smile drooped for a fraction of a moment before she remembered she was supposed to be in charge.

She had never seen eyes like his before. A deep gray as to be almost black, his eyes had the clarity of one of her grandmother's thoroughbreds. They were framed by the same dark, long lashes. She found her gaze drawn to his narrow hips and long legs, assessing him as she would the value of a potential stud.

Prudence grasped a nearby rail for support and yanked her gaze back to his eyes.

"Saddle up my horse, please." The please was a nice touch, she thought. If only she could have controlled the tremble in her voice that seemed to have found its way from her knees.

Had he noticed?

The corner of one eyebrow twitched, but the rest of his expression remained as calm as Smuggler's Bay on a windless day.

Prudence met his gray gaze, fighting the urge to squirm.

Had she presumed wrongly? Had she just issued orders to a new boarder that had yet to be added to the books? Not a good beginning, to be sure!

She opened her mouth to clarify her mistake when, like a statue coming to life, he set the blanket and blade down on a hay bale.

"Yes, ma'am." His voice was soft, but firm.

Prudence let a small sigh of relief escape. She hadn't been wrong. Now that the tall, dark-eyed stranger had resumed his proper role, she could resume hers. Maybe if she asked a few get-to-know-you questions, she could put him at ease.

"When did my grandmother hire you?"

It was an easy enough question, but when his eyes met hers, she could almost see him calculating his response in their gray depths.

He turned his back to her to peruse a line of saddles hanging on the wall. "Last week. Just arrived today."

The answer was frustratingly thin. Prudence considered the few words with which he had gifted her. He had a soft accent. Not harsh. Not guttural. Almost musical. Certainly not American. At least not fully.

"English?" she asked, as miserly with her words as he had been with his.

Surely her grandmother wouldn't hire an English stable master. That would be akin to inviting the proverbial fox into the henhouse. Or was he a sympathizer? Grandma Rachel had an ability to judge people with uncanny accuracy almost from the moment she met them.

"Welsh, actually." He turned in his water-filled world to give her a head to toe perusal that left her skin singed in its wake.

Payback for her earlier assessment of him?

Of course not. He was only sizing her up before selecting the proper saddle. So why did his gaze linger far longer on her hips than was necessary—or proper?

He turned back to the wall of saddles, leaving Prudence wondering if she met his standards. Probably not. She wouldn't make the best of brood mares. It wasn't in the Ashcroft bloodline.

From where had that thought come? Prudence shook her head.

"I've been in America for almost twenty years now, so perhaps I cannot claim to be Welsh either. Then again, I'm not really sure I ever was Welsh. Someone left me at the door of the Sisters of the Divine Mercy thirty-one years ago." He shrugged. "I could be French for all I know."

"You don't look much like a stable boy." Prudence interrupted him before he could analyze his muddy heritage further.

She cringed at her poor choice of words. He didn't look much like a boy at all.

There were lines at the corners of his eyes when he turned this time. "Thank you. I do believe that is the first time anyone has ever said that to me."

Was he laughing at her? Heat flared in her cheeks. Darn her red hair. With her complexion, even the slightest embarrassment set her cheeks aflame. There could be no hiding it.

"Not that one," Prudence snapped when he reached up to pull down a sidesaddle.

Why did men always assume a woman wanted to ride sidesaddle?

The man replaced the sidesaddle and pulled down a regular saddle.

"You'll pardon me for saying, miss, but you're not dressed to ride astride."

His voice was soft and soothing, as though he spoke to one of the mares. He was probably better with horses than people. Prudence glared at him. For some reason, she didn't like that they had that in common.

The stable master shrugged. "So which one is your horse?"

Prudence pointed. "The big red at the end of this row."

"That so?" The man eyed her again, his skepticism evident in the slow path of his gaze from the crown of her cap to the scuffed toe of her boot.

Prudence gritted her teeth against the insult. It was one thing to suggest she wasn't dressed for riding. That much was obvious. It was quite another to suggest that she couldn't handle her own horse.

With another shrug of indifference, the stable master set the saddle on the nearest bale and went to fetch Bolt from her stall.

The chestnut mare gave a sharp snort of protest when the strange man tried to put the bit in her mouth. Trained though Bolt might be, she only responded well to Prudence, and that was only when in the proper frame of mind.

Please, Bolt, just this once, behave, will you?

To Prudence's amazement, Bolt must have heard her silent plea, for in the next moment, she followed the stable master out of her stall like a puppy, hooves clacking against the stone floor.

"Begging your pardon again, but this is a lot of horse for someone as petite as yourself." Despite his spoken reservations, the stable master settled the saddle on Bolt's back.

While Prudence was determined to give him the benefit of the doubt, he seemed just as determined to find ways to irritate her. On any other day, she wouldn't have taken the bait, but today her frayed nerves were already at the edge.

"Are you suggesting I can't handle her?"

Bolt danced when he reached beneath her with deft hands to tighten the straps.

"Not at all. Just making conversation."

He nudged Bolt in the side with a knee to force her to exhale, then gave the strap one last tug before buckling it. As though bobbing on a wave, he dodged Bolt's sharp teeth when she swung her big head around.

"You just might want to keep those comments to yourself if you expect to have a long career at Ashcroft Stables." She reached for Bolt's reins.

"Sorry, miss. I shall endeavor to do so."

He sounded contrite enough, but she couldn't shake the feeling he found something amusing.

With one last glance at his face to assure herself that he wasn't smiling, Prudence grabbed Bolt's saddle and prepared to mount her.

"Argh!" She groaned when the buckle on her boot caught in the hem of her skirt.

Hopping on one foot, Prudence ignored the sound of her best petticoat tearing as she forced her way free. She really should have stopped by her room to put on her riding habit. She might have changed her mind about a ride now if not for the weight of his gaze on her.

Prudence gasped when a pair of large hands circled her waist. Before she could protest, she found herself hoisted through the air.

"Get your hands off me!" she said from atop Bolt's wide back. A ridiculous statement since his hands were once more at his side.

She quickly adjusted her position and tried to pull her skirts over her bare knees in order to reclaim what little remained of her dignity.

Bolt, spooked by Prudence's outburst and the sudden weight, lived up to her name. Had it not been for Prudence's extensive experience with the mare's temperament, she would have ended up in a heap right outside the stable door while her horse rode off into the setting sun.

As it was, she was still struggling to regain her balance by the time she reached the first rise. The cool breeze from the ocean caught her skirts, and they billowed up, settling well above her knees. Once more she could feel the stable master's gaze boring into her back. She chanced a glance back at the stable just in time to see him repress a toothy grin.

She would speak to her grandmother about dismissing him in the morning.

Chapter Two

Prudence allowed the chestnut mare to set her own pace over the thawing earth.

The musty scent of newly awakened soil filled the air as Bolt's hooves kicked up clods of matted grass and mud. The setting sun cast golden edges to the soft lavenders and pale pinks of the early spring flowers. Swallows swirled above, dipping low into the meadow to collect dry grasses for their nests.

Prudence scarcely noticed any of it.

Instead, a pair of clear, gray eyes filled her vision. On any other man, she would have called his face handsome, his grin infectious. Perhaps if her humiliation weren't the source of his amusement, she might find him so.

Prudence tamped down her irritation. She had spent years being laughed at, taunted for simply being a girl. But with her return to Ashcroft, she had put that behind her. It would not happen again. She would not allow it.

Bolt surged forward, threatening to pull the reins from her grasp.

"Easy, now." Prudence gave Bolt a reassuring pat on the neck. "You always were one to sense what I'm feeling weren't you, girl?"

Bolt nickered in response.

"Well, we won't let him get the best of us. Let's

just enjoy our ride and put him out of our minds, shall we?"

If only it were that easy.

He had picked her up as though she were no heavier than a child. The heat of his hands about her waist, the sensation of being lifted into the air had been shocking. And perhaps something else. Thrilling?

Like a puddle, the warmth spread from her waist to her cheeks, her arms, her limbs, her... Prudence squirmed in her saddle as the memory of his heat touched her in places his hands would certainly never linger. Nor any other man's for that matter.

What had her grandmother seen in him? He hardly seemed the type to be a stable master.

Rachel Ashcroft had always been faultless in her judgment. If she saw something in a man, Prudence hesitated to second-guess, but with her grandmother's illness, perhaps her keen eye for character and ability had dulled.

In her mind's eye, Prudence admired the man's broad shoulders, his power evident from the way his brown woolen coat stretched over them. But being accustomed to hard work was only the half of it. A stable master needed to be able to give orders as well as receive them. Her few minutes with the new man had left her with the sense he was unaccustomed to taking orders—from anybody. Giving them, perhaps. But not taking them.

That would change in time. He would soon learn that Rachel Ashcroft's granddaughter was not someone to be trifled with, nor laughed at.

Prudence chuckled when Bolt chose her own route down a soft slope. Like her horse, she would give her intractable stable master free rein in his domain. But in the end, he would learn to follow her lead.

Prudence leaned back in her saddle, providing her mare with what counterweight she could to help her retain her footing. On flatter ground, Bolt surged forward, and Prudence pulled back on the reins once more.

"I know you want to run, and we will, but I need to think for a while."

Bolt's ear flicked as though she didn't care to hear her master's excuses, but she settled into a more sedate canter.

Prudence set the matter of the irritating stable master aside and tried to focus on her conversation with her grandmother. She hated to disappoint Rachel Ashcroft, but she really had no intention of getting married.

Somehow there had to be a way to please her grandmother without shackling herself to an overbearing man, one with whom she felt a mutual disregard, but who felt a need to meddle in her business.

Prudence clicked her tongue and guided Bolt away from a patch of muddy ground toward a less treacherous looking stretch of meadow atop a rise.

Suppose she did become engaged? Would an impending wedding give her grandmother the strength she needed to recover?

Bolt gave a nervous whinny.

"Don't worry. It needn't be a real engagement." Prudence told her mare as though the animal had read her thoughts. "Once Grandma Rachel recovers, I will find a way to dissolve the engagement. Then everything will be as it should be."

There was, of course, one major flaw in the plan. A fake engagement required a willing partner.

Richard would be the most likely choice. Prudence rarely had difficulty persuading her childhood friend to participate in her schemes.

Bolt snorted and shook her dark mane.

"You're right. Richard won't do." Her grandmother had already declared Richard unsuitable.

An image of the stable master, all long lean limbs, strong back, and broad shoulders sprung to mind. Bolt started when Prudence scoffed aloud.

An unexpected thrill coursed through her at the idea, but she shrugged it off. She needed someone who would agree to a temporary betrothal, not sire her children. The stable master made perhaps an even poorer choice than Richard. Unlike Richard, the stable master hardly seemed the cooperative type.

Bolt slowed to a stop at the top of the rise and bent her head as if to enjoy the view of the stream meandering through the valley below before it emptied into the ocean in the roar of a distant waterfall.

Prudence remained content to sit atop Bolt's broad back. She needed to work out her plans. She swung her leg over to sit sidesaddle, then smoothed her skirts back over her legs until only the badly scuffed toes of her boots peeked from beneath.

Unfortunately, the only men Prudence really knew aside from Richard were her classmates. She went through a roster in her mind, there were a few that she heard had already wed, but the rest she rejected as being insupportably arrogant, impossibly boorish, or just downright unacceptable in every way.

Prudence snorted, and Bolt whinnied and danced sideways, forcing her to grab the saddle to keep from tumbling off. She gave her mare a half-hearted pat, and Bolt stilled.

Not that they would have found her appealing either. Her classmates had taken great delight in teasing her about her red hair, her lack of curves, her unfeminine alacrity for mathematics. And those were their kinder taunts, the ones reserved for her presence. She didn't want to think about things they said when they didn't think she was within earshot.

Despite their animosity, she supposed any number of them could be convinced to marry her in order to expand his family's holdings. Men like them considered it their duty to marry wealth. And when it came to wealth, an Ashcroft was a catch of the first order, even if she was part of the bargain.

Nevertheless, there was no way any of them would be content to leave her with the running of the business once they were married. Marrying a former classmate would be as good as signing over Ashcroft.

Of course there were other candidates in Rhode Island and even beyond the colony's borders. That she had never met any of them might be blamed on the strict watch the Sorensons had kept over her. Might be, if not for the fact she had never asked to go to any of the balls or assemblies in Boston. She had been certain she could never measure up to Boston's ideal of a young woman making her entry into society.

Besides, any man she might have met would, most likely, be much like her classmates.

Prudence scratched behind Bolt's ear as she reasoned out her thinking. Perhaps she needed to set her sights lower.

It went without saying that she had no need to marry for money, and a poor man would not have the experience to run a business. Perhaps he might not even want to try. A poor man might simply count his blessings at making such a fortunate match and be content to leave Ashcroft & Sons to her.

Bolt shifted again and stamped a hoof on the muddy ground. Prudence absently patted her mare's silky neck.

She might even convince Richard to draw up a contract, ensuring that Ashcroft would remain hers and hers alone. Prudence tapped her lips with a gloved finger, ignoring the smell of horse. Surely, the estate could afford to give her husband a sufficient allowance, one that permitted him to do as he pleased while encouraging him to leave her and the business alone.

The sun flickered and dipped below the hills. Prudence looked skyward. It was still too dark for the stars, but Venus winked back at her.

Prudence lifted her leg to swing it back over Bolt's back. Sensing her mistress's willingness to move again, Bolt started down the hill before Prudence got her foot over the horse's broad neck.

"Bolt!" Prudence dropped the reins in her haste to grab the saddle lest she roll off Bolt's back.

The mare picked her way down the hill at first but gathered speed until she was racing toward the stream.

"Bolt, no, you can't jump that. It's too wide!"

Prudence could only imagine what thoughts ran through Bolt's animal brain, for the strip of muddy water had looked considerably narrower from their perch at the top of the hill. Of course, Bolt had little experience in jumping streams and probably not enough intelligence to make a wise choice anyway.

She leaned forward and tried to find the reins while Bolt's crimson mane slapped at her face. She grabbed a handful of mane both to save her eyes and to keep from catapulting forward as she felt around for the leather straps.

Prudence caught glimpses of the stream bouncing in her field of vision between strands of chestnut horsehair mixed with her own auburn locks.

She had very little time left. Bolt, in her inexperience, could easily injure herself on the slick rocks. Maybe even break a leg. Prudence groaned as she clawed through her mare's thick mane.

At long last, firm leather brushed against the tips of her gloves. Grunting, she lunged forward, grasped the reins, and gave a sharp tug.

Thinking back, the next few moments would remain a blur for Prudence. She would remember pulling on the reins just as they reached the bottom of the rise, yet before they reached the sandier ground of the ancient streambed. Perhaps Bolt skidded on the mud or perhaps she stopped too abruptly. Prudence would never remember for sure.

What she would always remember, however, was waking up lying flat on her back, the muddy ground chilling her backside and permanently staining her dress. She would also remember the stable master's face staring down at her with his stormy gray eyes and a ludicrous grin, the stars twinkling behind him.

"Having a good ride?"

Chapter Three

His face hovered mere inches away, gray eyes laughing, his grin filling Prudence's vision. One of his canine teeth overlapped the others. No wonder he didn't smile often.

"Go to hell," Prudence said, then instantly regretted it, not for the uncharacteristic vulgarity, but for the way it made her head pound.

Unperturbed, he held out his hand.

Eyeing it with distrust, she accepted it and allowed him to pull her to her feet. Regaining her balance, she winced and would have fallen to one knee had he not been there to grasp her elbow, the other hand at her waist to steady her.

"Whoa there," he said, in a soft, accented voice she imagined he used to calm the horses as well. "Perhaps you should take it slowly. You may have hurt yourself."

"I'm quite well, thank you."

Fine time for him to notice. After he yanked her up like a sack of potatoes...with legs. Prudence shook off the strong arm wrapped about her waist.

Without his support, she wobbled. He gave her an uncertain look but didn't reach for her again. She dismissed the fleeting sense of disappointment.

She attempted to brush the mud from her dress only to smear it in dark streaks while great, greasy clumps clung to the fingers that poked out through the holes torn in her linen gloves.

Ignoring her ruined dress, she tested her ankle. A stabbing pain made her suck in a sharp breath. Had she broken it?

"Bolt!" She glanced around for her mare.

While a broken ankle might mean a few weeks of bed rest for her, for a horse it could be a death sentence.

Bolt stood a few yards away, munching a tuft of last season's dried grass. When she heard her name, she looked up and eyed her mistress with curiosity, blades of yellowed grass clinging to the side of her mouth. Prudence gave her horse a scathing look when Bolt bent her head to pluck another mouthful.

"Stupid horse," Prudence muttered, returning her attention to her own injuries.

"You know, I had been wondering why you gave your horse such an unusual name." The stable master said as though he were unraveling a great mystery. "She is a fine horse, and, at first, I thought it must be because of her speed."

Prudence looked up from her inspection of her throbbing ankle. What on earth was he babbling about now?

Silver moonlight illuminated his profile, and it occurred to her that he had a fine face, for a stable master. When she first laid eyes on him, she had noticed the slight angle to his nose, as though it had been broken and not set properly. With that and the small scar under his right eye, she had taken him for a bit of a brawler.

Now, in the glow of the moon, he looked far more like a medieval knight than a tavern brawler. His nose, in profile at least, was straight and well matched by a square jaw line, high forehead, and strong cheekbones.

He would be quite easy to look at, if it weren't for that obnoxious grin.

"Now, I am thinking that perhaps you named her Bolt because she has a tendency to do just that."

Prudence followed his gaze just in time to see the rump of her horse disappearing over the rise, taking her owner's spirits with her.

Oh, Bolt, how could you leave me like this?

"Well, as long as you're all right, I have work to do. Mucking out the stalls and such." With a cheery wave, he turned and started up the rise.

Prudence scowled after him. Why did he have to be so damned jovial? He hadn't been like that when they first met.

She stepped forward, and a stab of pain tore through her.

"Wait!" Prudence gave a strangled cry, unable to bear the pain as she tested her ankle again.

Whether broken or merely twisted, she would not make it back to the house by herself.

The stable master turned. He didn't speak a word, but at least his irksome grin was gone.

Prudence winced as she hobbled forward. Even hopping on one foot sent great waves of pain surging up her calf.

"Don't just stand there like a clod," she spat out. "Come and help me."

"Back on your horse?" He looked about. "I'm afraid she's munching hay in her stall by now."

"No, you idiot, help me walk." Her ankle and foot throbbed in time to her heartbeat, and Prudence was in no mood to explain her predicament to this simpleton.

"Sit." He pointed to a mossy boulder embedded in the hillside.

Prudence thought about reprimanding him for ordering her about, but in her condition, she couldn't afford to have him leave her. She took a seat on the rock, shivering as the cold seeped through her damp skirts.

He lifted her foot and placed it on his knee. She wouldn't have imagined such a powerful man could be so gentle. When she winced again, his gray eyes were laced with pain as well

"Name's Evan…"

"Ow!" Prudence said when he reached beneath her skirt to brace her leg, his warm palm against her calf. There had no pain, but the intimacy had shocked her.

"Sorry, I didn't think my touching you there would hurt."

Had the corner of his lips twitched?

Prudence considered warning him against toying with her, but the sight of his long fingers picking at the laces of her boot distracted her. He had elegant hands for a stable master. He pulled the knot free, and the blood rushed to her injury.

"Argh!" Prudence grasped the boulder, the sharp edges biting into her palms.

"The surge of pain will only last a moment, and then you'll begin to feel better."

"If you say so." She tried to keep a sob from her voice.

He rubbed the bottom of her foot with the pad of his thumb until the tension seeped from her shoulders. Then he flexed her foot. To the left. To the right. Then backward and forward, keeping his keen eyes on her face the entire time.

Prudence, who had never been that fond of pain, made no pretense at bravery. She slapped him on the top of his head when his manipulation sent a stab of fire up her calf. That brought his grin back.

"The good news is that it doesn't appear to be broken, merely sprained," he said at last, setting her foot on the ground.

She immediately missed the warmth of his hands.

"Thank you, Mr. Evan. And the bad news is?"

He stood and placed his hands on his hips. "I'm afraid you're going to have to ride back."

"Ride what?" Prudence made an exaggerated pretense of looking around for her horse. "As you have pointed out, my horse has abandoned me."

"Ride me." He turned and presented her with his broad, wool-clad back.

"Excuse me?" The heat rose in her cheeks. Did he realize how inappropriate his suggestion had been?

"Come on. Hop on."

Nothing in the man's expression suggested an intended insult. In fact, he looked a little like Richard had when he had given her piggyback rides through the meadows.

But she was a grown woman now. Not a child of seven or eight.

"Never in a million years will I ride on your back." As though her dignity hadn't suffered enough! She rose, putting all her weight on her good ankle. "You will help me walk."

The stable master shrugged. "Fine, we'll try it your way. Here, put your arm around my shoulders." He bent at the knees so she could reach around his neck.

When he stood, Prudence's feet dangled off the ground, and her ankle throbbed from the strain of being suspended in midair.

"That won't work. You're too tall. How about if I put my arm about your waist?"

"Fine." He lowered her to the ground.

Prudence put her arm about his waist, and they started forward.

"Ow, ow, ow!" She stumbled. "That won't work either. I can't take enough of my weight off my ankle with my arm merely at your waist. You'll have to carry me."

"Carry you?"

"Yes, Mr. Evan. Carry me." Prudence said, glad for the darkness that covered the heat creeping up her neck.

"Carry you?" he said again, doubt in his voice.

He looked at the hill as though he could see through it to the land and house beyond. Then he turned to her and gave her a speculative perusal that reminded Prudence of the look a farmer might give a prize hog.

Oh, for heaven's sake. She wasn't that heavy. He had lifted her into Bolt's saddle like she was nothing.

"It's got to be half a mile. I could carry you up a flight of stairs, but I couldn't carry you for a full half mile."

Prudence tried to brush the image of him carrying her up a flight of stairs out of her mind. The only stairs she could picture were those leading to her bedroom. The image left her far more discomfited than her ankle.

"I offered to give you a ride, and I'm afraid you're going to have to accept." He turned his back toward her again, hunched forward and held his hands back, palms facing up. "Hop on."

She couldn't miss the way his breeches stretched over his muscular backside.

"I...I...I can't ride on your back with this dress on." Prudence grasped at the first thought that popped into her muddled mind.

He turned to face her. "You had no problems with your horse, and I assure you, my back is not as broad as hers." He turned back again. "The night is not getting any younger, Miss Ashcroft, so I suggest you get on so I may return you safely home before someone in the household starts to wonder where you've been."

That did it.

Most of the household staff liked Prudence, but some of them would take great delight in gossiping. The story of how she returned with the stable master, her dress covered in mud, would get juicier with each telling.

Mr. Evan groaned when Prudence stuck her good foot into his entwined hands. "You could have wiped your boot on the grass first."

"Sorry." She did her best to scrape the mud from her boots before trying again.

As before, her skirts were hiked up to her knees, and she wrapped one arm about his neck to support herself as she tried to tug one side of her skirt down using the hand that held her spare boot.

"If you strangle me, I won't be able to carry you back to the house," he said in a choked voice.

"Sorry," Prudence said again, ceasing her efforts to cover her knees.

"Oh!" Prudence gasped when he clasped his hands so his interlocked fingers supported her bottom.

Before she could protest, he started off at a good

clip so she had no choice but to press herself against his broad back and hang on.

Before long, his warmth seeped through the front of her ruined gown, a balm against the chill. Despite her previous misgivings, she laid her cheek against his shoulder.

She breathed deeply. He smelled good. Not at all like she would imagine a stable master might, of horse sweat and manure, but more like old wood and the salty breeze off the ocean.

His warmth surrounded her like a blanket. She snuggled closer and let her eyes drift shut.

Darkness blanketed the hills by the time they reached the edge of the manicured lawns marking the boundary between house and lands. She gave the stable master a tap on the shoulder to get his attention.

"Mr. Evan, you may let me off here."

"But we are still far from the house," he said, not slowing down a bit.

Evidently, her new stable master was a bit like Bolt. He needed a firm hand.

"Yes, and I would prefer no one from the house see my unusual mode of transport. Now let me down."

"Very well." He came to a sudden halt and dropped his entwined hands so the makeshift seat beneath her suddenly disappeared.

For the second time that evening, Prudence found herself sprawled on her backside on the wet ground. Very much like Bolt indeed!

Instead of looking contrite, he smiled down at her with his crooked tooth. "Would you like me to saddle your horse again tomorrow?"

"No, thank you." She rose to her feet with as much

dignity as she could muster when both her legs were full of pins and needles from lack of blood flow, and her ankle still throbbed.

"Something tamer perhaps?"

Prudence tried to brush the drying mud from her dress again but quickly decided her gown would have to follow her favorite boots into the fire as soon as she reached the haven of her bedroom.

"No, thank you," she said again, straightening her spine and brushing a loose strand of hair from her forehead. "I will not need you to saddle any of my horses tomorrow."

"That's too bad." He raised his chin to the dark sky. "I believe the rain may stop, and the day will be unusually fair. It's a shame to waste a day like that indoors. The back of a horse is often the best place to enjoy such fine weather."

His grin was gone, but the crinkles at the corners of his eyes remained.

Prudence's temper rose like steam in a kettle. Why couldn't he have left well enough alone? She might have cooled off in the privacy of her bedroom, and he would have been safe for another day. But no, he had to press her.

"Oh, I probably will go riding tomorrow. However, you will not be saddling anything, Mr. Evan."

"I won't?"

"No, you won't," she said, letting go of the last tentative hold on her simmering temper, "because I will have you released first thing in the morning."

"Oh, that's too bad," he said, as though they were back to talking about the weather again. "Well, have a pleasant evening." He doffed an imaginary hat, then turned and headed back to the stables.

Prudence watched him go in disbelief. He had to be the most irritating man in all of America. That or the biggest simpleton she had ever met. She really must speak to her grandmother about him in the morning.

Chapter Four

"I wondered where you had gone off to." Stu led Evan Foster's tall, black horse into an empty stall at the front of the stables. "I would have sworn you told me you were going to take care of Demon yourself, and the next thing I know, I see the old boy racing over the top of the hill, riderless, with this one following on his heels." He nodded his head toward the stall next to Demon's where a chestnut mare munched a bucket of oats.

Evan grinned. "Yes, I had to go out again. In the end, I did not need my horse, so I sent him back alone. Thank you for seeing to him."

Stu raised an eyebrow, waiting for an explanation.

Evan wasn't ready to give one. His former valet would have to wait until he made sense of it himself.

"Smells like rain again," Stu commented into the silence.

"Mmmm." Evan stroked Demon's velvety nose. "I can almost feel the storm on the horizon."

The very skin on his back felt charged with its power. Did that storm have a name? Sparks in its green eyes? Wisps of auburn hair that refused to be tamed?

Demon nuzzled his nose into Evan's palm then nipped at him playfully. Thunder rumbled in the distance.

"I had the most interesting encounter." Demon's

nostrils flared as Evan rubbed between them.

He hadn't meant to tell his former valet about the girl, but for the first time in his life, he found he wanted to talk to someone. Almost needed to. It was as if she might be a figment from the storm. If someone else knew about her, it would make her real.

A flicker of lightning lit the sky, illuminating gray clouds for the briefest of moments before they disappeared into the dark once again.

"With who?" Stu set the bucket of oats in front of Demon. "Rachel Ashcroft?"

"No. We arrived so late this afternoon, and I had almost as much mud on me as Demon. I thought it best to wait until tomorrow to begin my employment." He ran a hand across Demon's blue-black flanks.

Stu must have used the shedding blade to finish the job he had been about to start when Prudence interrupted him.

He patted Demon's side. "I've only met her twice, but I confess that I rather like the old lady. I'm looking forward to seeing her again."

"So who did you meet?" Stu leaned against the stable wall.

"A young woman," Evan answered, deliberately inciting Stu's curiosity.

"A young lady?" Stu straightened. He could be so predictable at times. "How young, exactly?"

"Too young for what you're thinking." Evan suppressed a grin. "I would guess she was not one and twenty, although she couldn't be far from it."

"One and twenty?" Stu frowned and considered. "That's plenty old enough for what I was thinking."

Evan snorted. "Not if she's Rachel Ashcroft's

granddaughter, it's not."

"If?" Stu asked. "What do you mean by if? Did she not say who she was?"

"No, she didn't as a matter of fact. She was too busy ordering her new stable master around."

"Stable master?" Stu hesitated, for a moment, his jaw hanging loose, then gave a barking laugh. "She thought you were the stable master? That is rich. Knowing your need for amusement, I'll wager you didn't explain circumstances to her either."

Evan couldn't suppress his grin any longer. "Of course not." He gave Demon one last pat on the flanks before turning to his former valet. "But even so, I could tell she was Rachel's granddaughter. She had all the toughness of the old lady, even though she looked like she might blow away in a stiff wind."

"A scarecrow then? That's too bad." Stu glanced about at the well-kept stable with its stone floors, oak beams, and brass fixtures. "Still, I don't suppose she'll have any trouble making a match considering what she stands to inherit. I hope you put in a good word for me."

A scarecrow?

Evan considered. He would not have characterized her as such. To be sure, his hands nearly circled her slender waist when he lifted her onto her saddle, and he barely registered her weight when she snuggled against his back. However, thanks to her stubborn refusal to ride sidesaddle, he had been treated to more than one glimpse of a softly rounded calf and shapely knee. No, she didn't resemble a scarecrow. Not in the slightest.

Besides, her eyes were a mossy green and full of life, not the dead eyes of a straw man. During most of their encounter, she had been frowning, her full lower lip tempting him to steal a kiss even while her displeasure was on full display.

"I'm sorry, Stu. You were saying?" Evan had not heard a word his friend had uttered for the last several minutes.

Stu's grin suggested he knew exactly where Evan's thoughts had been. "I was just saying that I wanted to thank you for finding me this position now that you're going back to sea."

"I wouldn't have recommended you to Mrs. Ashcroft had I thought you incapable of running a stable of this size," Evan replied.

"Stables," Stu corrected with some awe in his voice. "By my count, there are three of them, and there must be close to fifty horses. I wonder how many of them belong to the Ashcroft estate."

"From what I've heard, in addition to a profitable trading business, Rachel Ashcroft breeds the finest horses around. Although"—Evan watched Bolt snort at Demon through the slats between their stalls—"I've also heard the mares can be a bit unpredictable."

Stu chuckled. "Nothing you can't handle I am sure."

Bolt tried again to intimidate Demon. Having none of it, the big black gave her a snort that sent her side stepping away from him.

"I do find the more temperamental the animal, the more loyal they become when tamed," Evan said.

"You mean broken?" Stu asked.

"No, I don't believe in breaking man or beast. I prefer tamed."

Demon's snort interrupted any more discussion,

and the two men turned to see Bolt try to nip Demon through the slats.

Stu laughed. "Although, heaven help me if I don't keep those two apart. There will be no barn left standing."

****

The rain tapped against the crown glass windowpanes, soft at first, then harder as the skies opened up. Prudence moaned and pulled the coverlet over her head.

The rain hadn't woken her. She had been tossing and turning for hours. Every time she drifted off to sleep, a memory yanked her back to consciousness. Memories of the cruel taunts of the boys at school. Memories of her conversation with her grandmother. Memories of one absurdly handsome but all-too-irritating stable master. She pounded her pillow, then threw her head back into the divot left by her fists.

Thunder rolled in the distance, and the wind lashed waves of rain against her window. Prudence shut her eyes and focused on the monotonous sound, hoping it would help her sleep at last.

"Miss Prudence?"

Prudence cracked an eye open to find Mrs. Hatcher, her grandmother's housekeeper, standing over her, hands crossed in front of her white apron, eyes rimmed in red.

She sat up with a jolt and glanced at the walnut clock on the mantel. A quarter past four in the morning. A full forty-five minutes has passed since she last looked.

"What is it, Mrs. Hatcher?"

"I'm sorry," the elderly woman whispered before

her voice caught in her throat. She put a clenched fist to her tight lips, while the rest of her face bunched around her hand like a spent handkerchief.

No. It can't be...

Prudence threw back the coverlet and felt around on the floor with her bare feet for the slippers she kept by the side of the bed.

Her satin wrap lay at the end of the bed. She stood and threw it over her shoulders, stuffing her arms through the sleeves. She was already through the door before she had a chance to tie the sash and tug her long auburn hair from beneath the collar.

A parlor on the first floor of the house had been converted into a bedroom for her grandmother when her condition no longer allowed her to climb stairs. Prudence took the steps two at a time, heedless of the residual pain in her swollen ankle and the nightdress that tangled about her feet and threatened to pitch her headlong to the marble foyer below. She slowed only when she reached the set of French double doors leading to her grandmother's room.

A sniffle behind her told her Mrs. Hatcher had caught up with her. Prudence did not turn around. She needed all of her strength, and one look at the housekeeper's red nose and watery eyes would turn her into a simpering puddle of self-pity, something her grandmother had taught her never to be.

She swallowed and nudged the doors open.

At first, Prudence thought her fears had been for naught. Her grandmother lay on her bed just as she had left her the night before, her silver hair arranged artfully about her, manicured hands resting across her stomach, rouged lips curled in a serene smile. Her pale skin almost glowed in the candlelight that flickered from the sconces on the wall.

Yet Prudence knew her grandmother was gone. Even when ill, her grandmother's presence filled the high-ceilinged parlor. Despite her grandmother's body on the bed, the room was just empty space now. Bayberry candles helped to disguise the scent of death that hung in the air, a foul smell that grew stronger once one was aware of it.

Prudence forced herself forward and sat on the edge of the mahogany four-poster bed. Sinking into the silk quilt embroidered with the tiny tea roses that had been Grandma Rachel's favorite flower, she reached for her grandmother's hand.

Her grandmother's fingers were stiff, and the skin chilled Prudence, but she covered the hand with her own, hoping she might warm it, and at least some part of Rachel Ashcroft would seem alive again.

Behind her, Mrs. Hatcher gulped for air. She murmured her pardons and disappeared from the room. Prudence could still hear her as she sobbed and blew her nose just outside the door.

How healing it must be to be able to let go. Prudence swallowed her own tears. There would be time later to deal with the grief. Right now, there were more pressing matters to deal with than her own sorrow.

Ashcroft was hers now. She had gone to bed as the heir to the Ashcroft name and fortune. She had awoken responsible for dozens of household staff, hundreds of employees, and the livelihood of an untold number of merchants with whom her grandmother did business.

Until now, she had only considered the moment-by-moment, day-to-day responsibilities of running Ashcroft. Now that the sum total belonged to her, it was as if she were being pulled under by a great wave of concerns. The sheer weight was suffocating.

Feeling a little light-headed, Prudence pulled the cloying parlor air into her lungs. She needed to speak with Richard. As soon as possible. This morning, if he called on her. If not, she would send word as soon as dawn broke and the storm subsided.

Mrs. Hatcher had deserted her post outside the door, and except for the monotonous ticking of the French clock on her grandmother's mahogany bed stand, silence filled the room.

Prudence glanced at the ugly, little clock, with its gilded cherubs and ornate, scrolled hands. It would be morning soon. Dawn would bring the welcome end of a long night, but the start of perhaps an even more difficult day.

She should retire to her room to make herself presentable before visitors arrived.

Tick...tick...tick. The pendulum swung back and forth in its gilded cage.

Prudence rubbed her thumb across her grandmother's cold hand. Perhaps she could afford to sit by her grandmother's side for a little while longer.

Dr. Willis arrived first. As the clock chimed half past nine, she heard Gil, Grandma Rachel's ancient butler, open the door to receive him. Moments later, he announced Dr. Willis's arrival.

When Prudence didn't respond, Gil shuffled back to the hallway where he exchanged raspy whispers with the doctor before taking it upon himself to show the man in.

Dr. Willis's considering gaze fell first on Prudence before he turned to his patient.

Prudence tucked one wispy strand of hair behind her ear. She must look a fright. She still wore her nightdress and wrap and hadn't even taken the time to brush her hair. Her grandmother appeared more presentable than she did.

Prudence choked back a laugh lest Dr. Willis think her hysterical and insist she take some of the laudanum he kept available for such times.

Instead, the good doctor gave her a sympathetic pat on the shoulder. He must have taken her choked laughter for a sob. Prudence ducked her head and dabbed at her dry eyes with a handkerchief.

Dr. Willis stood over Rachel Ashcroft's body holding her wrist between his thumb and two fingers. He frowned.

"I'm afraid she is gone," he said in a voice as somber as an undertaker's.

Prudence nodded as though she appreciated his medical opinion.

For heaven's sake, she could have sent a message to him by post with that news. She hardly needed him to come all the way out here to state the obvious.

The doctor lingered a moment longer, but seeming to sense that Prudence didn't need his assistance or his laudanum, he cleared his throat and bade her good day. Prudence managed a polite nod and dabbed at her nose for good measure.

Except for the ticking of the clock, silence filled the room. Prudence let herself sink deeper into the comforting beat until the present moment, metered out by the swinging of the pendulum, was all that remained.

"Miss Prudence?" Mrs. Hatcher stood behind her. "There will be more visitors today. Would you like me to help you dress?"

She sounded more composed than before, but when Prudence turned toward her, the old lady's eyes were still swollen, and the tip of her beaked nose had turned almost crimson.

"Not just yet," Prudence said, her voice scratchy from underuse.

"Then perhaps you would like me to bring you some tea," Mrs. Hatcher suggested. "You have not breakfasted yet this morning, and it is fast approaching eleven."

"No, thank you. Perhaps later."

"Very well, miss." Mrs. Hatcher turned and shuffled through the parlor door.

The rain pinged against the plate glass windows with sharp little notes. Prudence watched the drops collect and run down the panes in translucent ribbons. If it continued to rain, it might deter the inevitable stream of visitors who would come to pay their condolences. At the very least, they would wait until the rain let up.

Prudence glanced out at the steel gray sky through the crack in the oppressive velvet curtains. She needn't hurry.

The parson arrived next. His overcoat snapped as he shook the rain from it.

Gil showed him into the parlor, not bothering to announce the man's arrival. A breach of protocol, but understandable given Prudence's earlier behavior.

The parson said a quick prayer over the body and then whispered, "Is she well?"

Of course she isn't well. Grandma Rachel is dead.

Prudence glanced up, realizing a little belatedly the parson had spoken to Mrs. Hatcher. His gaze wandered about the room, settling everywhere except on the nightdress and wrap Prudence still wore. The parson's concern was for her, not her grandmother.

Prudence cast him a wan smile. He nodded then averted his eyes to the window.

"Can I offer you a cup of tea before you head back out into the weather, Mr. Simmons?" Mrs. Hatcher ignored the parson's discomfiture at the disheveled appearance of her new mistress.

"Yes, that would be most welcome," he replied.

His gaze darted back to Prudence for a fleeting moment as he followed Mrs. Hatcher from the room. Prudence was certain she would be the topic of conversation once they were out of earshot.

Mr. Whitley arrived some time later but did not immediately enter the parlor. Prudence could hear whispered voices through the open doors. The marbled foyer had a wonderful way of amplifying sound, but she still could not make out the words.

Moments later, Mr. Whitley's leather shoes squeaked behind her.

"I've taken the liberty of arranging a service with the parson for this evening," he said, not bothering to greet her before getting down to business.

Mr. Whitley's brusque manner tended to put off people, but Rachel Ashcroft had always appreciated his efficiency. Prudence found it comforting as well.

She nodded to indicate she heard him. A thank you was in order, but she couldn't find the strength to speak.

Mr. Whitley seemed to take her silence as an indication to continue. Either that, or he decided to get on with the business of the day, with or without her consent. Regardless of his reasons, it suited Prudence fine.

"We will have the funeral the day after tomorrow when the weather, God willing, will be more cooperative. We'll keep it to a small family affair." He cleared his throat. Had he just remembered she was the only family Rachel Ashcroft had left? "Your butler has been given instructions to turn away all but Mrs. Ashcroft's most intimate friends."

"Thank you, Mr. Whitley," Prudence said, really meaning it.

Mr. Whitley paused as though he were going to say more, but then turned on his heel and strode through the door with the same squeaky, purposeful steps that had announced his arrival.

The last of the Ashcroft line. Mr. Whitley hadn't said those words, but when he mentioned family, he practically swallowed his tongue.

The ancestors had never been a prolific bunch, at least from what Prudence knew of the family tree. Her great grandfather had sired just one child, Grandma Rachel. Rachel Ashcroft had just one child before her grandfather had passed, Prudence's mother. And Prudence's parents had only managed to bear one child before they, too, went to their eternal rest.

Prudence was the last of the line. The last of the Ashcroft's yet, not really an Ashcroft at all.

She sighed. Unmarried and childless, she was likely to remain so if her past experiences with the opposite gender were any indication. Did it really matter if the family name died out with her grandmother?

"Oh, Grandma," Prudence whispered, "I know how much you wanted me to get married, but I'm afraid I'm just not cut out for it."

The worst part of it was the business would likely be sold off once Prudence got too old to run it. Without heirs, it would eventually pass out of Ashcroft hands anyway.

A weight as heavy as the gray storm clouds hanging low in the sky settled about Prudence's shoulders.

"I feel like I've let you down." She squeezed her grandmother's cold hand.

Had Rachel Ashcroft been alive, her grandmother would have reassured her that she could never let her down. While she had been adamant toward the end that Prudence marry, she would have found a way to make her granddaughter believe it would happen.

Of course, her grandmother could offer her no reassurances now.

"It's time to get dressed, dear." Mrs. Hatcher appeared as if out of nowhere to pry Prudence's hand from her grandmother's cold one.

Prudence looked up in confusion. "Mr. Whitley said the service would be tonight."

"Yes, Miss Prudence," Mrs. Hatcher said, her voice soft and kind, as though speaking to a child. "The service is set to begin within the hour. We must get you ready."

Prudence looked about her. The rain had stopped, and through the window, she could see the sun gliding over the precipice of a distant hill. The clock on the bedside table declared it to be half past six.

Chapter Five

A cold drizzle tormented the miserable crowd huddled around the gaping, black hole that would become Rachel Ashcroft's eternal resting place. Their expressions were as gloomy as the sky, the parson's familiar words as monotonous as the cold drops that fell one after the other.

The rain had started after daybreak, come down in torrents at times, then let up just enough to allow Parson Simmons to carry on with the service, but not enough to allow those in attendance the comfort of dry shoes or stockings.

Mrs. Hatcher had tried her best to cajole Prudence into taking an umbrella, but the mild-mannered, sweet-tempered housekeeper had never been very good at cajoling where Prudence was concerned. And Prudence simply hadn't felt like carrying her umbrella today. She was in the mood to be miserable, and if nature conspired to make her so, then perhaps that was as it should be.

Prudence scanned the solemn faces. The crowd was not as large as it had been for the service of two days ago, but then, that had been held indoors in the warm confines of Trinity Church.

Even so, close to fifty people huddled about the gravesite looking as though they had gone for a swim in bombazine and black linen.

Prudence's wandering gaze stopped on a familiar face. Mr. Evan watched her from across the casket and over the heads of those clustered around the grave in front of him. A drop of rain hung from the end of his slightly crooked nose before falling to the ground.

She nodded to him.

They had only met three days ago, but his presence comforted her. If only he could have been the one standing next to her instead of Richard on one side and Mr. Whitley on the other. Of course, as the head of Ashcroft now, she stood with Rachel Ashcroft's closest friends and associates, some of whom barely acknowledged her existence a few weeks ago, while Mr. Evan stood amidst a cluster of Ashcroft employees.

It was downright silly to think the sympathetic look in his eye had to do with anything other than a formal regard for his employer.

He gave her a nod, then turned his attention back to Parson Simmons' recitation of the requisite verses.

Prudence shivered. Well, what did she expect? His crooked smile? A wave? Her last words to him had been a promise to have him dismissed.

The head of an empire was a lonely place to be. She swiped away a rivulet of rain from her cheek with frozen fingers.

Even if her grandmother hadn't died that evening, Prudence never would have followed through on her threat. She might be quick-tempered, but her temper was more like a summer rain shower than this never-ending, bone-chilling drizzle. She may be quick to anger, but her ire fizzled out before she did any real damage. Usually.

Prudence shifted in her sodden boots. The stable

master couldn't know that. He didn't know her the way the few she was close to did. She had shown Mr. Evan only her worst side, and the man had probably spent the last couple of days worrying about his position at Ashcroft. After all, with Rachel Ashcroft gone, he now worked for her granddaughter. Her temperamental, obstinate granddaughter—or so he must think.

She really had treated him rather horribly, even though he had done nothing but try to help her.

Prudence folded her arms against the chill and the remorse that ate at her conscience.

Grandma Rachel always said people carried enough burdens without adding regrets to the pile. If you're sorry for something you should say so.

She would do just that, at the earliest opportunity. Later today, at the funeral breakfast, she would make amends.

The rain slowed, then stopped all together. Parson Simmons closed his Bible with a soggy snap. Around her the crowd filtered away, their murmurs of condolences blending into the slosh of rainwater still gushing from the gutters of the chapel.

Prudence looked up at the sky, smiling for the first time in two days.

****

Gil closed the double oak doors behind the last of the mourners with a sturdy click, and Prudence let out a long breath.

"There's that sigh again." Richard offered his hand to help her stand.

"I think after today I deserve to sigh as much as I should like." Prudence groaned and straightened legs stiff from sitting for hours.

Her tea had gone cold long ago, and its stimulating effects had worn off shortly thereafter. Her bottom ached, her shoes pinched, and she wouldn't be surprised to see blood stain her dress from where her whalebone corset dug into her side.

Worst of all, Mr. Evan hadn't come to the funeral breakfast. She hadn't been able to apologize and put things to right between the two of them.

Well, no matter. Grandma Rachel had taught her to take matters into her own hands when the situation demanded it. The time had come to do just that.

"Would you like me to stay?" Richard asked.

Prudence looked into Richard's eyes. Such sweet eyes. So warm. So comforting. Looking into her old friend's eyes was like slipping into a pair of well-worn slippers.

Except Prudence didn't feel like slippers just yet.

She shook her head. "No, but I thank you for the offer, Richard. I think I'd just like to go to my room to be alone with my thoughts and perhaps rest before supper."

Richard raised an eyebrow, and Prudence let her gaze slide to the floor. Perhaps years of experience had taught him to be skeptical whenever she said she wanted to be alone.

For heaven's sake, she was no longer twelve. It wasn't as if she would find a toad to stick in his coat pocket again. Or like she would wander off to climb the cliffs over Smuggler's Bay. Or ride Bolt at breakneck speed, teaching her to jump the hedgerows between the fields.

The edge of her lip ticked up before she had a chance to check it. Those things would have to wait until tomorrow.

Nevertheless, she could not let Richard know what she had in mind. Ever her protector, he would never allow her to visit the stable master alone. He would insist on accompanying her, and that wouldn't do. If Richard were there, she would have to either couch her apology in vague words or own up to what an obstinate fool she had been. She couldn't bear the idea of losing whatever regard Richard might have for her.

But perhaps it wasn't Richard she was so concerned about.

She needed to put things to right, to handle things in a way that would have made her grandmother proud. Only then would she repair the damage she had done to her own self-regard.

She used the back of her hand to brush an imaginary strand of hair away from her forehead, punctuating the movement with another sigh.

"Very well, then." Richard raised her gloved hand to his lips. "I shall be by in the morning to check on you."

It sounded more like a warning than a promise.

"Thank you." Prudence let her hand slip from his.

"Perhaps you would like to go riding?"

"That would be lovely." She feigned as much polite enthusiasm as she could muster. She walked Richard to the large oak doors in the foyer, forcing herself to take slow even steps.

Richard bent to give her a quick, brotherly peck on the cheek. "Tomorrow then?"

"Yes, tomorrow." Prudence heaved another sigh for good measure.

This time, Richard only hesitated a moment before

descending the granite steps toward his waiting horse. He took the reins from the groom and mounted the bay in one smooth, graceful movement. The horse whinnied and shook her dark mane.

Richard perused Prudence from the saddle for a moment.

She gave him a small wave, and he urged his horse forward and down the crushed gravel drive. She watched him go long enough to assure herself that her ruse had been convincing, and that he wouldn't come back and ruin her plans.

When she was sure she had seen the last of him until morning, she closed the massive oak doors, turned in a swirl of black silk, and bounded up the stairs toward her bedroom.

"Would you like me to send one of the maids to attend to you, Miss Prudence?" Mrs. Hatcher called from the bottom of the steps.

Prudence skidded to a stop on the landing and forced her breathing to slow. Had Mrs. Hatcher seen her take flight?

"No, no, thank you, Mrs. Hatcher. I am going to lie down for a while. Please see to it that no one disturbs me before dinner."

"Yes, miss," Mrs. Hatcher said before bustling back to whatever shadow she had emerged from.

Once in her bedroom, Prudence unfastened the bodice of her black gown. In her haste, one of the buttons popped and skipped across the polished wood floor with a *plink, plink, plink* before rolling to stop somewhere under her bed.

She would find it later. She had to be back before supper, or she would be missed. There was little time left to find Mr. Evan, make her apologies, and start their relationship anew.

Prudence's cheeks flamed. Their *business* relationship she assured herself. They had no other kind. He was her employee. It mattered not that circumstances had caused her to come into rather intimate contact with him three nights ago.

Her skin warmed with the memory of her breasts pressed against his strong back, the spicy scent of his skin, the way his muscles moved as he carried her so effortlessly back to the manor. She hadn't imagined a connection to him, had she? It felt much like the one she experienced when she rode Bolt, almost as if they were one being...yet it had been so much more with him. Perhaps it was because she had never really been that close to another living being before.

Prudence jerked open the door to her wardrobe and pulled out a light brown and green striped, woolen mantua and petticoat. They had to be the least attractive garments she owned, but the unseasonable chill had been made worse by the rain. No sense in freezing to death in pursuit of an easy conscience. She pulled it on over her chemise, then yanked a cap over her hair. She surveyed her haphazard appearance in the mirror then tugged on her cap until it sat at least somewhat straight on her auburn curls.

But the gown...Prudence grimaced at the way the dark orange-brown hue made her complexion turn pasty. She pinched her cheeks to add a touch of color.

It would have to do.

The simple gown was drab, not mourning attire exactly, but she doubted the stable master would be a stickler for propriety of that sort. More to the point, the modest dress did not accentuate her figure. Not in the slightest. Even the V-shaped neckline dipped only so low as to show the barest hint of a curve. That was for the best. After all, she did not want Mr. Evan to misunderstand the point of her visit to the stables.

Prudence ran her palms over the small mounds at her chest and down to her narrow waist. Who was she trying to fool? On the right woman, even this dress would appeal.

On her, any dress was as good as the next.

****

"Excuse me." Prudence interrupted a tall blond man giving instructions to a stable boy of about fourteen on the care of the largest black horse Prudence had ever seen.

"Here you go now, Davie." He handed the reins to the boy. "Do you think you can handle him?"

"Yes, sir," the lad said with a grin that had Prudence grinning back.

The boy led the beast past Prudence and between the rows of stalls. She admired the way the muscles beneath the horse's powerful flanks made his black coat shimmer in the filtered sunlight. Whoever rode this horse would have to be equally as powerful.

Had Grandma Rachel acquired a new stud that she had not been made aware of? Her grandmother always had a fine eye for horses. Not only could she spot those with the best bloodlines, she had a knack for knowing which were the most virile. While Prudence's grandfather and great grandfather had been responsible for getting Ashcroft & Sons' shipping business off the ground, the success of Ashcroft Stables had been largely Grandma Rachel's doing.

"Yes, ma'am," the blond man said, startling her away from her speculation about the stallion's potential. "What can I do for you?"

"I'm Prudence Ashcroft." She reached out her hand.

A grin split the man's face. Prudence thought it odd he should be so pleased to meet her, but it was a promising start. If he were the owner of the black and a new boarder at the stables, she would have a chat with him about allowing her to pair his stallion with one of her mares once she concluded her business with Mr. Evan.

"Stuart Malone." He took her hand. "Your servant, ma'am."

"Thank you, Mr. Malone." Prudence pulled her hand away when he held it just a bit too long. "Have you seen Mr. Evan, by chance?"

She glanced around at the immaculate stalls. They looked even cleaner than they had three nights ago. Mr. Evan was clearly a competent man.

"Mr. Evan?" He pronounced the name slowly as though he couldn't quite place it.

"Yes, the new stable master. Tall man, dark hair, small scar under his right eye." She swept an imaginary line under her own eye with a gloved finger. "Oh, and a slightly crooked nose."

She almost added *and the most intense eyes you could imagine*, but decided that even if Mr. Malone had met Mr. Evan, he might not have noted that detail.

"Oh, yes, Mr. Evan." The light of understanding shone in his face. "The new stable master."

"Yes. Have you seen him?" Prudence tamped down her impatience.

"I'm afraid he isn't here right now." Mr. Malone's cheek twitched.

"Ah, I see."

Prudence wanted to ask if he happened to know where he might be, but that small twitch in the man's cheek looked suspiciously like a repressed grin. Mr. Malone found her amusing for some reason.

Too bad. He was a rather handsome gentleman, but she didn't enjoy being laughed at.

She picked up her skirts, unnecessarily so as there wasn't a speck of dirt or manure on the stable floor, and strode, back straight as a plank, into the feeble sunshine.

Thunder rumbled in the distance, and Prudence glanced up. A line of towering white clouds, their edges marked by shadows, marched across the horizon. A cool breeze ruffled her cap.

She wished she could share Mr. Malone's amusement, but right now, her life seemed much like the weather. Moments of joy as short-lived as the sunshine and soon overshadowed by the ever-present rain.

Prudence drew in a painful breath. She shouldn't be so disappointed. She would have other opportunities to speak with Mr. Evan. Even if he intended on leaving, it wouldn't be easy for him to find another position as prestigious as the one he held at Ashcroft. And she had no intention of letting him go, so she could count on him being around for at least a little while.

Prudence leaned against the rough paddock gate. If she waited awhile, he might yet make an appearance.

Mazy had borne her foal within the last day. The gentle mare stood contentedly while the young horse gamboled about on spindly legs, then returned to his mother for nourishment.

How simple life was for the young. Not that she was old by any means, but with her grandmother's death, Prudence would be responsible for a great many things. While girls her age were dancing at balls, planning weddings, or nursing their newborn babes as Mazy did, she would be running a business and trying to keep the family fortunes intact.

She watched foal and mare for a while, arms folded across the top of the rough wooden planks, one booted foot propped against the lowest of them, while she waited for Mr. Evan's return. With every crack of a twig or clang of a bucket, she turned, hoping to see the man. And every glance about her met with disappointment for it was either a stable boy attending to a task or the ever-grinning Mr. Malone watching the boys at work—and studying her.

Prudence turned back to the paddock and rested her chin on her hands with a thump.

What did Mr. Malone find so fascinating that he would hang about the stables now that his horse had been rubbed down and given his bag of oats? She had done nothing to encourage him. Most boarders would have been long gone by now.

The thunder rumbled again, closer now. A shadow crept across the pasture. A breeze threatened to tug the cap from her hair. Prudence glanced up, and a large drop of rain landed on her cheek. She held out a hand, palm up, and several more drops pelted her upturned face.

Mr. Evan would have to wait another day for his apology.

Turning, Prudence studied the stable. She could take refuge until the rain stopped. It would be warm and cozy, and she would have Bolt to keep her company. However, she'd also have the annoying Mr. Malone plus a handful of stable boys. She might as well head back to the house where she could be miserable by herself.

Prudence looked back toward the main house and found she didn't want to go back. It would be filled with servants, ready to see to her every need. Even now, the warm glow of a hearth shone through the plate glass windows of a back parlor.

Servants didn't fill a house. With her grandmother gone, no one would be there to welcome her home. No one who hadn't been paid to do so, that is. No one would be there to wrap a warm blanket around her shoulders, give her a hug, then sit with her while she drank her hot tea.

A second path, little more than a dirt trail, led away from the house. Prudence followed it past the stables, past a copse of beech trees, past a briar patch that refused to be tamed, until she reached the little stone chapel and the family cemetery.

The gate creaked when Prudence opened it. Despite the care the groundskeeper took to ensure the gate stayed well-oiled, rust coated the metal, and the hinges never failed to squeak. As a child, she had often gone into the cemetery to retrieve an errant ball or other toy and imagined the gate squeaked to warn the dead of her arrival.

Of course, as a child, the dead in the little family cemetery were just names. Her smile faded as she came first upon the headstones that marked her mother and father's final resting places. She ran her hand over the granite. Brown lichens grew on the edges, and the etchings showed signs of weathering, but the steady drizzle had darkened the stone until the names and dates stood out in stark relief—*Emily Saunders, 1720-1744; Charles Saunders 1716-1743*.

She had never known either of them. Her father died before she was born, and her mother died soon after. Grandma Rachel had raised her. Prudence had even taken her grandmother's last name to avoid confusion.

She read the name on the headstones again. *Saunders*. She knew her real name but had never really thought of it as hers. More like a middle name, inscribed on the records page in the family Bible, but never used again.

Was it odd that, as a child, she had never wondered who her parents were or what it would have been like to have a mother and father? Perhaps it signified some defect in her character, some lack of familial instinct or maternal bonding ability.

Her grandmother had told her tales about her mother. But that Emily Ashcroft had been like a character in a story, someone her grandmother made up to keep a young girl entertained.

Her grandfather's headstone lay a few feet away. He had died a couple of years after her mother. Sometimes, when she was drifting off to sleep or daydreaming in the library, she thought she could remember the smiling face of an older man beaming at her while he held her high above his head. She had always imagined it to be a distant memory of her grandfather, but the more rational side of her attributed the memory to fanciful thinking. At most, she had been three when her grandfather passed. She couldn't possibly remember his face.

Prudence trailed the tips of her fingers over the lichen-covered stone. Other than her grandmother, these people were the only real family she had. How could she not even be curious about who they were?

An ache settled in her heart, and she grieved for the first time in her life for the loss of family she had never known.

The rain turned from drizzle to shower, and the curls around Prudence's face plastered to her forehead and cheeks. Her cap had long since ceased to provide any protection against the elements, and it lay against her hair like a deflated mushroom. She pulled it from her head, stuffed it in her pocket, and picked her way through the mud to the fresh mound of dirt over her grandmother's grave.

The stonemason had yet to deliver the headstone. Only a small, wooden cross marked Rachel Ashcroft's grave.

Prudence sucked in a painful breath and stared at the marker that didn't even bear her grandmother's name. It all seemed like such unfinished business, as if the delivery and placement of the headstone would signal the true end of her grandmother's life and the beginning of her own lonely existence as the head of a family of one.

Prudence sank to her knees in grass still muddy from yesterday's burial and the trampling of dozens of pairs of feet. If only the placement of the headstone could end her pain. She would have to live the rest of her life without her grandmother and as the last living

Ashcroft in the family line. Her shoulders slumped under the burden that had become hers and hers alone.

The skies opened up just as the emotions Prudence had been holding back for so long did the same. Rain melded with tears to run down her cheeks in rivulets and drip from the end of her chin. Only the thunder rolling overhead muffled the sobs that racked her body.

Prudence would have fallen face first into the muddy mound had not a pair of strong arms encircled her shoulders. She turned into them, not caring for the moment whose arms they were, but knowing her pain was more than she could bear alone.

"It's all right, let it out," a resonant, male voice said.

A hand stroked her back.

That was all the encouragement she needed. She curled her fingers around handfuls of soft but sodden linen and poured out her misery into a limp neck cloth.

Her sobs subsided into hiccups, and a pair of strong arms tucked beneath her knees. The stranger cradled her against his chest and stood.

"Put your arms around me, sweetheart," he whispered in her ear.

Prudence didn't have the strength to protest had she wanted to, so she did as he asked and snuggled into his warm embrace.

He smelled good. Fresh. Like the rain mixed with pine and the spicy scent of the man beneath.

She buried her face in his shirt.

So familiar.

Prudence mustered the strength to open her eyes just enough to study his profile through the shadow of her lashes.

Mary Jean Adams

Once again, she found herself in the arms of the stable master. Once again, he had come to her rescue. Once again, he carried her back to the house, but this time she didn't care. This time, she would give herself over to the moment. Let the staff gossip.

Chapter Six

Prudence took a deep breath and grasped the cold brass knob. Beyond lay the Ashcroft library. The few guests that had arrived in the past half hour to hear the reading of her grandmother's will were inside. Gil had informed her not five minutes ago that they only awaited her presence in order to begin.

Grandma Rachel's headstone had been delivered. This last act marked the end of her grandmother's life. Once the reading was over, the estate and the business would be hers. Rachel Ashcroft would be truly gone from this world.

Squaring her shoulders, Prudence turned the knob.

"There you are." Richard came to her side and offered his arm. "I was beginning to think you had found something better to do."

"You know me." Prudence donned the brightest smile she could muster. "I love to look my best when there is an audience."

Richard scoffed. "Not that you don't look absolutely delightful, but I don't doubt for a moment that it was all your maid's idea. More than likely you only gave into her ministrations because you were delaying the inevitable."

"Hmmm, it seems that everyone is here," Prudence said, ignoring Richard's insightful and all-too-accurate observation.

Mr. Whitley stood behind a desk angled in front of the hearth that dominated one wall of the room. A portrait of her grandmother hung above the mantel. She looked down on the proceedings with a decidedly satisfied air, as though she were pleased her life's work allowed her to leave enough possessions to make such a gathering possible.

"I hope that I am as fortunate," Prudence whispered to the portrait.

"I'm sorry, what was that, Pru?" Richard asked.

"Oh, nothing. I was just observing how fortunate we are the rain has stopped."

"Oh, yes, of course." Richard cast a cursory glance at the sun streaming in through two arched windows on either side of the hearth.

Prudence gave an almost imperceptible shake of her head. Richard spent most of his time behind a desk. In all likelihood, he hadn't noticed it had rained almost non-stop for two weeks.

"I see Miss Ashcroft has arrived, so if you would all please take your seats, we can begin," Mr. Whitley announced in the booming voice he always used when he had an audience.

Richard led her to a chair in the front row and waited until she settled herself before taking his seat next to her.

Prudence glanced around at the rest of the assembly. The seats closest to her were filled with Rachel Ashcroft's business associates. Some she recognized. Some she didn't.

She nodded to Parson Simmons. He gave her a sympathetic smile and took a seat next to Mrs. Hatcher. A few others, mostly local farmers, household staff, and those who had been in her grandmother's employ for decades, took their seats toward the rear, giving Prudence a clear view of the back wall.

Her breath caught in her throat.

Mr. Evan stood, cocked hat in hand, just inside the French doors.

What was he doing here? Had he been summoned to stand by in case someone had need of a horse? No, that was absurd.

Besides, he wasn't dressed for the stable. Over a ruffled shirt and a neck cloth tied in a bow, he wore a green woolen waistcoat and cutaway coat. His taupe pants didn't look to be of the finest material, but they were well tailored to his tall frame. He wore the same knee-high boots he had worn two nights ago when he plucked her from the cemetery, but not a speck of mud remained.

Prudence narrowed her eyes at him. She supposed he had as much right to be at the reading as any other member of the staff, but while Rachel Ashcroft had been renowned for her generosity, Mr. Evan hadn't been in her employ for more than a week. Surely, he hadn't come looking for a handout. He didn't seem the type to beg or rely on the charity of others. She hadn't misjudged him, had she?

Mr. Evan nodded a greeting, and Prudence nodded back before turning away, her cheeks heating. How long had he been watching her watching him? For heaven's sake, she had been practically ogling the man.

There could only be one logical reason for his presence. He had come looking for her. While he might not be admitted if he called at the house, he could easily slip in amongst the other Ashcroft employees to attend the reading of the will. There would be no doubt that he would find her here as well.

Prudence fought the urge to fidget while Mr. Whitley waited for everyone to settle. Was it just her imagination, or could she still feel Mr. Evan's gaze heating the back of her shoulders?

Surely he wasn't concerned for his position at Ashcroft. She might have been rude to him on their first meeting, but did he think her so heartless that she would dismiss him after last night? She would have lain on her grandmother's grave and sobbed until the skies and her tears ran dry had he not found her there. Without him, she might have caught pneumonia and earned her own place in the family cemetery.

She hadn't even had the opportunity to thank him.

Instead of dropping her off a few hundred yards from the house, he carried her right up to the front door. She would never forget the look on Gil's face when Mr. Evan refused to relinquish her and demanded he be shown the way to her bedroom.

Only Mrs. Hatcher's sternest demeanor, saved for such occasions, convinced Mr. Evan that Prudence would be well cared for if only he would release her.

Prudence hid a smile behind her lace handkerchief.

Whatever his reason for wanting to speak with her, Mr. Evan would be waiting once the proceedings were concluded. At least she would have the opportunity to thank him for rescuing her a second time.

The solicitor cleared his throat, and a hush fell on the room.

The reading of her grandmother's will started with a few minor bequests. Some of the tenant farmers that had shown extraordinary potential over the years were given titles to the land they worked. Others on the estate staff were given sums of money to help them move forward in life. They were minor gifts compared to the Ashcroft fortune, but for the recipients, these arrangements could mean a new life, one lived on their own terms.

Pride swelled Prudence's heart. Leave it to her grandmother to continue to help people even after her death.

Mrs. Hatcher was to be given an annual income after her retirement so she could live out the remainder of her days without fear of want.

The solicitor read the will in his loud, clear voice. "She has been a friend to me as well as a godsend. She was with me when my daughter was born and when she was taken from me, as well as when my own dear husband followed my daughter to the grave. Agatha Hatcher helped me through those difficult times, and I can't imagine anyone better to have at my side as I make my own passing into the next life."

Next, Mr. Whitley read a name Prudence didn't recognize.

"Captain Foster is to be given full discretion as to the construction of the *Cythraul* and full command of her when she is finished. The ship is to be his to run as he sees fit, and upon a year of successful service to Ashcroft & Sons, the title is to be signed over to him."

The audience let out a collective gasp at the generosity of this bequest.

Prudence scanned the room, looking for the lucky captain. Neighbor whispered to neighbor, shrugged their shoulders, and craned their necks with her.

Who was Captain Foster? She had met most of the

sea captains in her grandmother's employ. Those she hadn't met, she had heard about. To have been granted such a generous and unusual gift, he must have won her grandmother's admiration.

Prudence froze in her seat.

Had he been more than that? More than a simple captain in her grandmother's employ?

Prudence scanned the gathering again, her eyes flitting from face to face.

She had been away at school for the majority of the past several years. Did her grandmother have a life she kept from her granddaughter? Had she taken a lover?

Prudence nearly scoffed aloud and swung back around.

She would ask Richard about it later and discover the truth behind Captain Foster. Her grandmother's paramour or not, Richard would know if the mysterious captain could be trusted.

Prudence's attention refocused on Mr. Whitley when he read her name.

"My granddaughter, Prudence Ashcroft, who is the light of my life and my one pride, shall inherit the bulk of my estate and sole ownership of Ashcroft & Sons," he paused and cleared his throat, "on the condition that she marry."

Gasps filled the library. One of them belonged to Prudence.

She would only receive the estate and the family business on the condition that she marry? Prudence snapped her lips shut when she realized her jaw had dropped to her chest.

Mr. Whitley waited for the buzzing to die down. When he had the majority of the room's attention once more, he cleared his throat again and continued.

"If she does not marry, she will be given the estate and lands plus a yearly allowance to be deposited into an account to which she has sole and full discretionary access. This amount will be enough to cover household expenses, personal necessities, and luxuries such as can be afforded by the estate and the annual income of the business. As business manager, Richard Bainbridge will be responsible for representing Ashcroft & Sons to my solicitors at Whitley and Jamison. They will determine the amounts to be deposited."

Prudence's lips tingled as the blood drained from them. Her grandmother had actually been serious about this marriage business. So serious she had outlined the provisions in her will.

The solicitor leveled a gaze at Richard from beneath the gray shrubbery that passed for his eyebrows.

"Richard, I need you to be strong." It was Mr. Whitley's voice, but Prudence could hear her grandmother's female tones superimposed over the solicitor's deep baritone. "I am quite serious about this, and I will come back to haunt you if my instructions are not carried out."

There was the muffled sound of polite tittering from behind gloved hands.

That was Grandma Rachel's sense of humor, all right. This hardly seemed like the time for it.

Prudence shot a quick glance at Richard and caught his smile before he could suppress it. She scowled, and he shrugged his shoulders as if to say he had nothing to do with it.

"Most of all," Mr. Whitley continued, "do not let

Prudence talk you into a marriage of convenience. You will both be miserable, and you will lose the most valuable possession either of you has—your friendship."

Mr. Whitley leveled his gray eyes at Prudence next, and she fought the urge to squirm. Good heavens, what more could there be?

"Prudence, I give you a grace period of three months from my death to select a man of your own choosing. After that time, Richard will need to approve of your choice, and I give him leave to choose for you."

Prudence thought she heard Richard groan, but she couldn't be sure over the growing voices of those around her.

"Richard, remember, I need you to be strong," Mr. Whitley read from the page, raising his voice above the din of speculation.

This time, a snort mixed with the polite chuckles.

"Prudence, if you refuse to marry, you shall be granted the allowance as I described. However, the running of Ashcroft & Sons will be left to Richard. Upon his death, the business shall be bequeathed to his heirs, as you will have none. While you remain unmarried, your part in the business shall be strictly limited to those tasks Richard deems suitable to your experience and temperament. In short, you will work for him instead of the other way around."

Prudence cast a sidelong look at Richard. He had managed to suppress his smile even though his eyes crinkled at the corners. Did he enjoy this humiliation?

"Richard, remember, you must be strong," Mr. Whitley said again, his voice squeaking on the final word against the strain of repressed laughter.

Around her, the audience no longer tried to hide their amusement. Even Richard couldn't stop from chuckling. Prudence gave him a nudge with a sharp elbow and glared at him. Turning to her, he bit his lip, but she could see the laughter in his hazel eyes.

He *would* find humor in this situation. After all, if she didn't choose a husband, he would have to choose one for her. Either that, or she would forfeit her part in running the business, and it would fall to him and his heirs. He had much to gain from this little arrangement.

Grandma Rachel had evidently considered that possibility as well.

"Richard, I trust you with my granddaughter and my empire. However, lest you be tempted to dispose of any man of Prudence's choosing, might I remind you that if she remains unmarried, she will be working for you, and you will be in the unenviable position of having to tell her what to do." Even the dour Mr. Whitley could no longer keep from laughing as he finished the sentence.

He pulled a lace handkerchief from his sleeve to dab at his eyes, then composed himself enough to continue. "Finally, Prudence, I know it is fashionable to wear mourning attire for at least a year, but I don't want you to. Black crape will swallow you up and make you even more ghostly looking than me. And besides, wearing pastels and other more cheerful shades will make it easier for you to attract a husband. Like a flower to the bee, as I always say."

Laughter bounced off the walls as Mr. Whitley snapped the book shut. "That's it, ladies and gentlemen. I wish to thank you all for coming today."

Prudence remained seated, while chairs squeaked

against the parquet floor as those around her rose to their feet. She should do her part as hostess, thank them for coming and see them off, but she really did not wish to face anyone at this moment.

With a cautious glance at her, Richard did his best to usher those that lingered from the room.

Mr. Whitley eyed Prudence. Unfortunately, she could not avoid him just now. She met his steady gaze with one of her own.

"You may inform me when you've made your choice." His smile dissolved, but his eyes were warmer than she had ever seen them. "Otherwise, three months hence, I shall work out arrangements with Mr. Bainbridge for your allowance to be deposited into an account to which you shall have sole discretion and full access according to Mrs. Ashcroft's wishes."

"Thank you. Mr. Whitley." She thrust her hand at him. "You shall be hearing from me shortly."

What he would be hearing, she had no idea.

Mr. Whitley hesitated a moment before taking her hand, but once he did, he seemed reluctant to let go.

"Prudence, I am sorry for your loss. Rachel Ashcroft was a remarkable woman, and she loved you more than life itself. She wanted only your happiness and security," he paused, "but, perhaps, not necessarily in that order."

Prudence nodded but said nothing. As soon as Mr. Whitley released her hand, she turned and fled through the study door.

A few people lingered in the foyer, waiting to offer their condolences or perhaps for an opportunity to speak with her about some business or estate matter. She was, for the next three months anyway, the head of the business and the household.

Mr. Evan waited among them, his hat still in his hands. Prudence rushed past him, without a second glance.

If only he could rescue her once more.

Chapter Seven

Prudence strode along the gritty path that edged the cove just above where the beach met the land. On any other day, she might have shucked her shoes and stockings and walked along the shore, letting the sun-warmed sand squish between her bare toes while she explored the flotsam left behind by the retreating tide.

Today, however, she had more serious thoughts on her mind. She took the route toward the top of the cliffs overlooking the bay. Even as a child, this barren windswept vantage point had been the place where she sorted out her most perplexing problems.

She would not lose the business. Grandma Rachel had run it profitably after Grandfather died, and so could she. Although she didn't have her grandmother's experience or her skill with people, Richard would help her avoid any poor decisions. Between the two of them, she had more ambition than Richard, but he had the experience and the wisdom. Together, they almost added up to one Rachel Ashcroft. Almost.

Prudence paused for a moment to consider that her grandmother's will did not necessarily require that she marry. She and Richard would be partners regardless of who owned the business.

She kicked a small stone and watched it skip along the path then veer over the edge of the cliff.

No, it wouldn't be the same. She resumed her

course. It was in Richard's very nature to be more cautious, and if she worked for him, she might not have as much sway when it came time to take a few risks.

Prudence topped the rise, and the sight of the sea, spreading out before her like a bright blue blanket, made her breath catch. The cool, salty breeze brushed at her face, making everything about her seem fresh and new, and full of possibility.

Perhaps this was why she climbed the cliffs when something troubled her. It wasn't that she always resolved her troubles at this height, but compared to the wonder of the ocean and the vastness of the sky, her own personal problems faded into insignificance.

****

Evan Foster's legs ached from trying to catch up to Prudence Ashcroft. The route she had taken gradually sloped up until it topped a cliff overlooking the beach. Evan glanced over his shoulder toward the stables, now some miles distant in the valley below. He would have caught up to her by now, but she strode with such purpose that he had been forced into a jog to make up the ground.

He wasn't unaccustomed to exercise. However, standing on the rolling deck of a ship or a vigorous ride through the countryside was exercise of a different sort. Clearly, Miss Ashcroft took this path often and had grown inured to the exertion. Had the worn path beneath their feet been entirely of her making? It wouldn't have surprised him.

Evan wasn't certain what caused him to start out after her when he saw her pass the stables, the lavender bow on her straw bonnet flapping behind her like a pennant in the breeze.

At first, he had been curious about her destination. Wherever it might be, she seemed determined to arrive as quickly as possible. Yet, nothing lay in the direction they were headed except the Rhode Island countryside and a cove favored by smugglers for generations. Furthermore, she appeared to be having a discussion with some imaginary companion. He was still too far away to hear what she said, but her lips moved and she kept waving her hand in the air as though punctuating her points. Every now and then, she stopped, placed her hands on her hips, and stared out at the sea.

With a grunt, Evan picked up his pace. He wanted to catch up with Prudence Ashcroft before the local constable decided she had taken leave of her senses.

When he pulled within hailing distance, Evan cupped his hands around his mouth. "Miss Ashcroft! Ahoy there."

She stopped her pacing and turned to watch him climb the last few yards to join her.

"Good morning, Mr. Evan." She squinted at him in a way that had nothing to do with the sunlight reflecting off the bay.

He shouldn't be surprised. Judging from the way she had charged from the room yesterday, he guessed the stipulations in her grandmother's will had come as something of a shock. He considered for a moment that he should have let her lick her wounds in peace, but there was nothing he could do now. He trudged the last few feet to join her at the top of the cliff.

"Good morning, Miss Ashcroft." Evan doffed his hat and tried not to gasp for air.

"What brings you out here this morning?"

From any other woman, the question might have

been the opening to polite conversation. From Prudence, it sounded more like a demand for information.

"Just taking my morning stroll, ma'am," he replied, thinking how pretty her eyes were when they flashed in the morning sun. At times, they looked almost transparent, at other times, dark and murky. "How are you faring this morning?"

Prudence's gaze dipped to her feet, and Evan felt a twinge of regret. Yes, he should have let her lick her wounds in peace.

After a moment's hesitation, she glanced up. "I am doing well, thank you."

Her bronze brows knitted together as though she wanted to say more but didn't know where to begin. Evan waited for her to choose.

As if donning a mask, the uncertainty disappeared, and Prudence gave an embarrassed tinkle of a laugh. "I'm glad you joined me, Mr. Evan."

The embarrassed laughter did not fit Prudence's personality well. It sounded like an affectation she had picked up because she thought it expected of her. He much preferred the other Prudence Ashcroft. Stubborn. Willful. Intriguing.

"Are you? Why is that?"

"Well, I don't really know where to begin, but I feel I must apologize for the way I've treated you."

Prudence started walking along the footpath that skirted Smuggler's Bay, and Evan fell in beside her, his feet swooshing though the long grass at the path's edge.

"How did you treat me?" he asked.

"Poorly. I ordered you about as if you were a servant when all you've done is come to my rescue."

Prudence cast him a sheepish grin. "Twice."

"But I am a servant," Evan pointed out.

Or at least Prudence thought him a servant. In time, she would find out who he really was, but he rather enjoyed being the stable master for now. It allowed him to see a side of Prudence she might not show once she understood the full truth. Besides, Stu wouldn't mind if he borrowed his identity for such a good cause.

"Well, yes, I suppose so, but stable master is an incredibly important position, especially at Ashcroft. Why, your role is nearly as important as Richard's."

"Richard? Do you mean the stuffy young man sitting next to you at the reading?"

Did anything lie between Richard and Prudence? Evidently, her grandmother didn't think so, but guardians were often the last to know.

"Richard is...*was* my grandmother's man of business." Prudence swallowed. "I guess he's mine now."

A comely blush stained her cheeks.

"For the next three months, anyway," Evan couldn't resist adding.

Seeing Prudence blush over the man left Evan feeling...well, he wasn't sure how he felt exactly. What did he care if his employer was spoken for? What did he care if the man was a stodgy-looking fool? He didn't.

"Yes, well anyway, I hope you'll accept my apology for the way I behaved." She showed admirable self-control, but Evan detected an underlying tightness in her voice.

He turned toward Prudence, surprised to see pain instead of anger lingering in her eyes. Perhaps he had misunderstood the reason for the color in her cheeks. Perhaps her thoughts had been on her predicament and not on the man seated beside her.

Who was the fool now?

"I can only imagine how it must feel to lose someone you love so deeply," Evan said, his voice conveying the sincerity of his words.

Prudence's shoulders relaxed as if an inner defense had crumbled. "Have you never lost someone like that?"

"I have never loved someone like that."

Prudence gave a small nod of acknowledgement, but Evan didn't detect pity in her green-eyed gaze. He could almost see her processing his words, coming to grips with his statement, and filing it away. He could grow used to talking with a woman who didn't need to pry into his background and make more out of it than it deserved.

A flash of sunlight on a distant sail caught his eye. He turned to watch a schooner coming about. "Looks like they are patrolling the bay again."

"Yes," Prudence agreed, the tight set of her jaw giving away her thoughts. "Most likely, they are on the lookout for smugglers."

"Smugglers?" Evan feigned ignorance. "Here in Rhode Island? What do they smuggle?"

"W…well." Her gaze darted about. "I hear there are some who smuggle tea, others Madeira. I suppose there is no limit to what they might smuggle considering the British controls on our imports and the outrageous duties they charge. Of course, that is all hearsay," she hastened to add. "I only know about it through conversations I've overheard in town. Perhaps the tales were exaggerated."

"Perhaps," Evan agreed.

Evidently, Prudence was not entirely in the dark on certain aspects of her family's business. He found the idea of keeping Rachel Ashcroft's secret from her granddaughter an unpalatable one. Of course, if she didn't learn to control her expressions, it wouldn't be a secret for long.

"So tell me about Ashcroft & Sons," Evan said.

Prudence's eyes widened. "What do you want to know?"

"Well, for starters, where are the sons?"

Prudence laughed. "I'm afraid you're looking at him."

Evan took the reply as an invitation to peruse her lithe figure. "I don't believe it."

A blush crept to her cheeks again.

"It's the family curse, I'm afraid. There never were any sons. My great grandfather's surname was Wainwright. He immigrated to America with his young daughter and not a penny in his pocket after his wife ran off with a duke."

Prudence clasped her hands behind her back as she strolled and recounted her family's history. Evan wondered if she realized the position of her arms had a delightful way of making her pert breasts appear more prominent. Probably not.

"In America, he met up with my grandfather, John Ashcroft, and they started the business. Not only were they successful business partners, but my great grandfather genuinely liked John and did everything he could to marry him to his only daughter."

"He must have succeeded," Evan interjected, trying

to keep his gaze from straying from Prudence's face.

Prudence gave him a wry smile. "I understand she put up quite a fuss. My grandfather could be a bit heavy handed."

"He beat her?" Evan asked. Surely, no man would raise a hand to Rachel Ashcroft.

"Oh, no, of course not." Prudence waved her hands. "He simply tended to like to have things his way while my grandmother liked to have things her way. Nevertheless, theirs was a marriage filled with great joy."

"But only one child?"

"Yes. Great Grandfather never remarried so Grandma Rachel remained an only child and my mother hers—"

"And you were your mother's only child," Evan finished for her.

"Yes, the sad secret behind the family name is there are no real Ashcrofts left. I am, in fact, a Saunders." Prudence gave a small shrug of acceptance. "I suppose you're thinking that it is unfortunate there were no sons to inherit the estate."

"No, I'm thinking it probably made it easier not having to split the inheritance with anyone. Or, heaven forbid, be at the mercy of an idiot brother who inherited the lion's share, then through mismanagement, a game of chance, or whatever ill-fate awaited him, managed to lose it all only to come begging for what little was bequeathed to you."

Prudence laughed. "My, you do have a flair for the dramatic, Mr. Evan."

Evan laughed with her. He had never met a woman so easy to talk with. But then again, the sisters had always been more interested in his immortal soul than in his thoughts. After escaping their clutches, he spent much of his youth aboard ship with no opportunity to talk with women, except the whores who weren't all that interested in a scrawny young lad with no money.

Listening to Prudence made him wonder what it would be like to actually be friends with a woman. She and that Richard Bainbridge were friends, perhaps more. When Bainbridge wasn't hovering at her side, his hungry gaze followed her about the room.

"Did your grandparents and your parents marry for money and not love?"

Prudence cocked her head, and he realized how impertinent the question must sound coming from a man she thought of as a servant. He hadn't meant to overstep his bounds; he just didn't like thinking about Prudence in the arms of the all-too-perfect Bainbridge.

"No, Great Grandfather never remarried. Grandma Rachel told me he kept a portrait of his wife in his bedroom until the day he died. And Grandma Rachel was desperately in love with my grandfather, although…"

"Although?" Evan prodded.

"Oh, it's nothing." Prudence waved a dismissive hand but stared at the ground as she walked.

It didn't appear to be nothing the way she chewed her lower lip, but Evan decided not to pull on that thread too hard lest he unravel the rapport he had managed to build with his employer.

"How about your mother?" he asked instead.

"My mother?" Prudence glanced up. "I'm afraid I didn't really get a chance to know my parents. I am told my father died in a hunting accident, and my mother died soon after of a broken heart."

"Then it wasn't for lack of trying, was it?" Evan gave a knowing nod.

Prudence stopped walking and turned toward him. "What wasn't?"

The wind toyed with a dark red curl that had crept from beneath her bonnet to play across her forehead. Evan clasped his hands behind his back to keep from reaching out to tug at it.

"It wasn't for lack of trying that your great grandfather, grandfather, and father only managed to sire one child apiece."

When he finished his explanation, Prudence's cheeks were as crimson as the curl dancing in the sun.

"No, I suppose it wasn't," she said, her tone crisp.

Prudence turned on her heel and resumed her brisk pace up the rise leading to the top of the cliff. Evan jogged to catch up, considering whether he should apologize for the outrageous remark. He reached for her elbow, intending to stop her progress so he could at least make a proper apology. She whirled around before he had the chance.

"The theory is that Ashcroft women are too scrawny." Prudence held her chin in the air as though daring him to contradict her, but the dejected tone in her voice told Evan all he needed to know.

"Scrawny?"

Prudence lowered her chin a notch. "Yes, as in too thin."

Evan shrugged. "That's a first, but then what do I know of medicine?"

"Dr. Willis agrees with you for what it's worth. When I was about eleven, I heard some local boys talking about it, and I worked up the courage to ask him." She hid a giggle behind her hand. "His face looked like a beet, freshly pulled from the garden. He answered my question but told me it was not a proper topic for young ladies. I never thought a doctor could be so easily embarrassed."

Evan stood still, enraptured at how the emotions played across Prudence's expressive face. One moment, the pain of the childhood taunts shone in her green eyes. The next, they sparkled with merriment as she remembered grilling poor Dr. Willis on the nuances of female fertility. Evan decided to take advantage of her momentary flash of good humor.

"Besides, I wouldn't say scrawny." He gave her a head to toe perusal that had Prudence crossing her arms over her none too ample chest. "More...athletic."

"Athletic!" Prudence snorted. "Thank you very much. I feel so much better now."

"Isn't athletic good?" Evan admired the rising color in her cheeks.

"Not if you're a woman looking to catch a husband," Prudence said.

"If you're looking to *catch* a husband, I would have thought athletic was preferable."

Prudence bubbled with laughter. Evan grinned at her, letting her enjoy the moment.

When her laughter died down, he turned serious. "Is that what you want? To catch a husband?"

"That's not the point of this discussion, Mr. Evan," Prudence admonished him in a soft voice.

"That's not an answer either, Miss Ashcroft."

Prudence sniffed and turned her face toward the cove. "Perhaps not, but is the answer important? My grandmother has forced my hand." Her eyes scanned the horizon as though she were looking for something. "You must understand that since you were at the reading of the will."

"So how do you propose to catch a husband?" Evan hoped to avoid the questions his presence at the reading might bring. "Despite my earlier assertions, I believe it would appear rather unseemly if you attempted to run one down." He gave her another head to toe inspection. "Besides, you don't appear to have the bulk to wrestle one to the ground."

Prudence's laughter swelled his heart. He loved the sound of it, perhaps even more so when he was the cause.

"Money, Mr. Evan." The laughter in her voice faded.

"Money?" Evan's blood ran cold, but he tried to make light of her words. "I'll admit, I am new to Rhode Island, but I am not aware of a market where young ladies can buy a husband."

"Aren't you?" She turned and started walking back down the hill. "Money has purchased more than one husband for unmarriageable ladies throughout the years."

"Unmarriageable?" Evan asked. "Are you speaking of yourself?"

Prudence shrugged. "Perhaps that is a bit strong, but I must be realistic."

"What about love?" Evan walked faster to catch up with her. "Your grandmother found it. Your mother found it. Why can't you?"

"Love?" She said the word as though it tasted sour. "Mr. Evan, I suspect you've made a wager or two in your life. Am I right?"

"On many things."

Of course, he would never have bet that he would be standing on top of a cliff, arguing the merits of marrying for love with a woman who seemed determined to reject the possibility.

She stopped and faced him, hands on her hips.

"Reality dictates that I face the fact that my chances of marrying for love were never that great to begin with. What odds would you lay on my chances of a man falling in love with me, or me with him for that matter, within the next three months?"

"I admit those are not odds I'd take, but then neither would I bet against it."

"Why not?"

"Because I prefer a sure thing, Miss Ashcroft."

Chapter Eight

Prudence steadied herself against the ornamental table in the hallway outside her room.

Had she really just fled from Mr. Evan? No. Of course not. An Ashcroft would never flee. She simply bade him a good day before making her way back down the path. Alone. As close to a run as the loose soil would allow. She slumped against the table, one hip supporting her. She had fled.

But why?

There was nothing sinister about Mr. Evan. Quite the opposite, in fact. He had come to her rescue twice, yet hadn't tried to use that fact to gain any sort of advantage. He seemed quite ready to accept an apology for her behavior, all the while proclaiming an apology unnecessary. While he wasn't as deferential as the average Ashcroft employee, neither had he been rude.

A little familiar, perhaps. Her face warmed. But not rude.

So why had she panicked?

There had been something in his eyes. But what? Friendliness? Appreciation? Desire?

No, the latter just wasn't possible.

Prudence studied herself in the ornate mirror above the table. The muted afternoon sunlight streaming in from the tall windows at the end of the long hall gave her flushed face a soft glow but did nothing to hide her disheveled state.

She tugged off her formerly white cap, and a layer of grit fell from the ruffled brim. Hair pins bounced and danced across the table. Her lopsided chignon melted away, and her hair tumbled over her shoulders in a tangle of auburn curls.

It could *not* have been desire she read in his eyes. He would have to be mad to desire a woman so lacking in refinement.

But there had been something there. She had seen it in his eyes. Sensed a connection unlike anything she had ever felt before, with anyone.

But then, she had never met anyone like Mr. Evan before. Talking with him was even easier than talking to Richard. So much so, that she let down her guard and almost told him the whole of her marriage plans. She certainly shared more than she would have with Richard.

Green eyes contemplated her from the mirror.

Perhaps that was why she fled. Perhaps she simply wanted to avoid giving away her plans. Not that Mr. Evan could hinder her in any way, but she didn't care to have him privy to her innermost thoughts.

Her reflection arched an eyebrow.

No, it was more than that. She hadn't fled from Mr. Evan so much as the seed of an idea that he had planted. She chewed her lower lip and gave her mirrored counterpart a pensive look.

Maybe…just possibly…there might be a chance… could she fulfill her grandmother's wishes without ceding her rightful place at the head of Ashcroft?

"Would Mr. Evan do?" she asked her reflection.

Green eyes warmed.

He seemed curious, but not overly inquisitive. She had been tense and ready for a barrage of questions when he pointed out the patrol boat in the harbor. However, his interest had been more polite than concerned, as though they were discussing the latest gossip over a cup of tea.

She no longer considered him a simpleton. Not a man of business to be sure, but then a stable master required a certain kind of intelligence. If not with numbers, at least with animals. More to the point, he seemed kind and easy to be around. If nothing else, she could certainly be friends with him. Couldn't she?

But would he agree?

Prudence frowned at her reflection. That might be a challenge.

But then again, he was a stable master. Surely the money would entice him, even if she could not.

I wouldn't say scrawny.

The corner of his lips had turned up as he said those words. He might have been teasing her, but had she detected a certain…*appreciation* in his voice? More than once, she caught his gaze lingering on her bodice.

At the time, she thought him to be judging her poor taste in fashion. The gown she wore was at least ten years out of fashion, and as was her custom when she walked the path along the cliffs or rode Bolt through the meadow, she had worn jumps instead of stays.

Some considered the lack of formality a sign of a disreputable character, a looseness of morals. But thinking back, she couldn't detect any sign of disapproval in his handsome face.

But what had she seen in his dark eyes?

Prudence ran a hand down the front of her bodice.

While fashion dictated a conical shape, her shape would better be described as a tube. Although her waist was narrow, her chest was hardly much wider. Even when she wore a corset, tying it tight enough to press her breasts upward made her chest appear even smaller.

Prudence sighed and dropped her hand. Did she really want a man who would find her appealing anyway? One who might insist on his marital rights?

Her reflection arched the other eyebrow.

These fledgling feelings that so upset her stomach and disquieted her nerves would go away in time. She was sure of it. And it wasn't as if Mr. Evan would suffer. With his newfound wealth, he could well afford to satisfy his needs elsewhere.

An unexpected tightness settled in her chest.

Should he happen to want her, then... She gave her unflattering reflection a dismissive glance.

No, her proposition would need to remain a business arrangement. No good could come of thinking about that which she would never have.

"Did you have a good walk, miss?"

Prudence started at the sound of Netty's voice. She whirled to face her maid.

"Yes, Netty, thank you."

How long had she been there? She studied Netty's beautiful, impassive face. Had her maid been lurking in the corner, watching her?

"Can I get you some tea, Miss Ashcroft? You must be positively exhausted after your walk."

Netty's tone seemed vaguely disapproving, but not enough to warrant an admonishment. Besides, it could just be her imagination.

The knot in Prudence's stomach unwound.

"Netty, I would like some refreshment, but not tea." The path she was about to embark upon called for something stronger than tea. "Perhaps a glass of Madeira. Bring it to my room, please."

Netty paused for a moment, almost as if unsure she had heard her mistress right. A flash of something unfathomable crossed her face, then disappeared.

"Yes, miss." Netty gave a half-hearted curtsey and vanished down the back stairs.

Prudence and her green-eyed reflection eyed each other with approbation. She would need strength, but she also felt like celebrating. If all went well, her troubles would soon be behind her.

****

By the time Netty knocked on her bedroom door, serving tray in hand, Prudence had settled herself at the writing desk, blank parchment in front of her, quill poised above it.

Netty set the silver tray containing a bottle of Madeira and a crystal goblet on the desk beside her.

Prudence composed the beginning of her note in her head while she waited for her maid to leave. Netty didn't move.

Prudence glanced over her shoulder. Had Netty's gaze been on the parchment?

"Shall I pour for you, miss?" Netty's smile looked like an afterthought.

"No, thank you. That will be all, Netty."

Netty's calico skirt and petticoats rustled when she shifted her weight, but she didn't move toward the door. "Would you like some light in here, Miss Ashcroft? Perhaps I can open the curtains for you?"

"No, thank you, Netty."

"Something to eat?"

"Thank you, Netty, but no." Prudence gave her maid a hard look. "Now, I really do have piles of correspondence to catch up on this afternoon. I'd appreciate it if you kept me from being disturbed."

"Yes, of course, Miss Ashcroft."

With a haughty air, but a definite reluctance in her step, Netty left Prudence to her task. Prudence watched her go, almost envying the regal way Netty carried herself. She considered, not for the first time, what sort of history her maid had left behind before coming to Ashcroft.

She had been in Boston when Netty arrived at Ashcroft, but if memory served, Grandma Rachel had purchased her indenture to ensure the beautiful girl had a position where she would be safe from disreputable male employers who preyed on the less fortunate.

As their length of servitude was temporary, at least theoretically, Rachel Ashcroft hadn't insisted on the formal propriety of so many of the wealthy elite in the colonies. At Ashcroft, even maids like Netty wore calicoes and other fine fabrics with brightly printed designs. Though often cast-offs or fashions that had gone out of style, Grandma Rachel felt it gave them a sense of individuality that would serve them well once they earned their independence. She hadn't condoned the practice of indentured servitude, but as long as she couldn't do anything about it as a whole, she looked for ways to help individuals who had been caught in its web.

Still, not everyone appreciated the help. Was Netty like an apple freshly fallen from the tree? Even though they might look bright and shiny, in reality their core had already begun to rot.

Prudence shook off the vague sense of wariness she always had when her maid was around. She would deal with that later. For now, she had a letter to write.

How did one go about proposing marriage to a man? She paused for only a moment before the words flew from her quill as naturally as if she spoke them aloud.

Mr. Evan,

 As you are aware, I must marry within the next three months. I have decided you are an appropriate choice and would ask that you agree to marry me as soon as can conveniently be arranged. I will have my man of business draw up the specifics and deliver them to you.

    Miss Prudence Ashcroft

Prudence frowned as she reread her note. The coldness of the words didn't seem appropriate for a man as warm as Mr. Evan.

She didn't want to get too far into the specifics of the arrangement. That was best left for a face-to-face discussion. However, she must not lead him to believe she felt nothing for him. Their marriage might be a business arrangement, but that did not mean they could not be friends. After all, she had a business relationship with Richard, and they were still friends.

Prudence crumpled the paper into a ball and tossed it into the smoldering embers in the hearth. It flared to life for a moment then crumbled to ash.

Satisfied no one could read her ill-crafted proposal should they find it when they came to sweep the hearth, she pulled out a fresh piece of parchment and began again.

My Dearest Mr. Evan,

Yes, that was how a woman should greet the man she planned to marry.

As you are aware, I must marry within the next three months.

Prudence considered crumpling the paper and starting again, but there could be no getting around the cold facts behind her proposal. Better to lay them out so Mr. Evan did not wonder about her purpose.

I have decided we would suit each other well, and I hope, after giving this careful consideration, you will come to the same conclusion.

Prudence tapped the quill against her chin. How old was Mr. Evan anyway? Twenty and four? Twenty and five? Maybe older, but certainly not yet thirty. Although a man of means might make an advantageous match in his early twenties, she had no idea at what age a man of Mr. Evan's means settled down. He might not even be contemplating marriage yet.

Then again, given his comments of this afternoon, it was clear he still considered love fundamental to marriage. Was *he* holding out for love?

She knew of muddle-headed women who still believed in romantic notions of love, but she had never heard of a man doing so. No, men were more pragmatic. He would gauge the advantages in a more practical light.

She didn't really need to spell it out in detail. The advantages of the union should be obvious, even to him. He would rise from the honorable but rather lowly position of stable master to head of an enormous empire. In title at least, he would also be head of

Ashcroft & Sons. With that, came respect and wealth beyond anything he was ever likely to have imagined for himself.

Recalling the words he had spoken at the top of the cliff, Prudence set quill to paper.

While a marriage to me may not have been what you had in mind, think of my proposal as the sure thing you were looking for. A marriage into the Ashcroft family will see you well-compensated.

Yes, that would do. She didn't want to imply too much. After all, Ashcroft would still be hers. While there was nothing she could do about the way society would view their union, when he came to discuss the particulars of their arrangement, she would make it clear the business was still hers, but that he would not go unrewarded.

Now to deliver it. Prudence reached for the bellpull, but her hand faltered. She could not simply call Netty back. The girl may not suspect anything, but she didn't trust her. Surely she would read it, and the entire household would know their mistress had been desperate enough to propose to the stable master.

Of course, there was always the chance Mr. Evan would not agree to her proposal. While she had money, she didn't have much else to offer, and he might have a more traditional marriage in mind. Her face heated as she imagined what that entailed. The embarrassment of having the household staff know she had proposed to the stable master—and been refused—would be more than she could bear.

Fanning herself with the letter, Prudence went in search of Mrs. Hatcher. She found her in the dining room polishing the furniture.

"Mrs. Hatcher, I wonder if you could do a favor for me?"

Mrs. Hatcher tucked the oily cloth into her pocket then wiped her hands on her apron. "Yes, of course, Miss Ashcroft. What can I do for you?"

"Will you send one of the lads to deliver this to Mr. Evan?"

Prudence held out the small yellow envelope that held the key to her future. Mrs. Hatcher had to give a small tug before she released it.

"Mr. Evan? I don't believe I'm acquainted with anyone by that name." She studied the unmarked envelope.

"Mr. Evan. The new stable master."

Prudence fought the urge to snatch the letter back and tell her housekeeper to forget all about it.

Mrs. Hatcher's brows furrowed even more than usual. "Now what would you be wantin' with that man?"

"I just wanted to thank him for his assistance."

From the fierce set of Mrs. Hatcher's jaw, Prudence could tell her housekeeper didn't need reminding of how she had been carried into the manor, dripping wet, in the arms of the stable master.

"He's been thanked enough. After I saw to you, I sat him down in my kitchen and gave him a meat pie while he and Gil shared a pint of ale." Mrs. Hatcher clutched the envelope in her bony fingers so hard it crumpled.

"He was here?" Prudence hadn't known Mr. Evan had lingered at the manor after releasing her, somewhat reluctantly, into Mrs. Hatcher's hands.

"He seemed worried about you." Mrs. Hatcher's eyes softened, but only for a moment. "Perhaps a little too worried. But don't you fret. Gil explained the way of things."

"What exactly did he explain?" Prudence was almost afraid to ask.

Mrs. Hatcher stuffed Prudence's note in one pocket then snatched the rag from the other. She began polishing the top of the table with renewed vigor.

"That you are a well-born young lady of high social standing. That despite being a girl, you attended one of the finest schools to prepare you to take your rightful place at the head of Ashcroft & Sons." Her voice rose and fell in an almost musical pattern as she made circles across the mirror-like surface. "That you have an impeccable reputation, and we intend to keep it that way."

"You said what?" Prudence clutched the back of one of the walnut chairs.

Prudence melted into the chair. On any other day, she would have been warmed by Mrs. Hatcher's confidence in her abilities, but the woman's newfound conviction had been ill timed.

"We, or rather Gil"—she glanced away—"simply explained that you are not for him."

"I really don't think that was necessary, Mrs. Hatcher. I'm sure Mr. Evan has no designs on me."

Not yet, but would he still be open to the idea after being warned off by her servants?

"Oh, posh!" Mrs. Hatcher placed a bony fist on one hip while she waved her rag around with the other. "You could see what he was thinking in those dark eyes of his. He's just like any other man that sees something he wants. He don't stop for a moment to think that maybe he can't have it."

She went back to polishing the table. "But Gil told him not to go sniffin' around your skirts."

"He told him what?" Prudence had never heard the phrase before, but the images it brought to mind were of the most vulgar sort.

"I'm sorry, dearie. I didn't mean to use such language with you. I was just rememberin' what Gil said."

Gil had actually used those words with Mr. Evan? Prudence had a momentary urge to crawl under the table.

Should she wait to deliver her proposal? Maybe he would think she had put those ideas into Gil's head. Perhaps he would think she was sniffing around his…whatever. Prudence shook the even more disturbing images from her mind.

No, she didn't have time to wait. She had three months to convince some suitable man to marry her, and so far, Mr. Evan was the only one she could think of.

"Mrs. Hatcher, I would appreciate it if you would have one of the lads deliver my note to Mr. Evan."

Mrs. Hatcher gave her the same wizened look she wore when Prudence had gotten into mischief as a child. "Miss Ashcroft, I know you're the lady of the house now, and I work for you. Still, I made a promise to your grandmother that I would keep an eye out for you. I served her for a long time, and a little thing like death doesn't wipe away my obligations to her. If you're cooking something up in that head of yours, perhaps you should run it by me before you run it by the stable master."

"I assure you Mrs. Hatcher, it's nothing but a thank you for coming to my rescue. It's what my grandmother would do, were she still here."

At the mention of Grandma Rachel, Mrs. Hatcher's defenses crumbled.

"Very well." She gave her new mistress a long look with skeptical eyes. "I'll see that he gets it."

"Thank you, Mrs. Hatcher."

She left the study before her stubborn housekeeper could change her mind.

Her plan set in motion, Prudence's heart lifted. Although not an intellect of the highest order, surely Mr. Evan had shown himself to be a practical man. Grandma Rachel must have seen some potential in him when she hired him to be the stable master at Ashcroft.

Not that she would have considered him a suitable match for her granddaughter.

Prudence paused, one hand on the banister. Or would she?

Her great grandfather and her grandfather had both been men of common means. While her grandmother had done her share of high-society entertaining, her true friends, those she invited to the manor for small private parties, came from all walks of life. She was as likely to have tea with the miller's wife as dinner at the governor's mansion.

Prudence climbed the stairs, deep in thought.

But the stable master?

Why not? Her grandmother would have wanted her to marry a man with whom she could be friends. Her admonition against marrying Richard, a man who was already her dearest friend in the world, indicated she wanted her granddaughter to have more. Still, it had been Grandma Rachel herself who removed that possibility when she demanded Prudence marry within three months.

Besides, what man could possibly refuse such a generous proposal?

Chapter Nine

Prudence's smile froze. "Mr. Evan."

Mr. Evan's eyebrows rose, suggesting he had noted the surprise in her voice. Prudence had been expecting her solicitor, not her stable master and soon-to-be fiancé.

She recovered herself. Or so she hoped. "Thank you, Gil, that will be all."

The butler left the parlor, and Prudence found herself alone with the one man she least wanted to be alone with at that moment.

She would have need of him soon enough, of course. But not yet.

First, she had to define her terms. Only then could she present them in the way that offered the greatest chance for a successful negotiation. To be less than prepared could spell disaster.

One look at Mr. Evan's dark eyes told her that negotiations might be futile. A vein pulsed in his forehead, and he opened his mouth to speak.

Mr. Whitley's squeaky shoes announced his arrival, saving Prudence from whatever vitriol Mr. Evan had been about to unleash. She had never been so glad to see the stuffy solicitor in her life.

Mr. Whitley gave Mr. Evan a cautious once over, then turned anxious eyes on Prudence.

"Thank you both for coming." She fought the

nervous giggle welling in her throat.

"I did not know we would have an audience for this discussion." Mr. Evan tossed his cocked hat onto the Queen Anne chair in the corner of the study.

Prudence's mind raced. What should she do now that they were both here?

"I needed to speak to Mr. Whitley about several matters." Should she bring up her proposal? "I planned to invite you to tea later." She might as well. The terms were fairly simple. "However, since you are here, perhaps we can address the matter between us." Now was as good a time as any to lay them out.

"There is no matter between *us*." Mr. Evan drew out the last word into a sound akin to a hiss.

"Then why did you come?" Prudence readjusted a flounce of lace over her forearm.

Did he mean to turn her down?

"Because I have the good grace to discuss these matters in person instead of by post."

"I didn't send my offer by post. I had Mrs. Hatcher ask one of the stable boys to deliver it."

Mr. Evan's eyes grew darker. Evidently, he didn't draw a distinction between postal rider and stable boy.

Prudence tried a new approach. "I am sorry about that. I don't have much experience in these matters. I thought putting it in a letter might allow me to get the words right. If it is the manner of my proposition that you object to, perhaps I can explain the details to you now, in person."

Mr. Whitley, whose gaze had been darting between them as if he were watching children playing a game of shuttlecock, held up his hands. "Perhaps someone can enlighten me as to the subject of our discussion and the need for my involvement?"

Prudence filled her lungs with air and prepared to launch into a well-rehearsed explanation. One she hadn't intended to give in front of a hostile audience.

"Mr. Whitley, as you know, I must be married within the next three months or I lose my inheritance."

"Yes, I am well aware of that." Mr. Whitley glanced at Mr. Evan. "But what does he have to do with that?"

"I have decided Mr. Evan and I will suit, and I want to work out the particulars as soon as possible. I'd like you to record our agreement so you can draw up a legal contract later."

"With whom?" Mr. Whitley's bushy brows came together until they formed a gray hedgerow above his eyes.

Good heavens! Hadn't he been listening?

"Mr. Evan, of course."

"Who is Mr. Evan?"

Prudence tamped down her impatience. "Mr. Evan." She waved her hand at the only other man in attendance. "The man who runs my grandmother's, or rather my, stables."

"She means me," Mr. Evan said.

"Ah." The understanding on Mr. Whitley's face lasted only a moment before his brows drew together again. "Miss Ashcroft, are you certain about this?"

"Mr. Whitley, I assure you, I know what I'm doing."

"I'm not sure that you do," he mumbled but took a seat behind the desk and pulled out a piece of parchment. He dipped a quill into the inkpot and meticulously wiped off the excess before saying, "Very well. Proceed with these…*negotiations*."

Prudence had only a moment to ponder Mr. Whitley's evident skepticism, before Mr. Evan took a step closer.

"Don't you think you should ask a man before you decide you're going to marry him?" his voice rumbled, low and dangerous.

Prudence fought the urge to back away.

Perhaps choosing Mr. Evan before she had gotten to know the man had been a mistake. She had never seen this side of him. Something about the way he looked at her now, dark storm clouds brewing in his gray eyes, made her light-headed.

"But I did ask you." She winced at the tight pitch of her voice. She took a deep breath and began again. "You received the note I wrote yesterday, didn't you?"

If Mr. Evan thought he could intimidate her, he did not understand Ashcroft women.

"I did, but usually a marriage proposal is done in person." He moved closer yet.

"Fine. Would it make you happy if I proposed in person?" Anything to get this over so they could move on to working out the details of their arrangement. "Mr. Evan, would you be so kind as to marry me?" Prudence said in a voice that would have made the most sanctimonious society matron proud.

"Why?" He drew so close Prudence could detect minute flecks of charcoal in his gray eyes, smell the slight hint of mint on his breath, feel the heat from his body.

With Mr. Evan this close, the intensity of his gaze pinning her to the spot, Prudence had a hard time even understanding the meaning of the one word question.

Why? Why what? Why did she want to marry him? Why should he marry her?

Evan stepped even closer as she searched for an answer.

The soft click of Mr. Whitley sticking the quill back in its holder made them both jump.

"I don't believe you are in need of a solicitor at this moment. However"—he opened the desk drawer and returned the unused piece of parchment—"should this discussion end in violence, I'd be happy to represent the survivor." He clapped his hat on his balding head. "Until then, I bid you a good day."

Prudence locked eyes with Mr. Evan, but she waited for the soft squeaking of Mr. Whitley's shoes to subside before speaking again.

"Why? You know why. I have to marry," she said in hushed tones even though they were alone in the room.

Mr. Evan advanced, and this time, she did back up. Her knees met the edge of the Queen Anne, and her legs buckled beneath her. She landed in the chair with a thump.

Rolling her hips to one side, she pulled Mr. Evan's flattened hat from beneath her and handed it to him. He tossed it across the room without glancing at it.

"But why *me*?" Mr. Evan said, clarifying his question.

He put his hands on both sides of her, grasping the arms of the chair and closing off any avenue of escape. Obviously, he wouldn't be satisfied until he had his answer.

Perhaps she should have insisted Mr. Whitley remain. He might have been able to talk some sense into Mr. Evan. Then again, the sooner she explained the details, the sooner Mr. Evan would calm down—and she could calm the riot of butterflies in her stomach.

Prudence straightened her spine, at least as much as she could with her intended hovering over her.

"Everyone accuses me of being rash, but I have thought this through."

Mr. Evan's eyebrow lifted.

"I have! I explained why I chose you in my letter. I think we'd suit each other well. Plus, I thought I'd be doing you a favor."

"And just what kind of favor would you being doing for me?" His gaze drifted to her neckline.

Prudence covered herself with her hand. Did he think her interest in him was physical? Beneath her muslin day gown, her body responded. So what if she was drawn to him? She could control her impulses. He need never know. It would be better for both of them if he thought this a purely business arrangement.

She folded her hands in her lap.

"I know the job of stable master is well-paid, but I would ensure you received a handsome annual allowance, one that meant you would never need work again. You could spend your days—"

"You're buying me?" Mr. Evan shoved off from the chair.

"No, of course not." Prudence shot to her feet. "It's not like that at all. As my husband, you have every right to the Ashcroft fortune. However, I need to make certain it is protected should you turn out to be a spendthrift."

The look of disbelief on his face told Prudence she had made a muddle of this.

"What of my husbandly rights?"

"Your what?" A flush crept to her cheeks as understanding dawned.

As a man he had certain needs, and perhaps he thought she expected him to... Even if she did, how long before a man as handsome as Mr. Evan tired of his plain wife? She'd rather not have him at all than lose him to another woman later.

She steeled herself to address such a delicate topic.

"That need not be part of our bargain." Her gaze dropped to the pattern of fruits and flowers running diagonally across the carpet. "The will does not stipulate that the union produce children. With your allowance, you will be able to attract female companionship of whatever sort your tastes run to."

Did his tastes ever run to thin, *athletic* redheads? Probably not.

Prudence raised her gaze. "As long as the arrangements are made discreetly, I will not intervene."

Mr. Evan said nothing, just stood in the middle of the room looking at her with those hard gray eyes.

"Why don't you sleep on it?" Her voice shook. "You'll get used to the idea and see that the match is advantageous for both of us."

"I don't need to sleep on it," Mr. Evan said, his voice dangerously low. "I will marry you—"

Relief flooded her and Prudence clapped her hands together. "Oh, that is excellent!"

"—on one condition."

"Condition?" The butterflies started their riot anew.

"Yes." He took a step toward her, and Prudence resisted the urge to back up again, lest she find herself pinned in the chair once more. "I will marry you, but no written contracts."

"No contracts?"

"Yes, the only contract between us will be our marriage vows. You will honor your vows, and I will honor mine."

"But are you sure—" Prudence hastily tried to recall the details of the marriage vows from the last wedding she had been to. It had been some years. What did they include?

"And our marriage will be legal." Mr. Evan added, his eyes as dark as storm clouds and nearly as dangerous looking. "In every way."

Somehow he had found the one for which she had been searching. Maybe it wasn't a vow exactly, but more of an expectation. Prudence thought she might not be able to breathe.

"You don't have to do that."

"It will be consummated, or I will have the marriage annulled on the grounds of frigidity."

The hated word brought back a flood of memories. The taunts of her classmates were as vivid as if they had been spoken right next to her. Her head swam, and hot tears stung the backs of her lids. She fought them, just as she had always done.

Prudence gasped when Mr. Evan strode forward and wrapped an arm around her waist. Like a steel band tightening, he pulled her to him. He slanted his lips over hers in a kiss that left her gasping for air when he finally released her.

"Don't look so crestfallen." His chest rumbled as he spoke, the vibration reaching to her core. "You've won, and winning won't seem so bad once you get used to the idea."

Chapter Ten

Moonlight illuminated the rocky path that led along the bluff. Far below, the small, narrow inlet the locals called Smuggler's Bay glittered as though strewn with diamond dust.

The pounding of Demon's hooves matched the pounding of the blood in Evan's ears. Despite Demon's sure-footedness and the moon-bright night, he was driving his horse too hard. Or perhaps the stallion was simply responding to his master's needs.

Being proposed to had certainly been a new experience. Countless women, on several continents, had propositioned him once he distinguished himself as a successful captain, but none had marriage in mind. A proposal of marriage took a certain audacity he admired. But then the daft woman told him he would be *compensated* for his troubles.

Compensated! Evan's pulse throbbed in his temple. She might as well have said *purchased*, like a ripe tomato at the market.

He should have seen that coming after their outrageous discussion on the bluff. Prudence Ashcroft had as much as confessed her plans to buy a husband. Evan had never stopped to consider he would be the one on the block. Not that he was opposed to the idea. The idea of having her lithe body writhing in passion in his bed had a definite appeal.

She, however, seemed to have something entirely different in mind when she proposed a union.

What did she mean she wouldn't hold him to his vows? She made it clear enough that she didn't expect him to be faithful. She also made it clear she didn't expect their marriage to be consummated. For some reason, she didn't seem to think he'd want to.

Did she not realize how beautiful she was? Perhaps not classically so, but she had a spark that called to him. Like most women, she kept her hair covered by a silly cap, but she could never quite seem to keep a few defiant auburn tendrils from spiraling against her long neck. He would free them from their prison the first chance he had. He couldn't wait to splay them across his palm, or better yet, against his bare chest.

Was her porcelain skin with its slight smattering of freckles even more pale and delicate beneath that atrociously high-necked bodice? Would the nipples that topped her creamy breasts be tight little peaks, like those of a virgin goddess? Would the curls at the juncture of her thighs be the same auburn color as her hair, or would they run to a darker brown?

Evan's body hardened, and he slowed Demon to a more reasonable pace. If she thought to hide herself from him, she would discover soon enough that the effort was futile.

He took a recuperating breath and looked out over the moonlight-dappled bay. Sheltered beneath the cliffs, a small ship bobbed on the waves. She wore no sails and no lights upon her masts.

Smugglers.

Were they Ashcroft ships? Evan scoffed and raised his face to the nearly full moon hanging low in the sky.

It lit the inlet and its occupants almost as effectively as a cloudy day.

He looked back at the small, dark figures pushing barrels about the deck like ants storing food for the winter. Whomever they were, they had chosen a poor night to bring in their cargo. While the cliffs offered adequate shelter, a darker night would have allowed them to slip into the inlet unseen.

Plus, there were rumors of a new customs agent. Regardless of whom the crown appointed, new agents all had one thing in common. They started their careers eager to be the first to collect the taxes due the crown from her rebellious subjects. Some had designs on a higher seat, perhaps even becoming the colonial governor. Others were simply loyal to the king and eager to punish those who objected to England's right to govern their affairs.

Whichever sort this new man turned out to be, he could pose a problem for Ashcroft & Sons. Perhaps even for Prudence herself.

A flash of cream caught his eye.

"Whoa, boy." Evan reined Demon to a stop so he could take a closer look.

A woman. There could be no doubt. Skirts billowed out behind her like a cloud drifting across the sand. She wore no cap and her hair floated free, flashes of red catching the moonlight. He recalled a painting he had once seen. It had been of Venus riding on a seashell, her own red curls covering her most intimate parts.

A spark of recognition sent a lump straight to the bottom of Evan's gut. This was definitely not Venus.

What in the hell was she doing here?

He was about to nudge Demon forward when another dark figure appeared on the sand, some forty feet away.

The commissioner? Unlikely. Not on a moonlit beach in the middle of the night.

Then who?

He presumed the man had been standing within the shadow of the steep cliffs. He wore a cocked hat and a dark cloak, but Evan couldn't get a good view of his face. He looked to be tall with broad shoulders, perhaps thin, although the cloak made that hard to discern. Unfortunately, it would not be enough to identify the stranger should he meet him on the street tomorrow.

Prudence ran toward the dark figure, and Evan's shoulders tensed as a fierce possessiveness overtook him. When she threw herself into the man's arms, his hands tightened on the leather reins.

Evan patted Demon's neck, more to calm himself than his horse.

So that was why she didn't expect to their marriage to be a real one. It had nothing to do with her feeling unworthy. Quite the opposite, in fact. She didn't want to hold him to his vows because she didn't expect to be held to hers, specifically the one about being faithful. He would put an end to that notion.

New voices drifted on the breeze, taking Evan's focus away from his errant fiancée. A small band of men picked their way down the rocky footpath. One slipped and nearly brought the rest of the party down as he slid forward on his rump. Rising, he uttered a crisp curse that carried all the way to Evan's ears.

English.

They weren't sailors either. It was difficult to tell

in the dark exactly who they were, but most wore hats, not the bandana tied around their head so many seamen favored. A long, thin shadow protruded above the shoulder of more than one man. Muskets most likely. Soldiers?

Evan glanced toward the beach. Prudence's lover rowed a small skiff toward the ship, but Prudence had disappeared.

Evan raked the shoreline. Where could she have gone? Had she hidden in the bottom of the boat? With her petite frame, she might have been able to flatten herself and cover her cream-colored gown with a blanket. He peered into the darkness trying to discern shapes from mere shadows.

The men on the shore loaded their muskets and shouted at the fleeing skiff. One fired off a shot that splashed into the water a few yards away from its intended target. He waded into the water, three or four steps, no more, then stopped as the waves lapped about his waist.

Evidently the rumors were true. While narrow inlets, coves, and bays dotted this section of the Rhode Island shoreline, smugglers favored this particular location because its deep bottom allowed them to bring a ship close to shore, within the protection of the rocky cliffs and away from the eyes of the men on the patrol boats.

Evan waited until the men picked their way back up the footpath and disappeared over the crest of a hill. Then he scanned the beach once more, looking for signs of Prudence.

Seeing none, he decided she must have been in the boat. He tugged on the reins, turning Demon back the way they had come.

"Enjoy your time, my dear." Evan muttered into the darkness. "Once we are married, you shall never see your lover again."

Evan let Demon set his own pace down the incline that led back to Ashcroft Stables. Occasionally, the big black horse snorted, his breath forming twin clouds of steam in the cool night air.

Evan spent the time deciding how he would break it to Prudence that her days of midnight trysts were numbered. He ached to put a stop to it tonight, but she had already gone to the man's ship. Unless he wanted to take a swim in the cold Atlantic, he could do nothing until morning.

Evan rounded a corner, passing a smaller cove, one not large or deep enough for smugglers but an ideal place for lovers to meet. Why hadn't Prudence and her lover met here? It would be no effort at all for him to have rowed his skiff a little further, rounding the small point that separated the smaller cove from the larger. They would have been out of sight of anyone patrolling the area. In the smaller cove, Evan might not even have noticed the pair.

His breath froze in his chest. A pale figure inched along a rocky outcrop, auburn hair tumbling past her waist. She no longer wore her cream-colored gown. Instead, her calves shone white beneath the short hem of what looked to be her shift.

"Dear God, Prudence, you are going to kill yourself." Evan knew full well she could not hear him with the waves crashing against the rocks beneath her.

Evan urged Demon forward until they came to the top of the cliff. He could no longer see her from his vantage point, but he dared not alert her to his presence by calling down to her. For one, he didn't want to startle her and make her lose her grip. But more than that, he didn't want her to think twice about seeing him, her guilt evident, and try to climb back down. The woman clearly had no regard for her own safety.

Instead, he dismounted and stood a yard or more away from the top of the cliff, waiting with his heart in his throat for her to reach him.

When it seemed he could take it no longer, a slender arm poked above the edge and a thin hand searched for purchase. Evan strode forward and grabbed the arm, pulling a startled Prudence to her feet in one tug.

"Oh, Mr. Evan, I'm surprised to see you." Prudence managed to sound as if she had just run into him in a tearoom.

Admirable aplomb for a woman who had been caught climbing a cliff in her shift after a clandestine meeting with her lover.

"Not nearly as surprised as I am to see you."

His gaze swept her. Not that he was an expert in women's undergarments, but her shift looked more transparent than most. The puckered tips of her breasts poked at the soft fabric, and it clung to her legs. He lifted his eyes to her face. Her auburn curls lay plastered to her scalp and against her cheeks like rivulets of dark water.

"You're wet," he said, wondering how he could have missed that not-insignificant detail, almost as much as he wondered what would have possessed her to go into the water in the first place.

"Yes, I believe I am." Prudence hugged her arms

across her chest and ground the words out between chattering teeth.

Evan shook his head. "Do I even want to know where your gown is?"

"I had to leave it behind. I couldn't climb the rocks with it on." Prudence said, as though that explanation were enough.

"We must be at least three miles from Ashcroft. Did you plan to walk the entire way back, wet, half-clothed and"—he looked down—"barefoot?"

"It's even more difficult to climb rocks with shoes on," she said.

"Your name is like a cruel joke, isn't it?" He tore his coat from his shoulders and draped it around her.

Prudence glared at him but tugged the lapels across her chest. The brown wool cutaway, which normally skimmed the tops of Evan's knees, draped to mid-calf. Huddled within his coat and her hair plastered to her head, she looked like a child just after a warm bath, although her pale lips served as a reminder of how cold the Atlantic in early May could be.

A sharp whistle from Evan brought Demon to his side. He swung into the saddle, then reached down to haul Prudence onto his lap. She snuggled against his chest, and he drew an arm about her waist to secure her while he held Demon's reins with the other hand and nudged the stallion forward at a leisurely pace.

"Do you normally meet your lover on a secluded beach in the middle of the night?" Evan whispered into her ear once Prudence stopped shivering.

"My what?" Prudence shot up, her head cracking Evan's chin.

Evan shut his eyes for a moment while he waited

for the stars to clear.

"I am so sorry!" Her slender arm darted out from within his coat to touch a tender spot on his jaw.

Her fingers were like ice, but they burned him all the same. Evan dropped the reins to grasp her hand in his. This was no time to be distracted by his little temptress.

"I asked if you normally met your lover—"

"He's not my lover."

Evan searched her face. Experience had taught him to know when a man lied. Women were generally even easier, but he had never met anyone as transparent as Prudence. Her eyes held only truth.

So if not her lover, who was this man she embraced so freely in the middle of the night? Not a brother or an uncle. Three generations of a single child being born into the family removed that possibility. Potentially a cousin, but even that was unlikely. He had done his research. Of all those present at the reading of Rachel's will, Prudence had been the only blood relative.

Although he wasn't her lover, that didn't mean the man didn't intend to be. She might not be guilty, but she might not be fully aware of the man's intentions either. He tightened his arm around her.

"Let's say I believe you for now."

"For now?" Prudence sputtered.

Evan continued as though she hadn't spoken. "I'd like to know what kind of man would leave a woman to fend for herself on the beach?"

"I am perfectly capable of fending for myself." She yanked her hand away from his.

"Yes, I can see that you are." Evan plucked at a strand of hair drying against her cheek. "But whether or not you can fend for yourself, what kind of man would leave you to do so?"

Prudence batted his hand away. "One who was concerned for my safety."

"Your safety?" Evan snorted.

"Yes, those men were after him not me. He knew if he drew their attention, I could slip away."

"So you decided to go for a swim?" Evan's own head swam as he tried to make sense of her logic.

"No, there are rocks that lead around the point separating the two coves. I use to go that way all the time as a child, but I forgot how difficult it could be in the dark, and I slipped."

She said it as though it were akin to tripping on a pebble. It could have happened to anyone.

"What if your plan didn't work?" Evan tried to shut out the image of Prudence being swept away by an undercurrent before she managed to clamber onto the rocks. "There were at least six of them. One might have decided you were a more interesting catch."

"We would have claimed to be lovers," Prudence said in a voice so low Evan had to strain to hear.

He felt his own heat rising. "That certainly would not have ensured your safety. I'm guessing those men were soldiers somehow connected to the customs office and that your *lover* is a smuggler. Had they caught you, they would have simply held you as bait."

Prudence stiffened. "They couldn't have held me for long. I'm an Ashcroft."

"The last thing you need is to connect the Ashcroft name to a smuggler. I suggest you disassociate yourself with this man."

"But he—"

"Remember, you promised to honor your vows. If I recall, one of those is to be faithful."

"I told you he's not my lover, and I haven't made any vows yet."

Evan ignored her. "And the other is to obey me. I'm beginning to see why your grandmother thought you needed a husband."

"And I'm beginning to think this wasn't such a good idea," Prudence mumbled against his chest.

Chapter Eleven

"Let's see, how shall we do your hair tonight?" Netty swept Prudence's thick, auburn tresses atop her head. "We want it to look extra special. After all, he might be there."

Prudence glanced up from the hairpin with which she had been absentmindedly toying. "I don't know who you're talking about, Netty."

She did, of course. However, Mr. Evan was the last person she wished to discuss with her maid. It would fuel the fires of gossip, and unfortunately, they needed no kindling at the moment. For the second time in a week, he had carried her, soaked to the skin, into the manor house.

"Why, your betrothed, of course." Netty flashed innocent eyes at Prudence.

Prudence wasn't fooled for a moment.

The girl was fishing for details, and who could blame her?

She had pleaded with Mr. Evan to use the servants' entrance, but he refused. Breaking free of his strong arms had proven a fruitless effort. In the end, she buried her face in his chest while he explained to the startled servants that he intended to take his fiancée upstairs and have a long talk with her.

Mrs. Hatcher had come to her rescue, following them up the stairs while arguing that talking could wait until Prudence had a hot bath. When Mr. Evan didn't appear willing to budge, she threatened to take her rolling pin to his head if he remained one second longer in her mistress's bedroom.

Faithful Mrs. Hatcher. Should Prudence ever have wondered why Grandma Rachel kept her on all those years, she didn't now. Inside the demeanor of a mouse beat the heart of a lion.

But Mrs. Hatcher's rescue had come too late to preserve Prudence's reputation. The glint in Netty's eyes said all she needed to know about the gossip in the servants' quarters. Their mistress had come home in the arms of a man wearing only her shift. If not for Mr. Evan's explanation that she was his fiancée, and Prudence's silence on the matter, her reputation would be in tatters. It was shredded enough as it was.

Prudence eyed Netty while her maid rummaged through a jewelry box. Did the servants know Mr. Evan was the stable master? Not that she cared, but that would certainly make the story juicer.

He had only been in her grandmother's employ for a few weeks, but there was the possibility, the *slight* possibility, that many of them had not yet made his acquaintance. Mrs. Hatcher and Gil would know, of course, but their loyalty could be counted on.

She hoped his secret could be kept at least until after tonight. It would be so much easier to introduce him simply as Mr. Evan, her betrothed, than Mr. Evan, her betrothed and stable master at Ashcroft. Egalitarian though some of her grandmother's friends and business associates might be, it would drive their curiosity. Others might not be so reserved in their response. Some saw it as a personal affront when anyone of what they deemed the *lower sort* attempted to better his station by marrying up.

Prudence gave a small huff. She covered it with a cough when Netty looked up from the tress she was winding around the crown of Prudence's head. Common. Simple. A working man. Whatever type of person Mr. Evan might be, he certainly didn't seem to Prudence to be one of the lower sort.

Besides, once they were married, he wouldn't be the stable master anymore. He would be her husband and master of all of Ashcroft. Prudence's mouth ticked up at the corner. At least of that which she allowed him to be.

Netty held up a strand of pearls, a question in her bright blue eyes.

Prudence shook her head. The pearls were beautiful, but they were also quite real.

While the Sheridans were almost as wealthy as the Ashcrofts, their annual dinner party was more of a casual affair, held in honor of neighbors and business associates. The guest list would include many local shopkeepers and merchants. Real pearls would be far out of reach of most of the attendees. Even the flamboyant Mrs. Benoit would likely be wearing Roman Pearls, iridescent glass beads filled with wax. Prudence couldn't wear pearls while everyone else wore wax.

The strand of pearls flowed like water from Netty's palm into their velvet home. Netty set the bag back in the box then held up a simple hairpin of gold filigree. Prudence nodded. It would have to do.

Netty artfully placed the pin atop a curl where it would be shown to its best advantage. "There. You look absolutely stunning."

"Thank you, Netty."

"You're welcome, Miss Prudence." Netty collected the unused jewels and left the room.

Prudence turned her head one way and then the other, studying her appearance in the mirror. Perhaps *stunning* went a bit too far. Nevertheless, her attire was well suited to tonight's performance. Whether she would play her part well or not, remained to be seen.

Unfortunately, gossip traveled faster than a plague. News of her supposed tryst had undoubtedly reached the ears of servants outside Ashcroft, and the Sheridans were her closest neighbors.

Theirs was the first invitation she had received since coming home from school. It was the first invitation she had *ever* received that hadn't been intended primarily for Grandma Rachel. No doubt, the Sheridans had caught wind of the servants' gossip, and that meant he would be invited, too. After all, the evening's entertainment wouldn't be complete without seeing how she and Mr. Evan behaved in close quarters.

Prudence set a hand against the riot of butterflies in her stomach. This must be what it felt like to be an actor about to take the stage for the first time.

How should she act? Prudence hadn't the slightest notion. She had never played a part in any of Rhode Island society's intrigues. Now that she had become involved in a situation that at least resembled an intrigue, she wished she had paid more attention to how she was expected to behave.

Should she ignore him in public? Pretend the incriminating incident never happened? Or perhaps they should play the loving couple, maybe even announce their engagement tonight. If there were any in all of Newport who didn't yet know, they would learn of it soon enough anyway.

A shiver ran through Prudence. What if he didn't come? What if he had second thoughts about their engagement and chose to break it off tonight? She would be humiliated.

Prudence buried her head in her hands. Tonight's guests might consider this entertainment, but it was all too real to her.

****

Prudence ignored the stares of the other guests boring into the side of her head, her back, her face. No matter which direction she looked, gazes slid away as though any eye contact had been mere happenstance, nothing more. Prudence knew better.

She was acquainted with most of the people in the room, but not well. She had never really mingled with the neighbors closest to Ashcroft. For the last few years, she had been away at school then busy with her tutors in Boston. But even when she was younger, her grandmother's wealth and status meant most of the neighbors, including the children, kept a respectful distance. Only Richard's constant presence prevented her childhood from being a lonely one.

However, there were others in the room she knew quite well. And, frankly, loathed.

Prudence sipped her punch, its sweetness stark against the bitter taste in her mouth as she watched the men whom she had known since they were little more than boys. Their sartorial splendor, powdered wigs atop their heads and English lace peeking from every cuff and hem, didn't change who they were in her eyes.

These were the classmates who had made her life a living hell. In the last four years, most had graduated from prestigious institutions of higher learning and were destined for important positions in the colonial government or in business. This would be their last summer in Rhode Island for some time, perhaps forever. She had heard rumors of a few going directly into trade, perhaps spurred on by need but more likely by ambition.

She glanced around, trying to guess the fortunes of each of them. If their gazes lingered, she glared at them over the rim of her punch glass, defying them to taunt her in the Sheridans' ballroom. It had been four years since she had seen most of them, but in their pretentious looks, she couldn't help but see the taunting faces of the adolescents they had been.

Suddenly, like a weight removed from her back, the pressure of all eyes upon her eased, and Prudence glanced up. Mr. Evan stood in the entrance to the ballroom.

She had never been so glad to see anyone in her life. At least she wouldn't be left to face the wolves alone.

Even if he hadn't been the second half of tonight's entertainment, Mr. Evan would have drawn attention. Undoubtedly, he had borrowed his suit of green silk velvet, but it fit like a glove across his broad shoulders and narrow hips. The only ornamentation, a piping of gold and silver, ran down the edges of his lapels. Even his neck cloth was understated, tied beneath a collar that extended nearly to his ears and made him look even taller and, perhaps, slightly menacing.

He wore his dark hair tied back in a simple tail. No

periwig or powder hid his thick, ebony locks. In more traditional colonies, it might be seen as a political statement, a rebellion against the formality that served as a symbol of a man's position in society and fealty to English customs. In Rhode Island, such a statement would either be embraced or frowned upon, depending on the company one kept.

Prudence decided she rather liked it. Tonight, even the shop keepers had dug out their finest, and compared to the embroidered, frilled and powdered guests around him, Mr. Evan's elegant but minimalist attire made him appear somehow more of a man.

He turned to Mrs. Sheridan, and the middle-aged woman beamed up at him as though she had discovered a prize on her doorstep. Mr. Evan bent and whispered something near her ear that made the woman blush and fan herself.

Was her fiancé flirting with their hostess?

A sudden surge of female possessiveness propelled Prudence forward, but a cantankerous voice from along the back wall stopped her mid-step.

"I hear he grew up in an orphanage in England."

Mrs. Grendel. Prudence had heard the voice since she was a child. Most of Newport had due to the old lady's dual misfortunes. First of all, she liked to gossip. Unfortunately, she was also hard of hearing and assumed everyone else was as well. Prudence had been the subject of her famous harangues more than once.

"Shush, Mrs. Grendel," her hired companion, Miss Avery, said.

"Don't shush me, girl. I know what I'm talking about. Thinks he can become one of us just by marrying the Ashcroft heiress."

Prudence really did wish Miss Avery wouldn't hush her companion so much. She could be almost as annoying as the old woman at times. And besides, Mrs. Grendel had finally hit upon a topic worth listening to.

Prudence had known Mr. Evan grew up in an orphanage, but he claimed to be Welsh, not English. Perhaps Mrs. Grendel had the details wrong.

Besides, what did it matter where he grew up? The Ashcroft fortune had been built by men of average means and a doubtful lineage, as had most of Rhode Island. Women like Mrs. Grendel loved to pretend they were some sort of American aristocracy. If Grandma Rachel's accounts were correct, Mrs. Grendel was the great granddaughter of a man who had chosen America over debtors' prison.

She scanned the guests, some staring with open curiosity toward the door, others whispering behind fans or gloved hands. Perhaps they didn't mean to be cruel, but she knew all too well how barbed a whisper could be. Prudence sipped her punch and marveled at her sudden urge to protect her fiancé, all six-foot plus of him, from her neighbors.

"Thinking about me?"

The voice in her ear made Prudence jump, and a small droplet of punch dripped down her chin and landed just above her neckline. Mr. Evan came to stand in front of her just in time to watch it form a crimson trail over one soft lobe and snake its way down the valley between her breasts.

"Here, let me get that for you," he said, without a hint of suggestion in his tone.

Prudence's face heated until she imagined she was as red as the punch. "Don't you dare!"

"Very well, then." Mr. Evan surveyed the assembled guests. "Why don't you introduce me to your friends?"

"They're no friends of mine." Prudence covertly dabbed at her chest with a silk handkerchief.

"Oh, come now. I see the way all the men follow you with their eyes. They are as fascinated with you as I am." He pursed his lips. "The women, too, it seems."

"It's not me that has them captivated. It's us." Prudence jammed the stained handkerchief back in her reticule. "You do realize we are tonight's entertainment, don't you?"

"Ah, so that explains why I received an invitation to a party given by people I've never met." Mr. Evan's sardonic tone suggested he had already figured out the reason for the invitation. "As I see it, we have two choices. Either we give them what they want or we don't. Either way, we should enjoy ourselves, don't you think?"

He looked down at Prudence as though the decision were entirely hers.

He was right. They could behave as well or as poorly as they chose. They could have a pleasant evening or not. It really made no difference to those around her. They had been invited to provide the entertainment for the evening, and their audience didn't care a whit how they felt about it. Certainly no more so than the audience at the theater cared about whether the actors enjoyed performing their parts. In the end, they might as well enjoy themselves.

"Very well." Prudence hooked a hand around Mr. Evan's elbow. "Let's go meet some of my *friends*, shall we?"

Prudence led Mr. Evan into the ballroom and toward a small cluster of elderly men. She didn't yet have the nerve to introduce him to anyone who knew her well, and these men seemed harmless enough. She recognized most of them as local merchants, the ones who bought the goods Ashcroft & Sons imported. During hard times, her grandmother had floated more than one business loan or allowed them to sell goods on consignment. Chances were excellent these men would have a vested interest in fostering a strong relationship with the new owners of Ashcroft.

Now, if she could just remember their names.

"Ah, Miss Prudence, how nice to see you again." An elderly man sporting a well-fashioned wig that marked him as prosperous, whatever his business was, held out a hand to her.

"Mr. Cowper." She dug his name from the recesses of her memory. She set her gloved hand in his, and he gave it a squeeze. "It is good to see you again, too, sir."

"I was so sorry to hear about your grandmother, my dear. She will be profoundly missed." His eyes held true kindness.

"I thank you, Mr. Cowper," she said, deciding she had chosen the first introduction well.

It was now or never.

"Mr. Cowper, might I introduce you to my fiancé, Mr. Evan? Mr. Evan, this is Mr. Cowper."

Mr. Cowper made an elegant bow. "Delighted to make your acquaintance, sir."

Mr. Evan returned the bow.

"What brings you to Newport, Mr. Evan?" He turned sparkling eyes on Prudence. "Aside from the obvious attractions, that is."

Unexpected panic tightened like hands around Prudence's throat. How much would Mr. Evan tell Mr. Cowper? She should have thought to take him aside and discuss it before making the rounds.

"Oh, Mr. Evan is a cousin of mine." Prudence concocted her own story and whispered a silent prayer that Mr. Evan would be willing to follow her lead for once. "A distant cousin," she added, noting the confusion that settled on Mr. Cowper's face. "He is visiting here from, um…Portugal."

Now what had made her say that? Mr. Evan cocked an eyebrow at her as if to ask the same thing.

"I see, sir. Are you an importer as well?"

Mr. Evan opened his mouth, but Prudence answered for him. "He is, Mr. Cowper." She recalled some of the products her grandmother had imported from Portugal. "His company imports the most beautiful blue and white tiles you've ever seen."

"I see," Mr. Cowper said again, with an interest that set Prudence's insides to squirming.

What kind of corner had she backed herself into? Aside from his dark hair and tanned skin, Mr. Evan didn't look remotely Portuguese. To make matters worse, she suddenly remembered Mr. Cowper had been a business associate of her grandmother's for years. His company specialized in a type of elegant porcelains made in only one country in the world. Portugal.

"*Sim, Senhor*. They are called *azulejos* and are common in my homeland." Mr. Evan gave a smart little bow that looked surprisingly European.

Prudence almost giggled with relief even as she wondered how on earth Mr. Evan knew what the tiles were called when she couldn't even remember herself.

130

Perhaps he had spent time in Portugal after leaving Wales. What she didn't know about her fiancé could fill volumes.

After a brief but animated discussion about the prospects of covering the homes of Rhode Island with the traditional Portuguese tiles, Mr. Cowper said, "Well, sir, I congratulate you on your upcoming nuptials. I've known Prudence since she was a young girl, and she is something special. I wish you both well."

"*Obrigado, Senhor*," Mr. Evan said, with such a pronounced Welsh accent that Prudence suspected he amused himself at the expense of her nerves.

When Mr. Cowper didn't seem to notice, she decided the introduction had gone as well as could be hoped, and the time had come to move on to deeper waters. Leaving off the Portuguese inspiration, Prudence introduced him to one after another of her schoolmates, neighbors, and assorted associates of Rachel Ashcroft's. For the latter, she had to dig deeply to recall names and the basis for their association. It made her realize how being away at school had distanced her from the business.

Mr. Evan chatted amiably with each of the people he met, amazing Prudence with his ability to discuss matters of all kinds. For a stable master, he knew a surprising amount about the business of importation.

With the society matrons, he mostly listened, nodding at their wisdom. At one point, Prudence stifled a chuckle behind her fan as he enthusiastically agreed with the octogenarian, Mrs. Carter, that hooped skirts were positively scandalous.

He readily joined in on discussions of business and

political matters with the men, and Prudence found herself feeling rather proud of her future husband. He might not have the same education and training as the men around him, but they were so taken with his business acumen that they treated him as an equal. They even listened to his advice, hanging on every word.

Even Prudence's old schoolmates seemed to have forgotten the taunts they had leveled at her over the years. While she wouldn't exactly call them friendly, they treated her with a certain level of respect. She supposed there was something to be said for having a fiancé at one's side, especially one that still radiated a certain air of masculine strength despite his fancy clothes.

The doors to the ballroom opened, and a soft draft brushed Prudence's face. She glanced up to see who had entered, eager to continue her introductions to all comers. Her heart seemed to stop beating.

Please. Not him. Not now.

Prudence's gaze darted about the ballroom. She could duck out onto the balcony, but she dare not go alone. She could easily run into one of her less-than-friendly schoolmates. Inviting Mr. Evan to join her on the balcony was out of the question, too. She didn't want him to get the wrong idea.

Prudence spied a door just to the side of the long buffet table. It was probably used by servants, but at the moment she didn't care where it led. Even the kitchen would do.

"Mr. Evan, I wonder if you might excuse me. I'm feeling rather weary." Having never been faint in her life, Prudence had to conjure up images of what she had seen other women do in such a condition. She patted her décolletage with her gloved hand and attempted a wilted look intended to emphasize her frail condition. "I believe I'll find the lady's retiring room if you don't mind."

Mr. Evan's brows drew together over his slightly crooked nose. "Would you like to return home?"

The idea had its merits, but right now, her old nemesis barred the way. She could hardly grab Mr. Evan's elbow and drag him to the door without being seen.

"No, that's all right. I think I just need a few minutes away from the heat of the crowd."

"All right, then," Mr. Evan said.

"Don't be too long, Miss Ashcroft," Mr. Pettigrew said. Prudence remembered him as one of the bankers her grandmother had visited from time to time. "The dancing will be starting soon, and you won't want to miss the opportunity to dance with your fiancé."

"No, of course not, Mr. Pettigrew. Thank you for reminding me." She gave him a smile she hoped appeared convincing then headed for the small door.

Prudence cracked open the door only to have her suspicions confirmed. Had guests been meant to head in this direction, the hallway would have been lit with wall sconces, and there would be servants stationed at every turn to provide directions. After the bright light of the ballroom, this particular passage seemed as dark as a cellar.

She glanced over her shoulder to be sure no one watched then ducked inside.

At least she was unlikely to run into *him* back here. She could linger awhile then peek into the ballroom to gauge when she could safely collect Mr. Evan and leave. Prudence relaxed against the wall, ready to wait out her nemesis for however long it took.

Chapter Twelve

"Would you excuse me, Mr. Pettigrew? I think I need to check on my fiancée," Evan said the moment the loquacious banker paused to catch a breath.

Mr. Pettigrew had been expounding on the rebellious behavior of some of his fellow "Rogue Islanders" as he called them. Evan would have listened with interest at any other time, but right now, he was concerned for Prudence.

"Yes, of course. You should do that."

Mr. Pettigrew scanned the guests around him, caught the eye of one, and was off without another word.

Evan opened the door through which Prudence had disappeared and was surprised to find a narrow corridor on the opposite side. He turned to scan the ballroom, as though she might have slipped past him while he was engaged with Pettigrew. There was no sign of her among the brightly dressed guests mingling about the buffet tables and dance floor. He turned and took a few hesitant steps into the darkness.

"One, two, three. Now twirl. No, Peter, you take Celia's hand and walk counterclockwise." Prudence's lively voice pierced the gloom like a ray of sunshine.

"What's counterclockwise?" a young voice asked.

"It's this way, silly," and even younger voice answered.

Evan followed the sound up a flight of stairs, each step creaking under his tread. Nestled in the farthest corner of the house, the door to a room stood open, warm yellow light pouring from within. Evan crept toward it.

Prudence stood in the middle of what looked like a nursery surrounded by six children of varying ages. With what little he knew of children, Evan judged the youngest, a girl, to be about three while the oldest was a boy of no more than eight or nine.

Prudence demonstrated a dance to the oldest boy and another girl of about six or seven. She twirled about in time to the music drifting up from the ballroom. The boy screwed up his face, clearly confounded by the steps. The girl, who looked enough like the lad that Evan surmised she was his sister, pursed her lips as though she would like nothing more than to throttle him.

Evan stood in the doorway of the nursery, enthralled. He hadn't even considered whether Prudence wanted children. Hell, he hadn't even considered whether he wanted them. But here she was, delight shining on her flushed face, surrounded by them. It was where she belonged.

If he had any control over it, the notion that Ashcrofts could only have one child would be put to rest.

"I want to dance, too!" the youngest wailed, tugging at Prudence's skirt.

"Of course you do, Elizabeth."

She scooped the toddler up and twirled about the room with her. The joy on the little girl's face nearly matched Prudence's. Evan ducked into the shadows of the hallway when an enthusiastic pirouette that had Elizabeth giggling in delight brought them close.

"I want a new partner." The girl who Prudence had been instructing said with a stamp of her foot.

"Fine with me, Celia." Her brother rolled his eyes and plopped into a settee at the edge of the room. "Why don't you ask him?"

All eyes turned toward Evan. Prudence stopped twirling just an arm's length away. She turned and teetered precariously with little Elizabeth still in her arms. Evan reached out to grab her elbow and steady her.

Prudence's cheeks were flushed from exertion and her eyes bright with merriment. Elizabeth ducked her face into Prudence's shoulder, turning only slightly so she could cast a sidelong glance at the strange man who had captured her new friend's attention.

"I can't dance with him. He's much too tall," Celia said.

Neither Evan nor Prudence turned her way.

"Miss Prudence could dance with him," one of the other children suggested.

"Yes, you two dance together." Celia took Evan by one hand and pulled him into the center of the room. "Lizzie, let Miss Prudence set you down so she can dance with the man."

Prudence seemed reluctant to let the child go. Elizabeth had to struggle a bit, but it was clear Celia's commands were meant to be obeyed.

In the end, Evan found himself in the center of the room with Prudence standing in front of him, clearly expecting him to comply with Celia's wishes.

"I don't dance," Evan said.

The merriment on Prudence's face dissolved.

"Sure you do," a girl with twin brown braids running down her back said. "Miss Prudence told us that all men dance. Isn't that right, Miss Prudence?"

Prudence flushed. "I suppose there are some men who don't dance. Perhaps they don't know how. Or perhaps they don't enjoy dancing."

"That would be me," the boy grumbled.

"Oh, shut up, Peter." Celia cast her brother a withering look that made him slump even further into the settee.

Prudence gave the children a wan smile, and Evan felt like the worst sort of cad. Somehow, he had doused the candle that had burned brightly not a moment before. He salved his guilt with the truth.

"That's it. I don't know how." At least he didn't know the steps of the Americanized dances being performed in the Sheridan's ballroom. "I never had a teacher like Miss Prudence to help me learn," he said, settling on a simpler answer he hoped the children would accept.

Celia put her small fists on her nearly nonexistent hips. "You don't look so tall after all. Miss Prudence can teach you while she teaches me. You will be my partner."

Evan almost laughed at the idea of learning to dance by partnering with a demanding six year old, but part of him was afraid to earn the little hellion's wrath. "I think it's actually time I collect Miss Prudence and return to the party with her."

His statement was met with collective groans and complaints from the children.

"Yes, I think Mr. Evan is right," Prudence said in a

breathy voice. "I've been away far too long, and I really must return."

Prudence took Evan's offered arm but had to drop it when Elizabeth ran up to her and held up her chubby, little arms. Prudence picked her up, closed her eyes, and gave the child a squeeze as though she might never see her again. After a long moment, she set her gently on her feet. Prudence returned her hand to the crook of Evan's arm, and he escorted her back down the stairs and through the dark hallway.

Prudence had been so cheerful dancing with the children. Now, he sensed an emptiness coming from her.

Did she hate leaving the children that much? He longed to assure her that she would have her own someday, but since she still considered their marriage a business arrangement, he thought she might consider him a bit presumptuous.

Still he couldn't help but worry about the way she had simply faded before his eyes.

"Is something amiss?" Evan asked just as they came to the door that would take them back into the light and crush of the crowded dance floor.

"I'm just weary I suppose. Would you mind terribly if I asked you to escort me home?"

"Of course." Evan opened the door so she could precede him through.

He almost bumped into her when she stopped. She seemed to be scanning the room for someone. But for whom? Before Evan could find his answer, Prudence started forward again, her eyes directed at her feet.

Evan put a hand on the small of her back and guided her toward the foyer. If Prudence resented the assumed intimacy she didn't show it. Besides, it was the safest way to get her through the crowd since she seemed reluctant to look up.

What or who had gotten to her?

Leaving Prudence standing by herself in the foyer, Evan left to ask a footman to find their wraps. He returned just in time to see a thin blond man sidle up to Prudence. The way his eyes darted about reminded Evan of a lizard.

"Well, you've turned into quite the looker, haven't you?" His voice even had a lizard-like hiss.

"Hello, Simon. How nice to see you again." Prudence's words were as cold as the Atlantic in the spring, and she kept her gaze firmly planted on her feet.

"I didn't think you had it in you. In school, you were all brains and no beauty. Now look at you." His eyes raked her from head to toe. "I think your grandmamma would have been better off sending you to finishing school where you might have learned how to be a woman."

Prudence's chin shot up at the impertinent remark. Her face blanched when she saw Evan standing behind Simon. However, the fool was so engrossed in lodging insults, he didn't notice her reaction.

"Of course, I could teach you to be a woman." He took a step forward and reached out his hand as though to stroke Prudence's cheek.

His hand never made it. In a flash, Evan had Simon by the back of the collar. He yanked him backward, and only Evan's grip kept the man from stumbling.

"Hello. I don't believe we've been properly introduced," Evan said as though he didn't have a handful of Simon's collar clutched in his fist.

Simon's pale features flushed crimson. "Just who the hell are you?"

"I am Miss Ashcroft's fiancé. And you?"

Simon twisted and Evan let the man go.

"I am Simon Manley, and you would do well to remember it." Simon tugged his coat back in place.

Evan almost smiled at the intricate silver embroidery that decorated every possible edge: along the tails, the hem, the cuffs, and even around each buttonhole. When they caught the candlelight, the delicate flower petals looked almost like snake scales. He could just imagine the man asking his tailor for a suit of clothes that accentuated his reptilian-like features.

"Well, Mr. Manley, I can assure you, if I ever find you insulting my fiancée again, I will remember your name, although you might not live to regret it."

Leaving Simon huffing in the foyer, Evan grasped Prudence by the elbow and led her down the stairs to the waiting carriage.

Once inside, he sat across from Prudence, his knees brushing hers in the small conveyance. Prudence tucked her knees to the side and turned her face to the window.

"What on earth did you ever do to him?" Evan asked, his tone light.

"Nothing much," Prudence said, her voice flat. "I went to school with him is all."

"Let me guess. You got better marks?"

Prudence nodded, and her lips twitched. "I did."

"In all your classes?"

"Of course." The carriage window reflected her tentative smile.

Evan nudged her knee with his. "And at some point

along the way, you probably beat him at a foot race, too. Am I right?"

"Tree climbing," Prudence said, her smile turning into a grin.

"But that's not all, is it?"

"No." Her grin dissolved.

"What is it, Prudence?" Evan let his knee brush hers again, but this time in a reassuring manner, the way he might casually touch a troubled horse. Not demanding, just letting the beast know he was not a threat.

"I broke his nose." Her voice held neither remorse nor pride.

"He deserved it," Evan said. "I can't tell you how much I wanted to take a swing at him. I'm glad one of us had the opportunity."

Evan waited, but Prudence's smile didn't return.

"He's wrong you know."

Prudence turned to face Evan. "About what?"

"Something tells me you've always been beautiful, even as a child."

Prudence's scoff sliced the air between them. "I'm afraid he's not wrong. And he was lying about me turning into a looker. He just said that because he knew how much it would hurt me."

"Somehow, I doubt that. The way he looked at you told me he meant what he said. I don't trust the man."

Prudence shook her head. "It doesn't matter anyway."

"Why not?"

She pierced Evan with her gaze. "I have money. Looks aren't required. When we met on the cliff, I told you I could buy a husband. I proved it to you when you agreed to marry me."

Her words were sharp, and Evan bit back the urge to lash out with his own sharp words. In the pale moonlight, the pain already glistening in Prudence's eyes stopped him.

"I'm not marrying you for your money."

"Oh really? Am I supposed to believe you are marrying me for love?" Her harsh laughter told him how absurd she considered the possibility. "I suppose you've written sonnets to me but haven't had the opportunity to send them. Or perhaps you're growing roses out behind the stables. Maybe you're just waiting for the right moment to pick them. Or maybe you're even—"

"Is that what you want? Sonnets? Roses?"

"I'd settle for a dance," Prudence said in a voice so low it barely registered.

"A dance? You would accept that I am not marrying you for your money if I danced with you?"

She pinned him with her eyes. "What kind of man would refuse to dance with his betrothed? I could have taught you a dance that didn't even require a single touch."

Prudence gasped when Evan plucked her from her seat and settled her in his lap.

"I don't find the idea of touching you disagreeable," he whispered against her ear. "I just don't think the kind of dance I have in mind would have been suitable to perform in front of the children."

She whirled on him. "What is that sup—"

Evan cut Prudence's question off by claiming her lips.

He expected her to pull back, to struggle off his lap

and cower on her side of the carriage as soon as she realized what he had in mind.

She didn't.

Evan softened the kiss. Her lips were soft and sweet, with a hint of fruitiness from the punch she had drunk as she introduced him to her many *friends*. He sucked on her lower lip, and Prudence giggled.

Now that was a good sign.

He pulled away to look into her eyes just as the carriage rumbled up the drive to Ashcroft manor. They were murky, with pupils so large they nearly concealed the dark ring of green around them.

She slid off his lap when the carriage rolled to a stop. Evan opened the door and stepped down to help her out. Prudence stumbled on the first step, and Evan nearly had to catch her. The door to the manor opened behind him, and Evan hid a smile when he realized how close he had come to carrying his betrothed into the house for a third time.

Instead, he handed her off to her maid and watched as she wobbled up the front steps. Did he have something to do with her inability to walk? He hoped so.

A sudden understanding dawned on him. His fiancée wasn't so unlike himself. He, too, had grown up with a sense of unworthiness, fostered by years of cruelty at the hands of those who were supposed to care for him. He had found refuge in the sea and discovered, quite by accident, something at which he excelled.

Prudence had yet to find that at which she excelled. Unlike others of his sex, he didn't think women existed only for the pleasure of men. Surely, most of them wanted to be good at something.

Evan had also found people he cared about. Stu was more like a brother than a valet. And then there was his former captain, a man he looked up to as much as he might his own father, if he had one.

While Prudence had at least one person who loved her, perhaps she had known cruelty, too. He had seen the way some of the men she introduced as former schoolmates looked at her. Their mocking disdain had his blood boiling, and more than once he had been moments away from issuing a challenge. Thankfully, those introductions had been few and far between.

He stared at the door through which his fiancée had disappeared. Somehow, someway, he would convince her of her worth, a value that had nothing to do with the Ashcroft fortune. It was a task he looked forward to.

Chapter Thirteen

Evan arrived at the manor at precisely quarter to three. He had come as Prudence requested, but not exactly *when* she requested. She was within her rights to take him to task for the kiss, but he'd be damned if he would let her dictate all the terms of their courtship.

Evan whisked off his hat, and Gil led him to a room at the back of the manor. He would have sworn the man gave him a wink before shutting the double doors behind him with a soft click.

No, that was impossible. Even when they shared a pint and a meat pie in the manor's kitchen, the man never cracked a smile.

Evan surveyed the empty room while he waited for Prudence. It was a large rectangular affair with parquet floors and high ceilings. Sunlight shone through tall mullioned windows, bathing the walls in soft hues of lemon and cream. Chairs upholstered in red velvet were scattered about in small clusters, as though arranged for intimate conversation.

Evan was no expert, but he suspected the room was used for small gatherings or perhaps music recitals.

He tossed his hat onto one of the chairs. After what happened to his last hat, he considered retrieving it but then decided Prudence couldn't possibly squash two of his best hats in one week.

A pianoforte had been shoved into a corner, a piece

of sheet music still propped open as though waiting for someone to return. Evan walked over to the instrument and tapped at a key. The tinny note echoed against the high ceilings.

The soft swoosh of skirts sounded behind him, and he whirled around.

"Mr. Evan... I hadn't expected you to be here until four o'clock." Prudence held a stack of sheet music in her hands.

She seemed surprised to see him. Had Gil not announced his arrival?

"I wasn't free at four. I am now."

That wasn't precisely true. While he promised Stu he would be at the stables at four to look over a new mare, he could have changed the appointment. However, he hadn't cared for the way Prudence summoned him to the house instead of inviting him. The note she delivered to the stables even requested he wear clean boots.

"But I'm not ready." She strode to the pianoforte and set the sheet music on top.

"Ready for what?"

She looked as though she were ready for a quiet afternoon at home. She wore a muslin gown of soft cream and green stripes. Flowers he guessed to be violets lined the hem and trailed down the front of her bodice. Her neckerchief was plain with just a narrow trimming of lace. She had tied her auburn curls in a ribbon of periwinkle blue that matched the flowers in her dress. One tress escaped its prison and curled about her ear. Had he not known she was the lady of the house, he might have mistaken her for a young governess.

"I… ah…" Prudence glanced at the door.

"Are you expecting someone else?"

She returned a steadied gaze to Evan. "Yes, I am."

"Who?"

The last time she summoned him to the house it had been to propose to him in front of her solicitor. Did she now plan to break the proposal in front of the same witness? If she thought she would get out of their arrangement that easily…

"The musicians."

Had her voice trembled?

"Musicians? Are we having an impromptu ball? I told you I don't dance. Or at least not the kind of dancing that requires musicians."

"I know. That's what the musicians are for. I plan to teach you." Prudence folded her hands in front of her waist, making her look even more like a prim governess than before.

Evan found the look rather enticing. Like a naughty schoolboy, he considered the many ways he might get her to lose that calm demeanor.

"And I take it they aren't to arrive until four."

"Well, half past, actually. I invited you for four o'clock so we might have a chance to have some tea and get to know each other better."

"Before we dance, so to speak."

Prudence flushed, but she ignored Evan's innuendo. "We'll just have to have tea now."

"I'm afraid I can't wait. I have to meet someone at the stables at four," Evan said, eager to see how Prudence would react to his disrupting her carefully laid plans.

"Oh, but that's only an hour from now." Her

disappointment made her look even younger, but she recovered quickly. "Oh well, I guess it can't be helped."

"I'm glad you see it that way." He started toward his hat.

"I will just have to teach you to dance without music." She grabbed his hand and led him to the middle of the floor. "You stand here." Prudence stationed Evan in one spot, before backing up three or four paces. "I will hum the tune. Are you ready?"

"I don't seem to have a choice," Evan said.

Despite himself, he was eager to see how Prudence would manage without the musicians.

Prudence scrunched her lips to one side. "I suppose we should start with a minuet, and then we can move on to something more complicated.

Prudence hummed a few notes that left something to be desired musically speaking and held out her hand. Evan grasped it, and the last note ended with a squeak.

"No, no, no. Lightly. Pretend I'm something delicate like a teacup, not the handle of a bucket."

Evan loosened his grip.

"That's better. Now you bow and I curtsy."

Evan bowed low while Prudence dipped her knees and bowed her head.

"Ba…bum,bum,bum…4, 5…" Prudence half-hummed, half spoke the tune, making Evan almost wish they might dance in silence.

"Now what?" Evan asked when they were both straight again.

"Now we promenade in a sort of an arc." She waved her hand as though the concept of an arc might be difficult for him to grasp.

"Promenade?" It wasn't the geometrical concept

that had him concerned.

"Yes, promenade, as in walk. Like this." Prudence led him in a small arc, but whereas she took several mincing steps while she hummed her tune, he covered the distance in two giant strides so that his "arc" looked more like a square angle.

"No, you have to take smaller steps. Like a prance." She demonstrated a small stuttering step that looked almost like a skip.

"Prance?" Evan cocked an eyebrow. He fought back a grin. "I do not prance."

Prudence huffed. "Fine then, just walk, but try to take smaller steps."

Evan did as she asked, swearing to himself that if he felt this much the fool in private he would never do this dance in public. Even in Europe he had never really understood the fascination with the minuet. Just watching it was enough to put him to sleep. He found he didn't like performing it much better. He and Prudence were separated by far too much parquet.

He much preferred the soirees thrown by the peasants, gypsies, sailors, and other folk that the European monied class tended to consider unsavory. For himself, Evan found them very savory and their dances much more invigorating.

"That's better. Now you bow again. No, no, not to me, bow forward." Prudence said, when Evan turned to face her again.

"But there's nobody in that direction." Evan waved his hand toward a row of empty chairs.

"Yes, but there *will* be when we are at a ball."

Evan turned and bowed to one particularly overstuffed, red velvet settee that reminded him of a

French grandam—one without a head, of course. He even pretended to doff a hat for good measure.

Prudence rolled her eyes. "Now, take my hand."

Evan took her hand again, lightly this time, and Prudence walked around him in a small circle. Not sure what he was supposed to do, Evan tried to follow her lead but ended up walking straight into her path. Prudence bounced off his solid frame, and Evan had to wrap his arm around her waist to keep her from toppling.

"No, you need to stand still," she said in a breathy voice. "Let's go back to where you took my hand again."

Prudence repeated her move, then reached out for his other hand. Evan allowed her to take it, and waited for further instructions.

Prudence spun the other way, twisting Evan along with her.

"You're supposed to move with me!" The strain was beginning to show in her flushed face, and she no longer bothered counting out the beats.

"Are you sure this is the dance we should start with?"

Prudence dropped his hand and put her fists on her hips. "Really, this is the simplest of dances. If you would just follow my instructions, I'm sure you'll have it in no time."

She looked and sounded all too much like little Celia.

"Perhaps we can try another dance that I know."

The prim governess returned, "Really, Mr. Evan, I don't think this is the time or place for a dance of the sort you have in mind."

"Now look who's having impure thoughts. I was referring to a dance that I learned while I was in Europe."

"I thought you didn't know how to dance."

"I don't," Evan said hastily. He didn't want her renewing the absurd notion he had refused to dance because he didn't want to dance with her. "But this dance looked exceedingly easy. The couple dances together in time to the music, with the man taking the lead. To me, that seems much easier than following a set of predefined steps."

"Together?" Prudence's eyebrows knit in confusion.

"Yes, like this." Before she could protest, Evan slid his arm about her waist.

"Oh," Prudence said, her eyes as round as her lips.

"Then, I take your hand in mine." Evan grasped her hand lightly and started to hum a tune he had first heard in Bavaria.

Prudence stumbled when his feet started to move.

"Just move with me," Evan said.

"I have to dance backward?" Prudence stiffened in his arms.

"Some of the time. At other times, I'll be the one dancing backward."

"Seems terribly random."

"Just follow my lead." Evan tightened his grip about her waist, and Prudence clung to his hand and shoulder.

He had danced many different versions of this peasant dance and with partners at all levels of skill during a brief expedition to Eastern Europe. Prudence was like none of them. Trying to lead her around the dance floor was like trying to tack in a full force gale. She simply wouldn't move the way he wanted her to.

Prudence laughed when Evan tried to whirl her around, and she lost her footing. "Are you sure this isn't dangerous?"

"I hadn't thought so, but now I'm not so sure." Evan laughed. "Tell you what, let's try something. Put your feet on mine. That way you'll get used to the feel of the dance."

Prudence narrowed her eyes at him. "You want me to stand on your toes? Are you sure I won't be too heavy?"

Evan snorted.

She took one tentative step onto his polished boot.

"*Oof*," Evan said.

Prudence slapped at his shoulder, but her voice held amusement. "I haven't even put my weight on you yet."

Once she had her full weight resting on his toes, Evan whirled her around the dance floor once more, humming the tune in her ear.

Her satin slippers threatened to slide off his feet several times, so Evan tightened his grip and pulled her up against his chest.

"Do they really dance this way in Europe, in public?" Prudence was breathless even though Evan had been the one doing all the work.

"Definitely." At least the villagers did. Evan pulled her closer.

"How very shocking!" Prudence giggled as he whirled her faster about the floor.

At the apex of one particularly aggressive twirl, Prudence's slippered foot slid off Evan's boot at the same time he lost his hold around her waist. He made a grab for her as she lost her footing and headed for the floor. Evan's fast reflexes and an uncommonly solid sense of balance acquired by living life on the moving deck of a ship, allowed him to ensure she fell on top of him instead of hitting the parquet.

"*Oof*," Evan said again, smiling into Prudence's shocked eyes.

"I am so sorry!" Prudence tried to pull away, but Evan kept his arms locked about her waist.

She stopped struggling. Her long auburn hair slipped over her shoulder and brushed his cheek like a sheet of satin. He thought he detected the slight hint of rosemary.

He could stay like this forever.

"Am I not heavy?" Prudence asked in a whisper.

"Yes, as a matter of fact you are." Evan gave her a wicked grin and flipped her over so she lay under him. "There, that's better."

It *was* better.

"I can see why the Europeans are fond of this dance," Prudence said, a becoming blush spreading across her cheeks.

Evan dipped his head, his eyes on her rose-colored lips. Would she let him kiss her again?

"I suggest we not try it at the Governor's Ball."

Evan froze, his lips just above hers. "The what?"

"The Governor's Ball." Prudence pushed at his chest so she could look into his eyes. "It's in two weeks. An invitation was delivered to the manor just today. That's one of the reasons I decided to teach you to dance."

Evan sprang to his feet, then yanked Prudence to

hers with a quick tug at her hand.

"I thank you for the lesson today, but I must get back to the stables so I'm there in time for my appointment."

"Oh, of course," Prudence said, sounding slightly bewildered. "Perhaps we could do this again sometime?"

****

"Stu!" Evan bellowed as soon as he cleared the threshold to the stables.

Stu appeared from Demon's stall, a hoof pick in hand. "What is it, Evan?"

"I need you to find me a dancing instructor. The best one money can buy." Evan leaned against the stable wall and released a frustrated sigh.

"A dancing instructor?" Merriment shone in Stu's eyes. "What on earth would you need a dancing instructor for? Unless...Oh, don't tell me. The lovely Miss Ashcroft has you dancing to a merry tune already!"

"Just do it," Evan said, in no mood for Stu's teasing.

Stu's smile dissolved. "Very well. How soon do you need him?"

"Now, dammit!"

He would not disappoint Prudence again.

Chapter Fourteen

A cool breeze tousled Evan's hair with gentle fingers as he guided Demon up the slope to the top of the cliff. The big black pulled at his reins, obviously eager to work out some of his pent up energy. Evan knew exactly how he felt.

His last encounter with Prudence left him aching with need. Their dancing lesson ended with her lying atop him, her soft, rosemary-scented hair falling over one shoulder, her breasts pressed against his chest, her hips against his hardening body.

Had she not mentioned the Governor's Ball, how might the afternoon have ended? Would he have suggested they continue their dance in the privacy of her bedroom? Or perhaps he would have been content to take her right there on the parquet floor.

Evan grunted. He was as bad as Demon, sniffing after Bolt even though the mare was not in season.

Demon snorted as though objecting to his master's thoughts.

Rider and horse cleared the top of the rise, and Evan scanned the horizon to the west. A single tree stood off in the distance surrounded by meadows still golden from last summer's grasses. He considered spurring Demon toward the tree, racing some imaginary foe, when a lone rider caught his eye.

So she did prefer to ride astride rather than

sidesaddle. This time, however, her skirts were hiked only to mid-calf. She still showed a ridiculous amount of leg, but at least she wore brown riding boots instead of the impractical kid boots she had worn on the day they met.

Prudence rode for the tree, her long auburn curls fluttering in the breeze, her white cap flopping at her back with each of Bolt's strides.

Evan nudged Demon with his knee, prepared to join her in a real race, when the shadow of a man separated from the trunk of the tree. He yanked Demon's reins so hard the horse nearly stumbled.

The man appeared to be waiting for Prudence, but for what purpose? The hair on the back of Evan's neck stood up, and every muscle in his body tensed.

A portion of his concerns were answered when Prudence waved a hand in greeting. The man waved back. At least she knew he was there, but that still didn't explain why Prudence would ride out to meet a man in the middle of a meadow without a chaperone.

Was this perhaps the same man she had met on the beach? He was tall and thin, but beneath the shadows of the old oak, Evan could detect no more defining characteristics.

Bolt trotted up to the tree, and Prudence slid from her saddle even before coming to a full stop. The man stepped forward until a drop of sunlight glinted against golden hair. Evan held his breath, waiting for him to step farther into the light that would reveal his identity. He released it in a frustrated rush when Prudence stopped the man's advance by throwing herself into his arms.

He had to be the same man. She claimed they

weren't lovers, and he believed her. Still, she obviously knew him well enough to be free with her affections.

An old friend of the family perhaps? But then why meet in the meadow? Was he unwelcome at the manor?

It occurred to Evan that should either Prudence or her mystery man look over their shoulder, he and Demon would stand out in stark contrast to the sea of golden grass and the blue sky behind them.

"Come on, boy, let's find a place to hide." Evan clicked his tongue and guided Demon behind a copse of trees.

Feeling a bit like a schoolboy with a jealous crush, he watched the pair face each other beneath the tree's sheltering branches. Prudence reached out and grasped the man's hands in hers. Her lips moved, but Evan was too far away to hear her words.

Demon nickered and nudged his nose into the small of Evan's back.

Unwilling to take his eyes off Prudence, Evan waved a hand behind him. "Settle down, boy. I can't go down there where I am not wanted."

Demon whinnied.

"Shush! We're upwind. She'll hear us if we're not quiet."

Evan stopped paying attention to his impatient horse when the stranger leaned in and placed a lingering kiss on Prudence's lips. So Prudence might have been telling the truth when she said the strange man wasn't her lover, but she never said she didn't intend him to be.

****

"What was that for?" Prudence asked when the shock of Richard's kiss wore off.

Had he been any other man, any other besides Mr. Evan, his cheek would have been stained with the imprint of her palm. But Richard had been her closest friend nearly all her life. That he hadn't tried to steal a kiss before now was perhaps more shocking.

"To tell you the truth, I've wanted to do that since I was about ten, but you were younger still so I thought I had better wait. I never seemed to find the right moment though. Then you went away to school, and now you tell me the rumors of your betrothal are true. I figured this was my last chance. I do hope you'll forgive me for taking it."

"Of course, Richard." Prudence released his hands so she could take his elbow. "Let's take a turn about the meadow, shall we?"

They walked through the dry grass, their boots kicking up early spring insects and seeds from last year's clover.

"Richard." Prudence hesitated and looked up at him. "Do you love me?"

Richard slid a glance toward her then cast his gaze at the horizon. "Yes and no."

"Yes and no?"

It wasn't the response she had been expecting. Deep inside, she suspected Richard had loved her since childhood. No man would have looked after her as faithfully as Richard had if he didn't harbor at least a deep affection.

Richard turned to face her, holding her hands in his. "Prudence, I will always love you. At one time, I even thought we might have a future together despite your grandmother's admonitions, but tell me something." He glanced at their entwined hands.

"What is it, Richard?"

Richard raised his eyes to hers. "How did you feel when I kissed you just now?"

Prudence thought for a moment. She hadn't recoiled at the touch of Richard's lips any more than the touch of his hands on hers. Had she not had something to compare it to, she might have thought it to be what a kiss was supposed to be.

But she did have something to compare it to.

"It was pleasant."

"Pleasant, huh?" Richard gave her a wry smile.

"Pleasant is good, isn't it?" She didn't want to encourage him, but on the other hand, she couldn't bear hurting her dearest friend.

"Sure, pleasant is good. I thought it pleasant, too, but don't you think kisses between people who love each other, I mean love each other as more than friends, ought to be more than *pleasant*?"

At one time, Prudence would have given anything to marry a man whose kisses she found pleasant. A man who found kissing her to be pleasant was more than she ever dared hope for.

Until she kissed Mr. Evan. Her face warmed. His kiss had been no light touching of lips. He had kissed her thoroughly, hungrily. She had returned his kiss with just as much fervor. Richard's kiss paled in comparison.

Richard chucked her under the chin with his knuckle. "Don't worry, sweetheart. One day the woman in you will awake, and you'll understand what I mean."

Prudence tucked her hand back into the crook of his elbow and nudged him forward, hoping he wouldn't notice the heat spreading across her face.

"So, tell me about this man you plan to marry," he

said as they walked.

"Well..." Prudence considered.

How could she describe a man she barely knew? He was handsome, but her friend didn't need to know that. He wasn't as accomplished as Richard, but it seemed somehow disloyal to say so. The feelings he engendered in her weren't something she had ever tried to put into words.

She didn't feel alone anymore.

The admission shocked Prudence. She had never considered herself lonely. Not really. Richard had always been there for her. Even when she was away at school and living in Boston, he found time to write to her, often several times a week. When his own schooling and then business allowed, he came to visit as well.

She realized now that even though she wasn't lonely, she was alone. She had dreaded what the future would bring. She supposed she always knew their friendship couldn't remain as it had been forever.

Rachel Ashcroft saw what her granddaughter had been loathed to admit. If she and Richard married, it would change their relationship.

But that was bound to happen eventually anyway. If he didn't marry her, he would find some other woman to marry. And his wife likely wouldn't care to see her husband spending quite as much time with another woman, childhood friend or not.

With Mr. Evan, Prudence felt more secure about her place in the world. It was like everything somehow seemed right, and even if things did go terribly wrong, she had someone she could count on. Mr. Evan would be there for her, always.

She had never thought that she would want that, but now, she realized how very much she hated being alone.

"He's intriguing." Prudence settled on a completely inadequate description.

"Intriguing?" Richard grinned down at her. "That's high praise coming from you. Does he have prospects?"

Prudence tucked her arm deeper into Richard's. He had been such a good friend all these years. She was glad he felt the same way about their kiss. It would be a shame to lose her best friend over something so inconsequential. She needed someone she could talk to, and while the future remained uncertain, she welcomed his company now.

"Well, he's stable master at Ashcroft, but I'm not sure what his prospects are."

"He works for you then, does he?" Richard's face turned thoughtful. "You don't think it takes skill or intelligence to run a stable as large as Ashcroft?"

"I'm sure it does. I've just never seen any indication that he wants more out of life." She could hardly admit to Richard that lack of ambition was a qualification she required in a husband.

"If he never rises above the position of stable master, would you hold that against him? Remember, although you call me cousin, I am just the son of your grandfather's steward."

Prudence jumped to his defense. "And my business manager."

"But a common man, nonetheless."

"You know I would never hold his upbringing or his station in life against him or any man. It doesn't bother me if he's as poor as a church mouse and never chooses to involve himself in matters outside the stables."

"I'm sure it wouldn't," Richard said in a knowing voice. "Perhaps that's what attracted you to him, his lack of interest in bettering himself. If he doesn't get involved in the business, you can continue running things your own way."

She had been backed into a corner, again. Prudence opened her mouth to protest, but she couldn't come up with a single response. Richard knew her too well.

"I'm just teasing you, sweetheart. Whether he involves himself or not is immaterial. I will always be here to watch out for your interests."

"Thank you, Richard." Prudence squeezed his elbow.

"So, do you think you'll be able to convince him to attend the Governor's Ball? Or is that a little beyond the social skills of a stable master?"

"I think he'll attend. He doesn't dance, but he seems quite comfortable in society. Much more so than I would have expected." She recalled his knowledge of Portuguese, the little blue and white tiles, and his skill at the scandalous dance he claimed to have learned while in Europe. "In fact, I think he must have traveled a bit."

"That's unusual for a stable master, don't you think?" They reached the far end of the meadow and turned back toward the meeting tree. "Are you sure he is who he claims to be?"

"I'm certain I only know a small bit about him, but do I think he may be trying to deceive me? No. Unless he's uncommonly good at hiding his feelings, I do not sense that kind of animosity from him."

"Do you sense any other kind of animosity from him?" Richard asked, his voice tense.

"No, no, of course, not. In fact, he seems to enjoy my company as much as I do his. Perhaps he and I can be...friends." Prudence rested her temple against his upper arm. "Not as close as you and I are, of course, but friends."

"I know I don't yet need to approve of your match if you marry within the next two months, but I should like to meet this man for myself. I think I may attend the Governor's Ball after all."

Chapter Fifteen

"I've pulled everything out of your trunks, Miss Ashcroft. Would you like me to see what I can find in mine?"

Prudence ignored Netty's scarcely concealed sarcasm. She didn't blame the girl for being piqued. The carriage ride from Newport to Providence had not been an easy one, and being cooped up with strangers in the rooms reserved for servants would surely be enough to fray anyone's nerves. At least Prudence had the luxury of a room to herself. She could afford to show a little understanding.

"That's kind of you, Netty, but I can manage with what I have here. Why don't I just call you to help me dress once I've decided?"

"Very well." Netty bobbed a curtsy and ducked through the door, closing it with more force than strictly necessary.

Prudence stared at the pile of dresses that lay sprawled like fallen soldiers across her bed.

She had plenty of gowns fine enough for the Governor's Ball, but she had no idea what Mr. Evan would be wearing. She hated the thought of making him feel self-conscious by making his attire appear shabby.

Somehow, he had scrounged up something appropriate for the Sheridans' supper party. His suit of green velvet had been understated but elegant. Would he wear it again? Or would his benefactor, whomever he was, loan him another suit of clothes for the occasion? She hoped he hadn't felt compelled to spend whatever money he had just to live up to her expectations. She had none. As long as his boots were clean, she didn't care what he wore.

Prudence held up a gown of rose and cream striped muslin. It had always been one of her favorites. She loved the little ivory rosettes that lined the bodice and the sleeves. She set it back on the bed with a sigh. As charming as the dress was, it just wouldn't be right for a ball.

She rifled through the pile of dresses, rejecting one after the other for being either too informal or too showy or too provocative. She threw an emerald green gown with a low-cut bodice on the bed. No point in emphasizing her deficiencies.

From the bottom of the pile, she lifted a gown of blue satin and held it up. It shimmered in the fading sunlight.

Prudence bit her lip. The dress would be lovely in the candlelight. She had rejected it once already because she hoped for something less elegant to wear. Her hopes had dwindled with the last of her dresses. The time had come to reconsider her options.

This dress had a modest neckline, but the seamstress had managed to add a few darts in the bodice that accentuated what little God had given her. The white, English lace that fell from the sleeves added an elegant touch. Of all the gowns she had, this one was her favorite and her finest. If Mr. Evan showed up in anything less formal than the suit he had worn to the Sheridans', he would indeed look shabby standing next to her.

Prudence started to set the dress down on the bed, but her fingers wouldn't let go. What if she wore the dress but didn't wear any jewelry with it? She could have Netty sweep her hair up into a simple chignon.

A shadow fell across the room as the sun dipped below the horizon. Whatever she decided, she would have to hurry. Mr. Evan would be arriving soon.

****

Prudence's heart gave a little leap when the inn keeper showed Mr. Evan into the inn's private parlor. He wore a coat of midnight blue velvet embroidered in gray silk. As understated as his previous attire had been, this suit spoke of wealth. More than that, her blue satin gown looked as though it had been made to complement.

"Good evening."

Prudence studied his face. He didn't appear to be looking forward to the evening ahead. If anything, the severity in his features would have been more fitting for one headed into battle.

"Good evening." No sense in delaying the inevitable. "If you will just give me a minute, I will fetch my pelisse, and we can be off.

"Just a moment." He held out a box wrapped in silver paper.

"What's this for?" Prudence took the beautifully wrapped box from his palm.

"I believe a betrothal gift is customary."

"A betrothal gift?"

She knew of the tradition, of course, but she had never expected such a thing.

"We are getting married, aren't we?"

"Well, yes, but—"

"Open it."

Prudence did as he commanded. Beneath her trembling fingers, the silver paper fell away to reveal a black, hinged box. Inside lay a brooch of silver filigree in the shape of…she looked closer. A gargoyle?

Prudence picked up the delicate piece. "It's beautiful."

It really was. The hideous little creature somehow managed to look cuddlier than his larger, granite cousins that guarded the corners of old buildings. He had sapphire eyes and a lopsided grin that was more impish than evil.

Mr. Evan must have had it commissioned and, judging by the delicate metalwork, by an artisan of great skill. The gargoyle's blue eyes sparkled in the light from the fire as only true gems would.

"I'm glad you like it."

Prudence glanced up at him. He didn't look very glad. His brows were dark slashes above narrow eyes, and his lips were set in a thin line.

"I don't think I can accept this. It must have cost you a fortune!"

A muscle in his jaw twitched.

"Contrary to your belief, I am not marrying you for your money. In fact, you might say that *you* are marrying *me* for your money."

"Oh, but I didn't mean—" Her voice trailed off as his words registered. "What do you mean I am marrying you for my money?"

"The will stipulated that you must marry someone within the next three months or control of Ashcroft is passed over to your business manager." He spat the last words. "So, in essence, you are marrying me for your money."

Prudence found herself at a loss for words. On a basic level, he spoke the truth. She did need to get married in order to retain control of Ashcroft. But that wasn't her sole reason for marrying him. Somehow, now that she had decided upon Mr. Evan, she couldn't imagine spending the rest of her life with anyone else.

"What I can't yet figure out is, why me?" He pierced her with speculative eyes. "Why not Richard? The two of you seem suitable enough."

"You know my grandmother expressly forbade Richard and me to marry."

Besides, although she and Richard were friends, they were not in love. At least not in the way her grandmother thought a couple should be. But then again, she wasn't in love with Mr. Evan either. Was she?

"Your grandmother cautioned you against marrying him, but she didn't make it a stipulation of the inheritance. You could still have married Bainbridge."

"But I don't love him!"

Prudence regretted the words as soon as they were spoken. Hopefully, Mr. Evan wouldn't read more into them than she had intended.

"But surely you had other suitors who would have been happy to speed you to the altar."

His words stung.

"No, as a matter of fact, I did not. You were the only eligible man available. So, depending on how you look at it, you are either lucky or cursed."

"I guess we'll see who is lucky and who is cursed." Mr. Evan threw open the parlor doors and called for the innkeeper to bring her wrap.

****

The carriage ride to the governor's mansion took less than twenty minutes, but in the small dark box, it might as well have been an eternity. Mr. Evan sat across from Prudence, his brooding face staring out the window at the passing scenery. In such close quarters, the jostling of the carriage made contact unavoidable. When her leg brushed against his, she sensed his coiled tension even through her skirts.

Was it the ball that had him in such a foul mood? When she told him about it, he had left the manor so abruptly that she hadn't had time to have Gil fetch the invitation that arrived that morning addressed to him. It had come attached with a note asking if she could have one of her servants deliver it since Mr. Evan's address was unknown.

At the time, she had been relieved. No one yet knew he lived in the small cottage not far from the stables. Nor did they know his true occupation. She was beginning to believe it might be possible to keep up his ruse forever. Not that she cared whether he had been a stable master, but he might not wish anyone to know his background. Based on how little he talked about himself, she guessed Mr. Evan valued his privacy.

For two weeks, she waited for him to call on her. Ultimately, she gave up and asked Gil to have one of the houseboys deliver the invitation to the stables. She didn't even know he had accepted the invitation until he sent a terse message a few days later saying he would arrive to pick her up at eight at the inn.

At last, the carriage rolled up to the governor's mansion. A liveried footman dressed in blue velvet with gold embroidery opened the door and lowered the steps. Prudence noted with approval how the man's uniform colors so perfectly matched the Rhode Island seal. He even had a gold anchor embroidered over his heart. She was glad she and Mr. Evan had both chosen to wear blue as well. While her gown had been made in London, she felt somehow more loyal to her colony dressed in her colors.

Mr. Evan got out first then turned to give Prudence his hand. She navigated the narrow steps, holding her skirts to the side with her free hand.

They ascended the steps of the stately mansion, entering the bright foyer where another footman relieved Prudence of her wrap. She retook Mr. Evan's arm, and he led her to the ballroom where the butler took their invitations.

It occurred to Prudence she should have opened Mr. Evan's invitation before giving it to him. Had she taken a quick peek, she would at least know his Christian name. If they were going to be married, she couldn't go on calling him "Mr. Evan" forever.

"Right this way, Captain." The butler indicated the ballroom with a white-gloved hand.

Captain? Had he been speaking to someone behind them? Prudence glanced back over her shoulder in time to see the butler hand an invitation back to Mr. Sheridan before he waved the elderly merchant and his wife into the ballroom with the same precise gesture he had used just moments before.

The governor's butler was of the highest caliber. It seemed unlikely he would make such an egregious mistake. Mr. Sheridan was no sea captain. He had invested in several ships managed by Ashcroft & Sons, but he got seasick every time he stepped foot on one of them. Prudence was equally certain he had never served in any army. While most considered him a genius where investments were concerned, he had something of a weak constitution. Mrs. Sheridan would have lasted longer in the army than her husband.

Prudence cast a sidelong glance at Mr. Evan.

Jaw rigid, he surveyed the governor's guests as though any one of them might pose an imminent threat. Yes, she could imagine him commanding a regiment. He would frighten the poor devils so much no one would dare cross him. One sight of his steely glare and the enemy would flee.

She wished she knew what had happened to cause him to lose that crooked smile he had when they first met. And what had happened to the man who had been so concerned for her health after her grandmother's funeral? Or the man she had talked so freely with on the cliffs?

Had she made that man disappear? Did he find being married to her such an objectionable prospect that he had become a different man?

No, she was just being overly dramatic. He had still been kind and sweet even after he agreed to marry her. He even kissed her after that horrible encounter with Simon.

It must be the Governor's Ball. She knew he didn't want to come, and while she hadn't insisted on his being here, she had done nothing to dissuade him. Prudence cast her fiancé a sidelong glance.

I'm so sorry to drag you into this. The words echoed in her head, but now was not the time nor the place to say them aloud. They would get this ball behind them and start anew.

Across the room, Richard conversed with a small group that included several ladies and two gentlemen. Over the head of one petite young woman, he caught sight of Prudence and grinned. His friendly face did much to relieve the strain of the carriage ride, and she raised a hand to give him a small wave before she caught herself. One did not wave to a gentleman across a ballroom at the governor's mansion.

About the room, ladies wielded their painted silk fans with artful sweeps, flicks, and flutters, almost as if they were fencing imaginary foes. Prudence supposed there was a certain way of flicking her fan that would symbolize a friendly greeting to Richard, but she had never been schooled in the art.

Perhaps if she drew her fan about her in the shape of a parallelogram, he would get the hint. She giggled as she imagined herself waving and fluttering as though she were directing carriage traffic on Orange Street in Boston.

Her laughter drew a glare from Mr. Evan. Lord, how would she get through this evening with such an ogre at her side?

"Mr. Evan, if you prefer, you could join the gentlemen in the card room. You need not stay with me."

"Are you so eager to get rid of me?"

Prudence realized with some alarm he was no longer looking at her. Instead he had his gaze fixed on Richard.

"No, I adore your company." She couldn't quite manage to keep the sarcasm out of her voice, even though she was the cause of his misery. "But you don't seem to be enjoying yourself. I thought perhaps you would be more comfortable with cards than standing around watching people dance."

"I don't play cards."

Prudence studied his face. He didn't dance, except for one unusual sort of dance that would surely cause a scandal in the governor's ballroom. He didn't play cards. Did the man spend his entire life in the stables with the horses?

"I guess I could teach you how. It would probably be less dangerous than dancing."

Judging by his scowl, her attempt to lighten the mood had failed.

The orchestra played a few notes and couples filled the dance floor. To her surprise, Mr. Evan grasped her hand and tugged her into the middle of it all.

"But you don't need to—"

He gave her a dark, determined look.

The dance was a simple country dance that required very little skill and left much room for conversation between pairs of couples. Mr. Evan executed the moves flawlessly, conversing politely with the other dancers and even managing to promenade in steps that were small, yet somehow manly.

"You've been practicing," Prudence said when they came back together again.

"Yes, I bribed one of the stable hands to teach me the steps. However, should they play the dance I showed you, we will not be able to join in as he flatly refused to partner me in that one so I could practice."

Prudence laughed, but her laughter died away when she realized he hadn't smiled.

When the music ended, Prudence led the way to

the edge of the dance floor. She didn't think she could stand the strain of another set with him.

"Would you like some punch?" Mr. Evan asked.

"Oh, yes, please."

She watched him go. Given the crush of people at the Governor's Ball, she estimated it would be at least five or ten minutes before he returned. A blissful five minutes where she didn't have to suffer him glowering at her.

"My, don't you make a lovely couple."

Prudence whirled around. "Richard! How happy I am to see you."

She had the sudden urge to throw herself into his arms, but she resisted.

"Has your future husband claimed you for every dance, or did you save one for me?"

"For my oldest and dearest friend, I will always save at least one." Prudence took the arm he offered and followed him onto the dance floor.

"Perhaps I should have asked your fiancé for permission before I asked you to dance," Richard said after they had executed only a few steps.

"Why on earth would you do that? We are not married yet. Besides what does he care with whom I dance?"

"I don't know *why* he should care. Only that he *does*. In fact, right now, he looks like he's considering how best to kill me."

Prudence glanced over her shoulder to find Mr. Evan glaring at them.

"He's not the dueling type is he?" Richard asked, a note of worry edging through the attempt at a jest.

"Of course not." Prudence laughed off his

comment.

At least she didn't think he was. But perhaps he really was a brawler. He had gotten his nose broken somehow. She couldn't imagine what she would do if Mr. Evan should challenge dear, sweet cousin Richard.

"Don't worry, Richard. I will protect you."

Richard raised an eyebrow, but Prudence gave him a look intended to convince him of the seriousness of her vow. She would allow no harm to come to her dearest friend, even if she had to defy her fiancé.

The music drew to a close, but both Prudence and Richard remained on the dance floor.

"I don't know that I am comfortable sending you back to him alone. Perhaps you had best introduce me and get this over with."

"Don't be silly," Prudence said with a slight waver in her voice. "I'll be fine. You can meet Mr. Evan some other day when he's not in such a foul humor."

This time, it was Richard's turn to give her a look that suggested he wasn't joking.

"Oh, all right." Prudence gave an exasperated sigh. "I guess we can't put it off forever."

Mr. Evan didn't take his eyes off Richard as they approached.

"Mr. Evan, I should like to introduce you to my cousin, Richard Bainbridge. Richard, this is my fiancé, Mr. Evan."

"Your servant, sir," Richard said, executing the lowest of bows.

Mr. Evan did not bow in return. Prudence told herself it was due to the two glasses of punch he still held in his hands. Given the scowl he wore, she doubted they were the sole reason.

"Do you have a first name to go with the last?" Richard asked.

"I find Mister suits me well." Mr. Evan's voice was as hard as his face. "Still, I am more interested in your name. Prudence, I believe you called him cousin, did you not?"

"I did."

Where could Mr. Evan be going with such an odd line of questioning?

"As I recall, your mother was an only child, and your father's siblings all died before they had offspring. How is it that Richard is a cousin?"

"I am the son of her father's steward," Richard broke in before Prudence could explain.

"So, not a cousin then?" Mr. Evan directed the pointed question at Prudence.

"No, he's not actually a cousin, but I think of Richard as family." Prudence kept her voice cool, but inside she seethed. "What right do you have to question his relationship to me anyway?"

Did he think Richard unworthy of her friendship simply because he was the son of the steward?

"You seem to know a lot about my family. Certainly, more than I told you." She didn't even try to soften the underlying accusation.

"I need to know who I am marrying," Mr. Evan said.

"That goes both ways." Prudence could feel the precarious hold on her temper slipping. "Perhaps I should have paid a little more heed before I selected the man with whom I am to spend the rest of my life. For heaven's sake, I don't even know your first name."

"I believe it is time to go." Mr. Evan ignored her

outburst. "Say goodbye to your *cousin,* then meet me by the carriages."

Prudence stared after him in stunned silence. They had been at the Governor's Ball for little more than an hour, and he was ready to leave? They might as well. She would never be able to enjoy herself with him scowling at her the entire time.

"Well, that could have gone better," Richard said. "As your friend and the closest thing you have to a male relative, even though not actually a relative as your dear fiancé has pointed out, I'm not sure I should let you leave with that man."

Prudence considered defying Mr. Evan. After all, he really had no right to order her around. Not now. Not ever. Still, it might be better to get her fiancé and her best friend as far from each other as possible. At least until she could explain the true nature of her relationship with Richard to Mr. Evan.

Prudence patted Richard's arm. "Don't worry, he can't kill me tonight. We're not married yet, so he wouldn't get a penny of the estate."

Prudence signaled for a footman to fetch her pelisse.

"That's not funny, Pru," Richard said. "It might be true, but it's not funny."

Richard followed her out to the carriages pulling up in front of the mansion. Mr. Evan stood a few feet away in the midst of a cluster of elderly matrons, all vying for his attention like a flock of debutantes.

"Listen, Prudence, perhaps you should let me draw up some sort of contract for you," Richard whispered for her ears only.

"Contract?"

The suggestion caught her off guard. She had spent days wondering how she could convince Richard to draw up a contract, and here he was, suggesting it himself.

"Yes, an agreement that puts you in charge of your family's assets and protects them in case your fiancé should turn out to be a swindler," Richard said, as though she hadn't understood what he meant.

"You don't trust him?"

Why was she hesitating? The idea had been hers to begin with. There was just something about Richard suggesting it that rankled a bit. And although her marriage might be no more than a business arrangement, a contract would be inescapable proof of it.

"It's not so much that as I have this sense that he's hiding something," Richard said. "I can't seem to shake it, and that worries me."

Prudence eyed Mr. Evan. "I don't know, Richard. It seems an awful way to begin a marriage. Let me think about it."

Mercifully, the Ashcroft carriage made it to the front of the line before Richard could press his case. He and Prudence joined Mr. Evan at the curb. The footman opened the door and lowered the stairs, and both men reached out a hand to help Prudence alight. Not wanting to slight either of them, she grasped both of their hands and found herself propelled into the carriage as each man vied to give more assistance than the other.

Just outside the carriage door, Mr. Evan and Richard stood toe to toe, glowering at one another. Next to Mr. Evan's dark features and stolid build, Richard appeared pale and thin—and nervous.

"Since you are not married yet, perhaps I should accompany the two of you."

The steadiness in Richard's voice filled Prudence with admiration for her friend.

"You think Prudence won't be able to resist me once we're alone?" Mr. Evan asked.

Prudence gasped. Of all the insufferable things to say.

Richard's spine stiffened. "No, I am saying that until Prudence is married she is under my protection."

"How is she your responsibility?"

Mr. Evan stepped a little closer, but Richard did not back down.

"Although, as you pointed out, she is not my cousin, my family has served hers for generations. Her happiness and her safety are my primary concerns. Promise me you will not harm her, and I will consider letting her go."

Storm clouds gathered in Mr. Evan's eyes, and Prudence balled her fists in her lap.

"I would never hurt a woman." Mr. Evan's voice was low and quiet. "However, I have no such compunction against taking you out, so I'd suggest you stand off."

Mr. Evan climbed into the carriage. Prudence shot Richard a look of gratitude mixed with reassurance just before her fiancé slammed the carriage door in the face of her dearest friend.

Chapter Sixteen

The Ashcroft business offices were in a bustling part of Newport, just a short walk from the wharf that accounted for so much of the family fortune. A bell chimed, announcing Evan as he opened the front door and stepped into the small, square room that served as the reception area.

A large, weathered oak desk consumed practically all of the usable space in the room. To its side sat two aged, but comfortable-looking leather chairs presumably reserved for guests. Other than the furniture, the room stood empty.

Instead of calling out, Evan decided to take his measure of the face Ashcroft & Sons chose to display to the casual visitor. Although a highly prosperous venture, the Ashcroft offices were plain compared to the offices of other shipping magnates. The carpet, woven in shades of crimson and royal blue, was faded and frayed from a multitude of boots. Instead of crystal chandeliers, sconces lined the walls. The white plaster had faded to yellow, helped along, no doubt, by decades of inexpensive tallow candles burning in their holders.

Evan nodded his approval, although no one was there to see it. These days, it was wise to avoid looking too prosperous. It kept the revenue collectors off one's back.

A solid young man of about eighteen or nineteen

materialized from the gloom of a back hallway. He had a nose bent worse than Evan's and looked more bodyguard than bookish. Like a troll assigned to guard the castle gate, Evan thought with uncharacteristic harshness. Then again, he had had far worse looking serve in his ranks, and in his experience, appearance bore no correlation to ability.

The boy eyed Evan, his face turned slightly askew. Evan knew the look well. Sailors whose eyes had grown clouded with age often had the same tilt to their head.

"Can I help you?" Despite his lack of years, the boy's voice reminded Evan of gravel being churned by a shovel.

"I'm here to see Mr. Bainbridge."

The boy squinted. "You have an appointment?"

"No, but tell him Captain Foster is here to see him. I believe he will wish to speak with me."

The boy looked doubtful but disappeared down the hallway. He opened a door at the back, and a soft ray of light lit the dark passage. Evan heard the boy grind out his request for a meeting.

"Send him in," Richard said in tones that were almost melodic compared to his secretary's.

Instead of showing him down the hallway, the boy left the door to Bainbridge's office ajar then lumbered through a side door like a troll escaping the light of day.

Evan stepped into Richard's office and stood in the center of a royal blue carpet only slightly less faded than the one in the lobby. Richard scratched notes in a book, seemingly oblivious to his presence. Evan coughed.

"I'm sorr—" Richard's voice caught in his throat.

Apprehension flashed over his features only to be replaced by understanding then a wry grin. He stood and came around the front of his desk.

"Captain *Evan* Foster, I presume."

Evan had to hand it to Richard Bainbridge. He was quick witted.

Richard crossed his arms. "At least she won't have to put up with you much if I can keep you busy hauling cargo."

Evan grabbed Richard by the collar and pushed him back against his own desk. A stack of logbooks clattered to the floor, and Evan considered briefly that he might have alerted the troll. While he clearly had the weight advantage on Richard, his secretary looked like he knew how to handle himself in a fight.

"Don't think you can have her all to yourself by keeping me at sea. If you lay a hand on my wife, I won't give you the courtesy of a duel. You'll be dead by morning."

Perhaps Prudence's lack of patience had worn off on him. Perhaps, even though their pending marriage was little more than a business arrangement, he didn't like the idea of another man being the recipient of Prudence's affections. Whatever it was, he found himself more often than not teetering on an emotional brink as of late.

"So that's how it is?" Despite being pinned to his own desk, his feet barely resting against the faded carpet, Richard sounded unperturbed. "Calm yourself man. I was only trying to lighten the mood. It might have been a poor jest, but that's all it was."

Evan loosened his grip on Richard's collar and let the man's weight slide to rest on his own two feet.

"In addition to warning me off Prudence, I presume you're also here to review plans for the *Cythraul*." Richard tugged his coat back into place.

Evan's anger ebbed, letting the more logical, and normally in-control, side of his brain take over. Perhaps the man was innocent. In his experience, the guilty were the most likely to fight back. If Bainbridge intended Prudence to become his lover, in all likelihood, the man would have already challenged him to a duel.

Richard strode to a table in the middle of the room and opened a drawer. He pulled out a roll of parchment, shoved a stack of ledgers aside, and then spread it across the ample space on top of the table. He pinned the edges of the parchment with an assortment of paperweights, including one that looked like the skull of a cat, and then stood back to survey the drawing.

He whistled in appreciation. "She's a beauty all right. I understand you gave the designer the specifications. For a captain, you know a fair amount about ship building."

Evan joined Richard at the table and looked down at his dream taken form on the crisp paper. The *Cythraul*. The name meant something akin to devil in Welsh. It had been what the sisters had called him for as long as he could remember. For reasons he wasn't even sure he understood, he found it gratifying to give that name to the ship that had become the symbol of his success.

"Did you manage to locate a source of copper?" He ran a finger along the keel.

"Yes, just as you instructed in your letter, we went straight to that mine in Wales...Myr...Myrd...Myrn...

184

or something that started with an M anyway."

"Mynydd Parys," Evan said. "It means 'mountain,' but it's the name of the mine, too."

"Yes, well, the man I sent was able to locate it and convince the poor fellows who work in that remote, rather desolate corner of the world that the Americans weren't such a bad lot after all." Richard snorted. "It was a close-run thing, though. Your name didn't do us a damned bit of good either."

Evan hadn't thought it would. He hadn't been to Wales for many years. "How about the bolts? Did you make sure they were the exact alloy I specified?"

"Yes," Richard said. "But why so precise? And what on earth made you think of copper in the first place?"

"Because, if you use iron bolts, they rust and defeat the purpose of the copper sheathing, and it wasn't my idea," Evan said, answering both questions with the same breath. "The Royal Navy's been considering the use of copper sheathing for decades. Mostly to protect against shipworm."

"Nasty things." Richard shuddered. "So why haven't they put their plan into action?"

Evan went back to his study of the drawings. "I suppose because it's expensive, and the war with the French hasn't left much in the government's coffers."

"When are you planning on breaking the news to Prudence?" Richard asked, not bothering to soften the change in subject.

Evan didn't need to ask what he meant. He had been expecting the question, or at least one like it from the moment Richard looked up from his books. He counted among his blessings that Richard was more rational-minded than his "cousin." There could be no predicting how Prudence would react when he did tell her.

"After the wedding." Evan picked up the compass and made a few quick measurements, ensuring his specifications had been followed.

"She thinks you're the stable master."

"I know." He set the compass down and ran his fingers over the lines of his future command. "But that's her problem. I never told her I was."

"Don't you think she should know who she is marrying?"

Evan snorted. "Why? So she can go off and find a real stable boy to marry? No, I think I'll let her leap into this one with both feet and her eyes shut. Maybe it will teach her not to be so rash."

"Do you love her?" Richard asked.

Love? Evan found the question as odd as it was unexpected. He might have anticipated it from a brother, if Prudence had one, but Richard was merely a friend of the family and her man of business. Was he testing the waters, trying to determine whether Prudence would still be available after the wedding?

Let him keep wondering.

"I'm a businessman. I made a deal with her grandmother that stands to earn me a lot of money and the ship of my dreams."

"And you'll be marrying into the Ashcroft fortune," Richard reminded him.

Evan shrugged. "That matters little. If she runs the business the way she runs the rest of her life, she'll be a pauper in ten years."

"That's hardly being fair," Richard said.

Evan straightened and looked him in the eye. "Tell me, do you always know what Prudence is thinking?"

"Generally, yes."

"So does everybody else. She wears every emotion on her sleeve and says practically everything that's in her head. The first time she comes face-to-face with a dishonest revenue collector, she'll lose everything. If she comes face-to-face with an honest one, she'll be run out of Rhode Island or spend the next fifteen years in jail."

To Evan's surprise, Richard's grin stretched from ear to ear. "You know, I'm actually relieved she chose you. I did not relish becoming her superior and attempting to tell her what to do. I, for one, am happy with our relationship just the way it is."

You'd better be, because your current relationship with my wife is all it will ever be. Evan gritted his teeth to keep the thought from escaping.

They spent the rest of the afternoon discussing the building of the *Cythraul*. Evan made a few changes to the plans, some based on his own knowledge of sailing and others based on suggestions from Bainbridge. For a man of business, Richard understood a fair amount about ships. He was no captain, and clearly not a sailor, but he understood the need for speed and was quick to pick up on the purpose of the changes Evan suggested.

More surprising was Richard's good nature. For a man about to have his would-be lover stolen from him, he seemed to harbor very little animosity. Nor did he seem particularly concerned that Prudence's fiancé wasn't who he claimed to be. Was he always this carefree or did she matter that little to him?

"If we make the changes here, she won't be able to

187

carry as much." Richard pointed to one of Evan's sketches.

"No," Evan agreed. "But she will be a fair amount faster."

Richard studied the suggested changes, then nodded his agreement. "If we lose the copper, we could lighten the expense."

The suggestion was perfunctory at best.

"In addition to protecting her from shipworms, she'll be faster. Don't worry. I am prepared to pay for it."

"You mean you will get your wife to pay for it." Richard removed the paperweights and rerolled the parchment.

"No, I mean I will pay for the changes." He didn't return Richard's grin. "My pockets may not be as deep as my wife's, but I expect to make a healthy return. It will be a worthwhile investment."

Richard nodded in approval, and Evan scowled at him. After spending one short afternoon with the man, he discovered he genuinely liked Richard Bainbridge. He found that annoying.

Chapter Seventeen

"They're both here?" Prudence decided she must have misunderstood Mrs. Hatcher.

"Sit still, Miss Prudence, or I'll never finish your hair." Netty spoke through the pins she held between her lips.

"Yes, ma'am." Mrs. Hatcher seemed rather surprised herself. "Both Mr. Evan and Mr. Bainbridge are waiting for you in the parlor."

"They came together?"

After the long, silent carriage ride back from the Governor's Ball, Prudence found it hard to believe Richard had dared come within ten feet of her betrothed. For reasons she could not fathom, Mr. Evan clearly disliked her oldest and dearest friend. It just didn't seem possible. Everybody liked Richard. Positively everybody!

"I don't exactly know if they came together, but they arrived at the same time. They both claimed to be escorting you to the assembly tonight."

"Thank you, Mrs. Hatcher. Tell them I will be down shortly."

Netty took the last of the pins out of her mouth and spoke to her mistress as if she were a child. "Not if you don't sit still you won't. You keep fidgeting, and I'll have to start all over."

Prudence willed herself to keep still. She didn't

care one whit what her hair looked like, but she hated to leave the two men alone in her parlor any longer than necessary—especially when her grandfather's dueling pistols lay in a case on the mantel.

As soon as Netty declared her ready, Prudence snatched her reticule from the bed and flew down the stairs, slowing only to catch her breath before throwing open the double doors to the front parlor.

Both men looked up. Richard wore his usual jovial expression. Mr. Evan's face was as icy as a Rhode Island winter.

"Mr. Evan. Richard." Prudence fanned herself. "How...nice to see you both here."

Mr. Evan raised an eyebrow.

Richard cast him a sidelong glance, then stepped forward. "Yes, I thought I'd stop by to ensure you had an escort to the assembly. I know how much you were looking forward to attending."

"Oh, yes, I am so looking forward to it." Prudence lied. "Let me fetch my cloak. I'll be but a moment."

The last place she wanted to be was at the Waite's assembly, and Richard knew it. The Waites fancied themselves among the upper crust of Rhode Island society, and they filled their home with guests they deemed worthy of their notice. There would be fops and coquettes aplenty, social climbers who thought that what one wore was more important than one's character. Nevertheless, wealth remained the primary criteria for inclusion on the guest list. It was the latter that had won the Ashcrofts their invitation over the years.

Then there were the political climbers, men who looked to England to further their station in life. They were vocal in their support of England's attempt to control trade between the Colonies and other countries and especially vociferous in their claim the Colonies should be grateful to the mother country for all they had.

These were the men she had to be especially careful around. They had been suspicious of Ashcroft for generations, and one hint of her family's extracurricular business arrangement would have them running to the governor. Despite Governor Hopkins being a merchant himself and the long-standing collegial relationship between their families, his political position would leave him no choice but to investigate.

Prudence inhaled a deep breath and held it, trying to calm her nerves. She understood the importance of appearances. Given her family's business dealings, she couldn't afford to snub the Waites and their objectionable guests, however much she might wish to.

Nevertheless, she had planned to attend alone. She expected to run into Richard. As her business manager, he was almost as prized as an actual Ashcroft. But she had no idea Mr. Evan had been invited. Perhaps they wished to waste no time winning him over to their way of thinking.

Would they be successful? The fops would make no headway, but Mr. Evan's political leanings could certainly be counted among the long list of things she did not know about her betrothed.

Prudence walked back into the parlor. To her relief, the dueling pistols were still on the mantel, both men were still standing, and there were no noticeable bruises on either of them. They seemed to be avoiding eye contact with one another, but that was preferable to a glaring match.

"We'd best be leaving." Mr. Evan reached for Prudence's cloak and helped her drape it over her shoulders.

"But—" Prudence paused. Had they both brought carriages?

"Mr. Evan's horse threw a shoe on the way here, so I offered him a ride with us," Richard said.

Mr. Evan scowled at him.

Richard offered Prudence an arm, but she turned it down with a slight shake of her head. Given the frown Mr. Evan already wore, she didn't care to give him cause to be angrier.

She and Richard walked side by side to the carriage with a surly Mr. Evan following behind them.

****

Prudence nibbled an asparagus stalk. The strain of sitting between Richard and Mr. Evan had taken a toll on her appetite. While Richard's glib chatter filled one ear, there was nothing but cold silence in the other.

"Would you like more of the suckling pig?" Mr. Evan asked. They were the first words he had spoken in half an hour.

"Oh, yes, please," Prudence said. Anything to give herself a respite from the dark cloud he carried around with him.

Prudence heaved a sigh as soon as Mr. Evan left the table. "I don't know how I'm going to make it through this."

"You mean tonight? I think you're doing rather well."

"I mean tonight, tomorrow night, the rest of my

life," Prudence said, annoyed at her friend for not recognizing the gravity of the situation.

"I rather like the man," Richard said.

Prudence turned in disbelief. "For heaven's sake, why? He's been nothing but cold and rude to you."

"If he's cold to me it's because he's in love with you." Richard popped an olive into his mouth.

"In love with me?" Prudence reached up a gloved hand to feel his forehead. "Are you feverish? Did you fall and hit your head?"

Richard swallowed the olive. "I'm quite serious, Pru. For some reason he's gotten it in his head that you and I are lovers, or at least potential lovers. If he thought we were actually lovers, I'm not sure I'd be sitting here with you tonight."

"That's nonsense, Richard." Prudence chewed another asparagus tip with slow deliberation as she thought back through the events of the past few weeks. "Still, I thought he and I might be able to develop a friendship, but since the Governor's Ball, he's been cold to me as well." She swallowed her asparagus. "Maybe it's because I kissed him."

Richard choked on his wine. "You what?"

"I kissed him," Prudence said. "Not after the ball, but before that. A couple of times, actually."

"I'm tempted to ask how his kiss compared to mine, but I don't think I could handle the shame."

Prudence glanced up at his handsome face, relieved to see the humor shining in his eyes.

"What does it matter anyway? When he agreed to the marriage, it was on the condition that we not have an intimate relationship," Prudence said.

Richard set his wine glass down with a thump. "He

agreed to that?"

"No, he didn't exactly agree to it." She considered how much of the details Richard could handle. "I promised him that he would not need to…uh…well that he need not concern himself with me."

"I see. What other promises were made?"

Prudence doubted that he really did see the full truth of what she had just shared. "Well, he made me promise to uphold my vows." She finished the explanation in her head. *And he promised me that the marriage would be consummated.*

"He expects you to obey him?" Richard rolled his eyes and drained his wine glass. "Has he got a surprise coming."

But he couldn't possibly have meant that he actually wanted to consummate the marriage, could he? It was just the duress of the moment.

"No, he didn't seem as concerned about that," Prudence said aloud, ignoring her inner voice. "He wanted me to be faithful. I didn't think that was much of a condition though, since I'm unlikely to receive an offer of a tryst."

Except she had. From him. Well not a tryst exactly, but an offer.

"And did you ask the same of him?" Richard asked.

"Oh no! I would never expect that of him." Prudence tried to ignore the confusing thoughts in her head and the even more confusing sensation in her belly. "In fact, I told him I would ensure he had an allowance large enough to cover the costs of female companionship. My only requirement was that he be discreet."

194

Richard's screwed up his face as if he were in great pain. "I'm beginning to understand why your Mr. Evan is in such a foul mood. For an intelligent woman, you can be utterly daft."

"What do you mean?" Prudence asked, but Richard's reply was cut short by Mr. Evan's reappearance, a platter of food in hand.

"Sir, I am convinced your fiancée is not altogether well. My sincerest hope is that you can cure her of her delusions." Richard stood, gave Mr. Evan a nod, then bent to brush a small kiss against Prudence's cheek. "I am off to find less dangerous company."

Mr. Evan looked like he wanted to throttle Richard, but as his hands were full, yet again, Richard escaped unscathed.

"What did you two talk about?" He set the platter on the table.

"Nothing much. Just life in general." Prudence speared a large chunk of pheasant and popped it in her mouth.

"What about life in general?" he asked.

"Noffing mouch," she said with her mouth full, then sputtered when the pheasant caught in her throat.

"If you think choking to death will get you out of answering my questions, you're wrong." Mr. Evan thumped the flat of his hand against her back.

Prudence waved off his hand and reached for her wine glass. Choking seemed preferable to being pounded to death.

A bellicose voice carried across the table. "But the tax is only fair. England has defended her colonies against the French and the Indians all these years. The Colonies should pay the tax and be grateful it is not higher."

Prudence rolled her eyes over the rim of her glass. The speaker was Mr. Wolkin, a man who seemed to think it his personal duty to uphold the status of the crown in America. Once he imbibed enough spirits, he could be counted on to share with all and sundry his feelings about the impure nature of Rhode Islanders, the rightful concessions due the king, and how Governor Hopkins failed to see either.

Around him, men of his ilk nodded, while his poor, beleaguered wife made a half-hearted attempt to get him to sit by plucking at his sleeve.

Wolkin drained his wine glass, a sure sign his diatribe had just begun.

"After all," he said, patting his ample belly, "children should be grateful to their parents. They owe their allegiance and whatever fortune befalls them to those who allowed it to happen."

Parents? Allowed it to happen?

Prudence took another fortifying sip of her wine and rose to her feet.

"My dear Mr. Wolkin, for many, this country was their only refuge from the tyranny that kept them scraping a living in the sewers of England. My own great grandfather came to this country to avoid rotting in a debtors' prison."

Mr. Evan laid a hand on her sleeve, but she ignored it. If he wanted to know what kind of woman he had agreed to marry, she would show him.

"Once here, their chances were little better. They lived in constant fear of attack from savages or starving to death when the crops failed. For those that worked hard, life in America was better. But it was through no fault of the English!"

What does she know? She's just a woman.

Prudence heard the muttering from the tables around her. She had grown accustomed to the words, or ones like them, from her days at the academy. They had long ago ceased to dampen her pride. Now, they fanned the flames of her passion.

One man she didn't recognize allowed her the dignity of a response. "English troops protected the Colonies during the war. Don't they owe England for the cost of that protection?"

"Perhaps," she said, feeling gracious toward the stranger for taking her comments seriously while the faces of those around him showed nothing but scorn. "But I think you must concede that many Colonists also fought in those wars, protecting their homeland and the honor of England. At the very least, doesn't England owe them representation in parliament so they may have a hand in determining what is just?"

Wolkin snorted, but behind him, another man nodded. It was progress.

Mr. Evan tugged again at her sleeve, but Prudence yanked her arm from his grasp. She would not stop now. Not when she had an audience, at last.

"And even if we owe some debt of gratitude to her for her protection during the war, does that mean we must stand for continued occupation?"

Prudence had heard the same thing from Grandma Rachel so many times. Tonight, the voice was her own, but she could almost sense her grandmother beside her. The final shreds of doubt fluttered away like ribbons in the wind.

Mr. Wolkin stood again. "This is what happens

when you try to educate a woman. Their brains are not designed to handle knowledge, and they lose their wits." He eyed Prudence directly. "And an understanding of their rightful place."

Many of the men around her murmured their agreement.

Prudence tightened her fists at her side. "It is you who have lost your wits, or perhaps it is your courage." A gasp from behind her made her pause, but it was too late to stop. "Certainly you have lost your willingness to see what is happening. British troops are moving east from the frontier. Are they boarding ships and sailing for home? No, they have ensconced themselves in our cities and towns. In some cases, no longer content with occupying barns and empty warehouses, they demand more comfortable lodgings in our homes."

Beside her, Mr. Evan stood and grasped her elbow in his hand. Prudence ignored him.

"It is no wonder we rebel every now and then. That we object to taxes levied without our consent. That we decide to boycott English-made goods. That we…"

"Prudence, that's enough," Mr. Evan said with enough force to break through the passions that were threatening to consume her. "I think it's time we take our leave."

"Yes, take her home where she belongs," a male voice said from the far corner of the room.

Prudence straightened her shoulders and let Mr. Evan lead her away from the table. If she couldn't at least count on her fiancé as an ally, there was no point in continuing the debate tonight. She would not forget his betrayal.

"She'll be bruised right proper before he's done

with her," Mr. Wolkin said, to the hearty guffaws of the men at the table.

Prudence dug her nails into her palms giving her fury the only outlet she had open to her.

****

"I got your message." Richard joined Evan and Prudence in the foyer. "Are you leaving already?"

A footman came and handed Prudence's cloak to Evan. She snatched it out of his hands before he could drape it about her shoulders, then she stood a good five feet away.

"Dinner went that well, did it?" Richard said with raised eyebrows.

"Someone raised the subject of taxes—" Evan said.

"Oh dear." Richard gave a knowing look in Prudence's direction. "And I take it our Miss Prudence did not do her name justice."

Evan snorted. "That would be an understatement."

Richard considered him for a moment. "Listen, I am in the midst of a game of cards with a couple of old fools with more money than brains. Why don't you take my carriage? I will find a ride with friends later."

"You trust me alone with her?" Evan asked.

"I would say she's safer with you than she is by herself, right now." Richard slid another glance in Prudence's direction. She appeared to be studying a potted plant in the corner of the foyer. "Besides, I think it's time we called a truce. My greatest wish is for Prudence to be happy, and for reasons I can't explain, I believe she might find happiness with you." Richard held out his hand.

Evan studied him for a moment, then grasped his hand. "Truce." Gripping Richard's hand, Evan pulled him closer. "But if you touch my wife—"

"Yes, yes, I know. I won't live to regret it or something along those lines." Richard grinned. "Perhaps that's why I'm putting my confidence in you. Prudence needs someone who loves her enough to protect her from whatever trouble she gets herself into."

Evan opened his mouth to protest but shut it again when a footman announced the arrival of the carriage.

"Well, I'm off to expand my fortunes." Richard waved a cheery farewell to Prudence, then ducked through the doorway leading to the card room.

As far as carriages went, Richard Bainbridge's was luxurious for a man of business. No doubt it had been financed by the Ashcrofts since he would be expected to carry important personages about town. Two passengers could sit on each side without so much as rubbing elbows. The way Prudence huddled up against the far side, a third could have fit between them.

Was she afraid of him, or just angry? No doubt, he had humiliated her in front of those arrogant bastards. But he had had no choice.

"Prudence—"

"Stay out of what you don't understand." Her words were muffled against the cushioned walls.

"What I don't understand?" A flame of anger flickered inside him.

"Yes." She turned to him, her face splotched with color. "How can you know what we have gone through? You grew up in Wales. I don't know how long you've been here—I don't know much about you at all—but you can't possibly understand the oppression we've seen."

She was right, she didn't know much about him,

but that wasn't entirely her fault. He hadn't shared much of himself, and what he had, hadn't been entirely truthful. It was time to change that.

"You don't think I understand oppression? I grew up in an orphanage where we needed protection from adults as much as from each other. I know more about abuse and oppression than you could ever dream of."

Prudence sniffed. "Were they cruel to you?"

"Let's just say that the Sisters of the Divine Mercy might have been divine, but they were not overly merciful." Someday he might tell her about his childhood. He'd have to. If they actually managed to go through with this marriage, she'd see the scars.

"Then why did you stop me?"

"Because one thing I learned in the orphanage is that you never give them a stick to beat you with. And that was something you were well on your way to doing."

Prudence stared at her hands.

"Come here," Evan said.

Prudence looked up at him with wide eyes. So she was at least a little afraid of him. He didn't care for it one bit.

He tugged at her hand. "I'm not going to hurt you. I would never hurt you."

Prudence slid across the seat to sit next to him.

Evan slid his arm about her and tucked her against his side. "I do want one more promise from you though."

Prudence stiffened beneath his arm. "What is that?"

"Once we're married I want you to trust me. You're probably the brightest woman I've ever known.

Hell, you're one of the brightest people I've ever met, but you're terribly rash."

Prudence straightened. "I'm rash? You're the one who has threatened to beat my cousin to a pulp more than once."

"He's not your cousin." Evan tucked her back against his side so she wouldn't see his grin. "But you're right. I'm not always in control either. I'm hoping that you will be a calming influence on me."

"Don't count on it," Prudence grumbled.

"Regardless, I want you to feel like you can talk to me. I am your husband, or I will be if we both make it through the next couple of days, and I want to feel like we are in this together."

Prudence sat up. "Deal," she said, offering her hand.

"In no way do I shake hands with my wife." He growled. "We seal this agreement with a kiss."

"But I'm not your wi—"

Evan claimed her lips, and Prudence melted against him.

Either the carriage driver made excessive use of the whip, or Evan lost track of time. Either way, they arrived at the Ashcroft manor far too soon. Prudence looked a little worse for wear with swollen lips and half her hairpins scattered across the floor of the carriage.

Evan helped her down the steps and handed her off to Gil who gave him a reproving look over the top of her tousled head.

Evan shifted uncomfortably in his seat as the carriage set off down the lane that lead to the stables. Two more days and he would be able to finish what they had started.

Chapter Eighteen

"It's time to go, Miss Ashcroft," Mrs. Hatcher said from Prudence's bedroom door.

Prudence said nothing, but her stomach answered with an irritated grumble.

She had been dressed since before dawn, and Netty had finished her hair well over an hour ago. That left plenty of time to dwell on her future husband and how little she really knew about him.

One question would be answered today for certain. She would finally know his Christian name. She could hardly imagine the parson marrying Prudence Amelia Saunders Ashcroft to a "Mr. Evan."

On the other hand, there were so many more important things she didn't know about him. For example, he calmed her fury after the Waites' assembly by kissing her senseless in the carriage ride home. It wasn't until about three o'clock in the morning that she awoke realizing she still didn't know whose side he was on. She could be marrying a Tory, for all she knew.

Prudence rose to wobbly feet and gave herself a once over in her full-length bedroom mirror. She should never have let Netty choose her wedding gown. The pale pink would look stunning on the dark-haired maid, but with Prudence's pale skin and auburn hair, she looked like a tarnished rose.

"It's not too late to change your mind." Mrs.

Hatcher's statement made Prudence realize she had been staring at herself in the mirror for several minutes.

"No, I'll be fine, Mrs. Hatcher." Prudence gave a weak laugh. "I just have a case of the pre-wedding nerves."

Mrs. Hatcher came and put her hand on Prudence's cheek. "I do believe that's normal, my dear."

For a moment, Mrs. Hatcher sounded just like her grandmother, and it was exactly the reassurance she needed.

"Oh!" Mrs. Hatcher exclaimed, when Prudence gave her an impulsive hug.

The ceremony was to be a small family affair witnessed only by Richard, a smattering of Rachel Ashcroft's closest friends, and a few household servants. Prudence had been surprised at how easily Parson Simmons agreed to perform the services in the Ashcroft ballroom, but the parson assured her that "God was not confined to certain buildings."

Walking slowly down the aisle, escorted by Richard—a concession from Mr. Evan that surprised her even more than Simmons' easy acquiescence—she realized just how handsome her future husband was. This time, he wore a suit of forest green velvet, embroidered with a gold trim that matched the gold buttons running down the sides of his coat and the smaller ones on his waistcoat. His coat tails were buttoned back to reveal the intricate embroidery beneath. His shoes were of a modest height and made of dark leather, their only adornment a pair of silver buckles.

He looked like a gentleman—a prosperous gentleman—instead of a simple stable master. But even his wedding finery couldn't hide the man beneath. His coat fit snugly over broad shoulders. His breeches stretched to accommodate well-muscled thighs, and silk stockings stretched over taut calves.

After what seemed an interminable walk, they reached his side. Richard gave her a peck on the cheek then dropped her arm. Prudence turned to face the parson, but out of the corner of her eye, she stole a glance at Mr. Evan.

His gray eyes regarded her with a fierce possessiveness. Her breath caught in her throat, and her bouquet of pink roses shook in her hand.

If she married this man, she would be his, forever, to do with as he pleased. The money may be hers, she would still own her thoughts, but her body would be his.

And her heart? What about that? Would he lay claim to it, too? Or would he allow it to wilt in her chest from neglect?

Prudence tightened her grip on her flowers until the wired stems dug into the palms of her hands.

The pain helped stiffen her resolve. She may not know much about her husband, but she would not start out expecting the worst from him.

"Dearly beloved..." Parson Simmons began in the ceremonial voice he used for special occasions.

Mr. Evan turned to face the parson, and she followed his lead. Although no part of her touched him, Prudence could feel his warmth enveloping her as firmly as an embrace.

She relaxed. If she married this man, she would no longer be alone in this world, no longer be the sole representative of the Ashcroft name. Not that he had agreed to become an Ashcroft. Of course, she hadn't agreed to become an Evan either. Come to think of it, they had never discussed the subject of surnames. Would he expect her to give up the Ashcroft name? The flowers in her hands trembled anew.

"Prudence?" Parson Simmons whispered.

"Pardon?" Prudence looked up to find an expectant look on his face.

Mr. Evan had turned toward her as well. They must have reached the part where she and Mr. Evan were to exchange their vows. How had that happened so soon?

Prudence took a steadying breath and turned to face her husband. She returned his grin with a scowl, although one that lacked complete conviction.

"…do you take this woman, Prudence Amelia Saunders Ashcroft…" Parson Simmons droned through the standard recitation of vows made by the groom.

By the grin he wore, Mr. Evan seemed happy to agree to each one in turn. Of course, he didn't have to promise to obey her. Why shouldn't he be happy? Then again, he also promised to be faithful, but she had already made it clear she didn't expect him to hold to that vow. Whatever arrangements he made were none of her concern, so long as he was discreet.

On the other hand, she would have to promise to be both faithful and to obey her husband. She didn't think she'd have any problem with the first vow. Lack of temptation would make compliance easy. On the other hand, the vow to obey would be a bit harder. Somehow, she was certain there would be plenty of that sort of temptation in the years ahead.

Parson Simmons turned to her next. "Prudence Amelia Saunders Ashcroft, do you take this man,

Captain Evan Foster to be your lawfully wedded husband?"

"I d—" Prudence paused as the parson's words sank in. "Wait. What?" she stammered.

This was Captain Foster?

Chapter Nineteen

Prudence stifled cynical laughter when Parson Simmons got to, "till death do ye part." That might come sooner than the estimable Captain Foster anticipated.

She pasted a smile on her lips when the parson pronounced them man and wife.

She kept the same smile plastered on her face all the way down the aisle, through the crowd of well-wishers, onto the back lawn, and between the lines of linen-covered tables that would soon hold a sumptuous wedding breakfast.

If her new husband felt her nails digging into the inside of his arm through the thick velvet he wore, he didn't comment.

She stole a glance at him. *Evan.* It would take her awhile to get used to calling him that. Even now, watching him smile and greet their guests, she thought of him as *Mister* Evan.

They reached the head table at the front of the lawn, and Evan held out a chair for her. Facing him, she dropped her smile for a fraction of a second. For now, she would show him what an Ashcroft was made of, but she wanted to let him know that they would have a discussion later about the attributes of a good marriage, honesty being chief among them.

Evan had the good graces to look sheepish, even if

he did it with that damned handsome lopsided grin of his.

As soon as the guests were seated and the wine poured, Richard stood and raised his glass. "If I may have your attention, please." He waited for the crowd to quiet. "I would like to propose a toast to the greatest partnership ever formed."

Prudence sipped her wine.

Partnership? It seemed an odd word to describe a new marriage. Of course, this wasn't a real marriage. As Evan had pointed out, she married him for *her* money. Perhaps a partnership was the best description for such an arrangement.

Her grandmother's friends seemed to appreciate the value of a good match, and there were murmurs of approval and calls of "hear hear" from all corners. They had not a romantic bone among them.

Prudence was so busy considering a fitting retribution for the man seated next to her that she didn't register the rest of Richard's toast. When he returned to his seat on her other side, he handed her a sealed letter.

"Your grandmother instructed me to give this to you after her death. She asked that I wait a few weeks, preferably until after you were safely married."

She took the pale yellow envelope from Richard. Her name was scrawled across the front in her grandmother's hand. She gave Richard a questioning glance.

"Don't look at me. I have no idea what's in it."

Her glance slid to Evan.

"Me neither." He looked just as curious as Richard.

Prudence slid a finger beneath the seal and opened the envelope.

My dearest Granddaughter,

I hope by now you have forgiven me for forcing you into marriage. I have every confidence you will choose wisely even if obligated to choose quickly. If not, I am confident Richard will choose wisely on your behalf. It is my sincerest belief that you will find someone to love who will cherish and protect you in return.

Speaking of that, I hope you like my gift. He cost me a pretty penny with that ship he demanded, but I think he'll be worth it. The winds are shifting, and I predict you will have need of the best captains and the fleetest ships. I wish I could be around to help you weather the storm.

But enough of such talk. You have Richard, and now you also have Captain Foster. He reminds me of your grandfather, strong and proud, but capable of great passion and even greater kindness. When I first met him, Captain Foster almost made me wish I were thirty years younger. But alas, if I can't have him, I hope you will take a liking to each other. Just remember to listen to your head, but don't ignore your heart's desires either.

"I'll be damned!" Evan said.

Prudence looked up to find both Evan and Richard reading over her shoulder.

Richard laughed. "You've been outmaneuvered, sir."

"I thought I was getting the deal of a lifetime with

the ship. Little did I know I was getting the old lady's granddaughter in the bargain." Evan's crooked grin suggested he wasn't too put off by the arrangement.

"The ship mentioned in the will?" Prudence tried to figure out which man irritated her more.

"Your grandmother promised him a ship built to his specifications if he agreed to work for Ashcroft."

"But not as a stable master, I take it?" She folded the letter and handed it back to Richard for safekeeping.

"No, the stable master would be my former valet, Stuart Malone."

"So that's why that insufferable man keeps hanging about the stables." Prudence remembered her brief encounters with the handsome blond man who seemed amused at her every action.

"Ah, so you've met?" Evan asked.

"Yes. We've met."

"And he didn't tell you he was the stable master?"

"No. He seemed to find it more amusing to let me believe you were the stable master." Prudence mentally added Stuart Malone to the growing list of men who had earned retribution.

"What did you think he was?" Richard asked.

Prudence shrugged. "I thought he was a gentleman who had come to see his horse."

Evan put a hand to his heart. "You thought he was a gentleman and I was the stable master. I think my pride has been wounded."

"Your pride could use a little wounding," she shot back. "And you!" Prudence leveled an accusatory finger at Richard. "You are supposed to be my dearest friend. You didn't think to tell me my future husband wasn't who I thought him to be?"

Richard held up his hands. "Now hold on. I only found out a few days ago."

"It's your fault for making assumptions about people, my dear," Evan said in a calm voice. "Besides, I don't understand what has you worked up. I work for you. That gives you the right to issues orders, at least in a business sense, which I suspect you're dying to do."

"Perhaps I'll fire you." Prudence stabbed at a roast quail from a platter before them and let it fall to her plate with a plunk. "Perhaps I'll fire both of you."

"Fine by me. I'm sure you can find some other captain willing to bring in your rum and China black while George's men are as thick as locusts in the bay."

Prudence glanced up at him.

"Yes, I know all about your family business. Your grandmother hired me to be part of it, after all. But even if you fire me, I wouldn't recommend a divorce. I'm afraid even Rhode Island society, for all its liberal attitudes, doesn't look too fondly on divorced women."

"I could have the marriage annulled. We haven't consummated our relationship, yet." Prudence cringed when Evan's eyebrow shot up on the word "yet." She hadn't meant to imply a physical relationship was inevitable.

"On what grounds?"

"Inability. Yours to be precise." There. If he thought to embarrass her, she would show him she knew how to fight back.

A dark cloud passed over Evan's features. "My inability? To consummate the marriage? I can bring in a number of women who will happily attest that I do not suffer from such a malady."

Prudence stifled a twinge of pain. What did it

matter if he had a hundred discarded paramours? She had already given him permission to do as he pleased.

"I'm sure you could." She chewed a piece of quail without tasting it.

"On the other hand, how many male doxies could you produce to attest to your...abilities?" Although speaking to Prudence, Evan glanced at Richard.

"Don't look at me. I know nothing about her ability. That, you will have to discover for yourself."

Chapter Twenty

Prudence stood alone in her room, clad in the diaphanous nightdress Mrs. Hatcher had laid out on her bed. An artful combination of linen and Dutch lace, it came with a note that merely said "good luck." The flourish at the end of the "k" left no doubt as to the author.

"Sorry, Grandma, but he may never see me in it," Prudence whispered to her reflection in the full-length mirror.

Perhaps that wasn't such a bad thing.

Prudence assessed herself in the mirror. Her facial features were passable, eyebrows and lashes a shade darker than her hair, a straight nose with only the slightest bulb at the end, and lips that had a natural tint to them, even if they were a bit thin. However, the rest of her rather ruined the picture. The flowing nightdress did nothing to accentuate what few curves she had, and the pale fabric and lace-lined scoop neck only served to highlight the freckles she had accrued from years of galloping through the meadows on Bolt's back without a parasol or neckerchief.

Prudence tugged her long, unbound hair over one shoulder and spread it so it shielded at least a portion of her pale, spotted décolletage. That was better. It hid her worst feature and brought out her best.

With a groan, she tossed her hair back over her

shoulder.

What did it matter, anyway? Thanks to her stupid agreement, she would be the only one who would ever appreciate the way her auburn hair tumbled in waves that gleamed in the candlelight.

Prudence lifted the candle from atop her dresser. She padded on bare feet to her bed and pulled back the covers. After snuffing out the wick, she slid between the cool sheets, pulled them up to her chin, and stared at the ceiling. She watched the shadows cast by the trees outside her window as they swayed in the light breeze.

Some wedding night this would be. Certainly not the night she would have imagined… if she had ever dared to imagine a wedding night at all…which she hadn't. Like a restless child, she flopped onto her side and tucked her hands beneath her pillow.

She let her eyes adjust to the darkness in the room that had once been her grandmother's. Prudence had been content with a smaller one at the end of the hall, a narrow room she found cozy and comfortable, even if it had no hearth and had to be warmed by a brazier filled with hot coals. This morning, Mrs. Hatcher moved her things into this room, insisting she was the lady of the house now adding, "What would the servants say if she remained in a bedroom more than half a house away from her husband?"

As much as Mrs. Hatcher had tried to keep Evan from her, she now seemed intent to bring them together. She had given Evan the large bedroom adjoining hers. Through the walls, Prudence could hear him walking about, readying himself for bed.

Was he thinking about their agreement? After all, it was his wedding night, too.

Moonlight caught the gilt on the scrolls of her grandmother's wardrobe. In the darkness, they loomed like a pair of baleful eyes. Prudence gave a low moan and pulled the blankets over her head as though she could shut out the accusation they held. It didn't work.

It was only natural that he should be thinking the same thoughts as she. According to the conversations she had overheard among her schoolmates, consummation was an expected part of marriage even among those unions that were little more than business arrangements. Consummation was like the signature on the contract; a child the sand that dried the ink. They made it sound as though a man would have to be completely repulsed by his wife not to wish to bed her at least once. Was she so disagreeable that he wouldn't ask her to reconsider?

Surely, he couldn't find her that repulsive. He had kissed her…three times. But perhaps a kiss didn't require as much fortitude as more intimate contact with an unappealing wife.

In the room next door, a slow, steady *tap, tap, tap* progressed from one corner to the other. Was Evan pacing? Perhaps he worried that she would expect him to fulfill his duties as a newly married husband.

She reached for the pillow next to her, intending to hug it to her chest, when her hand slid across a crisp piece of paper.

Prudence sat up and fumbled for the flint. She relit the candle and held the small slip of parchment up to it.

Dear Prudence,

I know we haven't begun on the best of terms, but I wish you to know that I hold the deepest affection for you. I will do my best to be a husband you can count on and be proud of. In time, I hope we can be friends, if nothing more.

While I would not wish to disturb your privacy, I will be in the next room should you wish to talk.

Faithfully yours,
Evan

Prudence lifted trembling fingers to her lips. He hadn't expressed any desire for her, but he did at least wish to be friends. He had invited her to visit him, in his room, to talk. It was a beginning.

****

"Come in," Evan said when a timid knock sounded on his door.

He leaned against the mantel and sipped his cognac, trying to look as though he hadn't been waiting for her, hadn't been hoping she would come to him, hadn't been imaging what he would do if she did.

The door opened, and his breath caught in his throat. The flickering glow of the fire caught the red highlights in her hair, making it shimmer. Her nightdress was chaste, but the fire's glow outlined the shape of her body beneath the creamy silk, her pert breasts, her nipped waist, and her gently flaring hips. Beneath the ruffled edge, her bare feet poked out, a childlike incongruity to the temptress that the rest of his wife presented.

His wife.

The very idea stoked the flames of passion that had been smoldering since he first saw her. Now, he had every right to scoop her up in his arms, carry her to the wide bed that dominated the room, and make love to her tonight and every night hereafter.

He had every right to do so, but he wouldn't.

He had invited her to join him in his room, to talk, nothing more. He had expressed a wish that they could be friends. He never said anything about being lovers. It was inevitable, of course. Prudence's passionate nature decreed it, but she would have to discover that for herself. Not that he didn't intend to help her along.

"I'm glad you came," he said, afraid to say more.

Her eyes flicked to his open shirt, and he realized he should have had more concern for her maidenly sensibilities. He reached for the waistcoat that lay flung across the back of a chair.

"No, no, please. This is your home. You should be comfortable." She stepped just inside the door and looked around at the room as though seeing the dark wooden paneling, the leather chairs, and the mahogany furniture for the first time. She chuckled. "Ashcroft has been without a man's touch for so long that this must be the only room that lacks a floral motif."

The comment was so banal, Evan felt himself at a loss for words. Finally, he said, "I knew it was different somehow."

"It was my grandfather's room. Mine is next door. The door I came through connects them." She sounded as if she were giving a tour.

"Did that room belong to your grandmother?" *Ach!* He sounded like he was taking one.

"It did. But she never used it." Her voice trailed off and color rose to her cheeks. "Anyway, I hope you find your room adequate to your needs."

Needs? He had found it totally inadequate, at least until she showed up.

"Yes, it's perfectly adequate. Thank you."

"Yes. Thank you, too. For the invitation that is." Despite being a vision of loveliness in her simple linen nightgown, her long hair flowing in a cascade over one shoulder, her demeanor turned business-like. "I came to apologize for my anger today. I have a weakness, you see."

"Is that so?" He wondered if she counted among her weaknesses the way her chest flushed when she was embarrassed.

She gave a self-deprecating laugh. "I like to be in control, and naturally, that means I'm not fond of surprises. When I learned that I was marrying Evan Foster, ship's captain, and not Mr. Evan, stable master, well, you can imagine my surprise."

"I should have told you," Evan said, meaning every word.

"Yes, you should have," she agreed, evidently not ready to shoulder all the blame for the rocky start to their marriage. "Why didn't you?"

Evan shrugged. "I suppose I liked that you were content to marry a stable master. I know you had your reasons, but I admired the fact that they were your reasons and not somebody else's."

"Contrary to what you might think, I wasn't marrying you because you were the stable master."

"You weren't?"

The flush that crept across her chest and up her cheeks gave him hope that her real reasons were more promising.

An oppressive silence hung in the air. He took a sip of his cognac to prevent himself from filling it.

When he just about couldn't take it anymore, she

said, "I thought you were simple."

Evan choked on his cognac. "Simple?"

"Yes. Not unintelligent exactly, but not worldly either," she said, no apology in her tone or words. Just the truth.

"That's hardly flattering."

He supposed he should find her honesty a comfort, considering how dishonest marriages in her circles could be. Instead, talking with her was like looking at a madly spinning compass, dizzying and disorienting.

"Well, don't let this go to your head, but I realize now how wrong I was. You're anything but simple."

"So what am I then?" He held his breath.

"I'm not sure." Prudence closed the door behind her, and Evan's heart bucked like a ship running headlong into a swell. "I know you're sure of yourself, but other than that, I don't really know what you are. I find myself completely befuddled whenever I am around you."

She assessed him, her dark brows knit together, as though he were a puzzle and not a man.

Evan came away from the mantel and stood before her. "I will tell you anything you want to know, but you must tell me one thing first. Why did you want to marry a simpleton?"

"I told you, I like to be in control. A simpleton was unlikely to involve himself in my affairs. In my *business* affairs," she hastily amended. "But evidently, you know all about the family business and are even part of it."

Evan put his finger under her chin and tipped her face up to look at him. "I won't try to wrestle control from you, you know. I only hope you will come to me if there is anything I can do to help."

"So you can solve my problems for me?" she said, defiance in her eyes.

He dropped her chin. "No, so we can solve them together."

Prudence's shoulders relaxed. "I'd like that."

If Prudence were any other woman, he would have kissed her senseless right then. But she wasn't. Being with her was like navigating in shallow waters. Once you knew where you were, things became easy. Until then, it was best to take it a bit slow.

"Then we can agree to forgive each other? Me for not telling you who I really am, and you for thinking I am a simpleton."

Prudence nodded, and a contemplative silence fell between them.

The business portion of their talk over, Evan decided it was time to press on matters of a more personal nature.

"Would you like to sit down? You could join me in a glass of cognac."

Prudence didn't speak, didn't move. She simply looked at him as though expecting something from him.

"Would you prefer something else? I could ring for some sherry." He thought the sweet, tawny wine that so many women enjoyed to be vile stuff, but at this moment, he would grant her any wish just to get her to stay with him awhile longer.

"Yes," she said. "I want out."

Chapter Twenty-One

The firelight caught Evan's charcoal-colored eyes until they glowed about the edges like smoldering embers.

"We've been married for less than"—he glanced at the clock on the mantel—"less than twelve hours, and you want out?"

"No, you misunderstand me." What had she meant? The words had come as much of a surprise to Prudence as to Evan.

"Then, pray tell, what do you mean?"

Prudence grappled with the tumult of emotions and half-formed thoughts, but as usual, her own impulsiveness had backed her into a corner. She had no time to sort it all out, let alone come up with a response that saved her pride. At least not one Evan was likely to believe. In such a situation, she did what came most natural to her. She told the truth.

"I want out of my promise."

She hoped he wouldn't make her spell it out. It would be humiliating beyond words.

"Let's see." Evan leaned against the mantel. His crisp shirt opened even wider, displaying an alarming amount of hard, male chest. "Putting aside our marriage vows, I can think of two promises you made. One, you promised to be faithful, and two, you promised that you would not require me to bed you. Tell me you haven't decided cousin Richard is the man for you after all."

Prudence almost choked. "Mercy, no."

"Then I take it you are asking me to make love to you?"

"Yes," she said, her face feeling as if it might catch flame.

Prudence kept her gaze trained on him, a desperate attempt not to show how much power he had over her at this moment. Not to show how much she wanted him, despite all her protestations that theirs was purely a business arrangement. If her grandmother had taught her anything, it was to not flinch during a negotiation.

She could still hear Rachel Ashcroft's instructions, given when she was all of seven and riding with her grandmother in a carriage on their way home from some meeting or another. *Silence is power, my dear. State your demands then wait for the other to respond.* While she couldn't remember the particulars of their discussion, Prudence doubted this situation was what her grandmother had in mind.

While she waited, Prudence argued with herself, rationalizing her actions against her intentions. She hadn't come to his room expecting to become his lover. She had promised him she would not hold him to that part of the marriage. She would honor his wishes if he turned her away, as he surely would at any moment. Yet the sight of him readying for bed, in a state of domestic dishabille, had her imagining what being his lover would be like. As usual, that which she imagined she had spoken aloud without so much as a thought. Perhaps not everything, but enough that she could no longer hide behind vague innuendo and hopeful imaginings.

The single word *yes*, soft and husky, played over and over in her mind until it sounded like a plea.

The fire crackled in the hearth, its golden-orange light playing over the features of Evan's face, casting shadows that made his expression hard to read. On the mantel, the clock ticked away the seconds. With each tick, what was left of her pride shriveled a little more.

She turned to go.

"No, wait." His voice was hoarse, as if the fire had sucked the air from the room and made it difficult to breath, let alone speak.

Prudence half-turned but didn't meet his gaze. "No, it's just as well. I shouldn't have asked. It wasn't fair of me to promise you one thing and then immediately go back on that promise. My only defense is that it was a request, not a demand."

Waiting for him to say something, anything, she studied the dark grains in the wood beneath her feet.

The floor creaked under the weight of Evan's step.

"Good, because although you might be able to issue orders to me as Captain Foster, here I am simply Evan, your husband."

Husband. The word, spoken almost as an endearment, drifted over her, caressed her. It wasn't the term of mastery that she had always considered it to be, but of something else. An indefinable essence that spoke of a life filled with companionship, and perhaps, of more.

Or had she only heard what she wanted to hear?

Despite his sweet words, her stubborn assumptions about marriage refused to die easily. "Oh, yes, I forgot. I am the one who is supposed to obey you."

Evan set a hand on her shoulder and turned her to

him. "I would never make you do anything you did not wish to do."

"Nor I you."

As if she could. How many times had she felt his strength against her? He had carried her into the house more than once as if she were no more than a child. He had twirled her around the dance floor, making her feel as if she were a part of him. Even now, she could feel his strength flowing into her from the palm of his hand against her small shoulder. For reasons she couldn't quite explain, she knew he would never use that strength against her. Only to protect her.

Laughter rumbled deep in his chest, a sound that flowed over her, warm and liquid, like honey and butter melted together and drizzled over toast. "As I recall our agreement, I never promised that I would stay out of your bed, nor keep you out of mine." He leaned down, his face so close his warm, cognac-scented breath brushed her cheek. "As I recall, I promised quite the opposite."

He brushed his lips over hers. It wasn't so much a kiss as a promise of one. Ribbons of pleasure rippled to the tips of Prudence's bare toes.

"Now what was it you wanted me to do?" he asked, his voice as soft and sensual as his lips had been.

"I wanted you to..."

He nibbled the line of her jaw. The ribbons tightened, drawing her closer to him.

"Sorry, come again. I didn't catch that." His words brushed against the sensitive shell of her ear.

He was going to make her ask again. She didn't mind. Unless he was an exceptionally cruel man, and she didn't think he was, he would fulfill her request.

Her entire body thrummed with anticipation.

"I want you to make love to me."

"It would be my pleasure, Wife," Evan said before his lips claimed her in a bruising kiss that left her trembling in his arms.

So unlike kissing Richard.

Prudence nearly giggled at the inappropriate thought, but she couldn't help comparing the two men. Richard's lips had been soft, tentative, and closed. Evan's lips were hard, his mouth open. Where Richard's kiss asked for permission, Evan's kiss demanded she give herself over to him.

And Prudence wanted to. Oh, how she wanted to.

She kissed him back as hungrily as he kissed her. When he flicked the tip of her tongue with his, she instinctively opened her mouth further, inviting him in. He retreated, and she made a low desperate moan in the back of her throat.

"Patience, my sweet." Evan set his forehead against hers, the heat of his breath caressing her face. "We have all night. There is no need to rush things."

She pulled back to look into his eyes. "Patience was never one of my virtues."

A wicked grin crossed Evan's face. He pulled back, and for one devastating moment, Prudence thought he might send her away. Her stomach flipped when he scooped her into his arms.

"*Oof*," he said, giving her that lopsided grin she had come to love so much. "Just as solid as ever, I see."

Prudence threw her arms around his neck and hid her smile in his chest as he carried her to his bed.

Evan laid her down on the coverlet, and she shivered when he pulled away. He glanced toward the fire. The flames had died down till only burning embers remained.

"You're cold," he said.

"No, I'm fine." She wanted him lying next to her, warming her body with the heat from his own, not off in the far corner of the room stoking the fire.

"No, I wouldn't want you to take ill, or me either for that matter. It would be a poor start to a marriage, and I don't think we should press our luck."

He strode to the hearth. Squatting on his haunches, he added several logs to the remains of the dying fire. He jabbed at the embers with the poker, while Prudence willed them to light. Flames roared in the hearth before Evan seemed satisfied.

"There, that's better." He glanced at Prudence. "Sure I can't get you a glass of brandy?"

"No." Prudence propped herself up on her elbows and shook her head.

"Madeira?" A teasing light shone in his eyes, and a smile tugged at the corner of his lips.

"No," she said, with more emphasis.

"Would you like anything?"

"Yes. You." Spoken as though she were lord of the manor instead of him, it was too late to soften the request.

Evan came to stand beside the bed. Instead of looking irritated at her demands, his face showed a certain manly pride, as though she could demand all she liked, he knew who remained in control of the situation.

"Patience, my wife."

"I am trying." Prudence reached a hand up to him, and he clasped it, entwining her fingers in his. "But it seems I am a slow learner."

Setting one knee on the side of the bed, he leaned over and brushed a kiss against her lips. "Don't worry. I am an excellent teacher, and I'll stick with you for however long it takes."

She quivered beneath his touch. If one small brush of his lips caused such a reaction, how would she survive their lovemaking?

"I want to see you."

She had done it again. Said the first thing that popped into her head. Would he think her too forward? Too demanding? It was in her nature to be straightforward, but perhaps there were times when she could at least try to be more demure.

"I'm right here."

His grin told her he was being deliberately obtuse. At least he didn't sound offended. Or repulsed.

"All of you," she said, emboldened by his apparent acceptance of her forwardness.

How accommodating would he be if she gave in to her sudden urge to explore the sharp angles of his face, the dark curls at the nape of his neck, or the hard planes of his chest? Even the firm roundness of his backside that had heretofore been hidden beneath his coats made her palms tingle with anticipation.

"Ah, well, I aim to please." He stood and pulled his shirt from the waistband of his breeches then drew it over his head.

Prudence held her breath. At the academy, she had become something of an expert in the male anatomy, at least from the waist up. Her schoolmates had taken every opportunity to offend her by removing their coats and shirts in her presence. But they had been boys. She could see that now. Her husband was a man.

His tanned skin glowed in the firelight, shadows licked around the hard angles and curves of his chest. A smattering of dark curls crossed the geometric planes, then thinned to a narrow line that ran into the waistband of his breeches.

He lacked the paunch of the country gentleman, that doughy roll, acquired from a life of indolence and indulgence. They tried in vain to hide it behind waistcoats and too-high breeches, but like dough punched down in its bowl, it rose again, flowing over the sides in ever-growing proportions.

Evan, in contrast, had the body of a working man. Lean and hard. She reached up to touch him, running her fingertips down the washboard pattern of muscle, almost relieved to find warmth instead of cold, hard granite.

Evan closed his eyes and lifted his chin as though focusing on her exploration. Then, without warning, his lids flew open, and he stepped deftly out of her reach.

She curled her hand and let it fall back to the bed.

"Patience, my love." He grinned, a look of satisfaction, like a cat with a bowl of warm cream.

My love. Prudence's heart sang, her disappointment forgotten. It might only be an expression, one said in the heat of the moment. But in the privacy of his bedroom, with the ephemeral shadows created by the soft glow of the firelight, it was easy to believe in love. For tonight, she would.

Keeping his gaze on her face, Evan undid the buttons of his breeches, taking more care with them then Prudence thought they were worth. She cursed the buttons that held the fall front, then more down the middle, as well as the laces that held them tight below the knees. She had always thought a lady's gown to be ridiculous in its intricacies, but a man's breeches weren't much better.

Freed from the restraints, Evan shimmied out of his breeches and small clothes. She recalled a sketch of Michelangelo's David one of her classmates had shown her, intending to shock her with the image. Prudence had been secretly fascinated with the beautiful Greek figure, male, yet elegant and almost feminine in the way the artist captured the smooth flowing lines of the young man's legs. And as for his more private anatomy, well, clearly the subject the artist had in mind had been no more than a boy.

Evan reminded her more of DaVinci's anatomy drawings, skin stretched taut over muscles that stood out in stark relief.

A muscle just above his right kneecap quivered, reminding her that this was no artist's rendering she so openly admired, but a flesh and blood man. Her husband. Hers, as the parson had said during the wedding ceremony, to obey, serve, love, honor, etcetera, etcetera. Prudence had trouble recalling the exact words of the promise, but one thing she did remember clearly. While her pledge started with a vow to obey her husband, his started with the pledge to love her. If she could hold up her end of the bargain, could he hold up his?

Prudence reached out again, intending to pull him closer.

Evan stepped back. "It's not fair that I stand here shivering while you're still fully dressed. I think I'll just warm myself by the fire for a while."

"I'm hardly fully dressed, but if you insist."

Surprising herself with her boldness, Prudence yanked her nightdress over her head and tossed it into the corner. Despite the warmth in the room, her nipples puckered from the sudden rush of air, and from anticipation as well. "Now, we're on equal terms."

"As it should be." Evan stood by the side of the bed, his height forcing her to lean back so she could look up at him. "As it always will be."

He smiled at her, his slightly crooked tooth winking in the light of the fire. Through a fog of wanting, it occurred to her that beauty truly was in the eye of the beholder. Somewhere between their first meeting in the stables and this moment, she had grown to love his crooked smile. It gave him a warmth, a vulnerability he might have lacked otherwise. The ordinary nature of the thought, the sheer absurdity of having it while he was towering over her, both of them naked, made her want to laugh out loud.

"Something in my countenance amuses you?" he asked, his grin growing wider.

"Not at all." Prudence barely managed to choke back the laughter in her words. "I was just remembering how arrogant I found you when we first met."

He slid down beside her, one foot still resting on the floor, the other tucked beneath him. "And have you changed your mind?"

Although he had lowered himself to her level, his face still held nothing but male self-possession and pride.

"Not one bit," she said.

"Good." He leaned over to claim her mouth with his.

She let him explore but gave equal measure with

lips, teeth, and tongue. Though they were just inches from each other, with no clothing to separate them, naught but their mouths touched. Prudence could feel the heat from him radiating against her breasts, and she longed to close the distance.

As though he could read her thoughts, Evan raised one hand to cradle her cheek in his palm. He slid the other hand between her shoulder blades to support her as he used the pressure from his kiss to lower her onto her back.

His knee wedged between her thighs, he still kept his distance. Prudence placed her hands against his chest, ran them over his broad shoulders and around his back. She tugged at him, intending to pull him down on top of her.

Evan didn't budge. His lips still occupied with hers, he didn't laugh so much as rumble.

Prudence tilted her chin, pulling her mouth from his so she could suggest that perhaps this wasn't the best time for a lesson in patience. Her words died when Evan's lips ran a path from her cheek, across her jawbone to a spot just below her ear. Whatever she had intended to say melted into in a languid sigh.

Since he was being so uncooperative, Prudence let her hands do a little exploring of their own. She marveled at his shoulders. Round and firm, she couldn't even fit one of them into the palm of her hand. From there, her hands traveled down the hard ridges of his back. Every now and then, her fingertips ran into tiny little lines that felt almost like the seams of a dress. Were they scars? From the number of them, she gathered his tales about the sisters hadn't been exaggerated.

Anger surged within her. No matter what sort of little devil he had been, no child warranted such abuse.

Evan mumbled something unintelligible against her neck, and Prudence sensed that her intrusion into his past wasn't something he welcomed. Someday he would trust her with the details. Someday she would show him he could.

She ran her hands around the curve of muscles at his sides to trail them back up his chest. Her palms brushed against his nipples. She stopped to thumb them, wonder filling her at the way they tightened at her slightest touch. She knew men had them. She had seen them on the boys at school. She just never knew they were as sensitive as her own.

"Turn about is fair play," Evan said, his breath warming her neck.

She had only a moment to consider what he meant before his mouth covered the tip of one of her breasts.

Prudence gasped and arched her back. She had been wrong. There was no way Evan's nipples were as sensitive as hers. His mouth on her breasts had her writhing beneath him, her will lost to his touch.

"Evan," she breathed. His name was a plea, although she didn't quite know for what.

"Do you like that?"

It wasn't really a question. She could tell he already knew the answer from the self-satisfied arrogance in his voice. Infernal man knew exactly how to touch her to make her lose what little control she possessed.

"Yes," she gasped.

Evan suckled harder.

"Evan," Prudence said again. She had thought it

would take forever to get used to using his Christian name. It was another thing she had been wrong about. She loved his name. She could have said it over and over again. *Evan. Evan. Evan.*

"Yes, my sweet?" Evan said.

"Evan." She savored the sound on her tongue as she spoke his name aloud. She needed to be closer, to hold his body against hers. But how could she say the words when she could barely think?

Evan leaned his body into hers, giving her exactly what she craved even though she hadn't asked.

"Am I crushing you?" he asked.

"No." Her answer sounded a little strained, but she hoped he hadn't noticed. His weight against her felt so strong, so solid, so comforting.

He nudged his other knee between her thighs widening them until he could settle himself between them. She could feel his arousal against her, hot and hard. She had seen him naked and aroused, yet she didn't feel afraid. She wanted to feel him inside her. She needed him inside her.

"Evan, please."

"Not yet, sweetheart." He breathed against her neck. "This is your first time. You need to be ready."

"I am ready." Her voice held a note of impatience.

"Trust me, my love. I don't think you want to rush this."

She did trust him. More than she had ever trusted anybody. More than she thought she ever would.

While his mouth claimed her lips in a kiss that left her breathless, he reached down between her legs to touch her in places so intimate she could barely name them.

Though inexperienced, she wasn't completely naïve to the workings of her own body. Riding astride had taught her much about the small nub of flesh that could bring both pleasure and pain when it came into contact with friction from her clothing. But she never dreamed it could be the source of such heated sensation in the hands of her husband.

Evan dipped his thumb into the dampness between her folds and brought it back to the source of that pleasure, stroking Prudence until she arched her back against the bed and gave a cry that sounded suspiciously like a sob.

The stroking stopped and just when she thought she might be able to breathe again, Evan parted her folds with his fingers and inserted one into the dampness. He stroked her, applying a pressure that left her dizzy with need.

It was like jumping off a cliff.

The thought came to Prudence through the fog of her desire. When she was about eight, a neighbor boy had dared her to jump off one of the cliffs. Prudence could barely remember which one—which boy or which cliff. She did remember that it had seemed impossibly high, even though it was probably one of the shorter cliffs between the bays where the rocks were fewer and the water deeper.

Eager to prove herself, she had stripped down to her chemise, took a running start toward the edge, closed her eyes, and jumped. She remembered having the oddest feeling of not being certain whether she were falling or flying.

She felt much the same way now.

Evan withdrew and settled himself between her

thighs. She opened her legs wider, in clear invitation. He entered her slowly, tentatively at first.

Prudence wanted more. Instinct drove her hands to his hips. Her nails dug into his buttocks as she pulled him forward and arched her hips up until he had buried himself deep within her.

Evan didn't move. He seemed to be waiting for something.

"Are you in pain?" he asked.

Somewhere in the deep recesses of her mind she could remember hearing something about the first time being painful and that a woman would bleed. Although she could feel Evan stretching her, it didn't seem particularly painful. More of a gratifying fullness. It would probably be even more pleasing if he would just move.

"I'm fine," she said, touched by his concern, but not sure how to let him know what she wanted from him.

Slowly, Evan withdrew and thrust forward again. Prudence could feel his control in the taut muscles of his back. He was holding back. She wanted to fly again, and he was restraining her.

Prudence ground her hips up to meet his when he thrust forward. For heaven's sake! What did she have to do to get the man to lose control?

Evan thrust again, and again, faster now, and Prudence forgot her frustration. Instinctively, she moved in time to his rhythm, not knowing which one of them set the pace.

She ran her hands up and down the sides of his back, grasping, urging him on. His muscles rippled beneath his sweat slick skin. He no longer held back but seemed to be driving forward, straining for something just out of reach.

Then she felt it. It started with a slight tingling as sweat broke out on her own brow, then the heat spread, across her cheeks, down her neck, and through her belly to where she and Evan were joined.

Prudence writhed with her own sense of urgency, but she lost control of her movements. Her thrusts turned jerky and out of time with Evan's. With a growl, Evan grabbed her hips and steadied her as he brought her rhythm to his. For once, Prudence was glad to let him take the lead.

She retained just enough presence of mind to feel him swell inside her moments before he gave one last powerful thrust and spilled his seed. She held onto him, letting the sensation of falling, or floating, or soaring slowly fade.

Chapter Twenty-Two

Prudence awoke to the brush of something warm and soft against her forehead.

"I hate to start out our new arrangement this way, but I must abandon you for a while."

It was a man's voice.

She sat up, eyelids fluttering, and glanced about at unfamiliar surroundings. It wasn't her bedroom. Nor her bed. She blinked. A man sat on the edge of it.

A wash of cool air and a flood of memories made her clasp a blanket to her naked breast.

She was a married woman now. A *really* married woman. They had sealed their bargain, just as Evan promised they would. The room swayed.

"How long will you be gone?"

The mundane reality of the question helped slow the room's motion.

"A day or two." Evan rose and buttoned his waistcoat. "I'm headed for Boston. If the weather stays fair, I'll sail this afternoon, have the ship unloaded tonight, and be back in your arms tomorrow."

Tomorrow? He must think her a simpleton. Even the sailing to Boston harbor would take at least a day to round the cape. The unloading of the cargo, perhaps another day. Then there was the trip back. Three days at least.

"What is the cargo?" She tried not to let her

238

suspicion show.

"Just household goods." He studied his neck cloth in the mirror. In the reflection, his gaze lighted on her then darted away like a startled sparrow.

"Will you be taking your new ship?"

He wasn't telling her something. Not that she had known him for long, but he had never refused to meet her gaze.

"The *Cythraul*?" He shook out his coat. "No. It will be some time before she's ready for her maiden voyage. In the meantime, I'll use one of the Ashcroft vessels."

He sounded so matter-of-fact, so business-like. How could he be like that after they had spent the night together? After they had been so intimate?

"But why you? The day after our wedding?"

She really ought to try to sound like she didn't care, but there was one problem. She did. More than she would have guessed. Certainly more than she cared to admit.

Evan shrugged. "We all do what we must."

Prudence picked at the velvet *fleur de lis* pattern on the coverlet while she tried to sort through it all. Ashcroft had plenty of captains. It made no sense that Evan should be the one to go if the cargo were nothing more than a run of household goods.

Besides, last night had changed things. Hadn't it?

Drifting off to sleep, wrapped in his arms, she assumed they would spend the day together, getting to know each other. Perhaps they might even repeat the pleasures of the night before.

She pulled at a loose thread then tried to tuck it back in when the design started unraveling. Unless, of course, he didn't mean to continue their physical relationship now that the marriage had been consummated.

Her hand stilled. Maybe he had a lover waiting for him in Boston.

"Will you miss me?"

His question brought her back to the present. She searched his dark eyes, looking for the truth they revealed.

Were they the eyes of a man looking at his lover or those of one returning to another? She tried not to see only what she wanted to see. Last night, she had almost managed to convince herself that he loved her, or at least that he might someday. In the harsh light of morning, the fantasy seemed utterly childish. The time had come to put her childish ways behind her.

"Of course not." Prudence tucked her trembling hands beneath the blankets.

She would not let him see how much his leaving hurt her. She had her pride, and perhaps he had no choice. Maybe he really did have cargo to deliver to Boston. For that matter, if he did have a mistress in Boston, why should she care?

"I've lived without you for nineteen years. What's one more day?"

"That's the spirit." Evan turned back to the mirror and straightened his already straight neck cloth.

"I could go with you." The suggestion spilled from Prudence's lips as soon it entered her thoughts. So much for her stoic attitude.

"An excellent suggestion…for another time. I'll be evaluating a potential crew on this voyage. With you aboard, I might not notice I have a crew." Evan strode to the side of the bed and kissed her brow, the sweetness of his words and his lips toppling what was left of the wall she had built around her tangled emotions. "Don't worry, sweetheart. I'll be back soon."

Swinging his coat over his shoulder, he departed through the door, leaving Prudence cold, naked, and alone.

Listening to the clop of hooves fading into the distance, Prudence rose from the bed. Suddenly, every muscle in her body felt stiff, even some she didn't think she had ever used before. She left her nightdress where it lay, a puddle of lace and linen in the middle of the floor, and padded over to the mirror.

Aside from a slight abrasion on her chest—she had a vague memory of Evan's whiskers scratching her— she didn't look any different. Were the green eyes looking back at her those of a married woman? One who had experienced the joys of the marriage bed? And it had been a joy, more than she had ever anticipated. Even though she had practically begged Evan to make love to her, she hadn't expected her world to fall out from under her.

Prudence turned away from the mirror and snatched her nightdress from the floor. Pulling it over her head, her gaze fell on the rumpled bed sheets. They certainly had made a mess of things. The coverlet lay half off the bed, the top sheet rested in a pile by the headboard, and the bottom sheet had come untucked from one corner and was peeling back to reveal the tufted mattress cover.

A knock sounded at the door.

"Yes?" Prudence called.

"Captain Foster requested that I bring you some fresh water, ma'am," Netty said through the closed door.

Prudence eyed the bed. She could hardly ask Netty to wait while she made it up.

"Come in, Netty," Prudence said, in a resigned voice.

Netty entered, gave Prudence a quick curtsy, then carried a washbasin, pitcher, and fresh towels to the dresser. She didn't seem to notice the bed.

The maid picked up the old basin and the used towel next to it, then turned to her mistress. "Shall I bring you some tea or coffee, ma'am?"

Had her gaze just flicked over her shoulder to the bed? Prudence couldn't be sure.

"No, thank you, Netty. That will be all I need for now."

"Yes, ma'am." Netty curtsied, bowing her head so Prudence couldn't read her expression.

Once Netty had gone, Prudence decided she was just being foolish. What did it matter what her maid thought? She and Evan were married. What they did together was their business, no one else's.

Prudence bent forward to straighten the bed the best she could, then decided it would be better to just remove the sheets and have them sent to the laundry. Evan would appreciate having fresh sheets when he returned. Maybe he would find her in them waiting for him. If he had a lover in Boston, she could make him forget about her. The notion put a spark in Prudence's step and her mood.

She had folded the coverlet and the blanket and was about to tug the bottom sheet from the mattress when a sudden realization made her knees buckle.

There was no blood.

She had been a virgin. Virgins were supposed to bleed, weren't they? Everybody knew that. Even she knew that.

Prudence shook out the top sheet. She and Evan really had made a mess of the covers. Maybe she had been on the top sheet and the blood hadn't had a chance to soak through to the bottom. She searched every inch for even a spot, then did the same to the blankets, the coverlet, and finally the bottom sheet.

Nothing.

Prudence went to the dresser and poured water over the wash rag in the basin. Lifting the hem of her nightgown above her thighs, she propped a foot on a stool and gently washed herself, taking care as she discovered she really was more tender than she realized.

She inspected the knobby cotton fabric. There were small, bright red dots. So she had bled, but just the tiniest amount, and certainly not enough to be noticed by Evan. She didn't think virgins were supposed to bleed profusely, but from the stories she had heard, the blood should at least be visible on the sheets.

Had Evan noticed? Her knees grew weak again, and she sank against the dresser. He must have. Maybe that was why he had been so distant.

She put a hand to her forehead and tried to think. Evan had made it clear that he thought Richard and she were lovers, or at least had the potential to be lovers. Had last night convinced him they had been?

Maybe he hadn't gone to Boston at all. Maybe he had gone to kill Richard.

****

"Would you like some breakfast, ma'am?" the

cook asked when Prudence wandered into the kitchen.

Prudence glanced up. "What? Oh, I'm sorry, Mary." Prudence peeked at the lantern clock hung against the wall. Well past ten. Mary would already be planning the midday meal. "Just some jam and bread will suit me this morning."

Prudence took a seat at the rough kitchen table normally reserved for servants and only glanced up when Mary set a plate of warm bread, a crock of jam, and a pot of tea before her.

She stared at the steam swirling from the spout of the silver teapot as though she could divine a proper course of action in the hazy tendrils.

Should she try to warn Richard? It probably wouldn't do any good. Evan knew where the offices of Ashcroft & Sons were, and he had at least an hour's head start. That was enough time for him to reach the office, and if Richard weren't in, to obtain the address of his townhouse from Richard's secretary and be well on his way.

Even if she did know exactly where he was, there simply wasn't enough time to catch him. Besides, how could she explain circumstances when she barely understood them herself? She had to leave it up to Richard to convince Evan that she and Richard had never been lovers and never would be.

Her stomach tightened. If Evan refused to listen, could her poor, sweet Richard defend himself?

"I was just making a bean soup for luncheon, and I happen to have a little too much ham." Mary set a plate with a couple of succulent looking slices before Prudence. "I thought perhaps you might like some with your breakfast."

"What? Oh, yes, thank you, Mary," Prudence said, seeing the plate of ham on the table and the expectant look in Mary's eye.

Prudence cut into a slice of ham and pushed the piece around on her plate.

Mrs. Hatcher bustled into the kitchen. "Ah, there you are, dear. I've been searching high and low for you."

"Good morning, Mrs. Hatcher."

Why had she been so forward last night? Had she seemed more uncertain it might have made it easier to convince Evan. But, no, she had to practically demand that he make love to her.

"Will the captain be returning before supper?" Mrs. Hatcher asked.

He said he would return tomorrow. But if he were detained or decided he preferred his mistress to his wife, he could be away longer, much longer. That is, assuming, he had even gone to Boston and not to confront Richard.

Prudence glanced up. Mrs. Hatcher seemed to be waiting for a response of some sort.

"Oh, I think just dust the wainscot and refill the lamps."

Mrs. Hatcher gave Prudence a quizzical look, then understanding dawned across her wrinkled face. "I take it the master of the house won't be back for supper."

Heat rose to Prudence's cheeks when she replayed the conversation she had just had with her housekeeper. From the knowing grin Mrs. Hatcher was doing her best to hide, the old woman had a clear idea of who had her mistress's mind in such a fuddle. She doubted, however, that the woman had any idea the true direction her thoughts had taken.

Prudence pondered talking over her dilemma with Mrs. Hatcher. Although she had never known a Mr. Hatcher, there must have been one at one time. Somehow, she just couldn't find the words to approach the subject.

Gil stepped into the room. "Mr. Bainbridge is here to see you, ma'am."

"Richard is here?" Prudence jumped up from the table and knocked over her teacup. "How glad I am to hear of it!"

The furrows in Gil's brow deepened, but Mrs. Hatcher shook her head at him and set the teacup to rights. A knowing smile flitted across Gil's features before he resumed the passionless butler's expression he wore so well.

****

Prudence threw open the parlor door with such force that it bounced against the opposite wall.

"You're not dead!"

"It's good to see you too, Pru." Richard strode to her, grasped her hands in his, and placed a light kiss on her cheek. "I had a late night last night, drinking to the health of the bride and groom, but I didn't think I looked that poorly."

Her anxiety much relieved by his sudden appearance, Prudence couldn't help but smile at her friend's self-effacing humor. "Of course you don't, Richard. You are as handsome as ever."

"Pru, give it to me straight. Something has you in a dither, doesn't it?"

"Richard, how is that you can you read me so easily?"

"It's because I care about you, sweetheart." He gave her an impish grin. "Plus, I know that whenever you try your feminine wiles on me, you're hiding something."

Prudence considered sharing her concerns with him, but had no idea where to begin. Surely Richard had some experience with women, and he was a man, but in all their years as friends, they had never had a truly *intimate* conversation. How could she possibly ask him why she hadn't bled despite being a virgin? And how could she warn him that her husband might now be searching for him in order to kill him?

Richard narrowed his eyes. "What is it? Evan didn't do something to hurt you, did he? I don't care if he is bigger and meaner than me, I'll kill him."

Prudence shook her head. "No, it's nothing like that. I just woke to a disconcerting dream. That's all."

"Then I hope you're not prescient," Richard said, his usual jovial tone back.

"Me, too," Prudence said in a far more serious voice.

"Come on, Pru, you should be happy today." Richard held her hands out to her side and gave her a thorough once over with laughing eyes. "Although, I must say, you don't look any different."

Prudence's ears flamed, and she tore her hands from his grip. "You mind your manners, Richard Anthony Bainbridge. I am a married woman, and my husband might have a thing or two to say if he knew you were being forward with me." She gave her friend a rueful smile. "Or at least he might if he were here."

"He abandoned you on your first day as a married couple?" Richard whistled through his teeth. "He is a brave man."

"Either that or very foolish."

"When do you expect him back?" Richard asked.

"Evan said he had to run some cargo up to Massachusetts, and he would be back tomorrow."

"He chose today to make the Boston run? He certainly doesn't let barnacles grow on his bow."

Richard's knowledge of the trip to Boston took Prudence aback for a moment.

"So you know about this run?"

It made sense. Richard knew about all the cargo runs, large or small, from Massachusetts to Morocco. In her concern over other, more personal matters, it hadn't occurred to her to question him about the run.

"I suggested he might want to take the shipment himself." Richard glanced at Prudence's expression. "But I swear I didn't mean today."

"What is the cargo?"

"Just household goods." Richard set one hip on the side of the desk and turned his attention to a stack of ledgers.

He thumbed through them as though looking for one in particular.

Prudence set her hands on her hips. "My husband left me in our marriage bed to take a load of pots and pans to Boston?"

"Well, I might not have put it that way, but yes." Richard opened the ledger and flipped a few pages. "It's a shame, really. If he were going to leave your side tonight, I would have thought he'd want to put his new ship through her paces. It's a perfect night for it."

"His ship is ready?" Prudence asked. "Does he know that?"

"He must. He's been hanging out at the factory for days, overseeing every little detail. I think the workers finished it two weeks early just so they could rid themselves of him."

"I could have sworn he said the *Cythraul* wasn't complete yet," Prudence said, more to herself than to Richard.

"Maybe it wasn't ready when he told you that. She was supposed to be launched just this morning."

"Maybe." And maybe Bolt would sprout wings. Just this morning Evan said he would have to take one of the other Ashcroft vessels. She was sure of it. So why would he lie to her?

"What else is bothering you, Pru?"

"Richard, have you ever been with a woman?"

She hadn't planned to ask the question, but Richard had been her confidant since childhood. Somehow the words just slipped out.

However, Richard's expression reminded her of a rabbit that had run across her path in the garden last summer. From the panic in its round eyes, she knew it wanted to run, but fear rooted its feet to the ground. As soon as Prudence moved on without so much as a glance, the rabbit darted into the bushes.

She took pity on Richard in much the same way. "Oh, never mind. Of course you have. You need not answer that question."

Richard relaxed against the desk. "I'm relieved to hear that, but do I want to know why you asked the question in the first place?"

"Probably not," Prudence admitted. "I'm just wondering if perhaps...if maybe his going to Boston had something to do with me."

From the way Richard tensed up again, she was glad she hadn't phrased that last as a question.

"Now why would you think that? Did last night not go as planned?" Richard looked as if he really didn't want to hear the answer.

It was sweet of him to care enough to allow her to talk if she needed to, but Prudence decided not to burden him with the intimate details. She would find her answers some other way.

"As you know, he thinks you and I were lovers. Somehow you have to help me convince him we weren't." Prudence left her explanation purposefully vague.

"Pru, give him time. Give yourself time. And get rid of the ridiculous notions you have about what your marriage is and isn't supposed to be. One night with you in his arms, and he'll know that you and I were no more than friends and never will be."

"Maybe," Prudence said, not at all convinced.

One night with her had probably convinced Evan she had been *somebody's* lover, if not Richard's. On top of that, he didn't trust her enough to be honest about where he was going this morning. If he wasn't headed to a lover in Boston, where had he gone?

Chapter Twenty-Three

As the clop of hooves from Richard's horse faded into the distance, Prudence took a seat in a winged chair angled in front of the window. She picked up some embroidery from the side table. She had started the pattern months ago but lost interest soon after finishing the first green leaf in the morning glory design. At least it would keep her hands busy.

She threaded the needle with lemon-yellow silk and focused on the flower, determined to finish at least one. If she could do nothing but wait, she might as well accomplish something with the time other than simply fretting.

"A Mr. Manley to see you, ma'am." Gil stood at the doorway.

Prudence's needle slipped, and she poked her finger, dotting the center of the flower with crimson.

What could he want?

"Tell him I'm not at home, Gil."

Simon may be an absolute boor, but surely he understood it would be poor form to pay a visit to a newly married woman the day after the wedding. Did he hope to goad Evan into some sort of confrontation? She could not imagine what sort of confrontation would favor Simon.

"He told me to tell you this is not a social call. He is here on business." Gil held out a silver platter containing a small, white rectangle.

Prudence picked it up, and her heart sank when she read the script on the front.

Simon Manley, Rhode Island Customs Officer.

If ever she needed Evan, it was now.

"Show him to the study. I will be with him in a moment."

"Yes, ma'am." Gil shut the parlor door, his face revealing nothing of what he thought of a visit from a customs officer.

Prudence surveyed her appearance in the mirror over the fireplace. Her sunken eyes and wan face suggested she hadn't had much sleep. She hadn't, of course, but it mortified her to think Simon might spend his time imagining what she had been up to. Or even worse, read the distress in her eyes.

With a trembling hand, she pinched some color into her cheeks and tucked a few stray curls into her chignon. She still looked tired, but at least she no longer looked like she had just crawled from her bed.

Prudence entered the study to find Simon leaning against the desk much as Richard had, an open ledger in his hand. Unlike Richard, Simon's legs barely reached the floor. The toe of one cardinal-red shoe rested lightly against the carpet while his other foot swung back and forth, his heel clicking against the wooden desk like a metronome.

If he scratched the mahogany, she would send the repair bill to his office this very afternoon.

"Mr. Manley, how nice of you to visit us this morning."

Prudence congratulated herself on sounding gracious even though she longed to lecture her odious classmate on the propriety of a visit the day after her wedding and the ill-mannered behavior of rummaging through one's belongings uninvited.

Simon looked up at her with thin eyes. He shut the ledger but did not return it to the stack.

Prudence gritted her teeth. Not that there was anything in the ledger to incriminate Ashcroft. An ingenious bookkeeping system developed by her grandfather kept all but those who were part of the Ashcroft inner circle in the dark. A customs officer might look at the ledger until the end of time; he would not find a single record that implicated her family or their business associates in any wrongdoing. Of course, that wouldn't stop the new breed of customs officials from making insinuations until they got what they wanted. Many of them lived in a far grander style than their meager salary or circumstances accounted for.

Simon Manley would not get a penny from her.

"Unfortunately, mine is not a social call, Mrs. Foster." He cocked his head as though he expected her to correct his use of her husband's name.

"Is that so?" Her voice lost some of its controlled civility.

"Is Captain Foster at home?"

"He is not." She folded her hands at her waist.

It wasn't fear that had them trembling, but anger. That surprised her. For years she had lived in fear of the taunts and bullying of her classmates. Somehow having Evan on her side had given her courage even in his absence.

"Ah." Simon tugged at his mustache, a pitiful thing that bore a striking resemblance to the one worn by Mrs. Fitzgerald, the manor's head laundress. "Is he away on business?"

"I know not, Mr. Manley. We are newly married, and I'm not yet familiar with my husband's routines."

"He left without telling you where he was going?" Simon gave her a look of disbelief through heavily lidded eyes. "When do you expect him to return?"

"I'm not certain." She would be damned if she would tell him anything, even if she did know.

"Well, I suppose you will have to do." He came off the desk with a little hop. "As you may have heard, I have been appointed the new head of customs by the governor."

He eyed Prudence as though he expected some sort of response to the news. She said nothing.

"I wanted to speak with Captain Foster to see what he knew of smuggling in the area." His pink tongue shot out and swept across his thin lips. "As former head of Ashcroft & Sons, perhaps you've heard of it?"

Former head of Ashcroft? Prudence stiffened, then reminded herself that this was Simon Manley she dealt with. She would not take the bait he so obviously dangled in front of her.

"I have heard rumors, but I know no details." There, she had managed to capture a polite, almost conversational tone again.

"Yes," Simon said, drawing out the word into a hiss. "I assumed as much. After all, a family as loyal as the Ashcrofts would never make a move against the crown, would they?" His eyebrow ticked up.

Her grandmother had always cautioned her that when in doubt don't do or say anything that would reveal your position. This seemed a good time to heed her advice. Prudence stood silently and waited to see what he would do next.

Simon scanned the books on the shelves that lined the study. "You know, Mrs. Foster, I like to read. Of course, you probably know that since we went to school together some years ago. Still, there is one thing you may not know about me." He walked along the shelves. He appeared to be scanning the titles along the spines even though he kept speaking. "Of all the books I have in my library, do you know which one I love to read the most? The almanac. Can you believe that? I've had the finest education money can buy, and I still enjoy reading the almanac. Do you read the almanac, Mrs. Foster?" He gave her an expectant look.

Prudence shook her head, wondering if Simon's mind might have slipped a little since she had seen him last.

"No, I didn't think you would. Women, especially women of consequence"—he gave a little nod in her direction—"have little need for the almanac. It's more useful to men who earn a living with their hands. Farmers, for example, swear by the almanac for knowing when to plant their crops. It gives them insights into the weather."

"I suppose that would be useful," she said when his pause lasted just a little too long.

"Yes, it would." A satisfied twitch crossed his lips. "I wonder if sailors also use the almanac. Knowing the weather could be useful for one who plies the seas, especially those around our rocky coastline, don't you think?" Simon cocked his head again in that sharp quick way he had, so lizard-like that she wanted to laugh despite the tension in the room. "The almanac will even tell them when the moon rises and sets."

Simon strode to the window and looked out at the still bright sky as though searching for the ephemeral daytime moon. "Tonight, for example will be an interesting night. It's a waning moon, and it sets early. By midnight, it will be dark as pitch."

The locals called it a Smuggler's Moon. Did Simon know that? Probably. If he had been a customs official for more than a week, surely someone would have told him about the best time for smuggling—or catching smugglers.

With a dry laugh reminiscent of a bird choking on a seed, Simon turned from the window. "It would be an interesting night to go smuggler hunting, don't you think, Mrs. Foster?"

Prudence's stomach did its best to tie itself into a knot. Did Simon know where Evan was? Or was he trying to bait her to see how much she would reveal?

For the first time all day, Prudence was glad Evan hadn't told her where he had gone. It allowed her to lie to herself, at least for as long as it took to get rid of Simon. After all, Evan might simply be running a load of pots and pans to Boston. In which case, she had no need to worry.

"I'm sure I could find better things to do with my time, Mr. Manley."

"I'm sure you could." He drew closer to Prudence, his sweet, rather feminine cologne filled the dwindling gap between them, and she had to fight the urge to shrink from him. "Frankly, I am surprised to find Captain Foster away. Were I newly married, I should not leave my young wife alone the day after the ceremony."

The abrupt turn in the conversation toward the

intimate left her feeling as though she were on the heaving deck of a ship. When Simon laid a hand on her arm, Prudence's skin quivered in revulsion, and she thought she might be sick.

"Mr. Manley, I think it's time you leave. I shall send word when my husband returns." Prudence snatched the ledger Simon still held.

"Gil," she called in a voice just shy of a bellow.

"Yes, ma'am?" Gil appeared as though he had been waiting outside the door.

"Show Mr. Manley out, please."

"Yes, ma'am." Gil ushered the reluctant customs officer toward the door.

Simon said nothing, but over his shoulder he gave Prudence a smug look that said he'd be back.

The rumbling of Simon's carriage wheels had long since died away, and yet Prudence still stared at the door to the library. If only Evan would return. Their personal arrangement aside, she had more urgent matters to discuss with him now.

Chapter Twenty-Four

"Come in," Prudence called from her seat at the window when a knock sounded at the library door.

Mrs. Hatcher stepped into the room, a silver tray in her hands.

"Would you like some dinner, ma'am?" She didn't wait for an answer before setting the tray on a side table. She lifted the cover. "I brought you tea, biscuits, boiled potatoes, and a bit of cold beef." She pointed to each of the items as she named them just as she had when Prudence was a child.

"Thank you, Mrs. Hatcher. I will eat in a moment."

Mrs. Hatcher returned the cover to the tray with the stern expression of a governess who had heard it all before. "See that you do. You've been locked in this room all day, staring out that window. He'll be home soon. Starving yourself won't bring him back any faster."

"Mmmm..." Prudence gave an appreciative sniff as though the smell of dinner had brought back her appetite.

The less Mrs. Hatcher knew of her plans, the better. She settled a starched, linen napkin across her lap. The moment the door clicked shut behind her housekeeper, Prudence turned back to the window to watch the setting sun stain the sky with streaks of fuchsia and violet.

Somewhere in the dusk, her husband readied his ship and crew. But where? What could be so important that he would leave her the day after their wedding? Or was she so unimportant to him that she couldn't entice him to stay.

Prudence's lips drew tight. She was no mere heiress to be married and discarded the day after the ceremony was performed, the marriage consummated, and the fortune secured. No sir! She was an Ashcroft, and she wouldn't have it.

Prudence strangled the little voice inside her when it tried to remind her this was exactly the sort of arrangement she had proposed.

She turned back to the tray Mrs. Hatcher had prepared and lifted the cover. Her appetite had not returned, but she had eaten little all day. There could be no telling what the night entailed, and she needed her strength. She picked up a buttermilk biscuit and nibbled at it while churning the day's events over and over in her mind as though they might eventually congeal into an explanation that made sense.

Her gut insisted that Evan had not simply run a load of household goods up to Boston. But if not Boston, where? The questions had become distressingly familiar, but she ran through them one more time. Where could Evan have gone that would only take a day? One by one she picked through the possibilities and found satisfaction with none of them. Except, possibly, one.

And what was Richard's role in Evan's disappearance? Richard had the final say in which ships were dispatched and to where. It was highly unlikely Richard would not know where Evan had gone if he had indeed taken an Ashcroft vessel.

She would also lay odds that Richard's borrowing of the ledger had been a ruse. The way he searched the stack made it look as though he wanted a certain one, but something in the way he searched didn't sit right with her. It had been casual, too casual.

Richard's surprise at not finding Evan at home hadn't been feigned. He had come to speak to Evan, not to her. Considering the way he left so soon after discovering her alone only furthered her suspicions. In all the years she had known him, Richard had never been in a hurry to leave her side.

Lost in thought, Prudence chewed her biscuit, not really tasting it, barely remembering to swallow.

Then there was Simon's visit. It, too, seemed rather well timed. Had he really come to question Evan, or had he suspected Evan would be absent?

She threw the half-eaten biscuit back on the tray.

No, he couldn't possibly have known Evan would be gone. More likely, his visit had been intended to irritate her.

She considered her husband's first reaction to Simon. Evidently, his new position as customs official had granted Mr. Manley boldness, if not wisdom.

Her convoluted thoughts came back to Evan. If Richard hadn't sent him, where could he have gone?

She forced herself to consider the unthinkable. Did he have a lover in Boston? Had he found his wife so unsatisfactory in the marriage bed that he sought the comforts of another woman?

No, that would be impossible. Not that he didn't have a lover in Boston. He might have several for all she knew about him.

However, as a ship's captain, he had to know it was more than a day's journey to Boston and back, regardless of how one traveled.

Prudence snorted. Besides, if she were his lover, she would insist on more than just a few hours of his time.

Of course, there was always the possibility of a lady friend in Newport.

Prudence's stomach clenched around what little she had eaten, until she reminded herself that within the small community of Newport very little went on that she didn't hear about one way or another. From the moment they announced their engagement, Evan's every move would be assessed, with the society matrons looking for the slightest hint of impropriety— and the scandalmongers hunting for something juicier.

Having taken a tortuous route to a final destination, Prudence could reach only one conclusion. Her husband hadn't gone anywhere.

A sliver of a moon, a Smuggler's Moon, blanketed the landscape in a soft glow. Although the light cast long shadows from the maple trees in the yard, Simon had been correct. The moon would set again in a few hours, and by midnight, it would be as black as pitch and nearly as difficult to see through.

Prudence popped the last bit of biscuit into her mouth and poured herself a cup of lukewarm tea. The night was perfect. Now, all she had to do was be patient a while longer. How she hated being patient!

In the hallway outside her door, she could hear the maids, their duties complete for the day, heading toward their chambers on the third floor of the manor. She urged them onward with her thoughts.

A sharp rap sounded at the door.

Prudence snatched another biscuit and pretended to be in the act of buttering it. "Come in."

Netty poked her head in the door. "Do you need anything, ma'am?"

"No, thank you, Netty. I shall be retiring soon and will ready myself for bed."

"Very well, then. Good night, ma'am." There was an unmistakable note of relief in the girl's voice.

Prudence couldn't blame her. The maids were up before dawn, so naturally they went to bed as soon as their evening chores were done.

Gil, on the other hand, could be up for several more hours. However, right about now he would be retiring to his room with a bottle of brandy. It had been his way for years, and in return for his loyalty, Rachel Ashcroft had always pretended not to notice. She also made certain her monthly shopping list included two bottles of the same brandy, which she conveniently stored in an unlocked cabinet in the back hall.

Prudence kept the practice going, never knowing when she might need to avail herself of her butler's loyalty. Tonight might be just such an occasion.

Slowly, the sounds of the household died away, and the trilling of crickets drifted through the open window. An owl gave a soft hoot. Prudence rose as if on cue. Without bothering to take a light, she entered the now still hallway and climbed the darkened stairs to her own chambers.

Once in her room, she shed her gown of sprigged muslin, shift and corset, then pulled a chest from beneath her bed. Holding her breath, she opened the lid, cringing when the creak of ancient hinges threatened to wake the household.

"I knew you would come in handy someday," she whispered, pulling out a pair of boy's breeches and a tunic.

They had belonged to one of her schoolmates, a short, wiry fellow who always reminded her of a weasel. What he lacked in brawn, he made up for in pure nastiness.

After enduring a particularly scathing and public rebuke centered on her lack of feminine charms, she chose her method of revenge. While the boy swam in the pond, she stole his clothes. As expected, he had been punished for swimming naked on school grounds when he—and she—were supposed to have been studying their Latin.

She had meant to return the clothes. After all, what was the fun if the object of revenge never knew who had bested him? But when she saw his anger fully unleashed and his determination to discover who was to blame, her courage failed her. His clothes had resided in her chest since that day although she took them out from time to time when she thought she might have reason to climb the cliffs around the cove. Had she worn the tunic and breeches the other night, Evan might not have noticed her clinging to the cliffs. Unfortunately, she hadn't anticipated the arrival of the patrols and the sudden need to flee.

Prudence donned the breeches and tunic. The clothes weren't overly large, but she had to tie a belt around her waist to keep the breeches from slipping to her ankles. Once she was certain her clothing wouldn't abandon her at an inopportune moment, she crept down the back stairs of the manor and stole into the night.

Over years of walking when something troubled her, Prudence had worn a path from the back door of the manor to the steep cliffs that overlooked the rocky beach. She kept up a brisk pace in the dark, slowing only when the path drew near the golden light flowing through the open door of the stables.

Prudence ducked behind an ancient oak to listen. Would Mr. Malone, the real stable master, be up and about still? She peered around the rough, musty-smelling tree trunk. Shadows moved within, but she couldn't tell if they were made by man or beast.

"I got a pair of kings," a young male voice called out.

"That's good, Billy!" said a voice she recognized as Malone's.

"What does my hand have?" an even younger voice asked.

"Let's see here…"

Prudence crept toward the open door. For years an old ship's lantern had sat on the shelf just to the left of the door. The former stable master had kept it filled and a flint nearby so it would be available at a moment's notice to signal a ship coming into a cove at night. If it were still there, she would make use of it tonight. Her grandmother had made certain she knew the code used by generations of Ashcroft men.

Not that she knew exactly which men Evan had with him, but in the small, tight-knit Newport community, there was a good chance they would be Ashcroft regulars. They would know the signals, too, even if Evan hadn't found time to learn them yet.

She crept forward, listening to the sound of young voices laughing and joking with the stable master as he instructed them on the finer arts of playing poker. She should have known Evan wasn't the stable master as soon as he said he didn't play cards. Every stable master she had ever known had been an expert at poker. One had even tried to teach her to play but had given up while grumbling something about "leading a lamb to the slaughter." She had held three aces in her hand at the time, so his complaint had made no sense to her.

Prudence leaned against the door and peeked around it. Mr. Malone and the two boys sat cross-legged on the floor about ten feet away. She longed to lean in farther to get her bearings and to make sure the lantern still sat on the shelf, but she didn't dare.

Thankful she wore a brown tunic that would blend with the rough pine instead of some frilly dress, she reached around the door. Her fingertips found the shelf with ease. Holding her breath, she walked them forward until they touched cold tin. Her hand crept upward to a smooth flat pane of glass until she reached the pyramid-shaped top that had been perforated to let in air. She ran her hand over the small bumps until she found the handle. With the greatest of care to keep it from squeaking, she lifted the lantern from the shelf.

"Gotcha!" Mr. Malone shouted.

Prudence froze, her heart pounding so hard she thought she might choke on it.

"No, you don't!" one of the boys squealed. "I have a full house."

"By golly, so you do," Malone said.

Prudence slowed her breathing and willed her heart to a normal pace before she withdrew, unlit lantern in hand. Once she was certain the card players were focused on their game, she darted her hand in and grabbed the flint from the shelf.

The warm light of the stables faded, and the air grew cooler as Prudence neared the beach. She shivered in her thin tunic. If only her former schoolmate had been so kind as to leave a cloak by the side of the pond.

Putting her discomfort aside, Prudence stepped toward the edge of the cliff and surveyed the dark, seemingly endless expanse of water. She glanced up at the moon, already low in the sky. If her instincts had served her well, a ship would be coming into sight within the next few hours.

Prudence eyed the long shadow that stretched out from the heels of her slippers. Waiting on the beach would be wiser than standing on the cliff, her slender form outlined against the night sky. Dark as it would be once the moon set, while the moon was still out, she might easily be mistaken for a spy—or worse, an employee of the customs office. Even at night, a random assortment of villagers, thieves, and ruffians could be found roaming about, and most of them held the same generally low opinion of the king and his revenue collectors.

As an Ashcroft, she would be safe, but dressed like a man, she might not be given the opportunity to prove her identity. With the increased restraints on trade, many of her fellow Rhode Islanders seemed a bit too eager for a fight lately. Picking off a customs officer and claiming a case of mistaken identity could turn an ordinary man into a hero at the local tavern.

Prudence picked her way down the steep trail, sliding her back against the rocky wall to stay out of sight. Thankfully, the moon's glow lit the path, and she did not need the lantern. As if she didn't have enough to worry about from the locals, the lantern's yellow light would signal the shore patrols long before she had a chance to warn Evan.

Once on the beach, she sat down, her back against a massive boulder, to wait for the moon to set. She reached into a pocket sewn into the tunic to ensure she still had the flint. She withdrew it, rubbing it between her thumb and index finger, taking comfort in the smooth feel of the cool rock. She tucked it back into her pocket then hugged the lantern to her chest as though it were a life raft.

Click...click...click, click, click.

Prudence turned in the direction of the sharp little sounds, her pulse racing.

A stone rolling down the cliff? Probably. But had it somehow begun the journey of its own accord, or had it been kicked by a human foot?

She squinted into the growing darkness, not daring to breathe, and tried to make out shapes. With the moon setting, the shadows had grown long, and with what little light remained flickering off the waves, it seemed as if everything around her moved.

She heard the intruders long before she made out their forms descending with painful slowness down the trail, at first blending into the shadows then standing out in stark relief as they stepped into a shaft of soft moonlight. The voices, muffled by the surf, grew more distinct as the two men drew nearer.

"You won't have long to wait now."

Prudence held her breath and tried to steady the pulse pounding in her ears. She didn't recognize the gruff voice, but from the slight tremor, she guessed it belonged to an older man. He had a solicitous tone. Not that of a servant. More of an underling. Or perhaps a hired man.

"Whether tonight, or tomorrow night, or the next, it makes no difference."

The whine in the second speaker's voice made her blood run cold. This voice, she recognized.

So she had guessed correctly. Someone had told Simon about the Smuggler's Moon. Perhaps that same someone had told him about the cove, too. How else would he have chosen this particular one from the hundreds that peppered the shoreline around Newport?

Of all the landing sights, Smuggler's Bay was perhaps the most favored. The shoals were so treacherous that none but the best captains could pilot a ship through to the deep waters closer to shore. Something inside her told her this would be the place her husband chose to test his new ship.

Had Simon made the same assumptions about Evan? Or did Ashcroft have a traitor in their midst?

Prudence peered around the safety of the rock to try to get a better view of Simon's companion. Two men stood on the beach, one scanning the horizon while the other kept his gaze trained on the younger man's face.

They were no longer coming toward her, but they stood so close she could easily make out their words. Their faces were harder to discern.

In profile, she could see the older man's bulbous nose, short, nearly nonexistent neck and rounded shoulders. He looked to be wearing a knit cap, the top of which reached only to Simon's shoulders. From the curve of his back, Prudence guessed he had once stood much taller.

Simon, on the other hand, stood out like a parrot among pigeons. In the dark, his clothing faded to black, but the cut of his clothes and the silver buckles that caught the occasional flicker of moonlight suggested he still wore the same richly embroidered suit of purple velvet, silk stockings, and bright red shoes he had worn earlier.

Prudence bit her lip. A rather ostentatious if not inappropriate choice for daywear, it was surely unsuitable for a midnight walk along the shore. She could just imagine trying to take a stroll along the beach in shoes that sank into the sand with every step.

"You could be out here all night, every night, and see nary a trace of the ship you're looking for—unless, of course, I tell you she'll be here."

The man had stooped shoulders, one slightly higher than the other as though he had sustained a back injury. She couldn't see his face clearly with the moon dipping below the horizon, but something about the tilt of his chin or the way he spoke seemed familiar. Was he an Ashcroft man?

"And how do you know who will be where?" Simon's contempt for his companion was obvious.

Prudence held her breath, waiting for his answer.

"I have my sources." The man seemed unperturbed by Simon's high-handed treatment.

"Well, so do I," Simon said. "Although she may not think she's a source, I can read her like a book. I know he'll be here—or at least he will if you were right about the drop point."

"Oh, aye, sir. This is the spot he'll choose for his first voyage. It's deep, and it's relatively calm. The shoals are narrow, but that won't mean a thing if he's as good a captain as they say he is."

"Good. I didn't come back to this God-forsaken colony to be denied." Simon spoke more to himself than his companion.

The older man sucked on his teeth. "'Course, that don't mean he'll be hauling tonight."

"What do you mean?"

"It's his first voyage. If all he's doing is testing his crew, why would he bother with cargo?" Prudence could practically sense Simon's animosity from her hiding place behind the bolder, yet the older man spoke as though he had nothing to fear.

"Doesn't matter," Simon said after a long pause that had Prudence breaking into a cold sweat. "I will have that women's head or her body, perhaps both if I find disfavor with her. Right now, I would be equally satisfied with either."

Prudence shivered and hugged her arms. Was he talking about her? She had only a moment to consider it before the older man spoke up again.

"There she is, just as I said she would be."

"Where?" Simon asked.

Prudence scanned the horizon. She saw nothing from her vantage point, but then, crouching behind her shelter, she was lower than the two men and could only peer south. If it were Evan, he would more than likely sail from the north. Steadying herself against the rock, calves and thighs burning, she straightened just a little.

"Rounding the point, sir."

After clearing the point, he'd have to find the channel that meandered through the rocky shoals into the deeper water of the bay. Unless one knew the shoreline well, navigation would be difficult. In addition to the deep water, the natural protection of the shoals was one of the reason smugglers had favored the cove since her grandfather's time.

"Can you tell what ship it is?" Simon asked.

"No, sir. Looks like a schooner, but not one I'm familiar with."

Ashcroft had plenty of schooners, but none of them new other than Evan's. The *Cythraul* had been in dry dock until this morning according to Richard. Even if the man had turned traitor only recently, it was possible he wouldn't recognize it.

Prudence's knees ached from crouching for so long, but she forced them to straighten. She froze in a half-crouch when one knee popped, but neither man seemed to hear it.

Keeping one eye on the men, she straightened fully and peered over the rock to scan the point.

There. A dark shadow against the dark sky. Prudence knew most of the ships in the Ashcroft fleet. She did not recognize the little vessel any more than Simon and his companion had, but even in the dark, she could see this was no ordinary schooner. When they were children, Richard had taught her many of the basics of ship design, at least enough to recognize a vessel built for speed.

With full sail and a light breeze, this ship looked as if it could outrun any other vessel in the fleet and probably the British Navy as well. Which was, after all, the point of such a ship.

"No lights, sir. Very little sail. I'd stake my reputation she's a smuggler."

"Of course, she's a smuggler," Simon said. "No need to stake something of so little value on it."

The man whistled through his teeth, ignoring his companion's touchiness. "She's a beauty. Don't think I've ever seen her like."

The ship's bow turned toward the shore.

Prudence gasped as reality hit her with the force of a blow. If the dark shadow gliding across the horizon was Evan's ship, danger awaited him. She had to warn him not to land tonight, not while Simon lay in wait on the beach. If he did have cargo, it most likely wasn't pots and pans bound for Boston.

But how could she warn him? Simon and his companion stood no more than twenty feet away. Even if they didn't hear her strike the flint, they'd see the light from the lantern as soon as she lit it.

The ship sailed nearer the secluded cove. Under minimal sail, she rode the waves, threading the currents past the sharp rocks that lay just below the water's surface.

Prudence could see men on deck, no more than dark, vaguely human figures, looking over the bulwark to the water below. In the distance she heard a voice. Probably the leadsman calling out the depth.

Prudence held her breath. A schooner such as this would have a draft of five feet or so, provided she weren't heavily laden with cargo. This one rode high in the water. Still, on such a dark night, an inexperienced crew could easily find their ship grounded.

No sooner did the thought come to mind than a sharp screech echoed across the water.

Prudence gasped.

"Who's there?" Simon turned toward her.

Like a startled deer, Prudence froze.

"Looks like a boy, sir," the older man said.

"Who are you, boy?" Simon's words sliced through the moist night air like a sword. "Speak up if you know what's good for you."

Prudence took stock of her options. The men stood between her and the trail leading up the cliff. She might easily slip by them on the sandy beach, but staying ahead of them on the trail was another matter. Even with Simon's absurd shoes, he would have much better footing on the gritty path.

Running the other way was a fool's choice. She would have to climb the face of the cliff, and Simon and his man could easily just take the trail themselves and wait for her at the top.

Prudence eyed the small schooner. It was still some distance out, but not so far. If she rode one of the currents between the shoals…

"I said, who are you, boy? Answer me." Simon took a step toward her.

Could Simon swim? She didn't remember him swimming with the rest of the boys at the academy. He had always been the one on shore who refused to take off his shoes lest he soil his silk stockings. She doubted he had changed his aversion to dirt since then.

Prudence sprang into action. Throwing the lantern at the two men, she dashed around the side of the boulder and headed toward the waves breaking along the shore. Behind her came the sound of startled oaths. Once she reached the water, she chanced a look back over her shoulder. The men still stood by the rock. What had made them give up so easily?

With the sharp crack of a pistol, she had her answer. She dove into the cold water, just as a ball whistled past her ear.

Chapter Twenty-Five

"Sir, I think someone is shooting at us from the beach."

Evan joined a young sailor at the bulwark. He strained his eyes, but all he saw were the dark, hulking shapes of the cliffs and the even darker shadows beneath.

"Are you sure, Peter? I don't see anything."

He tried not to sound accusatory. Peter couldn't be more than sixteen or seventeen, and he had eyes as sharp as an eagle's. Growing up a fisherman's son, he seemed to know the currents between the shoals better than anyone. Evan had already made up his mind that despite his youth, Peter would become an important part of his crew.

"I think that's what it was." Peter didn't sound so sure anymore. "I saw a flash, and I think I heard a report."

"Well, unless it's a cannon, and I'm pretty sure you would have been able to tell if it were, they can't hit us from the beach." Evan strained his eyes. "Still, we're in no hurry tonight. Let's drop anchor here and see if anything else arises, shall we?"

"Sir?" Peter asked as though he were afraid to voice his thoughts.

"What is it, Peter?"

"I think someone's swimming toward us." Peter's

reluctance to voice this new opinion was obvious.

"Swimming?" Evan scanned the dark water.

The idea of someone taking a swim, in the dark of night, in the cold Atlantic where the riptides could pull the best of swimmers out to sea, was insane. Whoever it was, he was clearly not of sound mind.

"There." Peter pointed.

In the distance, Evan saw flashes of white that could easily be mistaken for the breaking of small waves upon a submerged rock, but as he watched, they drew closer. Eventually, he made out slender arms, so fair they almost glowed in the moonlight, alternating over and over, as the swimmer made his way toward the ship. The swimmer stopped as he reached the side of the *Cythraul* and bobbed in the waves, pale arms sweeping back and forth just beneath the surface of the water.

Evan grimaced. He had been right. Clearly not of sound mind.

"Lower the ladder at once," Evan told Peter.

"Yes, sir." Peter signaled to one of his shipmates to help him unfurl the rope ladder over the side of the ship.

Evan waited for Prudence to scale the rope, but she seemed to be having a challenge with her grip. Her foot slipped, and he steeled himself to dive into the cold water, but she managed to find purchase at the last moment. At last, she came within reach, and he hauled her onto the deck like a fisherman pulling in his nets.

"S..s...s..ank youuu," Prudence said through chattering teeth as she hugged herself.

"Are you crazy?" Evan removed his coat and threw it around her shoulders. "What possessed you to go for a swim in the middle of the night?"

"They were sh...sh...shooting at me," Prudence said.

Evan sensed Peter's wide eyes on Prudence. He was an Ashcroft employee, but one so new he had probably never met his employer.

"Peter, have the cook heat some water and fill the tub in my quarters."

"Yes, sir."

Evan turned back to his wife, taking in the drenched tunic and breeches clinging to her shapely form. At least she hadn't taken her midnight swim in a nearly transparent shift this time. Evan's blood heated as memories of having that body beneath him little more than twenty-four hours ago flooded his mind. He banished the thought by reminding himself how many sailors died of illness after a swim in the cold sea. He had to get Prudence warmed, now. And he had to get answers.

"Who was shooting at you?"

"S...S...Simon," Prudence said, matter-of-factly despite her obvious difficulty getting her lips and tongue to form words.

"Simon was shooting at you?" Evan found it hard to believe, despite the man's obvious animosity toward Prudence.

"Well, I d...d...don't actually n...n...know that it was Simon doing the shooting. It m...m...might have been the other m...man."

Evan accepted a woolen blanket from one of his men and draped it around Prudence's shoulders. He tried to wring the seawater from her hair with a second blanket.

"Thank you, Thomas, that will be all for now." Evan tried not to sound irritable when he realized the man stood rooted to the deck not a half step behind him.

"Yes, sir," Thomas said, ogling Prudence over his shoulder as he returned to his duties.

Evan turned back to his wife. "What other man? Did you recognize him?"

Prudence considered. "No, but he looked familiar. I'm fairly certain he doesn't work for Ashcroft, but he could be a townsman."

"Perhaps his presence is mere coincidence—" Evan turned his eyes on his wife "—but yours is surely not. Mind telling me what you are doing here?"

"You don't seem happy to see me," Prudence said, her voice artificially light.

At least her shivering had stopped.

"I'm not sure I am," Evan said. "I thought I had left you at home, where you would be safe."

"Evan, I needed to warn you." Prudence laid a hand, fingernails an alarming shade of blue, against his chest. "I think Simon may be planning to use you to get to me."

Warn him? At the risk of her own life? Leave it to Prudence to give no thought to her own safety.

"You could have been caught in a current and swept out to sea." He forced the words past the knot in his throat. He could have lost her so easily.

"Nonsense." Prudence pulled the blanket tighter about her shoulders. "It's thanks to the currents that I was able to make it to your ship."

Jenkins, Evan's sailing master and a man of indiscriminate years but consummate skill approached, cutting through Evan's thoughts.

"Evening, ma'am." Jenkins nodded to Prudence.

"Good evening, ah, Mr. Jenkins, isn't it?" Prudence said as though she were in a drawing room in Newport having tea and not dripping seawater onto his deck.

Nevertheless, Evan couldn't help but be impressed. Prudence hadn't been back at Ashcroft long, yet she had clearly endeavored to learn the names of her employees. His lips twitched when he considered how long it had taken her to learn his true name.

"Yes, ma'am," Jenkins said, then turned to Evan. "Sir, shall we complete the run tonight or head back to port?"

At least there was one man among his crew who wasn't so bemused by his wife that he couldn't keep his mind on the job. He mentally added Jenkins to his list of permanent crew.

Evan turned his thoughts toward the situation at hand. There was no sign of Manley, but he couldn't take the chance that the little man would be waiting for him. By the time he sailed the *Cythraul* in, Simon would have had time to gather reinforcements. While Evan wasn't carrying anything incriminating, he didn't care to answer why he would be running his new ship into a deserted cove, one with an infamous history, in the middle of the night. The last thing he needed at the start of a new venture was to catch the attention of an overly zealous customs official, especially one who coveted his wife.

"Prudence, did you happen to notice whether Simon or the other man had a looking glass?"

A shiver racked Prudence's shoulders as she thought. He would have to get her out of those wet clothes and soon, or she would catch her death.

"No. Or at least I did not see one."

"Good. That means they should not be able to see the ship clearly in this light. Jenkins, weigh anchor and head back to port."

"Aye, sir." Jenkins brought a knuckle to his forehead. "Back to port." He turned to shout orders to the men.

Evan turned back to Prudence. "Now, we need to get you out of those clothes."

"Aye, sir." Prudence mimicked his sailing master.

Evan wondered if Prudence had intended the gesture as a subtle reminder that she was his superior, or if she just naturally bristled at being given orders.

Evan grasped her by the hand. The cold clamminess of her skin sent a wave of alarm through him. His superior or not, he had to get her warm. He led her down the ladder to his cabin below deck.

"Just finishing up, sir." Peter stepped aside so another man could bring in a pail of steaming water.

"Thank you, Peter."

As though he had lost the ability to turn his head, Peter's gaze remained fixed on Prudence. "Will there be anything else, sir?"

"No, Peter. We are heading back to port. You'll be back home in time to have breakfast with your mother."

"Aye, sir. Thank you, sir." Peter's face grew red to the tips of his ears, and he ducked out of Evan's quarters.

"That wasn't very nice, embarrassing the boy like that," Prudence admonished him once they were alone again.

Evan took the blanket and his coat from around her shoulders. "That boy is scarcely a year or so younger than you, and you obviously fascinate him. I don't particularly care to have my crew ogling my wife."

He untied the laces at her neck, and in one swift move, pulled the tunic over her head. Prudence wasn't wearing her shift, and her already puckered nipples shriveled even more. Evan longed to nibble on one of the rosy buds, but the goose bumps across her pale chest reminded him it was a reaction to the cold, not any particular desire she might be feeling.

Prudence crossed her arms in front of her chest.

"Cold?"

"Yes." Her green eyes darkened.

"Well, we have to get you out of those clothes, then you can take a hot bath to warm up."

"I don't suppose you have a roaring fire aboard ship somewhere," Prudence said, her teeth chattering anew.

"Fires are something we tend to avoid on wooden ships." He reached for the buttons on her breaches.

Where did she get these clothes anyway? Had she stolen them from Richard at some point during their misspent youth? He could just imagine a lanky, youthful Richard arising, naked and shivering, from the local duck pond only to find his clothes had gone missing. Being best friends with Prudence could not have been easy.

Prudence slapped his hands away. "I can do that."

"Suit yourself." Evan turned and strode to a sideboard where he poured two glasses of brandy.

When he came back to Prudence, glasses cradled in the palms of his hands, she was still fumbling with the buttons. Her hands shook so fiercely she had yet to undo even one.

"Here." He handed her a glass. .

"Damn these things, anyway." She took a sip of brandy. "You'd think they'd be easier to undo. However do men manage?"

"Generally, we don't soak our clothing in seawater and chill our fingers to the bone before we undress."

Goosebumps sprung out across her belly when Evan's knuckles grazed her cold flesh.

"So that's it, is it?" Prudence took another sip of brandy and closed her eyes. "Mmmm."

Evan grinned. He liked a woman with a sense of humor, even more so when she appreciated his best brandy. However, even the finest brandy money could buy wouldn't keep her well if she didn't get warm and dry.

"The warmth from the brandy is no more than superficial. We need to get you out of these and into the tub." Evan popped open the second button on her breeches and before she could protest, he pealed the wet fabric past her hips.

This time, she made no attempt to cover herself but took another sip of her brandy.

His wife wasn't the flirtatious type. But nor was she falsely modest, especially when it came to him. Her attempt to cover her breasts earlier had probably been because she was cold.

He liked that about her. Had she been a man, they could have been friends. Hell, they were friends.

He took her glass from her and ushered her into the oak tub.

"Ahhh." Prudence let out a sigh of satisfaction as she sank into the water.

Evan handed her glass back to her.

"This is almost as good as a roaring fire." Prudence accepted the glass of brandy. "I feel warm inside and out."

Evan considered telling her that he had even more pleasant ways to warm her in mind, but he held back. There were things that needed to be discussed.

"So now, tell me, what you were doing on the beach in the middle of the night, putting yourself in a position for Simon to shoot at you."

"I really don't know why Simon took a shot at me." Prudence sipped her brandy. "I suppose he thought I overheard something I shouldn't have."

For the moment, Evan decided to ignore her deliberate attempt to misunderstand his question. "Did he know it was you?"

Prudence shook her head. "I don't think so. The older man thought I was a boy."

"Yes, well they couldn't see what I can."

Prudence's chest turned a mottled shade of pink when Evan let his gaze slide over the smooth skin shimmering beneath the water. He leaned forward and let his lips brush hers. She tasted of brandy and seawater, an interesting and not unpleasant combination.

"Now, answer the first part of my question."

"Which was?" Prudence gave a slow blink.

Evan couldn't tell whether she was being deliberately obtuse or simply couldn't remember. Perhaps the brandy or the heat from the bathwater had made her sleepy. He liked to think that his kiss had affected her. If only his cunning little wife could be so easily distracted.

"What were you doing on the beach in the middle

of the night?"

"Waiting for you, of course." She said it as though it were obvious.

"But I told you, I had to run a load of goods up to Boston."

"Yes, you did." Prudence sat up in the tub and gave him a smirk with lips that were finally regaining some color. "But clearly we aren't in Boston, are we? You think I can't tell when my own husband is lying to me?"

"You mean your husband, the stable master?"

Prudence's face fell, and Evan immediately regretted reminding her that he had done nothing but deceive her since the day they met. He reached for the oak pail sitting beside the tub and filled it with water from the tub.

"I apologize for being evasive, but my story held a kernel of truth. I am sailing with a new crew. I wanted to see how they handled the shoals in Smuggler's Cove."

Evan tilted her head forward and poured the warm water over her hair.

When he finished, Prudence regarded him with solemn eyes. "Why didn't you tell me?"

Evan sat back on his heels. "I'm not sure. I think some part of me wanted to protect you. I was afraid you might want to come along, and I didn't want to put you in danger. With a new crew, the *Cythraul* could easily have been run aground."

Prudence gave a slight nod.

Her meek acceptance pricked his conscience. He needed to be completely honest with her. She deserved that much.

"And there was a part of me that didn't want to let you get close to me."

Prudence's gaze snapped to his face, but she said nothing.

"I've been on my own for a long time, and I never thought I'd meet someone with a will as strong as my own. I think maybe I was afraid to let you in, afraid I'd lose something of myself."

"Do you remember the promise I made to you?" Prudence asked in a small voice.

"You mean the one about being faithful?"

She gave him a rueful smile and rose from the tub. "No, the one I made in the carriage on the way home from the Waites' supper party."

Evan nodded.

"If I can manage to trust you, do you think you can find it in yourself to trust me?"

"I'm sure of it." Evan offered his hand to help her out of the tub.

He snatched a towel from the side table and wrapped it around Prudence's shoulders. She was still warm from her bath, but in the chilled air of his cabin, she would cool quickly. Part of him wished she had stayed home. Another part of him, specifically the part that lay below the buttons on the front of his breeches, was ecstatic to see her.

"Why didn't you wait for me at the manor? I told you I would be back on the morrow. What was so urgent that it couldn't wait a day?"

She colored, started to say something, then seemed to change her mind.

Evan tipped her chin toward him. "I am your husband, Prudence. Your secrets, whatever they are, are safe with me."

"That's just it. It's not a secret. I don't have any secrets from you."

"What do you mean, sweetheart? You're making no sense."

"I am a virgin." Prudence blurted, then paused. "Or at least I w…w…was."

Evan waited to see where she would go after making such a bizarre opening statement.

"I don't expect you to believe me. I don't know why I didn't bleed. I can't give you an answer to that. I know it is the way of things, but perhaps it isn't for me. Or maybe it's part of the curse. I don't know. All I can tell you is that I have never been with Richard or any other man."

Her words came so fast it seemed to Evan as though he were being buffeted about in a wave.

"Slow down." He laid a hand on her cheek. "Now, why again is it that I am supposed to think you weren't a virgin?"

"You don't trust Richard, and he said you think that he and I were lovers."

"I might have at one time, but not anymore."

"And because I didn't bleed."

"You didn't?"

Prudence looked incredulous. "Surely you noticed."

For reasons that made no sense to him, Evan felt the need to defend himself. "I know virgins are supposed to bleed, but it never occurred to me to check to see if you had."

Although he had never been with one, he also knew that virgins were supposed to feel pain the first time. He had worried about causing Prudence pain and gone slowly. When she hadn't appeared to be in any discomfort, he let his instincts take over.

He hadn't given it another thought until they weighed anchor and he had a moment to indulge in pleasant memories of the night spent with his wife. He assumed her adventurous nature had masked any discomfort. Like everything else she did, Prudence leapt in to making love with both feet and not much thought to the consequences. Not that he minded.

"Thank you for believing me. I know I haven't given you any reason to."

"Sure you have," Evan said.

"I have?"

"Yes, I believe you when you say you were a virgin because you are the worst liar I've ever met."

"I am not," Prudence protested. "I can lie with the best of them."

"Yes, and I am your distant Portuguese cousin." Evan reminded her of her most recent efforts at fabrication. "Eventually, Mr. Cowper is going to discover I am not Portuguese, and I'll have to come up with some plausible story as to why you thought I was. He might even expect me to explain why I went along with the misunderstanding." He leaned back against a table and nestled her between his thighs. "Being married to you won't be easy, will it?"

"We could still have the marriage annulled. No one need know it was consummated." The forlorn look in her eyes made his gut twist.

Was his wife falling in love with him? While he had no experience with love, from the moment he agreed to her terms, he had wanted something more than the business arrangement she proposed.

Of course, if Prudence were falling in love, his independent-minded wife would be the last to acknowledge it.

"Now, why would I want to do that?" Evan asked.

"Because of the curse." Evan rolled his eyes and Prudence added, "I know you don't believe in curses. I normally don't either, but this one is real. My grandmother was hexed by a woman who had fallen in love with my grandfather. Now, none of her heirs will ever have a male child."

"And you believe this?"

"Well, how else would you explain she only had a daughter and then my mother only had a daughter?"

"Luck? Coincidence? Fate?" Evan suggested.

Prudence crossed her arms over her chest, and her towel slipped lower. "I don't believe in luck, or coincidence, and isn't fate just another word for being cursed?"

Evan ran his finger along the edge of the towel. "You don't believe in luck or coincidences, but you believe in curses?"

"Yes." She backed away from his touch.

Evan caught her with his thighs before she could get very far.

"I never thought I'd say this, but you think too much. This is one time I'd rather you just follow your instincts. What do they tell you?"

"That there is a curse on my family." She looked at him doubtfully. "What do your instincts tell you?"

"That curses were meant to be broken." He pulled her into a searing kiss that left little doubt as to his intentions to do just that.

Chapter Twenty-Six

Prudence batted at the butterflies darting about her cheek, her eyes, her lips, her nose.

"Go away!" She forced her voice through her dry throat.

She rolled over, pulling a blanket of grass over her head and drifted back into the warmth of the meadow.

The butterflies tugged at her blanket. Prudence pulled it back. More of them gathered, tugging it farther from her shoulders. Prudence reached a hand out to swat at the aggressive insects. She could hear them laughing at her, their tiny masculine voices coming from far away. Funny. She would have thought butterfly laughter would be more feminine. Prudence sat up to stare into the all-too-cheerful face of her new husband.

She pressed her palms against her eyelids, blotting out the morning sun. "Do you always get up this early?"

"Early? It's after two bells in the forenoon watch."

"Pardon?" Prudence glanced around at unfamiliar surroundings. She wasn't in her soft summer meadow, but in Evan's ship, lying in his uncomfortably hard and narrow bed.

"It's after nine o'clock, sleepyhead." He tousled her hair as though she were a child.

"Is that all?" Prudence flopped back down into his

bed and pulled the quilt over her head.

"Well, I suppose you can go back to sleep if you want him to find you naked in here."

Prudence sprang back up. "Who?"

"Simon," Evan said. "He just set out from shore in a dinghy, and he's headed this way. Given the size of the two men rowing the boat, I'd guess you have about twenty minutes to make yourself presentable."

"Simon? Here? How can you be so calm? The man took a shot at me just yesterday!"

Evan laughed. "Relax, sweetheart. I don't suspect he came to finish the job. We don't even know what he's doing here. Perhaps he just wanted to extend his felicitations to the happy couple." Evan grew pensive. "Though I doubt that's all of it. He doesn't seem the type to go out of his way to congratulate the man who stole his love interest out from under him."

Prudence rose from the bed, wrapping the blanket around her naked body. "Love interest?" She snorted. "That man has no love for me."

Evan leaned back against a table and folded his arms over his chest. "No, I suppose it's not love, but he is not what I would call disinterested. There's a gleam in his eye that I recognize."

Prudence cast him a derisive look. "It's called hate. The man despises the very ground I walk on."

"I wouldn't be so sure."

Tugging her blanket tight, Prudence collected her sodden clothes from the floor. If only she had taken the time to lay them out to dry the night before. Alas, clothing had been the last thing on her mind during the night. It had been one spent in delirious oblivion to all but the way Evan made her body sing.

In the cold light of morning, the night's pleasures seemed an all-too-distant memory.

"Ahhh!" Her sigh was one of pure exasperation. "Even if these were dry, I could hardly greet him wearing boy's clothes. He'd know for certain it was me on the beach."

"Just stay in bed. We'll tell him you had a late night." Evan's eyes twinkled. "A very late night, and you're not up for receiving visitors this morning."

"We can't tell him that! He'd think we were up all night…" Her face heated.

Evan grabbed a handful of blanket as she strode by him, headed toward a limp stocking on the other side of the room.

"That sounds like a good idea to me." He tugged until she had to choose between going to him or collecting her things while naked.

Prudence chose the former. When she stood before him, he kissed her forehead and folded her into his arms. "I can't think of a better way to get revenge than to let him know you are happily married to a man who appreciates your charms. Besides, he's not likely to barge into my quarters insisting you receive him in the altogether."

"I don't think he's here for a social visit." Prudence ignored Evan's jest.

Her husband seemed none-too-worried about Simon finding her in a state of dishabille. Must be something to do with male pride of the conquest.

Evan drew back to look at her face. "What do you mean? Do you know more about this than you've told me?"

Prudence backed away. "He came to see me

yesterday."

"He did what?" Evan rose. "Why didn't you tell me this?"

"I started to tell you, but you distracted me before I had the opportunity."

"So why did he come to see you? I take it that he did not come to offer us his best wishes?"

"No, it seems my old nemesis has a new position. The governor appointed him customs officer." All vestiges of amusement vanished from Evan's expression, making Prudence wonder if she didn't have more to worry about than she knew. "Actually, he told me he came to see you. He told me that the visit could not wait."

"Did he say why he needed to see me?"

"No, he wouldn't tell me. Apparently, now that we are married, he believes all of our business affairs will be handled by you." The assumption still rankled, and Prudence didn't try to hide it. "Perhaps my inability to lie makes me more sensitive to lies in others, but he was either hiding something or fishing for information."

"Get dressed."

Prudence paused for a moment, waiting for Evan to turn his back or leave the quarters. When he didn't, she shrugged, tossed off the sheet and pulled on her salt-encrusted breeches. They were married after all, and besides, Evan was staring at the wall, deep in thought.

"Now what?" Prudence pinned her hair into a knot at the top of her head.

Evan surveyed her from the top of her head to her bare feet. "No, that won't do. It won't do at all."

"What won't do? At least if I'm dressed like this, he might not recognize me. Give me a hat, and I'll hide among the crew…"

Evan rose. "In the light of day, there is no way anyone is going to believe you are a boy. Follow me."

Evan pushed back a dresser on the opposite side of his quarters. Taking a knife from the top drawer, he used it to pry away a piece of the wall near the floor.

Prudence gripped the side of the hole and leaned in to stare into the gaping darkness. In the dim light, she could see a wall some three feet in. Was it a corridor? She glanced from side to side. Once her eyes adjusted, she could make out the distant shadowy forms of planks to both her right and left. Not a corridor then, but a secret hold of some sort.

She pulled her head back out. "What do you keep in here?"

"Only my most precious cargo." Evan brushed her forehead with his lips then hustled her into the darkness.

He replaced the piece of wall, and darkness enveloped her. The sound of the dresser scraping over the wood was like that of a tomb being closed.

"Evan, I really don't like dark places." Prudence shivered from a chill that had nothing to do with her wet clothes. She crossed her arms over her chest and hugged herself.

"Hush. It's just until I can get rid of him. In the meantime, you must remain absolutely quiet."

Prudence leaned back against the wall and sank to the floor. She hugged her knees, trying to quell the panic.

A small sliver of light about two feet above the floor beckoned to her. Prudence clambered to her knees and crawled toward it.

She peered through a small crack where the workmen had been a little less thorough when applying pitch between the planks. She couldn't see much from her vantage point. A few floorboards, the leg of a chair, some sort of brown leather. Evan's boots?

Prudence picked at the opening with her fingernails. If she could only widen it just a bit.

"Please don't pry apart my new ship."

"Sorry." Prudence sat back on her heels.

At least she could hear everything going on even if she could see nothing. It made her feel slightly less entombed. Of course, sound went two ways. Evan had made it clear that those in the room could hear her as well. She would have to be as quiet as a mouse. Quieter even, since a ship this new would be unlikely to have mice.

Or rats. Prudence shuddered at the idea she might not be alone in the darkness. She would rather face an overeager revenue collector than a rat—not that there was much difference in her opinion.

A sharp rap sounded on Evan's door.

"Come in."

Hinges gave a soft squeak and there was a shuffling of heavy boots.

"There's some bastard here to see you, Captain. Claims to be a customs officer. Looks like one, too, fancy suit and all. You'd think he was the king himself."

Prudence swallowed a giggle, Jenkins' distaste for customs officers, especially ones in fancy suits, was obvious.

"Send him in."

"If you say so, Captain."

There was more scuffling of boots, more than one pair this time, then a stifled oath.

"I can bloody well show myself in. And just so you know, I don't think I am the king. However, I am the king's representative, and I expect to be treated accordingly."

Prudence shrank back against the wall at the sound of Simon's voice.

"If I have my way, you will be." Jenkins' acerbic voice drifted off, the hinges squeaked, and then there was a sharp click of the door closing.

"What did he mean by that?" Simon asked.

"Just as you requested. You are the king's representative, and as such you deserve the same sort of deference we would give his majesty if he were here to collect the revenues himself."

"Yes, well, that's very good."

Given the way most of the men who served aboard her family's ships viewed the king and his representatives. Prudence thought Simon's acceptance of the explanation showed a certain naiveté.

"I suppose congratulations are in order." Simon's voice was as dead as a north wind in winter. "Although I don't know why you would choose to leave your bride so soon after your nuptials."

Evan said nothing, and Prudence could bear the silence no more. She crept forward to steal another glance through the small sliver between the planks. The brown leather hadn't moved. Either they were something other than Evan's boots, or he hadn't risen when Simon came into the room.

"You must have had something important to take care of to leave such a delightful woman all alone in that big house."

There was a soft rasp of papers being shuffled. Was Simon rifling through Evan's things the way he had absently picked over her ledgers? Surely, he wouldn't dare with Evan in the room.

The brown leather twitched.

"My bride can take care of herself, and I have business to attend." The leather twitched again. "Although I don't see how either of those is any of your business."

"Well, I suppose Prudence is none of my business, but as an old friend, I certainly care about her happiness." Simon's nasal voice held a casual tone that implied a familiarity with Evan that did not exist. "She was a lucky find for you. Tell me, was this a happy accident, or did you have an eye on marrying into the family when you accepted the position from the old lady."

Prudence clapped a hand over her mouth to smother a gasp.

Evan didn't respond, but through the crack between the planks, the leather moved up and down. Simon's question had agitated Evan.

Had Evan planned this whole marriage business himself? Had he accepted a position with Ashcroft & Sons with the express goal of taking over the company? Or perhaps he had had another plan in mind, but with her marriage proposal, Prudence had offered him an easier path. He had accepted her offer readily enough.

Prudence shook her head to clear the monstrous thoughts from her mind. Surely not. Her grandmother had called Evan a gift, one she had personally chosen for her granddaughter. Of course, that did not mean

Evan didn't have designs of his own. Perhaps she and her grandmother had been willing pawns in his game.

"So I suppose you will be taking over the business now?"

"What would I know about running Ashcroft & Sons? I'm just a simple sea captain."

"Are you? Just a simple sea captain, and yet Rachel Ashcroft has this ship built expressly for you. Seems there might be more to your story than meets the eye."

The hold grew stuffy as though Prudence had used up all the air. She forced her breathing to calm.

Simon continued when Evan didn't respond. "It's strange…I make it my business to know everything I can about the good citizens under my jurisdiction, but I can't find a record of an Evan Foster anywhere."

"I've moved around a lot."

"Really?" Simon's tone turned friendly again. "I have, too. Where did you live before you came to Rhode Island? Perhaps we've covered some of the same ground."

"I've lived aboard ship most of my life."

"I suppose you have." Simon's voice came from farther away.

Was he exploring the room? Prudence mentally ticked off the items she had worn, trying to come up with anything she might have left in the open. To her relief, she couldn't come up with a single thing.

"Tell me, on which ships did you serve?" Simon's voice was muffled as though his back were turned.

"Most recently, the *Mariposa*," Evan replied.

Prudence knew that ship. She belonged to an independent captain who was as likely to ply the triangle trade as he was to accept a legitimate job.

Mercy! She hoped Evan didn't plan to involve Ashcroft in that nasty business.

"The *Mariposa*, eh? I'll bet you have some interesting stories to tell."

"Not really," Evan said. "With the restrictions on trade, the captain couldn't afford to keep me on."

"What did you do after that?"

"Odd jobs."

"Like what?" Simon seemed determined not to let Evan get away with vague answers.

"Did some bricklaying. Had a stint as a chimney sweep. Considered heading up north to try my hand at trapping, but decided I'm not fond of frozen water."

"And then the offer from Mrs. Ashcroft fell into your lap."

Evan grunted an acknowledgement.

"Of course, by marrying the daughter, you don't have to content yourself with being just a sea captain. Now, you can have the whole business."

"Ashcroft belongs to Prudence."

"But she's a woman." Simon's incredulity seemed far less feigned than his friendliness.

Prudence's dislike of her former classmate deepened.

"She's an Ashcroft."

"Not really, of course." Simon lowered his voice to a conspiratorial whisper. "What with the curse and all, her grandfather was the last *real* Ashcroft. I suppose with no men to manage the business, Rachel Ashcroft was only too happy to throw you in the path of her granddaughter. She had to do it to save the family fortune from her incompetence."

Prudence could barely contain her fury. She waited

for Evan to defend her. If he didn't do it soon, she might just give into the urge to rip a hole in Evan's precious ship and throttle Simon herself.

"She has Richard to help her."

Prudence stifled a gasp. Did no one have confidence in her abilities?

"He's in love with her, you know. The man used to visit her at school. Stayed for days from what I've heard."

Prudence cringed. She did not need Simon replanting seeds of doubt in Evan's head. Right after she took him to task for not defending her abilities as the head of Ashcroft, she would explain that when Richard visited her at the academy, she had lived in the home of the Reverend Fitzgerald. Had it not been for the ever-watchful Mrs. Fitzgerald, her relationship with Richard might have developed into something more than friendship. Nevertheless, the stern Mrs. Fitzgerald had seen to it that they never had a moment alone during any of his visits.

"Though I don't understand why." Simon sounded more like he was talking to himself than to Evan. "As far as I can tell, she's never given him a bit of encouragement, never encouraged any of us for that matter. Mark my words. She's going to turn into a dried up old biddy."

The heel of Evan's boot ceased its rapid movements, and the air in the narrow hold grew even thicker. A trickle of sweat wound its way down Prudence's temple.

"Of course, maybe she is already," Simon said, seemingly oblivious to the change in atmosphere. "Maybe that's why you left her the day after your wedding. Couldn't convince her to spread those pretty little legs for you?"

The brown leather was there one moment, and then it was gone. Prudence fell back as something heavy slammed against the planks, blocking her view and plunging the dimly lit hold into darkness.

"I am the king's represent—" Simon's words were choked off.

"Jenkins!" Evan's bellow shook the planks.

Door hinges squeaked immediately. "Yes, sir?"

"Jenkins, help our guest off the ship." Evan's voice had returned to normal, but it still held an underlying current of restrained fury.

Something slumped to the floor.

"Come on, you. On your feet," Jenkins said, with a grunt.

"One more thing, Jenkins."

"Yes, sir?"

"Show him the same respect you would show the king."

"Yes, sir," Jenkins replied. "With pleasure, sir."

Chapter Twenty-Seven

Once again, Prudence was awakened from sensual dreams by the light brush of Evan's lips against her cheek. However, this time, when she opened her eyes, he had already moved off to tie his neck cloth in front of the mirror.

Prudence studied her husband while he dressed.

Although her anger had cooled, she had hoped they might have a word or two about her role at Ashcroft. Afterward, they might share more than words.

All afternoon her body had hummed with anticipation. Ever since she had met Evan, words had seemed inadequate. Either she wasn't very good at communicating, or he wasn't very good at listening, but their conversations left her feeling frustrated and out of sorts. Making love with him set everything right. She supposed they were both far better with physical communication than verbal.

By the time they reached the manor in the late afternoon, Prudence had been ready to suggest they forgo food in favor of the bedroom. Then she caught the hungry look in his eye when Mrs. Hatcher mentioned that supper would be ready momentarily, and she decided she could wait a little longer. Patience was, after all, a virtue.

After supper and a quick stop off in her room to snatch her nightdress from the wardrobe, Prudence followed Evan to his room and prepared for bed alongside her husband.

He had worn a dark and brooding look, as though he were considering matters of grave importance. Not wanting to intrude on his inner thoughts and not knowing how to get him to share them with her, she had said nothing.

She glanced at him before donning her nightdress to see if he might show the slightest interest, but he continued to stare into the fire as though it held the answers to some enigmatic mystery. At least he didn't send her back to her own room. Then again, she hadn't been certain he was aware of her presence.

Evan stared at the flames while Prudence studied his backside and pretended to be asleep. After twenty minutes or so, he finally shed his breeches, turned back the covers, and crawled into bed beside her. His half-hearted peck on her cheek and his muttered "g'night" left her bemused, frustrated, and more than a little agitated.

But now it was morning. Well, almost morning, since only the barest sliver of silvery gray could be seen through the lace curtains. Still, now that she was no longer preoccupied with his lack of interest in her, she found it a little easier to press him to share his thoughts.

"What is it?" She rose onto her elbows.

"I have to leave again." This time, he didn't give her a kiss on the forehead to ease the concern she was certain wrinkled her brow.

"You aren't just running another load of goods up to Boston, are you?" She repeated the lie he had told her the last time he left her alone in their bed.

Did she want him to lie to her? No, of course not.

"No, I'm not." He studied her face as though trying to decide how much to tell her. "Richard has a lead on a load of rum in Martinique that can be had for a good price."

Prudence narrowed her eyes at the bedroom door. Had she slept through the delivery of a note from Richard? It didn't seem possible given the tossing and turning they had both done throughout the night. More likely, Evan still did not trust her with the truth. The thought stung almost as much as his leaving.

"Ashcroft has plenty of captains here and in Martinique. Was there no one else available?"

Evan's willingness to leave at one suggestion from Richard, really at the mere hint of a suggestion since he sounded by no means certain the rum existed, spoke volumes about her husband's regard for her.

"It may take some negotiating with the owner. It seems he doesn't quite understand how difficult it is to bring rum into the Colonies now that the revenue men are getting bolder."

"Simon," Prudence said with some vehemence, the mere mention of the revenue collectors turning her thoughts to the man who seemed determine to make an enemy of them both.

"Precisely. Although, I believe Simon has more than the king's service in mind when he pursues his task with such diligence." The concern in Evan's eyes deepened.

"What do you mean?" Prudence asked, her own alarm bells ringing.

"Revenge," Evan said, his voice as cold as the word.

"Revenge?" Prudence repeated, the word tasting

metallic in her own mouth.

She didn't like Simon, nor did she trust him, but she had never thought of him as dangerous. Perhaps she should, since he had taken a shot at her yesterday, but then, he hadn't really known it was her, had he? Besides, revenge was an emotion so filled with hate that surely it required a motive beyond anything she had ever given him.

"On whom is he looking to get revenge? And for what?"

"You. Me." Evan sat beside her on the bed. "I'm not exactly sure who he considers the object of his revenge. Perhaps he doesn't either, but his goal has been thwarted, and he is not the type to take that lightly."

Prudence wasn't sure if it was the cold grayness of Evan's eyes or the thought of Simon hating her so much that sent the shiver up her spine. She tugged the bedclothes up to her chin.

"But why?" None of it made any sense.

"He wanted you, and I took you out of his reach."

Prudence snorted. "No, that isn't possible. Simon couldn't possibly love me. He's hated me since we were in school. I broke his nose, remember?"

"I didn't say he *loved* you. I said he wanted you. There is a difference." Evan sounded so logical as he explained the cold facts of reality.

Of course there was a difference between wanting someone and loving them. Prudence picked at a loose thread on the coverlet. Hadn't her husband proven that? He had shown her she wasn't the undesirable maiden bound for an early spinsterhood she had always considered herself to be. He had clearly wanted her.

The more she thought about it, the more she became certain he desired her as much as she did him. But could he ever love her?

She supposed she should be grateful. He could have found a way to stir his own arousal, make love to her in a perfunctory fashion, and then consider his future secured.

After all, once they consummated the marriage, there was no way for it to be annulled. The only other option was divorce, and despite her threats, he had to know she wouldn't submit the Ashcroft name to such a scandal. Her family fortune legally belonged to Evan now, and she had thrown her heart in for good measure.

"Stay away from him." Evan's words were hard.

Prudence's gaze shot back to his face. She searched his eyes for the slightest show of emotion. Did he care for her? Even a little? If he did, why didn't he stay and protect her himself?

"Yes, of course I will." She tried to make her tone light, reassuring, but the crack in her voice gave her away.

Evan rose. "Perhaps you should send for Richard. I'll be gone for at least a week. I'm sure he's been a guest of the household before, and his presence would be little cause for gossip among the servants."

Did she detect a note of warning again? Surely Simon hadn't managed to convince him there really was something to her relationship with Richard. Or maybe he was just signaling that, given the agreement she had made with him, he didn't expect her to be faithful either—just discreet.

"Isn't that a little like the fox guarding the hen house?" Prudence grumbled.

Let him think there was still something to their relationship. It would give him reason to stew while he was away. Perhaps he might even find he didn't care for the original terms of their agreement.

"Better to have a fox that loves you guarding you than one who is set upon devouring you." Evan grabbed his coat and strode toward the door.

"Fine. Maybe I will send for Richard."

Without another glance at his wife, Evan pulled the door shut behind him, leaving Prudence feeling more confused and alone than ever. There was only one thing she felt certain of. She and Evan would have been better off making love than talking.

Chapter Twenty-Eight

Prudence picked at the breakfast Mrs. Hatcher set on her bedside table. She didn't miss the disappointment mixed with concern on her housekeeper's face when Mrs. Hatcher returned an hour later to carry away the nearly full tray of cold food and tea. Prudence gave a sleepy yawn, as though she had just woken up, not been wide-eyed since dawn.

Once she was alone again, Prudence rose from her bed. It would be better to pretend that nothing was amiss, go about her day as usual, than to give Mrs. Hatcher undue cause for concern. Not that she could ever really hide anything from the housekeeper who had always been something more of an aunt to her.

Prudence opened the wardrobe on the far side of the room. She hadn't seen Netty much recently, but at least the girl had thought to stock her husband's wardrobe with some of her clothes. Although her gratitude dissipated somewhat as she picked through the odd collection. They were all her most unbecoming dresses. When Prudence had tried to wear the canary yellow gown to a lawn party, Netty had even told her it was all wrong for her coloring. So why would these be the dresses she picked?

Instead of going to her old room, Prudence chose a dress of dove gray muslin that was more suited to a maid's closest than the wardrobe of a newly married woman. It matched her mood, even if it did nothing for her appearance.

Once dressed, Prudence combed through her long auburn tresses. She considered asking Netty to come and help her arrange her hair, but that would give the girl a prime opportunity to pry into the state of her mistress's marriage. And once the girl had her teeth sunk into a bit of juicy gossip, she would certainly spread it throughout the household in a matter of minutes.

Because of the servants, Prudence would not invite Richard to stay with her. The more she acted as if nothing was amiss, the less likely they were to catch on to her misery and gossip about it.

Of course, she wouldn't be able to hide anything from Richard either. He would see through her façade within minutes and have her pouring her heart out to him as soon as they were alone.

If Richard really did love her as more than a friend, she couldn't put him through that. Even if he loved her only as a friend, there was always a chance he would take it upon himself to do something to solve her problems. When they were children, Prudence had been the one to get them into trouble, while Richard could always be counted on to get them out.

Prudence tied her hair back in a simple gray ribbon, then stared at herself in the mirror. Now what?

She reconsidered extending an invitation to Richard. They could at least while away the time playing cards or chess. No, games left plenty of time for idle conversation, even encouraged it. Richard would have her revealing all in the space of time it took her to consider her next move. Besides, distracted as she was, she would undoubtedly lose. She hated to lose.

She could always read. Prudence didn't dislike reading, but she doubted that anything she had in her library would be sufficiently entertaining or thought-provoking enough to distract her from her problems.

In the end, she chose a book of poetry by a collection of unremarkable poets and flopped down into an overstuffed chair in the library to read. Well, not read exactly. The poetry, being unremarkable, and Prudence never having much affinity for poetry anyway, she had plenty of opportunity to brood while she pretended to read.

A knock on the library door mercifully took Prudence away from a particularly woeful verse dedicated to the poet's cat.

"Come in." She closed the book on her lap, not bothering to mark the page.

"Pardon the interruption, Miss Prudence." Mrs. Hatcher wore a frown that cut deep ridges into her brow. "There are some men here to see you."

Prudence rose from her chair, clutching the book to her chest as though it were a shield.

"Did they say who they were or what they wanted?"

"Only one of them. He gave me his card." Mrs. Hatcher handed the small rectangle to Prudence.

Prudence almost groaned aloud as she read the familiar script.

"Tell Mr. Manley I'm not receiving today."

Mrs. Hatcher winced. "He told me he has a writ. If you didn't admit him, he has the legal authority to search the manor."

"Ransack is more like it," Prudence mumbled,

tapping Simon's card against her lips.

Did he know Evan was not at home? Probably. The coward.

"The thing is, the rest of the men look like..." Mrs. Hatcher paused as though she weren't clear how to describe the rest of Simon's entourage. "Well, they don't exactly look civil."

Prudence straightened her spine. "Well, we shall be civil even if they aren't. Show them into the library, Mrs. Hatcher."

Prudence longed to have Simon turned out on his ear, but if he had a writ, she had no choice but to admit him. At least by voluntarily allowing him and his men in, she might avoid having her home pillaged even if it would still be searched. She had nothing to hide, or at least no more so than any other Rhode Island merchant. And there was nothing here that would incriminate her. Let him search.

"Prudence... Oh, I beg your pardon. It's Mrs. Foster, isn't it? How nice it is to see you again." Simon's nasal tone was more pronounced than ever.

Had he sounded that cruel at the academy? No, his tone had been more spiteful then. Now there was an edge to his words that chilled Prudence to the bone.

"First, let me see the writ." Prudence held out her hand.

There seemed to be no point in maintaining a pretense of civility. She could do nothing to stop him, but the sooner they were done with this business, the sooner he would be gone.

"Of course. Of course."

Simon reached into his breast pocket and produced a folded piece of parchment. He gave Prudence that same cold smile when he handed it to her.

Prudence unfolded and scanned the document. It looked official enough, but this was the first time she had ever seen one. If only she had invited Richard for a visit. The offices at Ashcroft had been searched often enough. He would know how to discern a real document from a forged one.

Prudence handed the parchment back to Simon.

"Well, shall we begin?" His question was directed to his men.

"Just a moment." Prudence raised her hand.

One of the men, a brutish-looking fellow with a face that looked more like a lump of clay than a man, sneered at her, showing yellowed teeth. What was left of them anyway.

"Mrs. Hatcher, fetch Gil for me, will you, please?"

"No need, ma'am. I'm right here." Gil stepped through the door.

Bless the man for his loyalty. He had evidently been listening outside the door. Perhaps it was time to add a bottle of Madeira to the brandy in the closet.

"Gil, Mrs. Hatcher, assemble the staff. I want Mr. Manley's men accompanied throughout the house. None of them are to be left alone. Is that understood?"

"Yes, ma'am." The barest hint of a smile cracked his impervious demeanor.

"You don't trust me?" Simon appeared almost pleased.

"No, I don't."

How Gil did it, Prudence couldn't have guessed, but within minutes a virtual army of servants stood outside the doorway. Everyone, from the cook to the stable boys appeared at the ready. Even Netty made an appearance, although she eyed Simon like she were a cat and he, a bowl of cream.

She could have him. In fact, maybe a dalliance with Netty would rid him of his obsession with her. Not that she believed his obsession was based on desire, despite Evan's assertions, but her maid might serve as a distraction from whatever demons gnawed at Simon's soul.

"Thank you all for coming," Prudence told the assembled servants. "Mr. Manley is a customs official and has what *appears* to be a lawful writ of assistance."

She couldn't help herself when it came to the implication that Simon's authority might be anything but perfectly legitimate. The arrow hit its mark, too. Simon's snakelike grin melted a little.

"I'd like you to break up into groups and accompany these..." Prudence stumbled over her words as she assessed the rather motley assortment, "gentlemen as they search the manor."

"But why should we let 'em?" a young man asked. "There's more of us than there are of them."

At seventeen, the head gardener's son had a body so muscled he resembled a Greek statue. Unfortunately, his brain nearly matched that of a marble statue as well.

She had to ensure things didn't get out of control.

"No, Calvin. We have nothing to hide. Let them search. I would just prefer that the house be in one piece by the time they are through."

"And what do we do if they start destroying things, ma'am?" another man asked.

The man with the clay face bared his teeth.

"Just send one of your group for Gil or me. We'll take care of it. You're not to resist. Am I clear?"

There was a general muttering among the servants. The only thing clear was that many of them were none too pleased. She didn't blame them. This might be Ashcroft Manor, but it was their home, too.

The group dispersed, following Simon and his men as they went their separate ways down the long corridor and up the stairs to the floors above. A tall man with greasy hair and a pointed nose remained with Prudence.

"I'm to search the library with you, ma'am." The way he leered at her, Prudence half expected to see spittle dripping down his chin.

"That's all right. I prefer to remain out here in the hall where I can be available should anyone need me. You're welcome to search it by yourself. I'll just leave the door open."

The man's grin dissolved into something just short of a smirk.

Prudence held her ground, shoulders squared and eyes level. Short of dragging her into the room, something the writ most certainly didn't allow, he had no choice.

Pinning her with a malevolent gaze, the man strode past her and into the parlor. Prudence held her breath, half from fear, half from the stench of old sweat and cheap whisky that wafted after him.

As promised, Prudence left the door open. However, she couldn't bear to watch as he rifled through her books, tossing them to the floor when he found nothing of interest. She closed her eyes and didn't turn around when something fell to the floor and shattered. It was probably just a vase and nothing of great importance.

By the time Simon returned, Prudence's nerves

were nearly as shattered.

"Have you satisfied yourself?" She folded her arms across her middle.

A couple more of his men gathered behind him, followed by Netty. Clay face gave her a hungry look. Had he been the one Netty favored? Alas, there was no accounting for taste.

Allowing Simon to search the premises had been the right thing to do. Evidently not finding what he was looking for, he had finished quickly. The sooner she saw the backs of him and his men, the sooner she could get back to her…she looked down at the book of poetry she still had clasped in her hands. Spending the afternoon with mediocre poets and their cats was still preferable to an afternoon with Simon.

Simon smiled as though he had just swallowed a bug. "Mrs. Foster, I'm placing you under arrest for smuggling."

"Smuggling?" Prudence gasped. Two of the men grasped her upper arms, and her book of poetry tumbled to the floor. "But how? For what?"

Cunning though Simon was, he couldn't possibly have found evidence of smuggling in the manor.

Prudence stumbled when one of the men jerked her forward. Gil reached out, first to steady her, then toward the man as though to pry his employer from his grasp. The man gave him a shove that sent the aged butler sprawling against a side table.

Simon's eyes glittered as though he hoped she might do something rash.

Prudence glanced over her shoulder as the men dragged her toward the door. "Gil, find Richard."

"I'll find your husband, ma'am. He'll know what

to do."

"No, Richard will be faster." She couldn't tell Gil that Richard would know where Evan was, not with Simon hanging on every word.

Clay face shoved Prudence into Simon's waiting carriage. Her slipper caught on the upper step, and she stumbled forward, landing on her chin on the hard floor. Instead of offering his hand to help her from the floor, Simon waited until she righted herself then climbed in after her.

He took the seat across from her and studied her with his heavily lidded eyes. Prudence drew her gaze away to look out the rear window as the carriage pulled away from the manor. She could see Gil issuing orders to a couple of stable boys. When finished, they dashed away, intent on their mission.

She watched the figures grow smaller and smaller, her hopes diminishing along with them.

"So, it's to be Richard who comes to your rescue and not your husband. Trouble in paradise, perhaps?"

"My husband is away from home. But then you knew that, didn't you, since I told you yesterday."

The implication he had waited until she was alone hung in the air, but Simon refused to take the bait.

"Ah, yes, you did mention that." He picked at the fingers of his glove. "Then it is to be Richard. Of course, even now, my men are searching the Ashcroft offices. If they find the same evidence—"

"What evidence?" Prudence demanded.

He couldn't have found any evidence at Ashcroft because there was none. But the offices were a different matter. Yes, Richard had cleverly concealed it, but...

"You will find out soon enough at your trial."

"I am to have a trial then?"

"Of course you are to have a trial. England is a civilized country, and even though you live in this uncivilized land, you are still one of his majesty's subjects." He paused to consider his gloved hand. "However, I hope the gown you are wearing is warm. I hear Nova Scotia can be quite brutal this time of year."

Nova Scotia? She had heard that the admiralty trials had been moved to Nova Scotia.

Prudence looked out the window to watch the countryside pass and to give herself time to think.

So she would have a trial, if you could call an appearance before a judge appointed by the crown a trial. There would be no jury, and it would be incumbent upon her to prove her innocence to a judge who stood to gain a portion of the proceeds from any confiscated property. The odds were definitely not in her favor. If found guilty, she may or may not be jailed, but she would be left destitute.

She returned her gaze to Simon. "Are we going directly to Nova Scotia, or will I be allowed to send for a change of clothing before we depart?"

Perhaps, if she could send a note, she could find a way to warn Richard.

Simon looked as though he hadn't considered the notion, then his face brightened.

"It's a long way to Nova Scotia. A lot can happen along the way." He left his seat to take a position next to her.

Despite the layers of clothing between them, the press of his thigh against hers nauseated Prudence. She slid as near the side wall of the carriage as she could.

Simon scooted closer, filling the space she had just

vacated. "I could find a way to make this all go away."

She gave him a scathing glare. "You are the one who started all of this, why would you suddenly be willing to make it all go away?"

He seemed not to notice her scorn. "If I were offered a proper incentive…"

Prudence inhaled through her nose, a long drawn in breath that served to control her anger.

Was he asking for a bribe? It wouldn't be the first time a customs official had been bought off with a bribe, but usually such transactions were carried out in a more formal manner, not in the back of a carriage with the customs official's hand on the accused smuggler's knee.

A shiver of revulsion racked Prudence's shoulders. Her gaze returned to Simon's face in time to see his tongue swipe at his lips. They glistened in the afternoon sunlight streaming in through the carriage windows, and Prudence's stomach heaved.

Had Evan been right?

"If you become my mistress, I will drop the charges."

Simon's eyes grew soft, as though he actually held some small feelings of affection for her. He looked almost vulnerable.

"But I am a married woman!"

The softness in his eyes disappeared, and Prudence couldn't help but wonder if it had just been a trick of the light.

"With a husband who leaves you alone most of the time. It doesn't appear to be much of a marriage. I would have made a much better match for you. I come from an established family, and I see a bright future for myself. If my career keeps headed the way it is, I may even be appointed governor one day."

Prudence had no words to counter Simon's assertions. If anything, his sense of self-satisfaction seemed delusional.

"And when I am governor, I will rid this accursed colony of all the thieves, rogues, and smugglers who are such a blight on our kingdom."

Prudence chose her words carefully. She didn't want to encourage Simon's advances, but it didn't seem like a wise idea to antagonize him either. "I'm sure you will go far, but that doesn't change the fact that I am a married woman. Whether or not my marriage is a happy one is irrelevant."

Simon laughed, a vicious sound that chilled her to the marrow.

"I can solve that problem, too. You see, I know more about your husband than I've let on. In fact, I'd venture I know more about him that you do." Simon leaned back against the leather seat cushions, his self-satisfied smile daring her to argue that point.

Prudence couldn't. After all, with Simon's connections he might very well know more about Evan's past than she did. She remained silent, for once hoping he might keep talking and tell her what he knew.

"I know where your husband is headed, and I've sent my best ship to the West Indies to hunt him down." Simon said, being disappointingly vague. "Funny thing about the Navy. They may be British, but the law at sea isn't quite the same as it is on land. From what I hear, they don't require a trial to convict a man—nor to hang him."

Chapter Twenty-Nine

Prudence paced in the darkness. She was nervous, but that only accounted for part of her restlessness. Whenever she stopped pacing, an infernal cold crept into her limbs and refused to leave. She had made the mistake of lying down on the cold stone floor hoping to catch a few minutes of sleep. It took more than an hour of pacing just to get the feeling to return to her toes.

This had to be Nova Scotia. It was too cold to be anywhere else.

She had been blindfolded during the last part of a carriage ride that must have lasted for several hours. They had stopped only once so Simon could speak to the driver. She hadn't even been allowed out to see to her personal needs, which had grown quite urgent.

At least he hadn't renewed his offer to make Prudence his mistress, but she could still feel his reptilian stare on her even if she couldn't see him.

By the time they finally stopped, night had fallen, and hunger gnawed at her. She assumed they had stopped at an inn for supper. After all, even customs officials needed to eat. She had been wrong.

The carriage door opened to reveal a tiny harbor. Well, not really even a harbor since only a few fishing boats bobbed on the gentle waves. A greasy haired man stood at the bow of one, untying it from its tether. When finished, he pushed it a few feet away from the beach and nodded back toward Simon.

"Get in," Simon had said, shoving her down the beach toward the small dinghy.

They had rowed out to a ship waiting offshore. The men aboard didn't say much, although she caught a snippet of a crisp English accent here and there as they acknowledged Simon's orders. If they were surprised to see their superior in the company of a woman, they didn't let it show.

"Take her below." Simon pushed her toward one of the men.

Feet already numb from cold, she had been dragged down a ladder and thrown into a hold. She never would have believed it, but she had been actually glad to see a bucket that served as a privy in the corner. As soon as the heavy footfalls of the men died away, she used it, thinking it a sure sign of how dire her circumstances were.

The ship set sail almost immediately, and soon they were in open waters. With no light to judge by, she had no idea which direction they headed, nor how long the journey took. The increasing cold suggested north. Her hunger suggested a little more than a day. At the end of their journey, she was blindfolded once again and led off the ship. By the quiet sound of waves lapping against many hulls, but the lack of human activity, she decided it was a major port but probably night.

A short carriage ride later, she was shoved down a set of stone steps and into another prison cell. In that cold, dark hold, she remained for what seemed like several days and nights. No light shone into her prison through the barred window in the door, so she had no way to tell the passing of time. Periodically, she guessed once a day, a guard came to slide food and water under the door. Prudence had learned to snatch up the stale bread and moldy cheese before the rats got to it.

Waiting for her daily rations, Prudence snorted. Rats were another thing that had ceased to bother her during her ordeal.

Heavy footsteps sounded in the hallway outside the door, then she saw the small, welcome flicker of the guard's candle lantern. When he reached the door, he indicted with a grunt and nod of his head that she should step back. Once she had done so, the metal tray scraped against the stone floor as he shoved it under the door.

"Thank you," she said.

Prudence had given up trying to get the man to speak days ago. Since he never acknowledged her when she spoke, never even glanced up, she wondered if he weren't perhaps deaf. Still, she always remembered to say *thank you* whenever he brought her food. He might be her jailor, but for now, he was also her lifeline.

Prudence stooped to pick up the wooden bowl and a loaf of bread that resembled a small stone. At least the food had been reliable even if it were little more than slop fit for swine. She softened the hard bread in the thin stew and ate with gusto.

"Have you changed your mind yet?"

Prudence swallowed, the lump of bread sticking in her throat. Simon's voice made her lose her appetite in a way that not even moldy bread, semi-rancid meat, or the company of rats ever could.

She stood up, swiping crumbs from her lips with the back of her hand. "Changed my mind about what, exactly?"

"If you'll agree to be my mistress, I can get you out of here, clear you of all charges."

"What? Take me away from all this?" She made a dramatic sweep of the room with her free hand. "What could you offer me that would possibly be better than what I have now?"

Anger glinted in his eyes, and although heavy wood and the steel bars of the window separated them, she took an involuntary step backward.

"I don't think you understand the entirety of your situation. Posh though your surroundings may be, they are only temporary."

"Do you mean I am going to finally get my trial?"

Surely, even if they convicted her of smuggling, destitution was preferable to this dungeon.

"You'll get your trial. Only it may not be what you anticipated."

"What do you mean?" Her blood chilled at the eagerness in his voice.

"It seems the crown has decided to alter the charges." Simon licked his lips. "Tomorrow, you will be tried for treason."

"Treason?" Since when had smuggling been elevated to the level of treason? It was preposterous. Yet, the seriousness in Simon's tone suggested he wasn't lying.

"My husband will hear about this." Prudence's threat echoed against the cold stone walls. What would Evan be able to do about it even if he did arrive in time?

"Your husband? Your husband is dead by now, my dear. As I told you, I sent one of my best captains after him. His ship of the line will have turned that little schooner of Captain Foster's into toothpicks." Simon took a step forward. "And even if he does surrender, as I believe I might have mentioned, the laws at sea aren't as lax as those on land. His majesty's ships carry enough rope to hang a traitor one hundred times over."

A traitor? What had Evan done?

Prudence clenched her fists until her nails bit into her palms. It mattered little. Ashcroft had done nothing but evade a few of parliament's more odious import laws. She could be fined and her ships and other property impounded, but she had never heard of a merchant being charged with treason.

"You have six hours left before your trial begins. I suggest you use that time to consider which of your possible fates you prefer."

Simon wiped away a drop of spittle from the corner of his lips, and Prudence fought the urge to gag.

"He will come for me." She wished she felt as confident as she sounded.

With a growl, Simon stalked away.

Prudence stared at the bowl in her hands, her appetite gone. She needed to eat, needed to keep her strength up. She set the bowl on a rock that had passed for a chair for so many years it had a little divot worn in the center. Somehow, the rancid beef had lost its appeal.

How she longed to see a familiar face, one other than Simon's. Why hadn't anyone come to see her?

She supposed she couldn't blame Richard for not coming to her rescue. If Simon had put her on the first ship to Nova Scotia, perhaps Richard hadn't been able to find her. After he scoured New England, he would eventually settle on Nova Scotia, but by the time he reached her, would it be too late?

Of course, that was assuming Simon hadn't locked Richard up for some fabricated crime as well.

But Evan? Prudence blinked away fresh tears. Evan couldn't be dead, he just couldn't. She would know it. Prudence leaned forward, setting her forehead against the cold stones. For once the chill felt good, almost as if she had grown feverish.

If Evan were dead, she wasn't sure she could go on living. She wasn't sure she wanted to. She had begun to think her marriage to Evan might end up as happy as her grandmother's had been. While Evan didn't love her yet, they shared something. Despite her naiveté, she knew it went beyond a simple business arrangement, even beyond a simple matter of physical desire. They were friends, but also so much more.

Prudence gave a cynical chuckle. She really owed Richard for bestowing her with her first kiss. With that one simple gesture, he had shown her the difference between friendship and a desire that ran so deep it would last through the decades.

Her grandmother had known that sort of love and wanted it for her granddaughter. It was why she had not left Prudence to her own devices in finding a husband. Grandma Rachel knew she and Richard would almost surely have settled into a marriage that left them both content, but never fulfilled. Instead, her grandmother presented her with a gift.

Prudence sank to the floor. "Oh, Grandma, I'm so sorry, but I may have lost him already."

Cold seeping into her bottom, she buried her face in her bent knees.

"You're going to catch your death sitting on the floor like that."

Prudence's gaze shot up at the sound of the male voice. The guard stood at the iron bars. No, the guard's clothing, but not the guard.

"Evan!" Prudence shot to her feet. "You found me."

"Of course I did." He reached a hand through the iron bars.

Prudence clasped it as though it were a life line. "But how did you get past the guard? You didn't kill him did you?" As glad as she was to see Evan, she hated to think of the guard lying dead because of her.

"Funny thing that. The man seemed almost happy to see me when I said I had come for you. He didn't say anything, but I got the impression he was told you weren't to have visitors. As soon as I explained that I was your husband, he handed me his coat and hat, gesturing that I should switch with him. Even left the keys in here for good measure." Evan jangled his pocket.

"Then the guard turned around and pounded the back of his head. I'm guessing he thought I should knock him out."

"What did you do?"

"I did as he asked." Evan glanced at her face. "Don't worry, I didn't do any permanent damage. I probably didn't even hit him hard enough to knock him out for more than a few seconds. I just gave him a nice lump to serve as an alibi should anyone discover me down here. Hey, why the tears? I told you I didn't hurt the guard."

Prudence reached up a hand to the tears streaming

down her cheeks. With a sniffle, she wiped them away with her grimy sleeve. "Simon told me you were dead. He said he sent his best captain after you, and the *Cythraul* would be toothpicks by now."

"He did send his best captain after me. A man named Black Jack. And he found me all right."

Evan's grin was almost too much for Prudence to bear.

"But how is it that you're here?"

"Your former beau"—he chuckled when Prudence scowled—"is an idiot. I'm sure the crown didn't realize that when they appointed him tax commissioner, but they will realize it soon enough."

"He may be an idiot, but he hates me." Prudence glanced away. "Or at least I think he does."

Evan grew serious. "What do you mean?"

Prudence studied his face, his hardened jaw, his cold gray eyes, the angry slash of black eyebrows. Would he do something rash if she told him? Perhaps. But he had asked her to trust him, and she had asked for his trust in return.

"You were right about his…" She was about to say love, but it certainly wasn't any variant of that emotion that drove her nemesis. "…*desire* for me."

"What did he do? Did he hurt you?" Evan's grip on her shoulder was almost painful, but reassuring at the same time.

"No, but he did offer to make me his mistress in return for dropping the charges."

"I will kill him." It wasn't a vow, nor a promise, but a cold statement of fact.

Prudence reached through the bars to lay a hand against his cheek. "Evan, please, don't do anything rash. I couldn't bear…" Her words choked off into a sob.

Evan's face softened. He ran a thumb across her cheek to brush away a line of fresh tears. "Did you miss me?"

"Simon told me you were dead." Her voice caught on a sob. "How is it that this Black Jack, or whatever his name is, didn't sink the *Cythraul*?"

"Oh, yes, I haven't told you the rest, have I?" Evan's grin of almost boyish delight returned. "Well, you hit on the answer. It's all in a name."

"Evan, please, I have no patience for riddles."

"You have no patience for anything, my dear, but we'll work on that in good time." His look held a promise that left Prudence remembering their two nights together. "But Simon knew of Black Jack only by his reputation as one of the most fearsome, most courageous captains in the English Navy. No one can out sail the man."

"Yet you did?"

"Nope. I let him catch me. In fact, I sailed right up to him."

"But how is it that he didn't turn his guns on you as soon as you drew within firing range? I wouldn't think you'd even get close enough to wave a flag of parlay."

"Because I know Black Jack. If there is one trait he has in even greater abundance than courage and skill, it's curiosity. If he sees a small schooner sailing straight at him, with no other ships to back her up, he's not going to fire. Why should he? Even if my schooner took a shot at him from close range, the odds were still in his favor. Perhaps with any other captain, I could use the speed of my ship to play a game of cat and mouse.

326

Maybe even win. But not with him."

"I don't understand." Prudence felt as if her head were spinning. "How is it that you know him so well?"

"Because I know Captain Black Jack Foster."

It took Prudence a moment to understand what Evan had just said.

"Your father?"

"No, but the closet thing I had to one. When I ran away from the orphanage, he found me at the docks. Or rather I should say I found him. I had the audacity to try to pick his pocket when all else gave him a wide berth.

"He took one look at me and promised to let me keep the schilling I had just lifted from him if I worked for it aboard his ship. To this day, I'm not sure what he saw in that scrawny seven-year-old boy. Still, I'm glad he saw something."

"Me too." Prudence's tears flowed in a steady stream down her cheeks now. "But our time is short. You have to get me out of here."

"No. I can't do that."

"But why not?" Was he not going to rescue her? Had she misread the look in his eyes?

"Because I am not going to turn my wife into a fugitive and make her leave everything she loves."

Not everything. She wouldn't be leaving him.

"Is it the Ashcroft fortune? If it is, I don't care about that. I can learn to live without the money. We'll start anew."

An unfathomable look crossed Evan's features, and it made her stomach sink with despair.

"Prudence, I know what it's like to be poor. You don't."

His lack of faith in her stung, but then, what had

she ever done to show him that she was anything more than an overindulged heiress?

"That doesn't mean I can't learn to do without." She grasped the iron bars and pulled her face close so he could see her earnestness. "Besides, with your skills as a captain, we can build up our fortune again. Maybe in the West Indies?"

"Your optimism is one of the things that makes you so dear to me, Prudence." His crooked smiled seemed almost embarrassed. "I didn't realize how dark and dreary my life had been until I came to Ashcroft. Going back to that life now would be like weighing anchor with little hope of seeing shore again."

His sweet words were enough to be her undoing, but she pressed on. "It's not optimism. It's a statement of fact. We may have some hard times ahead of us, but I know we can do it."

"You would take that kind of chance on me?" He reached through the bars to caress her cheek.

"Evan, I love you. I'm not sure when I started loving you, but I know it with a certainty that I cannot deny. I love you with all my heart—"

Prudence's declaration was cut off as Evan drew her close and kissed her. The cold metal bit into her cheekbones, but she didn't care.

"I'm not sure exactly when I fell in love with you either," he whispered against her lips. "It might have been when I saw you riding off on Bolt, desperately trying to pull your skirts over those delightfully knobby knees of yours."

"My knees aren't knobby," Prudence protested, half laughing, half sobbing.

He loved her?

"Or maybe it was from the moment I saw you lying unconscious next to that stream. I thought my heart would stop."

"You didn't seem too agitated to me."

He really loved her?

"I think our fate was sealed the moment you snuggled up against my back and fell asleep."

He really loved her.

"So why didn't you tell me?"

"Because I knew from the moment I met you, from the moment you got it in your head that I was the stable master, that no one tells you anything. You have to come to your own conclusions. I knew in time you would realize you loved me, too. I was just giving you time to get used to it."

He kissed her through the bars again, a desperate, longing kiss that left them both a little breathless.

"Evan," Prudence said, pulling back so she could focus on what she had to tell him. "Simon said the judge elevated the charges to treason."

"Treason?" Evan's expression darkened. "That little snake. He thought he could drive you into his bed." Evan reached through the bars and ran a reassuring hand against her cheek. "Don't worry, sweetheart. As far as Richard and I can tell, this is just a simple smuggling charge. We haven't been able to determine what evidence Simon found, or claims to have found, but we're still ready for the trial."

"But, Evan, aren't all the trials being tried in the Vice-Admiralty Court now? I mean they brought me all the way to Nova Scotia."

If she were tried in the Vice-Admiralty Court, Evan and Richard might never have the opportunity to mount a defense on her behalf. Even if they did, the personal benefit the judge would receive from a guilty verdict stacked the odds against her.

Evan looked genuinely shocked. "Nova Scotia? Did he tell you that, too?"

Prudence nodded. "We rode for hours in his carriage, then he put me on a ship. I was locked in the hold for days."

"I really will kill him," Evan muttered. "You are in Providence."

"But how can that be?"

Had she just imagined that it had been days? Had the ship been tied up at anchor most of the time? No, she knew what a ship under sail felt like. They had sailed somewhere. Had it been just around the islands in the bay?

"I have no doubt it was all part of his plan to make you desperate." Evan cradled her cheek in his palm and brushed his thumb against her lips. "Dawn will break in less than an hour, and someone will be here for you soon. But I have a present for you before I go."

Evan reached into the pocket of the guard's jacket, withdrew a canvas bag, and handed it to her through the bars.

Prudence untied the drawstring and opened the bag. She reached in to pull out a loaf of bread so fresh it dented under her fingers. She held it against her nose, breathing in its scent as though it were the sweetest of blooms.

"Thank you."

"There's some cheese in there, too. I suppose you're probably tired of bread and cheese by now, but I could hardly fit a ham in that satchel."

Prudence gave a sputtering laugh. "No, this will do. How on earth did you know what I needed most?"

Evan gave a rueful glance around her stone prison. "Believe it or not, I've found myself on the other side of bars like these a time or two. I brought you some fresh water, too." He handed her a leather bladder. "I just wish I had thought to bring you a blanket."

"I can hide the satchel and the water bladder in my skirts so no one knows you were here. A blanket might be a bit more difficult to hide."

Evan grinned in appreciation. "Are all Ashcroft women this smart? If so, our daughter has a bright future ahead of her."

Prudence's heart swelled almost painfully in her chest. She hadn't thought she could love her husband any more than she already did. But with that one word, *daughter*, he told her he was willing to accept their future, whatever the Ashcroft fate might bring.

"By the way, there is one more thing I should tell you. I really didn't marry you for your money."

"I know that," Prudence assured him.

"No, you only know the half of it. I didn't need to marry for money because I have enough of my own. It may not be equal to the Ashcroft fortune, but even if you are forced to forfeit everything you own, we'll have enough to live comfortably in Newport, the West Indies, or wherever we decide to go."

Evan brushed her cheek with his knuckle. "I'd give you another kiss, but I think we've tempted fate enough already. I will see you in the morning, love."

And with that, Prudence was alone in her cell once more.

She ate her bread and cheese slowly, savoring

every bite. The cool spring water tasted almost as sweet as wine on her parched lips. She had to force herself to take small sips to make it last until the end of her meal.

When finished, she tucked the empty satchel and water bladder into the pockets she wore under her gown. Surely, if they were going to search her, they would have already done so.

Without Evan's reassuring presence, old doubts resurfaced.

He had married her for love, not for her money, but they were still married. That meant his fortunes were tied to hers. If she had to forfeit her wealth, there was nothing to keep the magistrate from coming after him. Maybe he hadn't understood the ramifications.

And since smuggling trials were no longer held in the civil courts, she would not be allowed a jury of sympathetic Colonists. With parliament's seemingly endless appetite for tormenting the crown's American subjects, smuggling cases were tried in the Vice-Admiralty Courts by judges who profited from the proceeds gained from forfeited property.

Despite whatever defense Richard and Evan had cooked up between them, there was little chance they would emerge from this with a penny to their name. She had no doubt she could adapt, but she hated to send him back to the poverty he had worked so hard to escape.

"Oh, Evan, I'm so sorry," she whispered through the bars of her cell. "I hope love really can conquer all because our future is looking rather bleak right now."

Prudence moved aside the congealed bowl of stew and sat on the rock to await the trial that might spell the beginnings of a true Ashcroft curse.

Chapter Thirty

Evan scanned the many faces in the packed courtroom. The gallery where the spectators stood wrapped around the edges of the room in a U-shape, broken only by the aisle that led from the double oak doors at the entry to the judge's bench at the opposite end.

On the witness list, he and Richard had been given a spot along the railing at the front of the gallery and along the main aisle where they could be seen and heard easily. Spectators pushed against his backside as they jostled for the next best position from which to view the proceedings.

Evan picked out a few Ashcroft employees among the crowd plus one or two merchants to whom Richard had introduced him. The rest were strangers.

He tried to guess their motivations from the expressions on their faces. They ranged from the ebullient, almost festive, to the taciturn and even angry as they argued and debated with one another. It seemed to be such a mixed crowd. Had they come to support Prudence or to revel in her downfall? Evan couldn't begin to guess.

He pulled a silver pocket watch from his waistcoat, flicked open the cover with his thumb, and glanced at the time. Nearly twelve minutes past the hour of ten, and still the attendants at the door were ushering spectators into the already overflowing gallery.

"Rather a lot of people here for such an insignificant trial, don't you think?" Evan said, resisting the urge to lash out when a beefy man in a leather apron gave him an inadvertent elbow to the ribcage.

"Insignificant?" Richard scanned the crowd, nodding a greeting to one or two when he caught their eye. "Your wife may be the one on trial, but don't think the Ashcroft family will be the only ones affected by the outcome. We may be in Providence, but it's through Ashcroft that many of these people keep food on their tables," he lowered his voice, "and rum in their bellies."

Evan ignored Richard's friendly, but almost condescending, know-it-all tone. He had earned the right. Ashcroft's man of business had proven his worth a hundred times over as they searched for any shred of evidence Simon might have uncovered. The man had connections from the highest levels of the provincial government to the lowliest street urchins. In the end, they drew the same conclusion. The reptilian-like tax commissioner had built his case on hearsay and innuendo.

"A friendly crowd, then? That's excellent." From across the open space of the courtroom, a man Evan didn't know nodded his head in greeting as if confirming Evan's statement.

Richard tilted his head and clucked his tongue. "Well, I wouldn't say all of them are friendly. There's always the one or two odd souls that hold a grudge."

As if on cue, Simon Manley strode through a side door to the left of the judge's bench. Evan couldn't decide which he found more obnoxious, Manley's purple velvet coat and breeches or the smug expression he wore under his absurd little wig. The man must have spent a fortune on it, but it did little to complement his sallow complexion.

Ah well, a lizard can't change his spots, or something like that, anyway.

As the accuser, Simon had been accorded one of two oak tables in front of the judge's bench. Making his way toward his assigned position, he had to pass by the railing that held back the spectators. He glanced up as he passed. When he caught sight of Evan not a yard's length away, he gave a startled hop.

So, you thought I was dead, did you? I am no ghost, I assure you.

As if he could hear Evan's thoughts, Simon paled, looked toward his feet and hurried on to his assigned place in front of the judge's bench. Once there, he laid the satchel he carried over his shoulder on the table, his hands visibly shaking.

Evan glanced around, expecting to see Simon's solicitor join him. Simon remained alone at the polished table, pulling a stack of papers from the satchel. He spread them out, adjusting and readjusting them until, seemingly satisfied, he clasped his hands behind his back and stared straight ahead.

Apparently, Simon would be representing himself. What a fool.

Having had time to compose himself or perhaps emboldened by the twenty or so paces that now separated him from Evan, Simon turned, his thin lips curling into a smile that would have befitted a snake. Evan would have challenged the little man to a childish staring match, had the side door not opened once again.

A bailiff led Prudence past assembled spectators to

take her place to the right of the judge's bench, roughly ten paces or so from Simon's position. She still wore the plain, gray muslin gown, but her face lacked the dark smudges from the last time Evan had seen her, and she had been given a simple but clean white cap. If Evan didn't know better, he might have mistaken her for a Quaker.

A short, rather portly fellow joined her, and they soon had their heads bowed together in consultation.

"Is that Adams?" Richard asked.

"It is." Evan studied his hired solicitor's almost slovenly appearance. He wore a suit of drab brown that might have been homespun. Even from a distance, Evan could see the wear on the heels of his leather shoes. The buckles looked to be made of brass.

Nothing in the lawyer's appearance inspired confidence, but then that hadn't been why Evan had hired him.

"Not much to look at, is he?" Richard voiced Evan's thoughts aloud. "Where did you find him?"

"Braintree," Evan said. He didn't mention the man had been tending his garden and had mud up to his elbows at the time.

"Hmmm." Richard studied the solicitor. "A maritime lawyer?"

"Yes."

"A *successful* maritime lawyer?" Richard clarified his question.

"Graduated from Harvard at the age of fifteen." Evan decided not to add that Adams had been between cases when he found him. Evidently, although not yet thirty, the young Mr. Adams had built a reputation for being brilliant but a bit hard to stomach.

Obnoxious had been the description provided by one of Adams' neighbors when Evan traveled up to Boston to fetch the man Rachel Ashcroft had told him to retain should he ever be in need of a lawyer. When the squeak of the garden gate announced Evan's arrival, Adams glanced up from the stubborn weed he was pulling, giving Evan the dour look of a man twice his age. Evan had wondered, and not for the last time, what brilliance Rachel could possibly have seen in the stout little fellow.

Adams invited him into the house to discuss the case and things went downhill from there. Evidently, even though he believed everyone should get a fair trial, Adams didn't approve of smugglers. Not that Evan admitted to smuggling, but Adams seemed to assume the entire world guilty.

Evan had had just about enough of the man's self-righteousness, when his fiancée interrupted the discussion to ask if the two men would like tea.

Pretty, vivacious and pleasant, Abigail Smith was almost everything her betrothed was not. She was also obviously in love with her future husband and expressed great confidence in his ability to defend Prudence. So, based on the personal opinion of a second woman, Evan retained Mr. Adams as his lawyer.

Evidently done conferring with his client, Adams straightened and glanced around, eyebrows drawn together over his beetle-like eyes as he stared down one spectator after another. Evan wondered if the man's scowl was purposeful or simply his normal expression. He tried to imagine a smile stretching the man's taut little lips and failed.

Once again, Evan hoped Rachel and Abigail were right about the lawyer's abilities because he wouldn't win this case on charm or sheer force of personality.

Prudence turned and scanned the crowd. Her green eyes sparkled like jewels in her pale face, making her look at once both defiant and vulnerable. She caught Evan's eye, and he gave her a reassuring smile. Her return smile looked forced at best. If only he could stand next to her to give her the strength she would need for the next few minutes.

Another door opened and an elderly man in a black robe and tightly curled wig entered.

"Oh dear," Richard said under his breath.

Evan gave him a questioning glance.

"That"—Richard inclined his head toward the judge taking his seat at the front of the room—"is Judge Everidge."

"Judge Everidge?" The name meant nothing to Evan, but then he wasn't as familiar with the good folk of Rhode Island as Richard.

"Everidge used to be the judge for cases tried in Providence, but ever since he was transferred to the Vice-Admiralty Court in Halifax, Judge Roberts has presided here. I guess the powers that be decided this case required Everidge's personal attention."

"Is Everidge likely to hear our case fairly?" Evan asked.

"The Court of Admiralty trials are biased under the best of circumstances. This happens to be the worst." Richard's look darkened. "Everidge is an adamant loyalist who would happily have all American merchants brought up on charges of treason."

The mention of treason and the memory of

Prudence's words just a few short hours ago sent a chill up Evan's spine. Had Simon found a way to get the charges elevated? Perhaps the new charges warranted a judge like Everidge.

"I hope Adams knows what he's doing," Richard said.

"Me too," Evan said, as much to himself as to Richard.

An attendant handed Judge Everidge a sheet of parchment. The conversation in the room faded away when the judge removed a pair of spectacles from his robe pocket and put them on. Even with this aid, he had to squint to read the print.

After several minutes, the judge looked over the top of his spectacles. He scanned the room until his gaze landed on Prudence. He studied her for a moment.

"Mrs. Foster?"

"Yes, your honor." Her voice was firm and clear.

"Formerly Miss Prudence Ashcroft, granddaughter of Rachel Ashcroft?"

"Yes, your honor," Prudence said again.

Judge Everidge gave a small nod that told little of what he was thinking and returned his attention to the parchment. Did the Ashcroft name mean something to the judge? Of course, it did. He was a Rhode Islander, and anyone within the state would know of the Ashcrofts. Perhaps the man was calculating what his take might be if Prudence were forced to forfeit the whole of the Ashcroft & Sons enterprise.

Everidge looked up again and cleared his throat. "Mrs. Foster, it says you have been charged with smuggling. What say you?"

While he waited for her answer, he scanned the

courtroom over the tops of his spectacles. What could he be thinking?

Prudence glanced at her lawyer who spoke for her. "My client maintains her innocence, your honor. Nor have we been informed of any evidence against her," Adams said in a surprisingly commanding tone. "Furthermore, your honor, my client was arrested in her home, detained for several days aboard a ship, and held in a cell with little food or water."

"Dear me." Judge Everidge's words of concern seemed contrary to his stern expression. "Well, then, we'd better get this trial moving forward so we can set things to rights."

Adams opened his mouth to say more, but then he shut it again. From his bemused expression, Evan could only surmise the judge had stunned him with his reply.

Evan was just as surprised, and he frowned at the judge. Had the old man been making light of Prudence's suffering? He began to wish he had rescued her last night, but of course, he had no way of knowing the odds would be so stacked against them.

No, it was too early to give up hope.

"Simon Manley—" Everidge looked up, his gaze finding Simon with little difficulty "—will you be so kind as to illuminate us as to the evidence, sir?"

Simon opened his mouth to speak, but the crowd, standing no more than a yard or so behind him, started booing and hissing.

"Excuse me!" Simon turned around, his face almost as purple as his coat. "I am Simon Manley, Tax Commissioner to Rhode Island, duly appointed by his majesty's representative, the Royal Governor!" To be heard above the din, he had to raise his voice more with each word until, in the end, he was almost shouting,

Everidge rapped his gavel against his desk, the sharp crack of oak against oak quieting the crowd. "Mr. Manley, perhaps if you turned this way and spoke to me, we could get this business done faster."

The crowd laughed, and the judge let it go for a moment before rapping his gavel again.

Simon straightened his coat, then stepped out from behind his table. He squared his shoulders and walked with imperious formality toward the center of the courtroom. Unfortunately on the way, one heel of his absurd red shoes must have hit a particularly slick spot on the polished walnut floor. His foot slid out from under him and only the flailing of arms and God's grace saved him from landing on his backside. A snort sounded from the back of the gallery, and several ladies in attendance held handkerchiefs to their lips.

Glowering at the crowd, Simon tugged his velvet coat back into place. It took him a moment longer to realize his wig was askew, but he quickly straightened that as well. Stifled laughter erupted through the gallery.

As much as Evan had begun to feel sorry for the little man, he hoped Simon's day wouldn't improve.

"Your honor," Simon tried, with little success, to make his nasal voice sound commanding. "On Thursday last, based on information I received from a reliable informant, I requested to search the home of Miss Ashcroft...I mean Mrs. Foster."

Simon's cheeks reddened a bit with his slight slip of the tongue.

"Mrs. Foster gave me permission to search the premises and even took the wise precaution of having her servants follow my men about the house to ensure proper conduct."

"What sort of improper conduct did she anticipate?" Judge Everidge regarded Simon over his spectacles.

Simon gave the judge an incredulous look. "To ensure no evidence was planted I suppose."

"And was it?"

"No, your honor, of course not." His voice nearly squeaked with indignation.

Evan wondered whether Simon's peevishness was due more to having his integrity questioned or his oratory interrupted.

"And what did you find?"

"As I was about to say, your honor, in the study Mrs. Foster uses to conduct business, my men discovered several invoices for shipments of rum from the French West Indies." He scooped his carefully arranged papers into a stack and held them up. "As you know, it is illegal to import French rum into the British territories."

Judge Everidge crooked his finger, and Simon brought the papers to the judge's bench.

"These invoices not only implicate Ashcroft & Sons, they also implicate the ship the *Cythraul* in the smuggling operation, your honor. I sent a ship after her to try to seize the *Cythraul*, but apparently—" he narrowed his eyes at Evan "—the captain was unsuccessful."

Evan gave Simon a little nod, and Simon snapped his attention back to the judge.

"Very well." Everidge handed the papers back to Simon. "Have you a witness that can testify to the authenticity of this evidence?"

"Yes, sir." Simon's smug expression returned. "Miss Annette O'Malley is Mrs. Foster's ladies maid. She attended the man who searched the study and found these papers, and she is willing to attest that no evidence was planted."

"Is Miss O'Malley present?" Everidge scanned the gallery.

"I am, your honor." Netty's voice came from the gallery and, as one, the crowd craned their necks to get a look at the girl. "I was there when the evidence was found, and I was watching them real close just to make sure there wasn't any foul play."

The maid's words sounded rehearsed, almost as if she were reading a script placed in front of her. For good measure, she plucked a handkerchief from her pocket with a mechanical flourish and dabbed at her eyes.

Evan glanced at Prudence who looked no more surprised than he at Netty's treachery. In fact, she seemed to be more focused on Netty's gown of sea foam green silk, a dress far more elaborate than anything one might expect a maid to own.

"Mrs. Foster often uses the study to conduct business, so I wasn't surprised. But, oh, I mean, to know that Mrs. Foster, a woman I always admired, could be involved in something so horrible as smuggling. I never would have imaged it, your honor." Netty's words grew more fluent as she warmed up to her role. "But there you have it. The evidence that it's true, all true, right in front of you."

She dabbed at her eyes again, wiping away tears Evan doubted existed.

"Well, that is surprising," Richard whispered. "I take great pains to ensure the loyalty of the staff at Ashcroft. I review the background checks personally. Netty O'Malley came from a family who has made a living off the Ashcrofts for generations. Even has a brother serving on one of our ships, if memory serves."

"Not so surprising." Evan shrugged. "That one followed me home one night and made me a little offer. When I refused, I should have known she wouldn't take it lightly."

"What kind of offer?" Richard asked.

Evan gave him one of those looks that are reserved for the truly naïve.

"Oh," Richard said as understanding dawned.

"Yes, yes, that will be fine," Judge Everidge said when Netty brought her handkerchief to her nose and blew with great abandon. "Wouldn't want to distress you anymore than you already are."

"Mr. Manley, is this the extent of your proof or is there more?"

"There is more, your honor." Simon licked his lips. "I have an eye witness. A man who served aboard the *Cythraul* and is willing to swear upon his honor to the charges."

Prudence paled at this. She gave Evan a quick glance over her shoulder.

"Yes, well, let us hear what he has to say. Call him forward."

Judge Everidge scanned the crowd as a young man came forward to stand at the rail.

"Peter," Evan gasped.

Chapter Thirty-One

"Now it's my turn to be surprised." Evan couldn't keep the disappointment from his voice. "Of all the men you referred to me, Peter seemed the most promising. His only fault is that he's in love with Prudence. I can't believe he'd turn out to be a traitor."

"So you're willing to attest to the charges, are you son?"

"No, sir—" Peter twisted and turned his broad-brimmed felt hat between thick, calloused fingers.

"No?" Simon shouted the word in a startled gasp. "But you—"

"Silence," Judge Everidge snapped. "The man is your witness. I suggest you let us hear what he has to say."

"I was threatened into appearing here today, sir, I mean, your honor." Peter gripped his hat with white knuckled fists and glanced over at Evan. "I thought they was gonna to press me unless I told them what they wanted to hear."

"He's been paid off!" Simon's pallid skin grew red as if he'd been out in the sun too long.

"God's truth, sir. I have not." Peter seemed to grow bolder in the face of Simon's accusation.

"Atta boy, Peter," Evan said under his breath.

Peter cast a shy glance toward Prudence. When he discovered her beaming at him, his ears glowed.

Simon wasn't willing to give up easily. "This boy has been bought off. I don't know what kind of lawyer Mrs. Foster hired, but I will bring him up on charges."

Adams sputtered with indignation, and Prudence laid a calming hand on his arm.

"Given time, I'm sure I can prove he paid my witness to give false testimony or someone else did." Simon's gaze darted around as though looking for the culprit. It landed on Evan. "Your honor, that man there"—Simon pointed toward Evan with a finger trembling with rage—"is the owner of the *Cythraul* and the accused's husband. I'm sure he had something to do with it."

Evan met Everidge's assessing gaze with what he hoped the judge took to be confidence, not arrogance. In his experience, many of the crown-appointed judges responded to timidity like a shark responded to blood in the water. On the other hand, arrogance didn't sit any better. The best course of action was to exude a calm confidence.

Judge Everidge's gaze slid to Prudence, and he winked. "It's nice to have a husband who comes to your rescue, isn't it?"

Prudence dipped her chin, and her cheeks took on a spot of color. "Yes, your honor."

"Argh!" Simon stamped his ruby-clad foot when he realized Judge Everidge didn't care one whit that the man who had undoubtedly paid off his witness stood not five feet away.

"Well, sir," Judge Everidge said. "I'd guess you'd better come up with a new witness. This one doesn't seem to be doing you any good."

A polite titter spread through the gallery.

"I have one more, your honor," Simon said in a tight voice. "I'd like to call Lydia Hendricks. She runs a local, uh, establishment and will attest to receiving smuggled goods."

A middle-aged woman in a violet gown even more flamboyant than Simon's velvet suit made her way to the railing. Her hair was swept high into an elaborate coiffure so large her hat, with its bright yellow plumes, could do no more than perch on one side like a tipsy canary.

"Mrs. Hendricks, I presume?" Judge Everidge asked.

"Yes, your honor." She waggled three bejeweled fingers at the judge. "Pleased to make your acquaintance."

Judge Everidge gave her a grin. "For the record, Mrs. Hendricks, what kind of establishment do you run?"

"I own a quaint little tea house in Newport." She flashed a becoming smile at the audience.

Laughter skittered throughout the courtroom.

"Brothel is more like it," Richard whispered in Evan's ear.

"Picked that one up, did you?" Evan asked.

Richard colored and cleared his throat.

"Mr. Manley just loves his tea."

The laughter in the courtroom grew louder.

"Mrs. Hendricks, do you admit to receiving smuggled rum from Ashcroft & Sons as Mr. Manley asserts?" Judge Everidge asked.

"Oh, no, sir. I never got a drop of it from Mrs. Foster or from anyone at Ashcroft. But still, there's plenty to be had for them that knows who to ask." She turned to Simon and her smiled dissolved. "Given Mr. Manley's preference for only the best, I'll bet he knows."

Simon's jaw dropped, and for a moment all he could do was stare at the woman. Finally he turned to Judge Everidge, his entire body quivering. "Your honor, as a loyal subject of the crown and the Royal Governor's appointed tax commissioner for Rhode Island, I do not partake of anything this woman has to offer."

Simon's lip curled as he glared at Mrs. Hendricks, silently daring her to deny his statement. The woman did not disappoint.

"And that's the problem." She placed two fists on her ample hips, her feathers bobbing as she spoke. "You do not partake of anything *except* the rum…"

"She's been paid off, too." Simon's rush of words drowned out whatever Mrs. Hendricks was about to say.

Judge Everidge waited for the laughter in the courtroom to die down before turning to Mrs. Hendricks. "Well then, madam, I guess that would mean you're excused as a witness."

"Thank you, your honor."

Mrs. Hendricks turned to make her way back into the crowd, but not before she cast a provocative glance toward the portly Mr. Adams. The young solicitor turned redder than the pomegranates Evan had sampled the last time he had been in Spain. Adams tugged at his collar, a vein pulsing in his forehead.

Judge Everidge regarded Simon over his spectacles. "Any more evidence you'd like to present, sir?"

"No, they've all been paid off. I don't know how they did it. I had Mrs. Foster in custody, and I have it on good authority that Captain Foster was in the West Indies negotiating with a Frenchman. It might have been Mr. Bainbridge…" Simon seemed to be talking to himself, turning over in his mind all the possible ways things could have gone so horribly wrong.

"Well, then, if there are no more—"

"Wait!" Simon's eyes darted about like a caged animal's until they landed on Prudence. "You can't let the slut go free. She owes me for what she's done to me."

Prudence's jaw dropped, and it was Adams' turn to lay a hand on her sleeve.

Although he hadn't been called to testify, Evan decided the time had come for him to speak.

"Your honor," he said in a voice that carried above Simon's manic ravings. "I will attest to my wife's virtue. Furthermore, I will demand satisfaction outside of this courtroom if it comes up again."

The assembled crowd answered Evan's statement with murmurs of approval. Simon, however, looked as if he had swallowed a spoonful of vinegar.

"Well then, if there are no more witnesses, I suggest we call an end to this farce."

"Farce!" Simon screamed.

With a nod, the two guards who had been standing placidly in the corner stepped forward to stand, one on each side of Simon. He glanced at them in horror.

"*Ei incumbit probatio, qui dicit, non qui negat,* Mr. Manley."

Mr. Adams nodded his approval while Simon gave the judge a confused look. Had Simon really been as

349

good a student as Prudence professed? It didn't take any great student of Latin to recognize the phrase.

The look on Judge Everidge's face suggested he felt the same disdain for Manley's ignorance as Evan.

"Mr. Manley," the judge said on a sigh. "I will not see an old and honored family, one that has contributed so much to the well-being of Rhode Islanders, dragged through the muck just to settle what is clearly a personal vendetta for you. This colony is under British rule, and while I might have been granted great leeway in how I see fit to enforce the rule of law, one is still presumed innocent until the accuser can prove otherwise." He took off his spectacles and stuck them back in his pocket. "Unless you have proof, sir, do not bring this before me again."

Judge Everidge stood, turned his back on a sputtering Simon, and with a flourish of his dark robes, made his way to the door.

With his attendant holding the door open for him, he paused, then turned and winked at Prudence. "I almost forgot. You're free to go, Mrs. Foster."

Chapter Thirty-Two

Evan pushed his way through the milling crowd toward his stunned wife.

Dodging one last well-wisher intent on shaking his hand or clapping him on the back, he reached Prudence and took her cold fingers in his. "See, I told you everything would be all right."

"Yes, but I never expected it to be this easy." She nodded to a man who shouted his congratulations over the heads of his neighbors.

"Nor I," Evan confessed.

He released Prudence's hands to hold one out to Mr. Adams. "Thank you, sir. My wife and I owe you a debt of gratitude."

Mr. Adams took the proffered hand, but the corners of his mouth were turned down even more than usual. "You're welcome, sir, but I don't see as how I did anything very great. Mr. Manley seems to have won the case for me."

"But you would have." Prudence took his chubby hands in hers. "I'm sure had Simon actually had a case against me, you would have disarmed it with your brilliance."

Adams looked into her eyes. "But I had hoped to launch my career with this case."

By the almighty! Was the man more concerned with himself than his client?

351

Prudence seemed not to notice. She gave him the sweetest smile Evan had ever seen. "I am certain you have a great future ahead of you, Mr. Adams. I know you are a man of exceptional abilities, and the world will speak your name with reverence one day."

Evan thought he might be sick, but Adams seemed to take Prudence's words to heart. Mollified he turned to go, his shoulders only slightly slumped as he shuffled away.

Prudence turned to Evan. "What?"

Evan cocked an eyebrow at her. "Speak your name with reverence? Really, did the man's ego need that much of a boost?"

"I am serious, Evan. Mr. Adams had a brilliant defense planned, and I never feared for our case." She laid her palm against his chest and peeked out at him from under her lashes. "But, truly, the credit goes to you for discovering such a brilliant lawyer."

Evan laughed. "All right, enough. I know when I'm being played."

He lifted the ruffle of her cap to kiss her forehead. Given a few years, Prudence would be just as capable of assessing and handling people as her grandmother. Perhaps, she already was if she had indeed detected brilliance in Mr. Adams when all he could see was a shabbily dressed, country lawyer whom no one else would hire.

Another man stopped just a few feet away, his hat in his hands.

"Congratulations, Captain Foster." The man lifted his face to Evan's. For a moment his awestruck gaze shifted to Prudence, but then yanked as if on a string back to Evan's face. Evidently, the crew of the

Cythraul weren't the only ones who got tongue tied in the presence of an Ashcroft. But then again, Evan was almost as much an Ashcroft as Prudence now. For some reason, that thought filled him with a sense of pride.

"My name's Seamus McGinley. Me son Billy works in your stables just as I did when I was a lad."

"I know Billy," Evan said. "He's a fine boy."

The man ducked his head. "Well, he can be a bit of a handful, but I know he'll make his way in the world working for you and Mrs. Foster. It was the same with me. Worked for her grandmother for years before she helped me get set up in town with a business of me own. I owe her the world and that extends to her granddaughter and to you. Fact is, most of us here are beholden to the Ashcrofts in one way or t'other." The man clapped his hat on his head, earnestness shining in his eyes. "If things went for the worst, we would surely have done somethin'. Not sure what it would have been, but we would have done somethin'."

Evan forced back a shudder at the look of purpose on the old man's face. In his travels, he had seen more than his share of normally peaceful people forced to violence when they felt they had no other recourse. He didn't care to see it happen in Rhode Island, nor to have Prudence in the midst of it all.

Evan stuck his hand out to the man, and after a moment of stunned silence, the man grasped it. "Well, we thank you for that, but luckily for all of us, things turned out as they should," Evan said.

"Bless you, they did," the man said, then left to join a gathering of men waiting for him at the door.

Evan turned back to Prudence and opened his mouth to suggest they take their leave when he was interrupted again.

"Captain Foster?" Peter said in a soft voice. "I came to say I'm sorry for my cowardly ways. I feel terrible for putting Mrs. Foster in danger."

Evan considered his young charge. He'd have to be tougher on the boy in the future, make sure he didn't cave in to fear when it really counted, but at least he had the courage to face up to his error.

The boy looked down at the hat he still held in his hands. "I'll understand if you don't want me on the *Cythraul* anymore." He forced his gaze to Prudence, and this time his face reddened in shame instead of shyness. "Your grandma gave me a chance when we, my family and me that is, was down on our luck and all. I'll always appreciate what she done for us. I can't believe I repaid her this way."

"Nonsense, boy. When Rachel Ashcroft saw something in a man, she was usually right." He gave Prudence a grin as they shared the private joke between them. "If she thought you'd be a good sailor, I think the best way to honor her memory is to prove her right. I'll see you back on the *Cythraul* in the morning."

"Do you really mean it, sir?" Peter's eyes shone with delight.

"Yes, but you'll be scrubbing decks for a few years," Evan added.

"Yes, sir!" Peter said, even more vehemently, the brightness in his eyes not dimming a bit.

He gave a little skip as he turned, and with just a few long strides, he disappeared through the door of the courthouse.

"In the morning?" Prudence asked.

So she had caught that. Evan cringed at the

implication. Married a little less than a fortnight, he had spent only two nights in her company. He wouldn't blame Prudence if she still had doubts.

"I got called away early from my last run so I was never able to finish the transaction. However, I—"

"Captain and Mrs. Foster," a silky voice interrupted them. Mrs. Hendricks grasped Evan's arm despite his having Prudence's hands in his. "I wanted to tell you how happy I am that this all worked out so well."

"Thank you, ma'am."

Evan could feel Prudence's eyes on him, assessing, judging. Did she think he and the madam were acquainted? Why wouldn't she? She barely knew her husband, and this woman had approached him as though he were an old friend, salacious delight shining in her brown eyes.

In truth, he had never met Mrs. Hendricks before, but that didn't mean he didn't know who she was. As soon as he learned of Simon's first visit to Prudence, Richard had had a man trail Mr. Manley to see what he could learn of the man's habits, habits that might be used against him should the need ever arise.

Mrs. Hendricks was their ace in a hole, and he had been quite surprised when Manley called her as his witness. He hadn't been worried though as he was certain Richard paid her more than Manley had, even though his agent had assured him that Mrs. Hendricks would have offered her assistance for free.

"Oh, t'wern't no trouble." Mrs. Hendricks gave Evan's arm a squeeze then turned to Prudence. "Your grandmother and I were old friends."

To her credit, Prudence gave Mrs. Hendricks a

polite smile.

"Yes, it's true," Mrs. Hendricks said as though she were used to the facts being disputed. "We met when she was only a little more than your age. I found her wandering the street in the middle of the night. I hadn't made my way in the world back then, not the way I have now." She gave her elaborate coiffure a little pat. "I thought she was competition if you know what I mean.

"'Course, when I got close, I could tell she was a lady, a real lady. The streets ain't no place for a lady, especially that close to the docks in the middle of the night. So, I closed up shop for the night and took her home with me. Gave her a bed to sleep in and some broth to warm her belly."

"Why was my grandmother wandering the streets at night?"

Evan smiled. He should have known Prudence wouldn't be able to contain her curiosity.

"Not sure of the details. Weren't none of my business. But I think she might have been angry at your grandfather. He showed up the next morning, his face all dark and stormy like. Scared me to my bones, so I went to get help. When I came back, the door was locked, and there were *noises* coming from the room." She gave a little cackle. "Weren't my face red when I had to tell the constable that it had all been a misunderstanding!"

"Well, I thank you for coming to my rescue as well," Prudence said, a touch of color on her own cheeks.

"Oh, it was my pleasure!" Mrs. Hendricks said. "In return for my help, your grandmother loaned me the money to set up my own establishment. She could have judged me, refused to have anything to do with the likes of me, but she weren't like that. As I said, she was a real lady.

"'Sides, what I said about that man was true. He does like his rum. Comes into my house, drinks my best stuff, then leaves. I charge him for the spirits of course, but I ain't running a tavern. He never chooses any of my girls. Just stares at them. Makes them so nervous they can't focus on what they're doin'." She emphasized her point with a shudder.

By the time Mrs. Hendricks took her leave in a whirl of violet silk and yellow feathers, both Prudence and Evan were stifling smiles.

"Well, that was interesting." Evan tried not to laugh aloud lest the departing Mrs. Hendricks be offended.

"I have to agree with you there," Prudence said. "My grandmother made some interesting allies in her time. Maybe I should spend some time down by the docks in the middle of the night."

The very thought made Evan's blood run cold. Instead he drew Prudence into his arms and whispered in her ear, "I think you and I can find better things to do, don't you?"

He felt her shiver when he kissed the shell of her ear.

"Evan," Prudence said, the seriousness in her tone prompting Evan to reluctantly release her. "Do you think Simon will retaliate?"

"I'll make sure he doesn't."

"But how—"

"Never mind that." Evan took her into his arms

again.

He didn't want to talk about Mrs. Hendricks, Simon, his ship, or the business. He didn't want to talk about any of it. He wanted to spend time with his wife, to get to know her the way he should, to start fresh. He wanted to talk with her, to tell her all about his life, all the things he should have told her from the beginning. As much as he wanted to tell her about him, he wanted to hear about her life, too. He wanted to hear all the stories about her childhood. He wanted to share her pain when she told him what it was like to be a young woman trying to hold her own in a world of men. He wanted to help her put that pain in her past where it belonged by making her realize she was worth more to him than all the money in the world.

Most of all, he wanted to make love with her. He grinned into a curl that had escaped her cap just in front of her ear. After all, they still had a curse to break.

Evan glanced around at the throngs still milling about. The victory, as the locals surely saw it, had left them in a festive atmosphere. They all seemed to be talking at once, but he heard snatches of conversation…*Ashcroft…helped me when…bless her soul*. The way they were extolling her virtues, he expected to hear someone suggest Rachel Ashcroft be elevated to sainthood at any moment.

Maybe he could sneak past them while they swapped stories, but if one more person interrupted them, he might just toss Prudence over his shoulder and force his way through the crowd.

"Excuse me, Captain Foster—"

Evan dropped Prudence's hands and spun to face this latest intrusion.

"Oh for the love of Go—" His words stuck in his throat. "Sorry, your honor, I thought you were someone else."

"Yes, I can see that." The old man's eyes twinkled. "I just came to give my regards to Mrs. Foster."

"Thank you, sir," Prudence said.

Richard extricated himself from a group of men standing nearby and came to join them.

"You are the spitting image of her." Judge Everidge gave her a kindly smile.

"Who?" Prudence asked.

"Rachel." The word came out in a thick whisper, and Judge Everidge cleared his throat. "I was an old friend of your grandmother's. Actually, I had hoped it would turn into something more, but she up and married your grandfather before I had a chance to win her heart."

Evan thought he detected tears in Everidge's eyes.

"I was glad she found happiness with him. I even thought of offering my suit after she lost him, but the one time I saw her, I could just tell she would only have one true love in her life. I contented myself with loving her until the end." He grasped Prudence's hand. "I'm sorry I wasn't able to be there for her funeral. I was in England when I heard about her death. I think the fates must have brought me home in time to help her granddaughter."

"Thank you." Prudence's eyes were as moist as the judge's now.

Richard gave a dramatic sigh after the judge took his leave. "I know just how he feels."

Prudence blushed and gave Evan a sidelong glance, but Evan just smiled. He had grown to like Richard

Bainbridge immensely. The concern he had shown for Prudence over the course of their ordeal had been almost as great as his own, but it had been the concern of a brother, not a lover.

"Are you going to be a problem?" he asked, his tone teasing.

"Only if you make her unhappy, old man." Richard didn't give Evan a chance to reply but left before Evan could get the last word in.

"There's nothing between Richard and me," Prudence said once they were finally alone.

"I know, but you still love him," Evan said, his words a matter of fact, not conjecture.

"Yes, but not the way I love you."

Evan drew her to him. "Oh, and how is that?"

Prudence turned thoughtful. "I don't know. Sometimes words fail me."

"Why don't you show me then," Evan suggested.

Prudence put her arms around his neck and pulled him into a kiss that no one dared to interrupt.

****

Prudence shut her eyes against the morning sun streaming in through the windows. She didn't think she had ever slept so late.

Memories of last night's lovemaking flooded her mind. She glanced to the other side of the bed just to be sure it hadn't all been a dream.

Evan lay next to her, his black hair sticking in all directions, dark shadows covering his jaw, his face pushed into the pillow so it distorted his features, bending his nose and pushing his lips to the side. He snorted and smacked his lips as though the sound startled him.

Prudence grinned. He'd never looked so handsome.

Light as a butterfly, she trailed her fingertips across his cheek.

Evan batted them away and pulled the blankets over his ear so only the top of his dark head showed.

Slowly, carefully, Prudence pulled the covers down, making sure to block the morning sun with her back so it didn't shine in his eyes and wake him before she'd had time to extract her own revenge.

This time, she trailed light kisses along the curve of his ear.

Evan mumbled something and scrubbed at his ear. Prudence put her hand over her mouth to stifle a giggle.

Growing bolder, she bent down and nibbled his ear lobe. Evan groaned, and Prudence's laughter came out in a puff of breath aimed right at his ear. She squealed as Evan grasped her shoulders and in one heart-pounding moment, pinned her beneath him on the bed.

"I caught you, my annoying little pest." He gave her a kiss.

Prudence giggled and drew a line with a fingertip over his unshaven jaw, across his neck, and down his breastbone. Evan hardened against her thigh.

Prudence grinned. "Pest am I?"

"Perhaps I've slept enough." Evan bent to kiss her again.

After a repeat of the night before, Prudence lay with her head against Evan's chest, listening to the slow steady beat of his heart while Evan trailed his fingertips over her back. Now that the wonder of their union had subsided, doubts about the future began to surface. She sighed.

"That didn't sound like a sigh of contentment."

Evan's voice rumbled in her ear.

Prudence rolled over. She layered her hands against his chest and set her chin on them so she could look into his face. "It's not you that brought about that sigh. It's Simon."

"You're thinking about another man?" His gray eyes were teasing.

"Of course not. I'm just concerned that we haven't seen the last of him."

Evan sat up in bed, and Prudence lay on her side, propping her head against the palm of her hand. While the discussions had turned serious, she couldn't resist playing with the line of dark curls twisting down the center of her husband's stomach.

"You need not worry about him. We've seen the last of him."

Prudence sat up fully, pulling the sheet against her naked breast. "Did you do something?"

"Nothing he didn't deserve."

"Oh, Evan. You didn't kill him, did you?"

Evan's eyebrows drew together. "Of course, not. I did not hurt a hair on that man's balding little head."

"How much did it take?"

"How much?"

"Well, if you didn't hurt him then I assume you bribed him. Although Richard probably handled that. He's gotten quite adept at determining a man's price to look the other way."

Evan snorted. "If only that worked with Manley as well as it did with his predecessors. No, that man's obsession is greater than his greed."

"So how did you get rid of him?"

"I bribed his superiors. It turns out they needed an

officer on the western frontier managing the interactions with the Indians. Someone with Simon's...*zeal* will fit the bill nicely."

Prudence shuddered. From what she had heard, the Ohio Territory was not a civilized place. Simon would either lose his imperiousness or be dead in a week.

"I don't suppose we ever will see him again," she whispered. "At least now, we can rest easy."

"I don't think so." The seriousness in Evan's tone had her searching his face. He gave her a reassuring smile that didn't quite reach his eyes. "Simon may have had an unhealthy obsession with you, but he's not the last customs officer we'll see. The Ashcroft name is too well known, too prominent. You will always be a prime target for the next zealot appointed by the governor."

"I can take care of them. You saw the support we had at the trial. There is no way—"

"Yes, there are plenty of people in Rhode Island who see things your way. I hate to think what kind of trouble you could get yourself in if I leave you to your own devices. I'll come back to find you rioting in the streets or trying to burn one of the revenue ships to the waterline. I'll just have to take you with me."

"I would never—Wait. What?" The meaning of his words penetrated Prudence's indignation.

"Ever seen the French West Indies?"

"No, but I'd like to. You'd actually take me with you?"

"It would be my pleasure." He gave her a slow smile that hinted to a hidden meaning. "But there is one small thing you should know."

"What's that," she asked, skepticism in her voice.

"Ashcroft is yours. But on my ship, I am in

charge."

"I agree." Prudence gave him the same sweet smile she had used to placate her lawyer.

Epilogue

Young Patience Ashcroft Foster had the lungs of a banshee. At least that's what her mother thought as she dragged herself out of bed in the wee hours of the morning.

In these last few weeks of night feedings, there were times when Prudence would have given anything for the custom of a wet nurse to come back. But then she knew she really couldn't bear to give up time with her daughter.

As she neared the nursery door, her daughter's wailing turned into a contented coo.

Prudence opened the door to find Evan tousling his daughter's shocking red curls.

"How's my little heiress?" he whispered.

The little girl reached chubby arms up to her father, clearly expecting to be picked up. Evan complied immediately, and Patience laid her head against her father's broad chest and stuck her thumb in her mouth. Evan bounced her gently in his arms.

"You know, I think you're getting bigger," he whispered against the top of her head. "One day soon, we'll be sending you off to school. Then I am going to get you into college."

"Good luck with that," Prudence said from the doorway.

"They'll accept her. Times are changing, and

women like you and Patience will lead the way."

Prudence laid a hand on her husband's shoulder and smiled down at her daughter. "That's fine, but she should get married, too."

"Why would you need anyone but your papa?" Evan asked the little girl, a pout in his voice.

Patience's heavily lidded eyes closed, and she released her thumb to give a contended sigh.

Prudence grinned. During the long months of her pregnancy, she had been worried about what would happen if she continued the Ashcroft tradition and gave birth to a daughter. Evan would hide his disappointment well, but she expected to see it nonetheless. Instead, the birth of his daughter had turned her strong, handsome husband into a fool, one that made her heart swell with love.

"She may not need anyone to help her run the business, but she will need to carry on the family tradition someday. She'll need to produce a daughter of her own."

Evan lay Patience back down in her bed. The little girl's limbs slowly relaxed, and her thumb drifted from her mouth although her lips still moved as though she were sucking.

"You know I don't believe in curses." Evan gave Prudence a look she knew well. One that was quite different from the look he had on his face moments ago.

"You still want to try for a son?" Prudence searched his face for a sign he was disappointed.

"Son? While I'd love to have a son, I'd be just as happy if we filled this big old house with daughters. Surely one of them will be tame enough to settle down and carry on the Ashcroft tradition while her sisters manage the business. That way, the burden won't fall to Patience alone."

"I don't know about that. Marriage isn't such a terrible burden." Prudence laced her arms around Evan's waist. "Not once you get used to it."

Historical Notes

Dear Reader,

Historical romance novels should never be confused with history books. The emphasis in a romance novel is and should always be the relationship between people. Events of the day, fascinating as they are, add color and context, but are never the story.

That said, for all those who love the history as much as I do, here are a few historical notes related to the time in which *Willing Love* is set that I thought you might find interesting.

~*~

Rhode Island—This little colony has fascinated me ever since I learned it was the last to ratify the Constitution and did so quite reluctantly in 1790 by only two votes. Rhode Island really was referred to as "Rogue Island" as Mr. Pettigrew refers to it in chapter twelve.

~*~

John Hancock—One of my favorite Founding Fathers, Hancock would only have been twenty-seven in 1764, but he was already a full partner at House of Hancock, his uncle's merchant business. The House of Hancock served as a loose inspiration for Ashcroft & Sons. When I asked my history-minded friends which historical figure they would look to if they wanted to learn more about smuggling, John Hancock was the man they all pointed to.

In 1768, Hancock's ship *Liberty* was seized in what has become known as the *Liberty Affair*. Hancock was accused of offloading a shipment of Madeira wine to avoid paying import duties. *Liberty* served as a revenue boat for the tax collectors until angry Colonists burned it to the waterline. Historians argue whether Hancock was ever really involved in smuggling as he was never convicted—although his ship was never returned—and historical evidence seems to be scant at best. It is one of history's intriguing mysteries.

~*~

Navigation Acts—These were a series of Acts enacted as far back as the 1650s that limited the importation and exportation of goods to and from the American Colonies. The essence of these acts restricted American trade so all goods had to be transported between English ports. Of course, this gave the crown the opportunity to levy duties on imports, and tax the Colonists at least indirectly. It also gave rise to the rampant smuggling that was so common in the Colonies in the years leading up to the Revolution.

When Evan Foster travels to Martinique to negotiate for a shipment of rum, it isn't the product that is illegal, but the port. Martinique at the time belonged to the French.

~*~

Writs of Assistance—Writs of Assistance are much like search warrants, but with a few major differences in colonial times. First of all, the holder of the writ didn't need to justify the need for the writ. Second, they didn't expire. When Simon Manley had his men search Prudence's home under the authority of the writ, he had no need to convince a judge of probable cause. It's very likely his office came with a general writ that allowed him to search anyone's property at any time and for any reason. Just imagine how this might rankle the revolutionary-minded Colonial!

~*~

John Adams—I hope that more than one reader picked up that Prudence's lawyer was none other than a young John Adams. I have to admit that my image of John Adams was greatly influenced by A&E's portrayal of him. However, he did once describe himself to Thomas Jefferson as "obnoxious, suspected, and unpopular." His writings and other historical notes lead me to believe that he might be one of the few people able to accurately assess his own personality

Nevertheless, Adams is another one of my favorite historical figures. And he started his career as a maritime lawyer. So many people know of his role in defending the British soldiers after the *Boston Massacre*, but he also represented Hancock in the *Liberty Affair*.

A word about the author...

Mary Jean Adams has been writing romance since she was in middle school—a fact her English teachers didn't always appreciate. She also loves history and telling the stories behind the stories of the founding of America. Today, she lives in North Dakota with her husband and two children.

http://www.maryjeanadams.blogspot.com

~*~

Other Mary Jean Adams titles
available from The Wild Rose Press, Inc.:
Le Chevalier
Caution to the Wind